ENVISI

THE CHANGING IDEALS AND IMAGES
OF NORTH AMERICAN JEWS

For Henry Siegman
visionary and activist

ENVISIONING ISRAEL

THE CHANGING IDEALS AND IMAGES
OF NORTH AMERICAN JEWS

Edited by

ALLON GAL

THE MAGNES PRESS, THE HEBREW UNIVERSITY, JERUSALEM

WAYNE STATE UNIVERSITY PRESS, DETROIT

Published in association with
The Ben-Gurion Research Center
Ben-Gurion University of the Negev

North American edition published by Wayne State University
Press, Detroit, Michigan 48201

Library of Congress Cataloging-in-Publication Data

Envisioning Israel: the changing ideals and images of North American
    Jews / edited by Allon Gal.
        p. cm. — (American Jewish civilization series)
    Includes index.
    ISBN 0-8143-2630-7 (pbk. : alk. paper)
    1. Israel and the diaspora.   2. Jews — United States — Attitides
    toward Israel.   I. Gal, Allon.   II. Series.
    DS132.E58   1996
    973'.04924—4c20   96-14959
                                                                    CIP
Printed in Israel
by E.M.N. Ltd., Jerusalem

Contents

Preface

This volume is based on the contributions to the international conference "Envisioning Israel: The Changing Ideals and Images of North American Jews" — that took place, 13–15 June 1993, on the Beer Sheva and Sede Boqer campuses of Ben-Gurion University of the Negev (BGU).

The conference was sponsored by the Center for the Study of North American Jewry and the Ben-Gurion Research Center, BGU. These centers, which initiated the conference, gratefully acknowledge the generosity of the American Jewish Congress (AJCong.), co-sponsor of the event. The conference was conducted under the auspices of the Israel Academy of Sciences and Humanities, Jerusalem.

AJCong.'s President, Robert Lifton, Executive Director Henry Siegman, Associate Executive Director Phil Baum, and the Director of the Israeli Office, Dr. David Clayman significantly contributed to the success of the conference. An organization that offered early support and encouragement was the Argov Center for the Study of the Jewish People, Bar-Ilan University, under its director, Professor Charles S. Liebman. The conference was also supported by Yad David Ben-Gurion, Tel Aviv, led by its chairman, Ambassador Asher Ben-Natan, and by the Organization and Community Relations Department of the World Zionist Organization — a department headed by Eli Eyal and directed by Rami Combloom. Additional assistance came from BGU's Department of History, chaired at the time by Professor Robert Liberles. Professor Amos Richmond of BGU provided constructive counseling as well as the good offices of BGU's Sede Boqer campus.

This volume is not a record of the conference proceedings but the result of a selection and editorial process. I am glad of this opportunity to thank my editorial committee colleagues: Professors Arthur A. Goren, Columbia University; Menahem Kaufman, The Hebrew University of Jerusalem; Charles S. Liebman, Bar-Ilan

University; Deborah D. Moore, Vassar College; Jonathan D. Sarna, Brandeis University; and Ze'ev Tzahor, BGU.

I am deeply grateful to Charles Liebman, who with unflagging good spirits and keen insight was constantly available to move the endeavor ahead. I owe a special debt also to Arthur Goren and Jonathan Sarna who invested so much of their time and wisdom in the conference and in this publication.

The generous support of Milton Forman of New York and Ludmilla and Harry Coven of Glencoe, IL, the friendly help of Barbara and John Weiss now of Nyack, NY, and the aid of a well-wisher who prefers to remain anonymous — all these were instrumental in the execution of the project.

I would like to express my appreciation to the Lucius N. Littauer Foundation, New York, for its generous help in financing this English edition.

Last but not least, it gives me great pleasure to thank Evelyn Katrak for her excellent copy-editing, the staff of Magnes Press for their kind cooperation, and especially Director Dan Benovici, who wisely and patiently advanced this publication to its fruition.

Its goes without saying that if it were not for the understanding and unfailing support of my family — especially my wife, Snunit, and our daughter, Keren, then still living at home — I would never have been able to undertake and complete this whole endeavor.

The conference was aimed toward an improved understanding — particularly in the ideological dimension — of the deeply entwined yet often problematic historical relationship between American Jewry and the Jewish community in Eretz Israel.

Paradoxically, the strong love of American Jews for the *yishuv* and Israel, and their lofty expectations of the State, often reflect an overriding urge for meaningful existence within the society where they live. The intensive envisioning of Israel undoubtedly entails a mythical element that serves to transfigure reality and provide spiritual and moral meaning for the survival of American Jewry.

This deep-seated urge for integration into American society, interwoven as it is with myths about Israeli society and ethos, is double-edged. On the one hand, the impulse is to present the American Jewish community as part of a normal and wholesome Jewish nation. A major natural expression of this quest is the stark emphasis on the triumph of Zionism in the homeland. The vision of Israel, in this connection, persistently tends to stress the vigor of Israel, its material successes and ingenuity, its elements of independence and symbols of sovereignty. The success of Israel, indeed, confers pride on and validates Jewish existence in the United States.

On the other hand, though in the same vein of Diaspora survivalism, the American Jewish myth of Israel tends also toward praising the Zionist endeavor to be responsive to those universal values of the general society that sustain the Diaspora. Prominent among these values are democracy, pluralism, equality before the law, civil rights, and minority rights. These and related values are at the heart of this aspect of the vision of Israel; namely, they are expected to be found — but at times are only imagined — in the Jewish state. This aspect of the vision conceives of the Israelis as the redeemers of the humanistic legacy of the prophets of old and as the creators of a singularly just and noble society.

Which aspect of this double-sided myth is dominant? The answer is something that historians and colleagues of other disciplines continuously reconsider and reevaluate. The articles in this volume, in any case, often analyze the envisioning of Israel as it has evolved between the two parameters of the myth: Israel as the great success of a stubborn nation that has unfortunately gone through extraordinarily tragic experiences; and Israel as evoking a unique promise of morality and justice — of being "a light unto the nations."

In my opinion, under the impact of the social-democratic pattern of the *yishuv* and the young State of Israel, the myth has tipped more toward transfiguring reality to provide ethical meaning to the survival of the American Diaspora. This I try to demonstrate in my "Overview," which is the opening chapter of this volume.

Part I, "The Zionist Ideals," concentrates on the expectations of some of the organized Zionist movements, and the built-in tensions between these ideals, and the *yishuv* and Israeli reality. Jonathan D. Sarna sketches changing ideals since the early nineteenth century and focuses on the "model state" conceptions of such progressive thinkers as Horace Kallen, Louis Brandeis, and Bernard Rosenblatt — prominent in the Zionist Organization of America at the beginning of this century. Michael Brown analyzes and describes the vision of Henrietta Szold, the founder of Hadassah (the Women's Zionist Organization of America) and its spiritual leader for decades. Szold immigrated to Palestine, considering the Zionist enterprise to be the best safeguard against assimilation, but still envisioned the desired state along thoroughly American lines. Arthur A. Goren examines the *halutz* ideal and the American Zionist pioneering movements whose radical faction promoted personal participation in the dotting of Eretz Israel with kibbutzim. The more typical American version of this ideal, however, was quite flexible and, paradoxically, was later further Americanized through the influence of the practical-minded leaders of young Israel.

Part II, "Religious Vision and Education," opens with David Ellenson's description and analysis of how the State of Israel, as both a religious ideal and a modern nation, is presented in the contemporary prayerbooks of the major liberal denominations — Reconstructionist, Reform, and Conservative. Stephen Sharot and Nurit Zaidman's essay investigates the multiple meanings of Israel for members of Reconstructionist congregations. Three dimensions of attitudes and behaviors were distinguished in their study: Israel's importance as a symbolic focus; its significance in the American-Jewish identity; and this denomination's perceptions of the religion and politics of Israel. Walter Ackerman discusses how American Jewish education, mainly religious, has been transformed since the prestate period, from idealization of Jewish efforts in Palestine and young Israel, to a much more realistic and balanced perspective shaped during the late 1970s (after the Yom Kippur War). With the changing times and perceptions, however, Israel has been depicted as worthy of American Jews' loyalties as much for its affinity with the values of American idealism as for its place in the Jewish heritage.

Part III, "Fundraising and Jewish Commitment," starts with a historical study by S. Ilan Troen that examines the work of two experts on the "economic absorptive capacity" of Palestine. Elwood Mead's report on rural society (in the 1920s) and Robert Nathan's on modernizing the *yishuv* (in the 1940s) suggest how views of Americans, both Jewish and gentile, were informed by intepretations of the American national experience. Mead's advice was resisted and Nathan's was accepted because the exportation of

American ideals ultimately depended on what local leaders believed ought to be transplanted. Menahem Kaufman's thesis is that the United Jewish Appeal's leaders tended to sympathize with liberal solutions for Israel's social and political problems. But what mainly marked their endeavor was the need — intensified in the wake of the Holocaust and by the War of Independence and the Six Day War — for Israel to be a center of rescue and rehabilitation. Deborah D. Moore looks closely at the meanings attached to the the Israel Bond campaigns in the l950s. Choosing Miami's Jews as a case study, she concludes that frontier visions of pioneering, building a democratic home, and defending it against enemies spoke to their situation as both newcomers to the region and Jews in a post-Holocaust age.

Part IV, "The Cultural Connection," discusses the ideological values embedded in literature and film of the post-1948 years. Sylvia B. Fishman examines depictions of Israel in current American Jewish fiction, using as examples Philip Roth's *The Counterlife* and *Operation Shylock*. For Roth, and for many of his colleagues, Israel is both an earthly Jewish state and also a state of mind in which one undertakes an evaluation of one's spiritual life. Stephen J. Whitfield discusses the movies *Exodus* (1960) and *The Little Drummer Girl* (1984). He concludes that, despite their great differences, both films are designed to suggest that Israel has engaged in violence only to protect its citizenry, and that the extremism of its enemies has sanctioned methods that were at times morally clouded. Actually, the movies tell us less about Israel than about the values and visions of the mass audience to whom they appeal.

The "Tangled Relations" between Israel and North American Jewry is the theme of Part V of this volume. Naomi W. Cohen points to a contradiction between the attachment of American Jews to liberal causes and their commitment to Israel, especially since the l960s, when important progressive circles, such as that of Democrat Jesse Jackson, aligned themselves against Israel, while conservative elements, such as the Christian Right, vigorously supported the state. This development may break the Jewish-liberal nexus, Cohen argues, and result in a polarization of American Jews' vision of Israel. Jerold S. Auerbach suggests that the proudly nationalist government of Israel in the years 1977–1992 disrupted the Brandeisian synthesis of Americanism and Zionism. Prime Ministers Begin and Shamir, who time and again confronted the American administration, forced American Jews to choose between Jewish-Israeli interests and their American liberal disposition and to ask themselves in all earnestness, Is the Jewish people one?

Steven M. Cohen suggests that with respect to American Jewish attitudes toward Israel one should distinguish between "attachment," "images," and "political orientation." Using these different spheres he argues that despite political events and processes that are presumed to have distanced Israel and American Jewry, the attachment to Israel in the decade 1983–1993 has not diminished. He proposes at the same time that a distancing process may take place in the long run. However, Chaim I. Waxman, studying "The Baby-Boomers and Israel," tends to see the distance between Israel and American Jewry in the context of the sharp decline of both American Jewish identity and identification. Waxman believes that the growing assimilation and the attenuation of the nature and intensity of American Jews' support of Israel are closely interrelated.

Jack Wertheimer examines two major cases of internal opposition to the American Jewish establishment's staunch support of Israel. The Breira group (founded in 1973) failed; but the later grouping, loosely composed of the New Jewish Agenda, the New Israel Fund, and Americans for Peace Now — who openly stood for Israeli democratic traditions and energetically cultivated Israeli partners — has demonstrated a much stronger vitality. The more these groups have allied themselves with Israeli stances and factions, Wertheimer concludes, the more their opposition has been considered legitimate.

A. G.

Overview: Envisioning Israel — The American Jewish Tradition

Allon Gal

Three distinct factors worked to shape American Zionism, including its vision of Israel: American civilization, American Judaism, and the Zionist enterprise in Palestine.

After the establishment of Israel in May 1948, and especially after the Six-Day War of June 1967, philo-Israelism persistently expanded and well overshadowed the defined historical Zionist movement. Since then, virtually all American Jewish community organizations have become supporters of the Jewish state and have developed some variation of "a vision of Israel." However, the above-mentioned three factors have remained central in shaping American Jewry's vision of Israel. Processes and events in the United States, Europe, and the Middle East, have also played their part in influencing the attitudes of American Jewry toward Israel. I will sketch in some of the relevant historical influences as the discussion evolves.

I. The Impact of American Civilization

American civilization played an extraordinarily powerful role in molding American Zionism.

The basic characteristics of the American tradition, which enabled American Jewry to be comfortable in the United States and shaped American Zionism significantly in the image of the American ethos, are well-known: lack of a medieval past; a deep-rooted separation of church and state; a long-established tradition of religious freedom; vigorous pluralism; the related widespread phenomenon of self-governing bodies and of denominationalism; and a mosaic of immigrant and ethnic groups.[1]

True, some aspects of the American ethnic reality were, for generations, discriminative and even oppressive. But against the backdrop of the great depression and World War II, and with the presidency of Franklin D. Roosevelt (1933–1945), who headed "a minorities coalition," the trend toward ethnic equality evolved. Later, acts passed in the 1960s and 1970s represented a meaningful application of the principle of equality and a reluctant acknowledgment of pluralism in the ethnic dimension of American life.[2]

Generally speaking, anti-Semitism has been a rather marginal phenomenon in the United States. Moreover, anti-Jewish sentiment has often been counterbalanced by a considerable philo-Semitic heritage. Although Jews were few in number in colonial America, a relatively large proportion took an active part in the American War of Independence. Last, but not least, Jews in the United States have enjoyed equality without having to struggle militantly for it; nor was this equality achieved at the expense of collective Jewish identity.[3]

All these characteristics left their mark on American Zionism, which expressed itself not in purely nationalistic terms, by seeking a

1   Seymour M. Lipset, *The First New Nation* (Garden City, N.Y.: Anchor Books/Doubleday, l967); Daniel J. Boorstein, *The Americans,* 3 vols. (New York: Vintage Books/Random House, 1958–1974); Herbert McClosky and John Zaller, *The American Ethos* (Cambridge, Mass.: Harvard University Press, 1984), esp. chaps. 1–3.

2   For succinct discussions see in *Harvard Encyclopedia of American Ethnic Groups,* ed. Stephen Thernstrom (Cambridge, Mass.: Harvard University Press, 1980); George M. Fredrickson and Dale T. Knobel, s.v. "Prejudice and Discrimination, History of"; Nathan Glazer and Reed Ueda, s.v. "Policy and Discrimination, Policy Against"; and William S. Bernard, s.v. "Immigration: History of U.S. Policy." See also Nathan Glazer, *Ethnic Dilemmas 1964-1982* (Cambridge, Mass.: Harvard University Press, 1983), 17ff.

3   For background, see Henry L. Feingold, ed., *The Jewish People in America,* 5 vols. (Baltimore: The Johns Hopkins University Press, 1992); Jacob R. Marcus, *United States Jewry 1776-1985,* 4 vols. (Detroit: Wayne State University Press, 1989–1993); Howard M. Sachar, *A History of the Jews in America* (New York: Knopf, 1992); David A. Gerber, "Anti-Semitism and Jewish-Gentile Relations in American Historiography and the American Past," in *Anti-Semitism in American History,* ed. idem. (Urbana: University of Illinois Press, 1987), 3–54; and see note 2, supra.

political substitute to group life in the United States, but rather as *complementary* to American nationality and American Jewish communal existence. This complementarity has meant that American Zionism (its major trends at least) have included a strong element of American identity and identification.[4]

American Zionism was bound to develop along typically American moderate lines from the social point of view as well. The vision of Eretz Israel (the Land of Israel) as a new and better society — a New Zion — was characterized as a remedy for American ills, not as a substitute solution. It was, in a way, the American dream coming true in a somewhat more favorable setting.[5]

Finally, the moderate, American nature of American Zionism gave it a pragmatic bent: its ideals were to a certain extent attainable in this world. Rather than dreaming up a "utopia" — an imaginary country with ideal laws and social conditions — American Zionism envisaged the Jewish community in Eretz Israel as the instrument for the absorption and refinement of Amercian goals. Thus, as we shall see, the ideal Israel — characteristic of the American tradition — was depicted as socially moderate, ideologically inclusive (rather than exclusive), voluntaristic, and achievable by free and practical people.[6]

The centrality of the American political culture in the shaping of the American Zionist vision notwithstanding, the role of the Jewish and Israeli factors should be discussed before elaborating on the vision itself.

4   See the works of Melvin I. Urofsky on American Zionism, esp. "Zionism: An American Experience," *American Jewish Historical Quarterly,* 53(3) (March 1974): 215–243. See also Naomi W. Cohen, *American Jews and the Zionist Idea* (New York: Ktav, 1975), xi–xvi, 142–150; and Ben Halpern, "The Americanization of Zionism, 1880–1930," *American Jewish History* 69(1) (September 1979): 15–33.

5   See the works of Allon Gal on American Zionism, esp. *Brandeis of Boston* (Cambridge, Mass.: Harvard University Press, 1980), chaps. 4–6. See also Jonathan D. Sarna's article in this volume.

6   See discussion in section IV, infra.

II. The Imperatives of American Judaism

Since the days of Woodrow Wilson, American Jews by and large have been liberals, and their liberalism has been central to their conception of Judaism. In particular, the non-Orthodox Jews, who make up the bulk of the community, perceive political liberalism as a constituent element in their understanding of what it means to be a good Jew. To this day, Jews continue disproportionately to support the more liberal party in the United States — the Democrats. Voting Democratic and identifying with liberal causes reflect a range of political and social attitudes, among them support for social welfare programs, sympathy for minorities, commitment to civil rights and civil liberties, dedication to the separation of church and state, and espousal of a nonmilitaristic, internationalist foreign policy.[7]

Most American Jews link their political concerns with their understanding of Jewish tradition. The distinguishing characteristics of the religious life of American Jews can be briefly summarized as personalism, voluntarism, moralism, and universalism. These traits, especially the last two, are pertinent to my theme. Moralism means that the religious person is distinguished not by his or her observance of rituals, but rather by the ethical scrupulousness of his or her behavior. Universalism conveys the idea that the Jewish tradition has a message for all people, not only for Jews, and that Judaism is open to the messages of other traditions and cultures. Further, Judaism is construed as being open to non-Jews, who may develop a variety of partial affiliations with the Jewish people.[8]

As American Jews developed their kind of Zionism in consonance with their Diaspora existence, they sensibly maintained their Jewish legacy in this process. They tended to be faithful to the moralistic and universalistic qualities of Judaism; only now have they extended

7   Daniel J. Elazar, "The Political Tradition of the American Jew," in *Traditions of the American Jew,* ed. Stanley M. Wagner (New York: Center for Judaic Studies, University of Denver, 1977), 105–130; Charles S. Liebman and Steven M. Cohen, *Two Worlds of Judaism: The Israeli and American Experiences* (New Haven, Conn.: Yale University Press, 1990), 96–122; Seymour M. Lipset and Earl Rabb, "The American Jews: The 1984 Elections and Beyond," *Journal of the Tocqueville Society* 6(2) (Fall 1984): 401–419.

8   Liebman and Cohen, *Two Worlds of Judaism,* 123–156.

their Jewish liberal dream to include Eretz Israel as well. In other words, Zionism in the American setting has not emerged against a distorted kind of Judaism typifying a group deprived of political power (a submissive and sterile, *galutic* kind of Judaism); rather, Zionism in the United States has come to be an extension — something that has complemented and *completed* Judaism. American Zionism has been an aspect, sometimes a culmination, of the enlightened Judaism that American Jews have long held dear.

Did the realities of Jewish Palestine inspire this kind of dream; or was the effect of these realities on the nature of the vision perhaps insignificant, even dissuasive?!

III. The Old and the New Zion

One might well expect to find in Palestine a Jewish society rather at variance with the values of American civilization and American Judaism.

The *yishuv*, and later Israel itself, were the fruit of classic European Zionism. This Zionism developed dynamically in continental Europe, where emancipation had failed to emerge (in the East) or foundered (in Central Europe). The Jewish Palestinian endeavor developed, then, as a substitute for Jewish life in the Diaspora — as a radical nationalist alternative to the failure of liberalism and emancipation. Naturally, this European Zionist response (especially in Eastern Europe) was characterized by a strong emphasis on nationalism — that is, by a persistent inclination to adopt nationalist values as the guiding criteria and the ultimate goal.[9]

Still, most of the Zionist pioneers in Palestine, ardent nationalists as they were, consciously tried to build a Jewish state essentially

9 For background, see Dan Horowitz and Moshe Lissak, *The Origins of Israeli Polity: Palestine under the Mandate* (Chicago: University of Chicago Press, 1978); idem, *Troubles in Utopia: The Overburdened Polity of Israel* (New York: State University of New York Press, 1989); and Allon Gal, "Independence and Universal Mission in Modern Jewish Nationalism: A Comparative Analysis of European and American Zionism (1897–1948)" (with responses by A. Eisen, A. Goren, Y. Gorny, and E. Mendelsohn, and rejoinder by A. Gal), *Studies in Contemporary Jewry* 5 (1989): 242–274.

different from the oppressive societies from which they had emigrated. The leading political trends in Palestine, and eventually in the World Zionist movement, were of a social-democratic, often socialist-democratic, nature. The pioneers, dreamers and doers, ventured to develop a democratic society distinguished by labor rights and comprehensive welfare system. Creatively they developed a mixed socio-economic system with a unique network of voluntaristic cooperative and socialist enterprises at its core.[10]

Zionism's political ties strengthened the democratic nature of the movement. For many decades, virtually until the State of Israel was established in May 1948, Zionism was a small, weak movement; it needed international backing for its growth. The Zionists found much of the vital help they looked for in two countries — Great Britain and the United States. Many historical factors combined to make these English-speaking countries hospitable to the main diplomatic efforts and intrumental in some of Zionism's greatest victories. The reasons are to be found in, among other things, these countries' Protestantism and its associated philo-Semitism. But perhaps even more important were their conspicuous democratic nature and particularly their ingrained pluralistic traditions, which provided a benign milieu for Zionist diplomacy to flourish. These "Anglo-American" traits gave Zionism some leverage in these countries. Zionists could establish power bases and wage an effective struggle to win public opinion. (The distinctive cultivation of public opinion was especially prominent in the United States.) Two of Zionism's historic victories — the Balfour Declaration (of November 1917) and the establishment of the State of Israel (in May 1948) — were won with English and American support, respectively. In fact the Zionist movement developed and gained influence largely by adopting the Anglo-American world's democratic political culture. Notwithstanding the many conflicts with Great Britain, the *yishuv* developed and matured to statehood as a British Mandate. The last

10   Horowitz and Lissak, *Israeli Polity*, chap. 6 and passim; Israel Kolatt et al., s.v. "Israel, State of, Labor" and Malka H. Shulewitz and Giora Lotan, s.v. "Israel, State of, Health, Welfare, and Social Security," in *Encyclopedia Judaica,* 1971. See also Harry Viteles, *A History of the Co-operative Movement in Israel,* 7 vols. (London: Vallentine-Mitchell, 1966–1970).

decade of the *yishuv* (1938–1948) was marked by the intensive political work in the United States of David Ben-Gurion, a labor Zionist who would be Israel's first prime minister, keenly emphasizing the shared values of the pioneers of Jewish Palestine and those of "the most developed and democratic of nations".[11] Zionism, which had been founded as a democratic and even idealistic movement to begin with, largely adhered to this socio-political pattern, thanks also to its close and constant involvement with Anglo-American democratic politics.

In conclusion, although Zionism was carried out in Palestine as an ethnic collectivist enterprise, it was developed by pioneering idealists faithful to democratic and social values. It was this path of progress that brought about a certain similarity between Jewish Palestine and the United States. This likeness, as well as the actual connection over the years between the successfully developing Jewish Palestine and the English-speaking world (now almost one hundred years' duration), served as an enriching fountainhead for the imagination and hopes of American Zionists. These Zionists envisioned Palestine as a better America — because there was some similarity between the two and because the Zionist endeavor in the old land of Zion did have some potential for becoming a New Zion.[12]

IV. The Vision of Classic American Zionism

It remains for us to see how American Zionists actually developed their vision of Israel and how they interwove it into their broader Zionist ideology.

It should be emphasized first that the major trends of American Zionism have always lacked the element so fundamental to classic Zionism — that is, immigration to Eretz Israel and personal participation in the building of the Jewish national home. Indigenous

---

11 Allon Gal, *David Ben-Gurion and the American Alignment for a Jewish State* (Bloomington and Jerusalem: Indiana University Press and Magnes Press, The Hebrew University, 1991), 15. See also Nadav Safran, *Israel: The Embattled Ally* (Cambridge, Mass.: Belknap/Harvard University Press, 1981), chaps. 4, 19–27.
12 For background, see Peter Grose, *Israel in the Mind of America* (New York: Schocken Books, 1984).

American Zionism never subscribed to the European creed of *shelilat ha-golah,* "negation of the exile" — not negation of the American Diaspora, anyway.[13]

But one must not of course restrict oneself to describing a movement as lacking a "normally" expected element. One must analyze what a movement *is* rather than what it is *not*. Doing so will reveal those elements that *positively* constitute American Zionist ideology.

A major characteristic of American Zionist ideology is its acceptance of the concept that has become known as "cultural pluralism." Though never officially adopted, this philosophy — which views the United States as a federation of national cultures and not merely of political and administrative units — has typified American Zionist thought since the early twentieth century. Embracing cultural pluralism provided the opportunity to create flourishing Judaism in the United States, a development that, in turn, would help to make America culturally richer and more democratic. True, the focus of Zionist interest has been on building an autonomous Jewish community in Palestine. But the successful development of the Jewish community in America and its constructive relationship with the pluralistic society at large have always loomed large in American Zionist thought and deed.[14]

Living in democratic and pluralistic America, Zionists looked for a *general American* rationale for creating the Jewish state against many heavy odds. They formulated a "mission ideology" that responded to this quest; that is, the endeavor to establish a Jewish state became more relevant in the American context once its *contribution to society at large* became evident. Also, acculturated

---

13 For the uniqueness of American Zionism, see the works cited in notes 4 and 5. See also Evyatar Friesel, "Criteria and Conception in the Historiography of German and American Zionism," *Studies in Zionism* 2 (Autumn 1980), esp. 286, 294–299; Allon Gal, "American Zionism between the World Wars: Ideological Characteristics" (in Hebrew), *Contemporary Jewry* 5 (1989), 79–90.

14 Sarah Schmidt, "Toward the Pittsburgh Program: Horace M. Kallen, Philosopher of American Zionism," in *The Herzl Year Book*, vol. 8, ed. Melvin I. Urofsky (1978), esp. 26–28; Gal, *Brandeis of Boston*, 147–162; idem, "Aspects of the Zionist Movement's Role in the Communal Life of American Jewry (1898–1948)," *American Jewish History* 75(2) (December 1985): 150–155 and passim.

American Zionists were inclined to imbibe elements of American nationalism that were themselves significantly shaped in the light of universal-individualistic tenets. Thus Americanized Zionists tended to perceive their particular nationalist aspirations as leading toward the realization of a set of enlightened universalistic values. This humanistic aspect served to bring the American Zionists' vision of Israel into significant accord with the ethos of the American people. Moreover, the relationship was even more intimate on account of the American ethos itself, which prominently included the idea of an American universal mission. For American Zionists, who tended to understand Jewish values and American ideals as congruous, Zionist mission-oriented ideology became a valid philosophical synthesis.[15]

Another basic characteristic of American Zionism is its inclination to stress the continuity of Jewish history and the positive relationship between Zionism and the Diaspora experience — past and present. Paradoxically, as I will soon clarify, this mental bent often caused Zionists in the United States to perceive the national enterprise in Palestine as akin to liberal America, a view at variance with the mind-set of their European counterparts.

Archetypal European Zionism understood Jewish history in a "negation of the Diaspora" context. As a logical consequence, European Zionist thought tended to idealize the ancient periods of Jewish sovereignty. For the European-born pioneers, return to the ancient homeland meant jettisoning the bulk of what had accumulated during the lengthy sojourn in foreign lands, which anyway had diminished in relevance. The flawed past included the Jewish life of the ghetto as well as Jewish weakness and submission vis-à-vis the majority society. European Zionists contrasted the objective of a sovereign homeland with the humiliation and oppression of the Diaspora period. Also, the ideal of reviving Hebrew culture was enhanced when compared to the sterile, faltering Jewish culture over "those two thousand years." Thus, their social-democratic tenets notwithstanding, their vision of Jewish Palestine emphasized

---

15   Allon Gal, "The Mission Motif in American Zionism (1898–1948)," *American Jewish History* 75(4) (June 1986): 363–385.

the values that presumably characterized the heroic days of old —
nationalist stamina and a purely Hebrew culture.[16]

Against this view, American Zionists tended to emphasize the
accomplishments of the Diaspora and to highlight the experiences
of those communities that had developed a rich Jewish life while
fostering fruitful mutual relations with the non-Jewish society at
large. Significantly, American Zionists tended to claim that a great
deal had also been achieved during the exilic period in terms of
moral values and spiritual traits, which Jewish Palestine would do
well to emulate. Even the troubles of life in the Diaspora were at
times interpreted positively — that is, as experiences that had left a
noteworthy legacy. Major trends within American Zionism urged the
Eretz Israeli Jews to appreciate the grievances of the Jews during the
long, agonizing exilic past, lest Israeli society not be properly ethical.
Jewish Palestine was expected to treat its minorities as Diaspora Jews
would wish to be treated by the majority society. This sensitivity
was of course most intimately connected with America's Jews being
a minority in their country. Hence, the tortured history of the Jews
among oppressive majorities, and the nature of Jewish Palestine in
this very connection, were constantly before their eyes. Both their
Judaism and their social ideology were structured to predispose them
to look eagerly for justice in this regard. A great many American
Zionists yearned for an Israeli model society — precisely regarding
the rights of non-Jewish constituencies and weaker groups — that
would inspire the entire world.[17]

All these factors and features combined to shape the American
Jewish vision of Israel to be not only democratic but also clearly
liberal, just, pluralistic — indeed, akin to the Jeffersonian vein of
the American ethos.

This way of envisioning Israel characterized such secular pro-
gressive Zionists as Horace M. Kallen, Louis D. Brandeis, Julian
W. Mack, and Bernard Rosenblatt. Great Zionist doer and thinker
Henrietta Szold envisioned Jewish Palestine in very similar pattern.

16 Idem, "The Motif of Historical Continuity in American Zionist Ideology,
     1900–1950," *Studies in Zionism* 13(1) (Spring 1992): 2–3 and passim.
17 Ibid., 3–20; idem, "The Historical Continuity Motif in Conservative Judaism's
     Concept of Israel," *Journal of Jewish Thought and Philosophy* 2(2) (1993):
     157–183.

Zionist leaders of Reform background — Richard J. Gottheil, Judah L. Magnes, and Stephen S. Wise — obviously conceived of the Zionist endeavor in terms of the American liberal-humanistic mission. In the Conservative movement, the emphasis was often on Zionism as an ethnic-cultural bulwark against assimilation. Still, this movement's nineteenth century legacy, as well as such of its prominent ideologists as Israel Friedlaender, envisioned Israel as an offshoot of a liberal, compassionate America. These personalities and their contributions reflect the nature of American Zionism, its vision of Israel included, during roughly the period of World War I and its aftermath, when Zionism became for the first time a potent factor in the Jewish community and general American scene.

The classic document of the period was surely the program adopted by the Zionist Organization of America at its convention in Pittsburgh in June 1918. Although it was the major American Zionist response to the Balfour Declaration, the Pittsburgh Program barely reflected any nationalist sentiment. Rather, it emphasized as its first item that American Zionists were "for political and civil equality irrespective of race, sex or faith of all the inhabitants of the land." Subsequent items suggested how to ensure in the projected Jewish homeland — through partial nationalization, extensive cooperation, and free education — the American ideal of "equality of opportunity." The national-cultural dimension was touched upon only as the last item of the program: "Hebrew, the national language of the Jewish people, shall be the medium of public instruction." This program (the work of Kallen, Brandeis, and Rosenblatt) was very American in two aspects hardly known to European Zionism. First, its entire cast was mission-oriented; second, it reflected the philosophy of "social-Zionism" — a democratically pluralistic and mixed economy unknown at the time among Europe's relatively doctrinaire political schools.[18]

18 Urofsky, *American Zionism*, 250–257; Schmidt, "Toward the Pittsburgh Program," 28–34; Bernard A. Rosenblatt, *Two Generations of Zionism* (New York: Shengold, 1967), 62–64.

V. Survivalism versus Universal Mission

In the years following World War I, historical processes and events working in different settings — nativism and anti-Semitism in America from World War I to the end of World War II; the fanatical Palestinian Arab nationalist movement, which collaborated with the Axis powers and aimed at undermining the *yishuv*; Britain's retreat from the Mandate at the most dire time for European Jewry; and finally, Nazism, the horrors of World War II, and the Holocaust — placed the existence of the Jewish people at the center of concern. The State of Israel, established in the wake of the Holocaust, came into being through a bloody and heroic defensive war (1947–1949). What was the effect of all this on American Zionist ideology and its vision of the *yishuv* and Israel?

One significant effect was that during the 1930s and 1940s survivalism emerged as a potent component of the American Jewish *mentalité*. In Zionist ideology, this process was evident in the downplaying of the universal mission rationale. At the same time, non-Zionist organizations, which under the impact of Hitler's war against the Jews gradually adopted a pro-Zionist program, conceived of Jewish Palestine as a haven for the remnants of European Jewry. Consequently, the prowess of the State of Israel — its military strength, the determination of its people, national unity and uniformity — gradually loomed larger in Amercian Jews' visions of Israel.

During the early 1940s a pair of eminent Zionist leaders — Abba Hillel Silver and Emanuel Neumann — ushered in a period in which the universal mission rationale of the movement was relegated to second place. Neumann, the zealous Zionist leader, was always more blatantly nationalistic than his distinguished Reform friend. He sympathized with the Revisionist movement, and his ideology of "Integral Zionism" had a clear common denominator with Ze'ev Jabotinsky's "Monist Zionism" — that is, the ruling out of the mission justification. According to both, the Zionist goal was defined and justified solely on the basis of internal Jewish needs. In July 1947 the ZOA convention elected Neumann as president, beginning a new era in American Zionism. The impact of the Holocaust began to sink in, and more than in the case of any other ZOA president

before him, his Zionist ideology focused on survivalism and on Israel
as an asylum-fortress.[19]

The history of B'nai B'rith is a case in point as far as the Zionization process is concerned. During the 1940s, under the leadership of
Henry Monsky, this non-Zionist order gradually accepted Zionism,
with the survivalist strain — or more precisely its defensive aspect
— becoming paramount in the process. That is, the Jewish state
came to be considered as a refuge and a bastion in the face of
anti-Semitic brutality. Perhaps even more survivalist than Monsky
(president of B'nai B'rith from 1938 to 1947) was Frank Goldman,
the next president (1947–1953), who was hardly interested in the
nature of the evolving Israeli society. The survivalist-defensive end
of B'nai B'rith's ideology was clearly demonstrated in the power
worship of the order's Anti-Defamation League. Within a month of
the establishment of Israel, the executive committee of the League
concluded that the strength and success of the new state would give
it leverage in its struggle against anti-Semitism in America. And
several months later the League leadership resolved that "Israel as a
Fighting Force" would be the first of the ADL's seven themes in its
pro-Israel educational work in the United States. This stance came
to characterize the League in years to come.[20]

During the 1940s, activists of the Joint (the JDC), the UJA and the
federations became "Zionized" under the impact of the Holocaust
and the desperate situation of Jewish refugees in post war Europe.
A historic turning point was reached in Atlantic City in December
1945 at the national conference of the UJA, when the delegates
directly confronted survivors of Nazi Europe. Huge contributions
for Israel as a place of refuge began to pour in after 1946. Still,
the emerging pro-Zionism of the Jewish establishment (with the

---

19 Marc L. Raphael, *Abba Hillel Silver* (New York: Holmes & Meier, 1989), esp.
    chaps. 4 and 10; Emanuel Neumann, *In the Arena: An Autobiographical Memoir*
    (New York: Herzl Press, 1976), 107 and passim.
20 For Monsky, *Proceedings of the Sixteenth General Convention of the Supreme
    Lodge B'nai B'rith*, Chicago, 29 March–2 April 1941, 40; for Goldman, *Summary
    of the Nineteenth General Convention of the Supreme Lodge B'nai B'rith*, Wash-
    ington, D.C., 18–22 March 1950, 2–3; Proceedings of Meetings of the Executive
    Committee of the ADL National Commission, 11 June and 12 November 1948,
    Anti-Defamation League Archives, New York.

CJF at its heart) was focused somewhat beyond mere survivalism. Leaders of the federations envisaged an Israel cherishing the core values of Judaism such as *tzedakah*. And they saw the Jewish state as representing a consummation of America's own values of democracy and equal opportunity. The federations' ideology was steeped in American values and even adopted the ideal of an American mission as a Jewish virtue to be pursued. Survivalism in the postwar civil religion of the federations assumed that Israel was a model society in the making. Therefore, even though Israel as an asylum-fortress was the Jewish establishment's main rationale for supporting it, an associated expectation was that the Jewish state would demonstrate freedom, compassion, and decency.[21] The historic shift of American Jewish ideology toward survivalism, then, did not cause the mission motif to vanish entirely, nor cause the total erasure of the vision of a model society.

Again, the dramatic change undergone by the organized Zionist movement has not made it homogeneously survival-oriented. Some veteran expounders of "missionism" — personalities such as Horace Kallen and Bernard Rosenblatt — lived to see the establishment of Israel and actively perpetuated their original attitudes. The progressive tradition did not die at once. Soon after the establishment of the State of Israel, during the Fifty-First convention of the ZOA, its leadership (Neumann and his associates) was accused by some delegates of dragging the organization away from the grand Pittsburgh Program; in response the leaders avowed loyalty to the Program and brought it to the floor for confirmation, which swiftly took place. This approval by no means meant that the ZOA of the 1950s was committed to the universal mission rationale, or to the Program's very progressive social order; it did mean, however, that despite the ascendency of survivalism, strong sentiments for democracy and a just society had stubbornly persisted.[22]

---

21   Allon Gal, "Universal Mission and Jewish Survivalism in American Zionist Ideology," in *From Ancient Israel to Modern Judaism: Essays in Honor of Marvin Fox,* 4 vols., ed. Jacob Neusner et al. (Atlanta: Scholars Press, 1989), 4: 73–74, 82–83; Jonathan S. Woocher, *Sacred Survival: The Civil Religion of American Jews* (Bloomington: Indiana University Press, 1986), chaps. 2 and 3; and see also Menahem Kaufman's article in this volume.

22   Gal, "Universal Mission and Jewish Survivalism," 74–79.

Moreover, the Hadassah organization patently steered clear of Neumann's pro-Revisionist course. True, since the early 1940s, Hadassah had espoused a more militant Zionism than in the years of Henrietta Szold's and Irma Lindheim's leadership. Under the presidencies of Judith Epstein (1943–1947) and Rose Halprin (1947–1952), for example, the organization abandoned its tilt toward a binational political solution for Palestine, in which it had previously evinced great interest. Still, Hadassah members and leaders continued to hope that the Jewish state would not only provide a solution for problems of Jewish nationalism but would also convey some universal message. The organization stubbornly opposed the efforts of Silver and Neumann to persuade the World Confederation of General Zionists (which at the time included the ZOA and Hadassah) to identify itself with the General Zionists, the conservative Israeli party. Eventually (in 1958) the Confederation split, when the grouping of Silver and Neumann (which assumed the name World Union of General Zionists) linked itself to the rightist camp in Israeli politics. Hadassah, on the other hand, adhered to its generally liberal, non partisan position. In the framework of the World Confederation of General Zionists, Hadassah often expressed its vision of Israel not just as a haven-fortress but also as an enlightened new society, pursuing a compassionate foreign policy, thus combining what Hadassah considered the noble Jewish prophetic heritage with the best of the American liberal tradition.[23]

Another source of mission inspiration for American Zionists was the Conservative movement (historically pro-Zionist). The movement already had a meaningful tradition (dating back to the nineteenth century) of a universalist vision of Israel. Louis Finkelstein, its long-time president and chancellor of the Jewish Theological Seminary of America (1940–1972), himself a reluctant Zionist, influenced the Zionist movement to become more responsive to the idea of Israel as the cosmic servant of God and mankind. Following the establishment of the State of Israel, and considering its rapid and vigorous development, apprehension arose that Israel might evolve as a separate and distinct national entity. Conservative educators and thinkers, eminent among them Robert Gordis, mooted the concern

23 Ibid., 76–78.

that Israel — detached both from its painful exilic past, and from the Diaspora's current vulnerabilities — might develop narrowly and chauvinistically. "The Jewish people," wrote Gordis, "which never abandoned its concept of morality and truth in all the ages of darkness, will not surrender its high tradition of spiritual integrity in the hour of its shining victory." He expressed the hope that "the people which gave the Bible to the world will feel impelled to go beyond preachment to practice and to transmute the promise of its ideals into glorious fulfillment", and that

> A small country may for the second time in history justify its title of the Holy Land by pointing the way for mankind to a nobler patriotism, an ethical nationalism, and a social system based on voluntary cooperation and flowering into freedom.[24]

An interesting case of an agency that was actively involved in the struggle against anti-Semitism and Nazism during the 1920s to mid-1940s, but which turned away from survivalist ideology, was the American Jewish Congress, led by Stephen S. Wise. In 1945, the Congress embarked on a program whose premise was that the well-being of the Jews depended on a liberal political and social climate, and it became increasingly involved in the promotion of social legislation, strengthening American democracy, eliminating racial and religious bigotry, and advancing civil liberties, as well as advocating separation of church and state. The Congress, always of strong pro-Zionist sentiment, envisioned an Israel responsive to these imperatives, and in time elaborated tools, among them American Jewish-Israeli "dialogues," designed also to pursue this vision.[25]

Significantly, some of the new American Zionist bodies — although Zionized under the impact of Nazism and the Holocaust — shaped their evolving nationalist concept in a rather universal mission oriented pattern. This was certainly the case with the Reform movement. Zionism had already made its small home within Reform

---

24   Robert Gordis, *Judaism for the Modern Age* (New York: Farrar, Straus, & Cudahy, 1955), chap. 6, quotation on 124. See also Gal, "The Historical Continuity Motif in Conservative Judaism," 164–165.

25   Melvin I. Urofsky, *A Voice that Spoke for Justice: The Life and Times of Stephen S. Wise* (Albany: State University of New York Press, 1982), chap. 20; C. Bezalel Sherman, in *Encyclopedia Judaica*, s.v. "American Jewish Congress."

Judaism at the beginning of the twentieth century, without Reform Zionists giving up the mission idea. During the 1930s and 1940s, however, the idea went through an interesting mutation: what was formerly seen as a message being carried by the scattered people was now conceived of as being fulfilled and disseminated by a model society in the ancient homeland (in conjunction with the Diaspora). A long list of Reform personalities, responsible for the Zionization of the movement, boldly drew on the social-democratic character of the *yishuv* and young Israel to effect this transformation. They were amazed that the Jewish pioneers — with their unique social justice achievements, cooperative and collective enterprises, and voluntaristic-democratic beliefs — "have not only made the desert to flower like a garden, but have made a way for the Lord in the erstwhile wilderness." The establishment of the State of Israel had naturally accelerated the Zionization of Reform Judaism. In the early 1950s, the first group of Reform rabbis visited Israel and reported that

> She [Israel] exists by the word of the very men who were her midwives, not to display trappings of sovereignty, nor even solely as a life-saving device, but because of the perennial and millennial objectives of the Jewish religion... Prophets must speak again from Zion for mankind. No one wants just another nationalism.

The visiting rabbis concluded on this note:

> It is a great thrill for the Israeli to see his flag flying over his president's house. But the high and noble sense of mission cannot come solely from pride in political independence. The spur of the ageless religious inspiration of Judaism must again and again be applied if Israel is to be more than just another state.[26]

Some of the non-Zionist elite organizations (as distinct from the more mass-based ones such as B'nai B'rith), made their way to Zionism (American-style of course) at a slower pace and with greater concern

26 Allon Gal, *The Changing Concept of "Mission" in American Reform Judaism* (Cincinnati: American Jewish Archives, 1991), quotations on 17, 18–19.

30 *ALLON GAL*

as to the nature of Israeli society. More organically integrated into the fabric of Amercian society, they were painfully distressed by the "dual loyalty" question. Thus they gradually cultivated pro-Israelism on their own terms — namely, shaping it to be sensitively responsive to American values and mores. This was the case, for example, with the American Jewish Committee which came only slowly to see Palestine as a place for Jewish refugees. It reluctantly supported the 1947 UN resolution to establish a Jewish state in part of western Palestine, and it emphasized time and again that American Jews were part of the American nation and owed their political loyalty only to the United States. Now, thanks to this very Americanism, they had strong expectations from Israel: they expected that all Israeli citizens, regardless of race, religion, national origins, or class, would enjoy full and equal political rights. Accordingly, the Committee persistently produced statements expressing the wish to see the Arab minority in Israel treated equally and fairly. Similarly it voiced the expectation that Israel would be based on a constitution which, as in the United States, would ensure separation of church and state. True, this attitude was a far cry from the lofty mission-oriented Brandeis vision, but it deviated at the same time from the stark survivalist vein prevalent, for example, among the ADL circles of B'nai B'rith.[27]

Following the developments and events of the 1920s–1940s, survivalist trends became potent for the first time in the record of American Zionism. Israel epitomized the right of the Jewish people to exist; the state's existence thus became a goal unto itself. On the whole, however, a kind of synthesis between survivalism and missionism emerged. The Jewish state was often expected to exhibit exemplary behavior à la liberal America. Furthermore, important groups adhered to the idea that Israel, by virtue of both its recent and its historic past, had a humanistic message to convey to the rest of the nations — the tortured people, now saved and loyal to its historic calling, at this point goes out to help redeem the world.[28]

27 Menahem Kaufman , "The State of Israel as Conceived by the American Jewish Committee, 1947–1948" (in Hebrew), *Contemporary Jewry* 3 (1986), 171–185.
28 For the synthesis see, e.g., the editorial, upon the proclamation of the State of Israel, in the leading organ of the American Zionist movement, *New Palestine,*

VI. Recent Trends and Issues

Until the late 1970s, Israel's wars for its survival further attenuated the mission aspect of American Jewry's vision. Israel's development as an increasingly "normal" Western society also contributed to this end. Consequently, the state's right to exist, whatever its social order and mores, has penetrated as the ultimate value to the very core of American Jewry's concept of Israel. But again, other processes and events have caused American Jews to look harder at and be more concerned about Israel's polity and politics. The War in Lebanon, the Palestinian uprising in the occupied territores, the attempts to change the Law of Return in defiance of most of American Jewry — these were among the major reasons for a renewed interest in and sharper sensitivity to issues concerning Israeli society and politics. The futurity of Israeli democracy, pluralism, and compassionate policies came to be a matter of grave concern for many American Jews. All these influences culminated in the greater confidence of American Jews in their own liberal convictions and, eventually, a synthesized vision of Israel. The security and well-being of the state remained at the top of the agenda; but the traditional expectation of an exemplary democratic society conducting decent and considerate foreign relations was also revitalized.[29] This new synthesis — of toned-down missionism and survivalism — was reflected in comprehensive treatises and declarations by the major streams of Amercian religious Judaism — the Reform and the Conservative.

The new Reform credo — "Reform Judaism: A Centenary Perspective" — adopted at the 1976 CCAR national convention in San Francisco, was quite survival-oriented compared to the Columbus (1937) and the Minneapolis-St. Paul (1962) statements. In a section entitled "One Hundred Years: What We Have Learned," the San Francisco document, written after the Yom Kippur War, clearly presented a survivalist viewpoint: "We have learned again that the

38(18) (18 May 1948), 4; In Hadassah's synthesis of survivalism and missionism it was latter element that loomed larger. See, e.g., Rose Halprin's treatise "We Herewith Pledge," *Hadassah Newsletter* 29(9) (May 1949): 2.

29   For background, see Sachar, *A History of the Jews in America*, chap. 24.

survival of the Jewish people is of highest priority and that in carrying out our Jewish responsibilities we help move humanity toward its messianic fulfillment." Still, the main ideological effort was directed toward working out a synthesis between survivalism and universal mission; the pertinent deliberation is worth quoting at some length:

> Until the recent past our obligations to the Jewish people and to all humanity seemed congruent. At times now these two imperatives appear to conflict. We know of no simple way to resolve such tensions. We must, however, confront them without abandoning either of our commitments. A universal concern for humanity unaccompanied by a devotion to our particular people is self-destructive; a passion for our people without involvement in humankind contradicts what the prophets have meant to us. Judaism calls us simultaneously to universal and particular obligations.[30]

Moreover, the mission impulse is present in the concluding article of the credo. The urge for survival is stretched beyond ethnicity and beyond narrow locality in order to give mankind's history a humanistically valid meaning. The movement has continued to envision Israel as a conspicuously enlightened state and has made tremendous efforts — including establishing its own kibbutzim — to make Israel into a state adhering both domestically and internationally to "a noble sense of mission."[31]

In September 1978, the Association of Reform Zionists of America (ARZA) was established in Washington, D.C. Its platform was an interpreted version of the Jerusalem Program (adopted by the 1968 World Zionist Congress). Item 3 endorsed the Program's social vision: "The strengthening of the State of Israel which is based on the prophetic vision of justice and peace."

> We do not envision a Jewish nation like other nations. We hope it will continue to be nourished by the moral, social, and spiritual teachings of our tradition, reaching back to Sinai, to

30 Quotations from *Central Conference of American Rabbis Yearbook*, vol. 86 (New York: The Central Conference of American Rabbis, 1976), 177–178.
31 Ibid., 178.

our biblical and rabbinic sources, to our Diaspora experience, to Israel's own social achievements.

And it boldly added: "Reform can augment the Zionist vision of the just society by calling for the same kind of concern with moral and social issues in Israel that we have advanced in America." In March 1993 ARZA's first journal was published, stating its religious relationship to the envisioned Israel. In addition to voluntarism and pluralism, it stood for "Social ethics together with ritual"; and "Universal concern as an intrinsic element in our ethnic character." And typically it concluded the statement with "Our common vision is that 'Zion shall be redeemed through righteousness'."[32]

In the fortieth year of Israel's independence (1988), the Conservative movement published its *Emet Ve-Emunah*, a comprehensive "Statement of Principles of Conservative Judaism." This treatise explicitly stands for the theology of the election of Israel, interpreting it as a moral and spiritual obligation of the Jewish people and of the State of Israel. One article, in particular, entitled "The Uniqueness of Israel," declares that "We do not view Israel as just another state of political entity; rather, we envision it as an exemplar of religious and moral principles, of civil, political and religious rights for all citizens regardless of race, religion, ethnic origin or sex." The article continues:

> We believe that the litmus test of the character of a democratic Jewish state is its treatment of and attitude towards its religious and ethnic minorities.... Jews should be particulary sensitive to the well-being of all of the various ethnic and religious groups living in the State of Israel.

And it concludes:

> [We] recall the prophetic injunction to our people to be "a

---

32 Ronald B. Gittelsohn, *ARZA — From Birth to Bar/Bat Mitzvah* (New York: Association of Reform Zionists of America, 1990), 7; *ARZA Newsletter* 2(4) (November 1978): 5; and *Journal of Reform Zionism* 1(1) (March 1993): i. See also Michael Langer, "Reform Judaism and Zionism as Responses to the Modern Age," in *A Reform Zionist Perspective*, ed. idem (New York: Union of American Hebrew Congregations, 1983), 3–17 and sections 10 and 11, 249–296 and 297–388, respectively.

covenant people, a light of nations." Israel reborn provides a unique opportunity for the Jewish people to be a holy people and a blessing to the nations. Consequently, it behooves Israel to set an example for other nations to build their societies on the principles of social justice, righteousness, compassion, and love for all citizens of all faiths and ethnic groups.

We hope that Israel will be true to the principles cited in its Declaration of Independence so that the State will continue to maintain the moral principles of our prophets and sages who never ceased calling for morality in government and international affairs. We look forward to the day envisioned by our prophets when "nation shall not take up sword against nation; they shall never again know war."[33]

The statement then elaborates on the principles embedded in that succinct expression as to the loyalty of the envisioned Israel to the values of justice, ethics, and dignity of man domestically, and an all-embracing constructive interaction with the world's nations.[34]

In 1979 members of the American Conservative movement who had immigrated to Israel, together with interested Israelis, established the Masorti (Traditional) Movement oriented toward the world Conservative movement. In its vision of Israel the Israeli Masorti movement stands for the basic Western values of human rights, and under the rubric "Tolerance and Pluralism," typical of the Conservative tradition, proclaims:

> The Masorti Movement emphasizes the Jewish belief that all people are created in God's image, entitled to liberty, freedom of thought and freedom of religious worship. The Movement considers the principles of democracy and religious humanism central to its world view.
>
> The Masorti Movement was a founding member of HEMDAT, a coalition of organizations that works for freedom of science, religion, and culture in Israel.[35]

33   The Jewish Theological Seminary of America et al., *Emet Ve-Emunah: Statement of Principles of Conservative Judaism* (New York: The Jewish Theological Seminary of America, 1988), 36–37.

34   Ibid., 37–40, 42–44, 44–46.

35   *The Masorti Movement* (Jerusalem: The Masorti Movement, 1993), 8.

Another development of Conservative Judaism was the establish-ment, in 1979, of the U.S.A. Merkaz and, in 1991, of the World Union of Merkaz, which works as the political arm of Conservative Judaism within the framework of the World Zionist Organization. The liberal and democratic nature of Merkaz is clear from its formal commitment to "ensure religious pluralism in Israel...; promote civil rights including Masorti representation on religious councils and full equality for women; encourage electoral reform so that extremist minority parties will no longer wield undue power."[36]

The concern of the Conservative movement, both American and Israeli, for the future of Israel's social democracy and its relations with the Arabs at home and abroad — were expressed loudly and clearly in a conference devoted to the theme "Zionism and the Conservative/Masorti Movement," led by the Jewish Theological Seminary of America in 1988. The vision of Israel as a democratic, ethical, highly sensible state was at the heart of this important gathering.[37]

The attitudes of the Reform and Conservative movements — which together comprise the vast majority of American Jewry and the core leadership of the organized community — demonstrate the vitality of the liberal tradition of American Jewry and Zionism. Recent surveys, which concentrate on Jewish-Arab relations and the peace process, sustain a similar conclusion. Whereas the mission rationale has generally been relegated to a minor position since the 1930s, the concern that Israel should be an enlightened polity has proven to be quite tenacious.

It is instructive that a questionnaire in 1989 listed three decidedly hawkish options, all of which were rejected by the sample. (The terms "hawkish" and "dovish" used in the questionnaire are of course colloquial, but for the researcher they are at the same time serviceable and clear.) Hardly any support was found for the forcible transfer of Arabs out of the West Bank; by smaller but still decisive margins the sample also rejected Israeli annexation of the West Bank.

---

36 MERCAZ's flier, distributed by its New York headquarters, March 1991.
37 John S. Ruskay and David M. Szonyi, eds., *Deepening the Commitment: Zionism and the Conservative/Masorti Movement* (New York: The Jewish Theologcial Seminary of America, 1990), esp. Introduction, Plenary Addresses, and Semi-nars 1, 2, and 6.

A question probing whether respondents agreed that "Israel should offer the Arabs territorial compromise in the West Bank and Gaza in return for credible guarantees of peace" was endorsed by about 40 percent, opposed by 30 percent. By a two-to-one majority the 1989 sample agreed that "Palestinians have a right to a homeland on the West Bank and Gaza, so long as it does not threaten Israel." Some questions explored attitudes to talking with the PLO. A plurality of the sample endorsed the impending U.S.-PLO talks. The statement, "If the PLO recognizes Israel and renounces terrorism, Israel should be willing to talk with the PLO," was endorsed by a solid majority.[38]

Considering these data and attitudes, it is little wonder that one finds American Jews, already in 1991, willing to support far-reaching compromises in order to advance the peace process in the Middle East. This dovish inclination is especially conspicuous when we consider the attitudes of the leaders of the community. The following are some of the major findings of the survey of over 200 leaders (all Council of Jewish Federations board members or presidents of local federations): a large majority is worried about Israeli rule over Palestinians. While expressing mixed feelings about settlements, most leaders are ready to freeze settlement in return for Arab concessions and U.S. loan guarantees. A huge preponderance of leaders disagrees with Shamir's "not one inch" stance, favors territorial compromise in exchange for a credible peace, and is open to a nonthreatening Palestinian state. A majority is open to returning some part of the Golan Heights in exchange for real peace with Syria. Although many leaders distrust the Arabs, almost all say enforceable peace agreements are possible; most are ready for Israel to talk to the PLO if the PLO is peaceful; and they support active American involvement in the peace process, including pressure on both sides to be more flexible. Overall, the leaders strongly prefer the Israeli left over the Israeli right; politically, most are liberal to middle-of-the-road.[39]

When it finally came to the Palestinian autonomy agreement and

38   Data and discussion are based on Steven M. Cohen, *Ties and Tensions: An Update. The 1989 Survey of American Jewish Attitudes toward Israel and Israelis* (New York: The American Jewish Committee, 1989).

39   Steven M. Cohen and Seymour M. Lipset, *Attitudes toward the Arab-Israeli Conflict and the Peace Process among American Jewish Philanthropic Leaders,*

Israel-PLO recognition, a survey (of late September 1993) demonstrated that the overwhelming majority of American Jewish opinion supports both initiatives. The key findings are that 90 percent of Amercian Jews view mutual recognition between Israel and the PLO as a "positive development from Israel's point of view," and that 74 percent support the autonomy agreement. With regard to giving up the Golan Heights in order to reach peace with Syria, about 60 percent are for yielding a small part or some of it, and 7 percent are for giving back most or all of it (as opposed to 27 percent who are against giving back any of it).[40]

All these findings, qualified as they should be, fall well into line with the liberal tradition of American Jewry and its compassionate vision of Israel.

1991 (Los Angeles: The Wilstein Institute of Jewish Policy Studies, University of Judaism, 1992).

40   Market Facts, "The Palestinian Autonomy Agreement and Israel–PLO Recognition: A Survey of American Jewish Opinion," (New York), conducted for the American Jewish Committee, September 1993. Typescript.

Part I

Zionist Ideals

A Projection of Amercia as It Ought to Be: Zion in the Mind's Eye of American Jews

Jonathan D. Sarna

Let me begin with a bold thesis. The Israel of American Jews — the Zion that they imagined in their minds, dreamed about, and wrote about — was for centuries a mythical Zion, a Zion that reveals more about American Jewish ideals than about the realities of Eretz Israel. In the late eighteenth and early nineteenth centuries, American Jews depicted Israel as a "holy" land, a land where desperately poor and scrupulously faithful Jews engaged in prayer and study; a land, in short, where the material life, values, and practices of Jews were precisely the reverse of American Jews' own. In the late nineteenth and early twentieth centuries, alongside this traditional image, a new one arose: the image of the romantic pioneer, the hard-working agricultural colonist, the brawny Jewish farmer — the answer, in other words, to those who claimed that Jews were mere parasites, racially incapable of "productive" labor. Finally, in the second decade of the twentieth century, Zionists like Louis D. Brandeis added a further twist to this image: Zion became for them a utopian extension of the American dream, a Jewish refuge where freedom, liberty, and social justice would reign supreme, an "outpost of democracy" that American Jews could legitimately, proudly, and patriotically champion.

All of these images, whatever truth they may have contained, took on mythic proportions in America. They embodied American Jews' yearnings and dreams, responded to their psychological, political, and emotional needs, and helped them to counter the malicious slurs of their enemies. The Zion of the American Jewish imagination, in short, became something of a fantasy land: a seductive heaven-on-earth, where enemies were vanquished, guilt assuaged, hopes realized, and deeply felt longings satisfied.[1]

This essay examines these historic American Jewish images of Zion in greater detail. It argues that such images developed from — and addressed — the needs of *American* Jewry and were, as a result, increasingly out of touch with reality back in Eretz Israel. Over time, this "Israel of American Jews" became more and more of an idealized dream world — no more realizable than the starry-eyed visions of a *goldene medina* that some Jewish immigrants to America brought with them when they sailed to Ellis Island. This in no way of course diminishes the significance of these dreams; for like all such dreams they reveal much about the mind of the dreamers — in our case American Jews. The dreams also took on a life of their own, influencing culture, philanthropy, and politics.

It is impossible in the space allotted to me to deal with all of these themes. I confine myself, therefore, to three little-known but I think revealing documents, each from a different century, that shed light on the image of Zion as it developed in America prior to 1948.

I

Let us turn first to a document from 1761. Early in that year, the leaders of New York's Congregation Shearith Israel received an unusual letter in Spanish from "the very Reverent Haham Haim Mudahy [Modai]." Raised in th Holy City of Safed and later a member of the Jewish court (*bet din*) of Constantinople, Modai was a distinguished Sephardic scholar. He was also an experienced emissary of the Jews of Safed, having traveled to Europe in 1749 to collect funds for his impoverished community. Now he was again representing the Jews of Safed, for they had just experienced a devastating earthquake (30 October, 1759) and urgently needed money to rebuild.

In his letter Modai described "the great misfortune and calamity

---

1   In these paragraphs, I have drawn upon my earlier remarks on this subject in *Commentary*, February 1988, 64–65.

which our brethren have suffered in the holy city of Zaphet [Safed] caused by the earthquake." He reported that both the synagogues and the house of study had been damaged, that many houses were totally destroyed, their owners losing all they possessed, and that 160 people had perished in the ruins. He begged the "illustrious gentlemen" of the Jewish community of New York for "prompt and liberal relief to alleviate the disaster which brought such terrible misfortune and unspeakable distress, a calamity from which God may deliver us and never again permit to befall children of Israel."

Haham Modai's letter was one of numerous appeals sent to the congregation through the years on behalf of suffering Holy Land Jews, and it encapsulated in its language the central images that Jews in Early America already associated with their brethren in Zion: the idea that in this case, Safed, was a "poor Kehila [community]," a "holy and suffering Kehila," and a "Kehila" whose leaders were deeply committed to "the continuous study of the Holy Law." To assist such a worthy community, Modai reminded American Jews, was a "mitzvah," and as such, contributions benefited donors no less than recipients. "I trust to Divine Grace," he concluded, "...that by your acts, Omnipotent God may redeem us from our bitter and prolonged captivity, and that He may bless you, prosper and increase you."[2]

The Land of Israel, in Haham Modai's day and into the early decades of the nineteenth century, was sparsely settled. It held a population of about 300,000, not more than 5,000 of whom were Jews. Disease and poverty were rampant, violence was omnipresent, and as a modern historian puts it, "the country displayed all the characteristics of a neglected province of a disintegrating empire," the Ottoman empire.[3] Such was the real Israel, which to my knowledge not a single American Jew of those days had ever seen. The Israel in the mind of early American Jews, in contrast, was an imagined Israel — a land of troubles, to be sure, but still a holy land,

2   *Publications of the American Jewish Historical Society* 27 (1920) 18–20; on Modai, see *Encyclopaedia Judaica.* s.v. I find no evidence to support the claim that Modai actually visited New York, as maintained by David de Sola Pool, "Early Relations between Palestine and American Jewry," in *The Brandeis Avukah Annual of 1932*, ed. Joseph S. Shubow (Boston; Avukah, 1932), 537.

3   H. Z. Hirschberg, *Encyclopaedia Judaica,* s.v. "Israel, Land of," Col. 293.

a land where in the midst of suffering and poverty Jews studied and prayed, and a land to which, in God's good time, all Jews would be restored.

Emissaries (*meshulahim*) collecting funds for the Jews of the Holy Land visited America's shores every few years from 1759 onward, supplementing the appeals from scholars like Haham Modai that arrived by letter. Some, like Haham Hayim Carigal, who visited the American colonies in 1772–1773, developed a network of Jewish and Christian friends and won wide respect; others failed miserably.[4] Whether successful or not, however, itinerants tended to reinforce the image of the Holy Land as radically other, altogether different from Jewish life as lived in the New World, and practically its antithesis. "You, protected by the liberal constitution of America, living in freedom, opulence and prosperity: turn your eyes to the horrible state of slavery and misery, under which our brethren are weeping in the Holy Land! and your compassionate hearts will be deeply affected," a typical fundraising epistle read, in this case a letter of 1838 seeking funds from the Jews of Charleston.[5] The American Jewish leader Mordecai Noah, in his 1825 address at the laying of the cornerstone of Ararat, his abortive Jewish colony near Grand Island, New York, underscored this same sharp distinction:

> They are the great sentinels and guardians of the law and religion and amidst the severest privations and the most intense sufferings, they have for centuries kept their eye upon the ruined

4   Pool, "Palestine and American Jewry," 536–548; Hyman B. Grinstein, *The Rise of the Jewish Community of New York, 1654–1860* (Philadelphia: Jewish Publication Society, 1945), 440–465; Abraham Yaari, *Sheluhe Eretz Yisrael* (Emissaries from the Land of Israel) (Jerusalem, 1951); David de Sola Pool and Tamar de Sola Pool, *An Old Faith in the New World* (New York: Columbia University Press, 1955), 396–405; and Salo W. Baron and Jeannette M. Baron, "Palestinian Messengers in America, 1849–79: A Record of Four Journeys," reprinted in S. W. Baron, *Steeled by Adversity* (Philadelphia: Jewish Publication Society of America, 1971), 158–266.

5   Letter of 24 Nissan 5598 (29 March 1838), quoted in Moshe Davis, *Igrot ha-Pekidim ve-ha-Amarkalim me-Amsterdam* (The correspondence of the *Pekidim* and *Amarkalim* from Amsterdam) in *Salo Baron Jubilee Volume* (Jerusalem, 1975), Hebrew section, 95. English version in Moshe Davis, *America and the Holy Land* (Westport, Conn.: Praeger, 1995), 107.

site of the temple and said, "the time will come — the day will be accomplished."

Here... in this free and happy country, distinctions in religion are unknown; here we enjoy liberty without licentiousness and land without oppression.[6]

America and Israel, according to these exaggerated conceptions, were polar opposites. Where American Jews cultivated commerce, neglected Jewish learning, evinced considerable laxity in their religious behavior, and enjoyed liberty and freedom, the Jews of Eretz Israel wallowed in poverty, suffered brutal oppression, devoted themselves to Jewish learning, and remained completely scrupulous in their religious observances. America, in this binary scheme, represented modernity's lures and perils, while Israel symbolized tradition and suffering with the promise of redemption. Each nevertheless needed the other, and as a result the two communities (like the Diaspora and Israel generally) developed a genuine sense of interdependence: material sustenance flowed in one direction, spiritual sustenance in the other. Again, it was Mordecai Noah who best articulated this symbiotic relationship, this time in his address at Shearith Israel on Thanksgiving Day, 1848, on behalf of Rabbi Jechiel Ha-Cohen's mission[7] seeking funds to enlarge a Jerusalem synagogue:

It has been said that the Jews at Jerusalem are indolent, are disinclined to labor, are only employed in studying the law, and devoting all their hours to prayer, and prefer leading a life of dependence and want to one of prosperous active industry. I thank them that they do so. Amid our worldly cares, [our] pursuits of gain, our limited knowledge of our holy faith, our surrender of many cardinal points — probably of necessity — I am thankful that there is a holy band of brotherhood at Zion, whose nights and days are devoted to our sublime laws, our

6 "Address of Mordecai M. Noah... Delivered at the Laying of the Corner Stone of the City of Ararat [25 September, 1825]," reprinted in *Publications of the American Jewish Historical Society* 21 (1913), 236, 244. On Noah, see Jonathan D. Sarna, *Jacksonian Jew: The Two Worlds of Mordecai Noah* (New York: Holmes & Meier, 1981).

7 Sarna, *Jacksonian Jew*, 156–157; Pool, *Old Faith*, 401.

venerable institutions. I wish them to remain so; I think it our duty and our interest to share our means with them — to repay them with the bread of life, for aiding us with the bread of salvation.[8]

Noah understood that the cause he advocated faced opposition, for by 1848 some American Jews had come to resent the appeals made to them by the Jews of the Holy Land. Influenced by the Enlightenment and by ideas emanating from European Jewish philanthropists, they wanted the Jews of Palestine to become self-sufficient, to abandon if necessary their focus on prayer and study for "prosperous active industry." But even if elements of the traditional relationship had come under attack, the central images developed over the previous century proved extremely resilient. The Holy Land during this period came to represent traditional religious values that American Jews paid homage to but never themselves expected to uphold. Contributions aimed at strengthening the Holy Land Jewish community compensated — consciously so in Noah's case — for American Jewry's own spiritual weaknesses, as if to bridge the chasm between modernity and tradition. American Jews gave no thought to emulating the behavior of Jews in the Holy Land, nor — barring supernatural intervention — did they imagine themselves returning there. Instead, Zion functioned for them as something of a counterlife: in conjuring it up, they caught a glimpse of a world that was practically the antithesis of their own, for better and for worse.

II

One hundred and twenty-eight years after Haham Modai's appeal to Shearith Israel, an unusual volume was published in Philadelphia entitled *Migdal Zophim (The Watch Tower): The Jewish Problem and Agriculture as Its Solution* (1889). The volume's author, Moses Klein (1857–1910), was an immigrant from Hungary described by his contemporaries as an "ardent worker in the cause of Jewish charity

8   Mordecai M. Noah, *Address Delivered at the Hebrew Synagogue in Crosby-Street, New York, on Thanksgiving Day to Aid in the Erection of the Temple at Jerusalem* (Kingston, Jamaica, 1849), 8.

and education." In Philadelphia, he served as the first agent of the Association for the Protection of Jewish Immigrants and later as an inspector of immigration and a manager with the United Hebrew Charities.[9] His real passion, however, lay in the movement to return Jews to the land through agricultural colonization. To his mind this was the only realistic solution to the problems of the Jewish people, and it was this message that *Migdal Zophim* sought to drive home:

> Poor souls!... there is no brighter future for you in New York than in Wilna; and no more prospect at Philadelphia and Chicago than in Lemberg and Bucharest! *Farming* alone seems to me to be your future destiny in this blessed country, and *colonization* only can solve THE JEWISH PROBLEM forced upon us for solution by Eastern Europe and Asia.[10]

Notwithstanding his tribute to "this blessed country," Klein devoted about a third of his book to a depiction of Jewish agricultural life in Palestine. First he translated from the original Hebrew a series of "descriptive sketches" of Palestine's Jews written by Joshua Stampfer, one of the founders of the pioneering Palestine Jewish agricultural colony, Petach Tikvah. Stampfer (whose words Klein echoed) sought to refute "the charge of 'idleness' usually brought against Jews of Palestine," emphasizing instead their many trades and occupations, and particularly their agricultural colonies ("which alone can solve THE JEWISH PROBLEM and secure to the 'Wandering Jew' the promised recreation"). Next Klein himself provided an elaborate description of Jaffa's Mikveh Israel Agricultural School, founded to teach farming to young Jews in the Holy Land, in the hope of eventually "extending practical farming amongst all the Jews under the Sultan's government." In a concluding addendum,

9 Henry S. Morais, *The Jews, of Philadelphia* (Philadelphia, 1894), 354; Maxwell Whiteman, "The Fiddlers Rejected: Jewish Immigrant Expression in Philadelphia," in *Jewish Life in Philadelphia*, ed. Murray Friedman (Philadelphia: ISHI, 1983), 91; Jacob Zausmer, *Footprints of a Generation: Essays and Memoirs* (in Hebrew) (New York: Histadruth Ivrith of America, 1957), 214. See also Jacob Kabakoff *Halutze ha-Sifrut ha-Ivrit ba-Amerika* (Pioneers of American Hebrew Literature) (Tel Aviv: Yavneh, 1966), 167.

10 Moses Klein, *Migdal Zophim (The Watch Tower): The Jewish Problem and Agriculture as Its Solution* (Philadelphia, 1889), 62–63. (Emphasis in the original.)

he offered a personal defense of the Jewish colonies in Palestine
to rebut critics who portrayed them as economically unviable,
charity-dependent, and utter failures. "The Jewish colonists who
till the soil of the Holy Land will advance onward and upward," he
prophesied, insisting that

> by pursuing agriculture as their calling, they will uplift them-
> selves and incite many others of their brethren, in enlightened,
> as well as in benighted, countries, to emulate their example,
> and earn their livelihood by the "sweat of their brow." Such
> was the occupation of our patriarchs, of our prophets, of our
> sages; and that which afforded them sustenance, yea, delight
> — because it instilled within them the feeling of dependence
> upon God alone — ought surely to effect permanent good to
> their latest posterity. Joined to the pursuit of agriculture, the
> dissemination of the pure Hebrew as a language of intercourse
> will be attended with inestimable benefits.
> We sincerely believe that the time will come when Jewish
> agricultural colonization will spread throughout the Orient,
> and that Palestine will be, as in ancient days, the centre of all
> such efforts.[11]

Klein's vision of an agrarian Palestine, a land where Jewish pioneers,
inspired by the patriarchs and prophets of old, worked productively,
tilled the ancient soil, revived the pure Hebrew language, cast off the
shackles of economic dependence, and served as an example to the
Jews of the Diaspora, reflected an appealing new image of the Holy
Land that in his day was beginning to take hold in American Jewish
circles. Like the earlier image of the impoverished settler who prayed
and studied all day long, this image too had some basis in reality.
Immigration had swelled the Jewish population of Palestine to the
point where charity dependence was no longer feasible. Within
the *yishuv*, a tiny group of "rebels" resolved to strike out for
independence from alms by tilling the ancestral soil "with their own
hands" and reviving Hebrew as a spoken language. Youthful Eastern
European immigrants brought with them similar ideals, ones shared
by many Christians, some of whom were simultaneously involved

11   Ibid., 20, 28, 31, 87–88.

in establishing agricultural colonies in Palestine.[12] What bound all of these populists together was their pronounced love for the land and their ideology of productivism, their fierce sense that the only honest professions were those that entailed the creation of goods, preferably through agriculture.[13]

News of the agricultural colonization of Jews in Palestine first reached the American Jewish community through its newspapers — potent sources both of Jewish information and for the shaping of community perceptions. Isaac Leeser, the foremost traditionalist Jewish religious leader of his day and editor of the important Jewish monthly *The Occident*, published a great deal of news about the Holy Land and its colonies and spoke out in favor of Jewish agriculture in Palestine as early as 1852. A year later he called on his fellow Jews to do "something useful for that land, to have an interest in its soil, and to try to elevate its inhabitants from the low degree of unlaboring idleness...to the rank of independent industrious freemen." In 1854, he even tried to organize a national conference in support of agricultural and vocational training in Palestine, but without success.[14] His rival, the Reform Jewish leader Isaac Mayer Wise, editor of the *Israelite* (from 1874, *American Israelite*), likewise published a great deal of Holy Land news and was for much of his life no less sympathetic to the cause of agricultural colonization. He urged support for the Society to Colonize Palestine, wished success to the Moses Montefiore Agricultural Aid Association, and as late as 1893 praised the early Hovevei Zion for their efforts "to settle as many as possible of our brethren in agricultural colonies."[15]

12 Moshe Davis, "The Holy Land Idea in American Spritual History," in *With Eyes toward Zion*, ed. Davis, (New York: Arno, 1977), 1: 16, cf. 43–44; Robert T. Handy, ed., *The Holy Land in American Life, 1800–1948* (New York: Arno, 1981), esp. 147ff.

13 On agricultural colonization in Palestine, see Alex Bein, *The Return to the Soil* (Jerusalem, 1952), 1–8; and Yehoshua Ben-Arieh, *The Rediscovery of the Holy Land in the Nineteenth Century* (Jerusalem and Detroit: Magnes Press and Wayne State University Press, 1979), esp. 102–104.

14 *Occident* 10 (October 1852), 361, and 11 (December 1853), 432; *Asmonean* 9 (10 February, 1854), 133 — all as cited in Maxine S. Seller, "Isaac Leeser's Views on the Restoration of a Jewish Palestine," *American Jewish Historical Quarterly* 58 (September 1968): 118–135.

15 *American Israelite* 40 (3 August 1893), reprinted in James G. Heller, *Isaac M.*

Wise's support for agricultural colonization underscores the allure of the new romantic portrait of the Jew that was emerging from Palestine. The image of the young Jewish farmer, perhaps a refugee from Russia, once the victim of pogroms and now productively tilling the ancient Judean soil, had an irresistible quality about it; even those opposed to Zionism, like Rabbi Wise, found themselves entranced. ("This kind of Zionism," he wrote, "will recommend itself to every good man and all who can spare even a little should contribute to it.")[16] The fact that such farmers remained few and far between — 5 percent of the country's Jewish population, according to Klein's figures[17] — made no difference. In Palestine, as in America, it was the *symbol* of the Jewish farmer that proved all important, and understandably so. As Professor Robert Alan Goldberg explains in *Back to the Soil*:

> Agriculture offered to "productivize" the Jew by removing him from the artificial and less worthy sectors of urban commerce and industry while providing him with a measure of dignity and self-worth. The Jew would claim the power of decision making and initiative along with the sense of fulfillment generated by hard work and land ownership while contributing in a real sense to the wellbeing of his fellow countrymen. Further, a return to the land promised an end to dependence...and the creation of a balanced economic structure, the absence of which had plagued the Jewish world in the Diaspora. No longer would anti-Semites be able to smear Jews as commercial parasites who fed upon the sweat of producing members of society. Jews, in turn, would be cleansed of the debilitating self-hatred produced when such slurs were internalized.[18]

Wise (New York: Union of American Hebrew Congregations, 1965), 595, see also 589–596; Melvin Weinman, "The Attitude of Isaac Mayer Wise toward Zionism and Palestine," *American Jewish Archives* 3 (January 1951), reprinted in J. R. Marcus, *Critical Studies in American Jewish History* (Cincinnati and New York: American Jewish Archives/Ktav, 1971), 1: 256–259.

16   *American Israelite* 44 (23, June 1989), as quoted in Heller, *Wise*, 607.

17   Klein, *Migdal Zophim*, 28, 35.

18   Robert Alan Goldberg, *Back to the Soil* (Salt Lake City: University of Utah Press, 1986), 38.

Agriculture, in short, became something of a Jewish panacea in the late nineteenth and early twentieth centuries. Jews considered it a sure remedy for anti-Semitism, for those aspects of Jewish life that (to their minds) fomented anti-Semitism, and for a wide variety of other Jewish group ailments as well. Most American Jews, despite these promised therapeutic benefits, eschewed the agricultural option for themselves and continued to live out their lives in crowded cities. But they rewarded with high praise (and with considerable economic assistance) those of their brethren who did return to the land, especially in Palestine, and they took vicarious pleasure in learning of their achievements — which, as a consequence, proponents greatly exaggerated. Again the Holy Land had come to symbolize to American Jews something of a counterlife. The new Jewish agricultural settlements — small in number, large in significance — pointed toward an alternative form of existence for American Jews: an idyllically pastoral Jewish life, built on values that they (and their non-Jewish neighbors) respected and supported, but did not practice, and a life that was very much the antithesis of their own.[19]

III

On 25 June, 1918, delegates to the Twenty-First Annual Convention of the Zionist Organizations of America, meeting in Pittsburgh's Soldiers Memorial Hall, unanimously approved a "Declaration of Principles" that came to be known as "The Pittsburgh Program." As finally published in the frontispiece of *The Maccabaean*, the official organ of American Zionism, the document ("for the guidance of the Organization in its work of restoring Palestine") consisted of six idealistic planks:

---

19 Significantly, Jewish agricultural utopias in America sometimes bore Holy Land names, such as "Palestine" and "Bethlehem-Jehudah." Symbolically, these names distinguished the colonies from the Americanized East Coast Cities where most American Jews then resided. See Uri D. Herscher, *Jewish Agricultural Utopias in America, 1880–1910* (Detroit: Wayne State University Press, 1981).

FIRST We declare for political and civil equality irrespective of race, sex, or faith of all the inhabitants of the land.

SECOND To insure in the Jewish national home in Palestine equality of opportunity we favor a policy which, with due regard to existing rights, shall tend to establish the ownership and control by the whole people of the land, of all natural resources and of all public utilities.

THIRD All land, owned or controlled by the whole people, should be leased on such conditions as will insure the fullest opportunity for development and continuity of possession.

FOURTH The co-operative principle should be applied so far as feasible in the organization of all agricultural, industrial, commercial, and financial undertakings.

FIFTH The system of free public instruction which is to be established should embrace all grades and departments of education.

SIXTH Hebrew, the national language of the Jewish people, shall be the medium of public instruction.[20]

The American Zionist movement was enjoying a period of tremendous wartime growth at this time, evidenced by a fourfold increase in membership since 1914. Delegates, amidst "a demonstration of unequalled fervor and earnestness," had just agreed to a massive reorganization of American Zionist activities, along the lines advocated by Louis Brandeis. Henceforward, American Zionism would be guided by a single national organization, the Zionist Organization of America, to which every Zionist would at least in theory belong. These developments, coupled with the November 1917 Balfour Declaration pledging British support for a Jewish homeland in Palestine, General Allenby's triumphal entry into Jerusalem promising "a new era of brotherhood and peace in the Holy Land," and Woodrow Wilson's fourteen-point list of American war aims made the Pittsburgh Program timely indeed.[21]

---

20 *The Maccabaean* 31 (August 1918); 237. Many scholars cite other texts of the Pittsburgh Program, which vary from this one in significant ways (see note 22), but this text would seem to be authoritative.

21 *The Maccabaean* 31 (August 1918); 237, 240, 254, 256; Jehuda Reinharz, "Zionism in the USA on the Eve of the Balfour Declarfation," *Studies in*

Horace Kallen, the well-known exponent of cultural pluralism, then still an instructor of philosophy and psychology at the University of Wisconsin, drafted the platform approved at Pittsburgh, and the document in its final version embodied ideas that he and like-minded colleagues had been thrashing out for several years. Kallen reviewed his formulation with "eight or nine" members of a secret Zionist fraternity that he headed known as the Parushim, and the document was subsequently modified by American Zionist leaders, notably Supreme Court Justice Louis Brandeis.[22]

Presumably at their insistence, one principle was deleted from the text at the last minute. Listed in Kallen's draft as principle five, it was the most radical plank in the document and echoed a refrain commonly heard in left-wing political circles of the day: "The fiscal policy [of Palestine] shall be framed so as to protect the people from the evils of land speculation and from every other form of financial oppression."[23]

Why this language was dropped from the official text is unclear; perhaps Brandeis objected to its jarringly negative tone. Whatever the case, the plank continued to circulate unofficially and certainly harmonized with the goals that Brandeis and the American Zionist leadership of his day espoused.

Taken together, the ideals that did find expression in the Pittsburgh Program — equality, public ownership, the cooperative principle, free public education, and the rest — bespeak a utopian vision of Zion, one that went beyond the agrarian dreams of Moses Klein

---

Zionism 9 (1988): 131–145; Melvin I. Urofsky, *American Zionism from Herzl to the Holocaust* (Garden City, N.Y.: Doubleday, 1976), 237–241.

22   Sarah L. Schmidt, "Horace M. Kallen and the Americanization of Zionism" (Ph.D. diss., University of Maryland, 1973), 261–263; idem, "The *Parushim*: A Secret Episode in American Zionist History," *American Jewish Historical Quarterly* 65 (December 1975): 121–139; idem, "Toward the Pittsburgh Program: Horace M. Kallen, Philosopher of an American Zionism," *Herzl Year Book* 8 (1978): 18–36; Horace M. Kallen, *Zionism and World Politics* (Garden City, N.Y.: Doubleday, 1921), 300–302. The frequently cited claim that Brandeis authored the Pittsburgh Program is shown by Schmidt to be erroneous.

23   Kallen, *Zionism and World Politics*, 302; see also Bernard A. Rosenblatt, *Social Zionism* (New York: Public Publishing, 1919), 10–11; and Naomi W. Cohen, *American Jews and the Zionist Idea* (New York: Ktav, 1975), 23.

to envisage not just agricultural settlements but a full-scale "social commonwealth." This Zion, a vision that proved enormously appealing to American Jews, combined Progressive-era American designs and European Labor Zionist ideals, linked them to (selectively read) traditional Jewish sources, and then projected them onto the landscape of the so-called New Palestine, described as "a land of waste places with few inhabitants, not many vested interests, and its future all in the making."[24] Social justice stood at the heart of this vision of Zion, and so did social engineering. The ultimate aim was to turn Palestine into what the Zionist leader Bernard Rosenblatt called "a laboratory for momentous experiments."[25]

Rosenblatt (1886-1969), born in Grodok (near Bialystok) and raised in the United States, was one of the youngest leaders in the American Zionist movement, and he brought to Zionism some of the new ideas that he had imbibed in the classroom of his "revered teacher," the distinguished Columbia sociologist, Franklin H. Giddings. Several of the planks in the Pittsburgh Program drew on ideas that he had formulated in articles written beginning in 1910; and in 1919 he published *Social Zionism* to "serve as an introduction to the study of certain planks in the Pittsburgh Program and its implication."[26]

Significantly, Rosenblatt had devoted a previous book, *The Social Commonwealth (A Plan for Achieving Industrial Democracy)* (1914), to the cause of "achieving 'social justice'" in the United States. That book won the approbation of Louis Brandeis, to whom it was dedicated, and put forward a variety of social, economic, and political proposals designed to bring nearer "that future day, when, instead of classes and masses, of the rich and the poor, we shall

24 Mary Fels, "The Pittsburgh Program," *The Maccabaean* 31 (August 1918): 240.
25 Rosenblatt, *Social Zionism*, 10. For a discussion of social engineering and Zionism, see Derek J. Pensler, *Zionism and Technocracy: The Engineering of Jewish Settlement in Palestine, 1870–1918* (Bloomington and Indianapolis: Indiana University Press, 1991).
26 Rosenblatt, *Social Zionism*, 12. On Rosenblatt, see Evyatar Friesel, *Ha-Tenuah ha-Tziyonit be-Artzot ha-Brit, 1897–1914* (The Zionist movement in the United States 1897–1914) (Jerusalem: Hakibbutz Hameuhad, 1970), 155–157; and Rosenblatt's autobiography, *Two Generations of Zionism* (New York: Shengold, 1967), esp. p. 41.

have one happy people, free in their industrial life as well as in their political life...the day when we shall reach the long sought port of pure Democracy."[27]

In the same year that the book appeared, Rosenblatt attempted to realize some of its most far-reaching proposals on a limited scale, across the ocean in Palestine. Many Jewish Progressives, following the lead of Louis D. Brandeis, came to believe at this time that Palestine, because of its relative desolation, could function as a testing ground for social experiments that proved impossible to implement in the United States. Rosenblatt followed suit, incorporating — at the age of twenty-eight — the Zion Commonwealth for Land Purchase and Development. Known later as the American Zion Commonwealth (AZIC), the corporation aimed to establish Jewish colonists in Palestine on the basis of the same "just land system" spelled out in *The Social Commonwealth* — one that emphasized "collective ownership of city land, industrial plots and sub-soil deposits." Revealingly, the very first article of the corporation's lofty constitution promised to make "social justice, in harmony with the ideals of the prophets of Israel...the cornerstone of the Jewish Commonwealth in Zion." A subsequent article in the same document set up a "Board of Shoftim [Jewish judges]" to serve "as the general arbitration court for the members of the community."[28]

By the time he published *Social Zionism*, Rosenblatt, under the influence of the Pittsburgh Program, had extended his social vision to apply to the Zionist movement as a whole. His volume, illustrated on every page with romantic sketches of Holy Land scenes (real and imagined), advocated the creation of "a model state in the Holy Land — freed from the economic wrongs, the social injustices and the greed of modern-day industrialism."[29] Cooperation formed the cornerstone of this plan, which envisaged the creation in Palestine of a "social-moral community of Jews — a true commonwealth." The

27 Bernard A. Rosenblatt, *The Social Commonwealth* (New York: Lincoln Publishing, 1914), 12, 189.

28 Rosenblatt, *Social Zionism*, 138–139, 149; Rosenblatt, *Two Generations of Zionism*, 62–65; Nathan M. Kaganoff, ed., *Guide to America-Holy Land Studies* (New York: Arno, 1980), 9–13; Cf. Nili Fox, "Balfouriya: An American Zionst Failure or Secret Success?" *American Jewish History* 78 (June 1989): 497–512.

29 Rosenblatt, *Social Zionism*, 13.

book advocated common ownership of all land, a system of profit-sharing, a version of the "single tax" (on land) to generate revenue, and other cooperative endeavors — including, in one chapter, the suggestion that the commonwealth promote scientific eugenics. Its major aim, however, was, as before, to promote the creation of "a model community [in Palestine] based on Social Justice." "Can there be," Rosenblatt asked his readers, "a higher or nobler mission?"[30]

In an appendix to *Social Zionism*, Rosenblatt reprinted from the *Menorah Journal* a syllabus he had prepared on Zionism's aims and objectives. In addition to supplying historical and explanatory information, the syllabus set forth many of the ideals that underlay both his own "model community" and the American Zionist movement as a whole in the wake of the Pittsburgh Program — ideals that continued to shape Zionist thought and the image of Israel in the United States for the next half century. To cite just a few examples, he wrote that "Judaism will be separate and distinct from the Jewish State in Palestine" and that "freedom of religion will be guaranteed." He promised "equal rights for all Palestinians" and "the principle of democratic rule and equal rights, as developed in America and England." Most important of all, he looked to the new state to provide "leadership in social and economic organization." Highlighting "Jewish co-operative efforts in Palestine," he reiterated that "Zionists are planning for the establishment of a model commonwealth" — a goal he defended not only on the basis of the Pittsburgh Program but on the basis of Theodor Herzl's writings as well.[31]

Reflecting back years later, Rosenblatt believed that these high-minded ideals stemmed from what he called "the period of youthful dreams about the kind of state that we would build in the land of Israel."[32] Actually, not all of his fellow dreamers were young; some, like Justice Louis D. Brandeis, the undisputed leader of American Zionism at that time, had been social idealist for decades. What Rosenblatt, Kallen, Brandeis, and other idealistically minded American Zionist leaders of that era all shared in common was the desire

30   Ibid., esp. 10, 41, 55–57.
31   Ibid., *Social Zionism*, 144–151.
32   Rosenblatt, *Two Generations of Zionism*, 53.

to create not just a Jewish state in Palestine but a utopian Jewish state, one that drew on American experience, took advantage of the latest in social, economic and political thinking, and conformed to prophetic teachings as they understood them. Thus conceived, the Jewish "model state" represented American liberal intellectuals' fondest and most romantic visions of a better world, one that the Pittsburgh Program sought to realize in Palestine, as a harbinger of what might be accomplished in America as well.

IV

The image of the "model state" endured in the mind of American Jews for over half a century. This longevity was due, in part, to its extraordinary political value as a symbol. A "model state" cast in the image of America served not only to defuse the sensitive issue of dual loyalty, it actually worked to strengthen the position of America's Jews by permitting them both to bask in the reflected glory of those engaged in building the state and to boast of their own patriotic efforts to spread the American dream outward. Louis Brandeis understood this intuitively and therefore regularly linked the "Zionist cause" with "the American ideal of democracy, of social justice and of liberty."[33] On a popular level, this claim became something of a Zionist mantra, repeated catechistically, often with a suitable quotation from the mouth of Brandeis himself — recognized even in his lifetime as a prophetic figure. The creedal statement, "We Believe," issued by the young women's Zionist organization, Junior Hadassah, for example, included among its various articles of faith the following:

> We, the members of Junior Hadassah, believe in the democratic way of life. We believe in it as young Americans who are born to it and who live by its principles.
> We believe it is our *obligation* to perpetuate the ideals of

33   Harris, "Zionist Speeches," 224, 246; See also Jonathan D. Sarna, "'The Greatest Jew in the World since Jesus Christ': The Jewish Legacy of Louis D. Brandeis" *American Jewish History* 81 (3–4) (Spring–Summer 1994): 346–364.

American democracy. As young Jews we are guided by our Jewish heritage of justice, humanity and freedom.

We believe that America's first function as a world power is to assure freedom for all peoples. As Zionists we have shared in building a national community in Israel on the firm foundation of democratic experience and social justice, but we know that only in a free world can this new nation continue to exist...

We see no division of loyalty but rather a strengthening of loyalties in our work for Israel. Associate United States Supreme Court Justice Louis D. Brandeis, a great American and ardent Zionist once declared: "There is no inconsistency between loyalty to America and loyalty to Jewry... Indeed, loyalty to America demands rather that each American Jew become a Zionist..."[34]

As this creedal statement of "beliefs" suggests, the image of the "model state" cast in the American mold had also come to serve an important religious function for its adherents. It offered American Jews, many of whom had become disenchanted with the traditional beliefs, rituals, and practices of Judaism, a sacred "mission" that both linked them to other Jews and infused their own personal lives with meaning — the lofty satisfaction that comes from pursuing work of transcendent importance. The fact that this rhetoric of mission, so prominent both in American thought and in Reform Jewish thought, was appropriated for Zionist purposes underscores the movement's secular-religious underpinnings. It sought to tap precisely the same kind of religious energy that motivated those who embarked on other great American religious missions, from the Puritan "Errand into the Wilderness" to their descendants' "Errand to the World." Like these missions, Zionism conjured up a grand vision of ardent young men and women earnestly engaged in the selfless task of creating a new and better humanity. "Our aim is the Kingdom of Heaven," Louis Brandeis once exclaimed, and the declaration reveals much about the kind of Zion that he and his fellow missionaries envisaged: nothing less than a heaven-on-earth.[35]

34   "We Believe: Our American Affairs Program," in undated (c. 1947) Junior Hadassah publication, Box 3, Junior Hadassah file, Miscellaneous Publications, American Jewish Historical Society, Waltham, Mass.

35   On the "mission motif" in American Zionism, see especially Allon Gal, "The

This utopian vision of Zion, linked as it was both to the self-image of American Jews and to their highest religious aspirations, had less and less to do with the realities of the Middle East.[36] While American Jews dreamed on about a "model state" where democracy and social justice reigned,[37] the Jews in Eretz Israel focused, of necessity, on security, resistance, and the need for new settlements. But this disjunction, as we have seen, was nothing new. All of the historic American Jewish images of Israel — from the early image of poor Jews engaged in study and prayer, to the later image of agrarian pioneers, to the twentieth-century image of the "model state" — spoke to the needs of *American* Jews and reflected *their* ideals and fantasies rather than the contemporary realities of Jewish life in the land of Israel. In creating these images, American Jews projected onto the Holy Land their American vision of an ideal society — sometimes a counterimage of their own lives and sometimes a new and improved version, reflecting the latest in Progressive social engineering. In either case, they expected their "model state" to embody all of the values that they cherished most deeply, values that they associated with America as it ought to be and the Zion of their imagination.

Mission Motif in American Zionism (1898–1948)," *American Jewish History* 75 (June 1986): 363–385 [the Brandeis quote is on p. 370]; and idem, "Independence and Universal Mission in Modern Jewish Nationalism: A Comparative Analysis of European and American Zionism (1897–1948)" (with responses by A. Eisen, A. Goren, Y. Gorny, and E. Mendelsohn), *Studies in Contemporary Jewry* 5 (1989): 242–274. For a different view of the rise of the mission motif in American Zionism, see Jonathan D. Sarna, "Converts to Zionism in the American Reform Movement," in *Zionism and Religion*, ed. J. Reinharz (forthcoming). William R. Hutchison, *Errand to the World: American Protestant Thought and Foreign Missions* (Chicago: University of Chicago, 1987), analyzes significant differences in the way that the missionary idea was understood, over time, by Americans. He begins (p. 1) with an arresting quote from Arnold Rose: "Don't apologize. All Americans are missionaries."

36   Cf. Anita Shapira, "Uri Zvi Greenberg—Apocalypse Now," *Zion* 56 (2) (1991): 173–192.

37   See, for example, Maurice Samuel, *Harvest in the Desert* (Philadelphia: Jewish Publication Society, 1944), esp. p. 315, where Zionism is linked to "the forces on which the progress of mankind as a whole depends."

Henrietta Szold's Progressive American Vision of the *Yishuv*

Michael Brown

The influence of America on the *yishuv* in the pre-1945 era has been underestimated or misunderstood to a considerable extent. Palestine and the United States were in competition for the bodies and souls of Eastern European Jews in the turn-of-the-century years and beyond. As a result of that unequal competition Zionists, in particular those who actually settled in Palestine, were inclined to resent everything about the American rival, especially its success. Moreover, because only a small percentage of the immigrants to Palestine in the prestate period came from the United States, American influence was not obvious. Among the leaders of the state-in-the-making an even smaller percentage came from the New World, only three of the first rank: Judah Magnes, Golda Meir, and Henrietta Szold.[1]

Szold is a case in point. To a degree and for a time she served as representative to Palestine of organizations and wealthy individuals in the United States; eventually she emerged as the representative of the *yishuv* to America. Her contributions have been widely acknowledged, as have her American upbringing, her attachment to her family in the United States, and her nostalgia for the American landscape.[2] That she drew apart from her American roots over time

---

1   For a discussion of the "American-ness" of Golda Meir, see Michael Brown, "The American Element in the Rise of Golda Meir 1906–1929," *Jewish History* 6 (1992): 35–50.

2   See, for example, Frederick Painton, "Henrietta Szold — American," article written for *Readers' Digest* in 1944 but never published, typescript, in Central Zionist Archives, Jerusalem (hereafter, CZA), File A125/29; Louis Lipsky, *A Gallery of Zionist Profiles* (New York: Farrar Straus & Cudahy, 1956), 142; Joan Dash, *Summoned to Jerusalem: The Life and Times of Henrietta Szold* (New York: Harper & Row, 1979), 224–225; and Sylva M. Gelber, *No Balm in Gilead* (Ottawa: Carleton University Press, 1898), 52, 191. Dash's work is

was recognized in her own day. The extent to which she exerted an Americanizing influence on the *yishuv*, however, the nature of that influence, and the degree to which through her personality and the institutions she shaped Szold helped to make America, its Jews, and its ways less alien to the Jews of Palestine have not been adequately considered.[3]

Ernst Simon, Szold's co-worker in education, compatriot in politics, and close friend, remarked in a eulogy soon after her death that Szold's "life's work" had been built upon three foundations: "her family heritage, Lincoln's America, and her encounter with" Eastern European Jews. In fact, Szold's responses to situations in Palestine, especially to the Arab-Jewish conflict and to the refugee crisis of the 1930s, were in large part conditioned by her earlier experiences in the United States with blacks and with Eastern European Jewish immigrants. Another significant element in her background was American Progressivism, what Richard Hofstadter defined as the broad "impulse toward criticism and change that was everywhere so conspicuous [in the United States] after 1900, when the already forceful stream of agrarian discontent was enlarged and redirected by the growing enthusiasm of middle-class people for social and economic reform." Although "rather vague and not altogether [a] cohesive or consistent movement," Progressivism promoted the use of science to bring order to a society perceived as increasingly chaotic and to improve it. Progressivism affected "the whole tone of American political life" in the turn-of-the-century years. To it can be attributed the technology and the notions of bureaucratic thought and scientific method that Szold brought to the health, education, and welfare institutions with which she was associated in Palestine.[4]

---

the most complete biography of Szold to date. Gelber, who had a career as a distinguished senior civil servant in Canada, lived in Palestine for some time and was the first graduate of the school of social work established by Szold.

3   The works that come closest to appreciating the American dimension of Szold's work in Palestine are Irving Fineman, *Woman of Valor* (New York: Simon & Schuster, 1961); and Carol Bosworth Kutscher, "The Early Years of Hadassah," Ph.D. diss., Department of Near Eastern and Judaic Studies, Brandeis University, 1976.

4   Ernst Akiba Simon, "Henrietta Szold — Mehanekhet Ha-Am" (Henrietta Szold — Teacher of the Nation) in *Henrietta Szold 5621–5705: Divrei Azkara*

Although she became a Palestinian, heart and soul, Szold never overcame or abjured her American upbringing. Many of her co-workers, especially those of Eastern European origin, resisted her American ways, at least at first. Over time, however, her sensibilities became better understood and also — more mellow; and the presumably superior technology she represented was accepted, at least in part. Willy-nilly — but often consciously — Szold served as an apostle of Americanism. It is on the American aspects of her faith and some of her "works" that this paper focuses.

I

Henrietta Szold was born in Baltimore in 1860. The Civil War and the issue of black slavery, the Spanish-American War, World War I, and especially the immigration crisis, which lasted from 1881 to 1914, were among her formative experiences. So too was the westernized Judaism of her father, Rabbi Benjamin Szold, who practiced a moderate traditionalism that emphasized spirit rather than letter. Rabbi Szold had been one of the few supporters of Lincoln in Baltimore, a border city with Southern sympathies. From him she acquired an approach to religion that stressed broad tolerance towards all people, including blacks and other minorities.[5] Her memory of viewing Lincoln's bier while perched on her father's shoulders acquired the status of personal myth. Such books as *Up from Slavery* by Booker T. Washington, the black American educator and social reformer, and *The War-Time Journal of a Georgia Girl, 1864–1865* by Eliza Francis Andrews helped to form her adult consciousness.[6] She rejoiced at

---

SheNe'emru beYom 3 beIyyar 5705 al yede Prof. Sh. Adler ve Dr. E. Simon baUniversita haIvrit (Henrietta Szold, 5621–5705: Words spoken in her memory on the third of Iyyar 5705 by Prof. Sh. Adler and Dr. E. Simon at The Hebrew University (Jerusalem: 1945), 7; Richard Hofstadter, *The Age of Reform from Bryan to F.D.R.* (New York: Knopf, 1956), 5. See also Robert H. Wiebe, *The Search for Order 1877–1920* (New York: Hill & Wang, 1967), 144–159. Unless otherwise noted, all translations are the author's.

5   Among other sources on Rabbi Szold, see Shmaryahu Levin, "MiSefer Hayyai" (From the book of my Life), *HaAretz*, 25 May 1934.

6   Henrietta Szold, speech to Aliyat Noar, Ben Shemen, Palestine, 24 December

the victories of black American athlete Jesse Owens at the 1936 Olympics in Berlin, because of which, she hoped, "Herr Hitler's race-conscious soul must be squirming." At one of her last Passover seders, the ceremony ended — at her request — with the singing of Negro spirituals.[7]

Only somewhat less influential in Szold's development was the "wicked, wicked war" of 1914–1918, perpetrated, she believed at the time, by "poor old wicked Francis Joseph." In 1917, as war fever gripped the nation, she declared herself "anti-war, and anti-this-war, and anti-all-wars." Even after the United States entered the fray, she maintained her absolutist position, to the chagrin of Louis Brandeis — head of the wartime Provisional Executive Committee for General Zionist Affairs, with which she was also associated — and other Zionist leaders, who feared that their movement would be branded as unpatriotic.[8]

Most indelibly inscribed in her memory was the era of mass immigration to America, "when the doors of the country stood wide open and the disinherited of many nations were permitted to crowd in." That period she saw as a golden age, when the United States was living up to its highest ideals and being rewarded by the vitality of the newcomers. Her vision of America as "a composite of nations" was similar to that articulated by Brandeis in *The Jewish Problem and How to Solve It* (New York, 1915) and by other advocates of the new doctrine of cultural pluralism. Szold believed that "each nation" or immigrant group represented in the United States "should apply the fundamental ideals common to civilized peoples in the way its history and traditions teach. That," she said, and not material prosperity,

---

1940, in CZA, File A125/188. See also Simon, "Mehanekhet," 8; Arnold Zweig, "Henrietta Szold on Her Return Today from America," *Palestine Post*, 5 February 1936; and many other sources. There is an incomplete record book of Szold's reading in CZA, File A125/250.

7   Henrietta Szold, Jerusalem, letter to her sisters Bertha [Levin] and Adele [Seltzer], n.p., 7 August 1936, in CZA, File A125/265; Gelber, *Balm*, p. 193.

8   Henrietta Szold, New York, letters, to "Mamma and All," n.p., 30 July 1914, and to "Mamma," [Maine], 3 August 1914, both in CZA, File A125/275; idem, New York, letter to Dr. [Richard] Gottheil, [New York], 13 May 1917, in CZA, File A125/302. On Brandeis's response to her position, see, Dash, *Jerusalem*, 118; and Kutscher, "Early Years," 162–163.

is "what is meant when...[America] is called the land of unlimited possibilities." She herself worked with the immigrants as a teacher. Americanization, she declared, was not "the opposite...to Jewish living and thinking." It meant simply the "process of acquiring [the] power of realizing [the] fundamental ideas and ideals of the Republic," the empowerment of the disfranchised, in the language of a later day.[9]

From these experiences Szold emerged as a not atypical American Progressive, with radical leanings in some areas and rather conservative views in others, a genteel reformer with strong views colored by both morality and aesthetics, "a liberal of the old school, a defender of the rights of the individual." To her last days she admired "the abolitionist spirit — unflinchingly just and true in the fashion of the day when the spirit of the champions of a great cause lingered in the air." She read *The Nation* and followed the influential social work journal *The Survey Graphic, de rigueur* for a Progressive, although by 1930 she had canceled her subscription to *The Nation*, disillusioned with its "superficialities" regarding to the Palestine issue.[10]

Szold held Supreme Court Justice Louis D. Brandeis, the wartime leader of American Zionism, in high esteem; and Brandeis, who paid her salary for years through a private arrangement with the Zionist Organization of America (hereafter ZOA), much admired her. Szold shared with Brandeis, a leading Progressive and an early proponent of the notion that "small is beautiful — and efficient," an appreciation for the little man, respect for labor organizations, a suspicion of great wealth, and a sense that "prosperity [had]...

9   Henrietta Szold [Jerusalem], letter to Mrs. Edith Gann Kniberg, Newark, N.J., 17 June 1934, in CZA, File A125/95; idem, "Extension Work Meeting," handwritten notes for speech [?], n.d., CZA, File A125/285.
10 Gelber, *Balm* p. 190; Henrietta Szold, Jerusalem, letter to her sisters Bertha [Levin] and Adele [Seltzer], n.p., 17 February 1939, in CZA, File 125/267; idem, letters; Jerusalem, to "dear Family," [United States], 22 November 1920, in CZA, File A125/256; en route to Marseille [sic], to Sisters, n.p., 17 June 1930, in CZA, File A125/262; Jerusalem, to sister Adele [Seltzer], n.p., 8 December 1933, in CZA, File A125/263; and Jerusalem, to Ellis Radinsky, League for Labor Palestine, New York City, 28 January 1943, in CZA, File A125/62. See also, transcript of her address to the *Survey Graphic*, New York, January 1936, typescript, in CZA, File A125/83.

something vulgar and repugnant about it."[11] She deplored "America's business greed [which] has deprived us of" beauty in our lives; and she was outraged when the United States withheld its assent to the British mandate over Palestine and Mesopotamia "in order to protect the interests of the Standard Oil Company."[12]

Szold's political tastes, although reformist, were decidedly middle-of-the-road. To her, Bolshevism and fascism were "both ugly [and] inconceivably barbarous." When conservative Republican William McKinley, during whose first term the "splendid, little" Spanish–American War had been embarked upon, was reelected president in 1900, she could find no "reason to rejoice." In later years she found Franklin Roosevelt too radical. Like many other Progressives, she considered him unacceptably unsystematic in his approach to the Depression ("too 'jumpy' for my taste," as she put it) and cavalier with regard to individual rights. On one occasion, she compared him to Hitler. When the Supreme Court declared the National Recovery Act, one of the keystones of FDR's New Deal program of economic regeneration, to be unconstitutional in 1935, Szold "wasn't surprised." She had disapproved of the president's "antics" from the start and believed that in politics, as well as economics, "he was acting impulsively to the point of irresponsibility." Wendell Willkie, the unsuccessful progressive Republican candidate for president in 1940, she saw

11 Louis D. Brandeis, letters, Boston, 11 March 1916, and Washington, 6 November 1925, both to Julian W. Mack, n.p., in *Letters of Louis D. Brandeis*, vol. 4, ed. Melvin I. Urofsky and David W. Levy (Albany: State University of New York Press, 1975), 115, 191–192; Henrietta Szold, Baltimore, letter to her sister Rachel [Jastrow], n.p., 25 October 1891, in CZA, File A125/17. See also her eulogy for Brandeis, delivered on Palestine Radio, 9 October 1941, the typescript of which is in CZA, File A125/15. On Brandeis as a progressive, see, among other sources, Allon Gal, *Brandeis of Boston* (Cambridge, Mass., and London: Harvard University Press, 1980); and Melvin Urofsky, *Louis D. Brandeis and the Progressive Tradition* (Boston and Toronto: Little, Brown, 1981).

12 Henrietta Szold, Jerusalem, letter to "dear Ones" (that is, her sisters and their families in the United States), 28 March 1926, CZA, File A125/260; idem, Rishon le-Zion, [Palestine], letter to "dear Ones," 14 April 1922, in CZA, File A125/258.

as an accurate "interpreter of [her own cherished] principles and attitudes."[13]

In religion Szold was also a centrist. Despite her affinity for Eastern European Jews, she rejected their Orthodoxy, which turned away from the modern world. But she also rejected Reform Judaism, which appeared sterile and removed from Jewish life and learning. For many years she was close to the modernizing traditionalists at the Conservative Jewish Theological Seminary in New York, such people as Solomon Schechter and his wife, Mathilda, Louis Ginzberg, and others. She studied at the Seminary, after making a required public declaration that she did not aspire to the rabbinate, and assisted Ginzberg with his research.[14]

II

Her Americanized values and faith provided Szold with guidelines and a mind-set with which to approach the political, religious, and economic minefield of the *yishuv* — not necessarily with success. Religion was a particularly thorny area. Although she recognized the intense commitment and humane values of the Labor leaders of the day, she was uncomfortable with the tendency of many of them to devalue religion altogether. She sought "a Zionism which stressed the positive worth of a living and growing Judaism"; but only Haim Arlosoroff, who had been educated in Germany, and a few others in the labor movement sympathized with that goal. The traditionalists, on the other hand, were foreign to her enlightened and scholarly spirit. Rabbi Abraham Isaac Kook, the chief rabbi of the Ashkenazi community from 1921 to 1935, was regarded by

13   Idem, Jerusalem, letter to sister Bertha [Levin, Baltimore], 15 April 1938, in CZA, File A125/266; idem, Baltimore, personal letter to Miss [Elvira] Solis, New York, 1 March 1901, in CZA, File A125/308; idem, Jerusalem, letters: to sisters Bertha [Levin] and Adele [Seltzer], n.p., 6 January 1939, in CZA, File A125/267; to sister Bertha [Levin], n.p., 4 December 1942, in CZA, File A125/274; to sisters Bertha [Levin] and Adele [Seltzer, United States], 31 May 1935, in CZA, File A125/265; idem, [Jerusalem], letter to Wendell Willkie, New York, 27 March 1944, in CZA, File A125/63.
14   See Dash, *Jerusalem*, 39–79.

many, even by secularists, as saintly. Szold, however, could see in him "not an iota of grace or even human-ness," she declared in 1922. The Orthodox Zionists of the Mizrachi were closer to her in spirit, but not quite to her liking, nor she to theirs. In her early years in Palestine she and a few American friends, including Magnes, gathered together on Sabbath mornings for the study of sacred texts or for an informal worship service. Those sessions, she wrote to the mother of poet Jesse Sampter, one of her American acolytes who also immigrated to Palestine, "save[d her]...from [spiritual] homesickness." In later years she attended the partially westernized Yeshurun Synagogue in Jerusalem, where a small circle of followers looked to her for spiritual guidance. On the whole, however, her Americanized religious sensibility proved irrelevant in the *yishuv*.[15]

In the area of Arab–Jewish relations Szold's American baggage was most evident and also ultimately irrelevant, if not misguided. Her pacifism, her commitment to cultural pluralism, and her empathy for blacks all came into play on this issue. Although her official positions often constrained her, she felt, not to "go beyond the expression of platonic sympathy," she supported the idea of a binational, Jewish–Arab state in Palestine. Already at the time of the 1921 Arab anti-Jewish riots, she came to believe that Jews bore some responsibility for Arab discontent. In the 1930s she lent tacit approval to the Brit Shalom organization, which sought to foster Arab–Jewish rapprochement; in the 1940s, when the Ihud was founded to promote the idea of a binational state, she served on its executive committee along with Martin Buber, Magnes, and others. (Many of the members of both the Brit Shalom and the

---

15   Henrietta Szold, "Tsu Haim Arlosoroff's Ershten Yortsayt" (On the first anniversary of Haim Arlosoroff's death), *Pioneer Woman*, June 1934, p. 15; idem, Jerusalem, letter to "My dear Ones" [her family in the United States], 26 January 1922, in CZA, File A125/258; idem, Jerusalem, letter to Mrs. Edgar J. Wachenheim, New Rochelle, N.Y., 30 May 1920, in CZA, File A219/4; Mrs. Shulamith Schwartz Nardi, personal interview with the author, Jerusalem, 26 March 1991. See also Simon, "Mehanekhet," 9; and Joan Dash, "Doing Good in Palestine: Magnes and Henrietta Szold," in *Like All the Nations? The Life and Legacy of Judah L. Magnes*, ed. William H. Brinner and Moses Rischin (Albany: State University of New York Press, 1987), 103–104; and Dash, *Jerusalem*, 196–199, 216–217.

Ihud were intellectuals or technocrats who had come to Palestine from the English-speaking countries or from Central Europe. Both groups exhibited many of the patrician, reforming characteristics of American Progressives.) Together with the writer S. Y. Agnon, the philosopher Shmuel Hugo Bergman, and others, Szold signed the self-critical 1939 "Manifesto against Internal Terror," which circulated in the *yishuv*. And in 1941 she angered many friends by issuing a public statement to the press equating explosive bombs thrown by Arabs at Jewish targets with stink bombs thrown by Jews at Arab targets. In 1942 she proved less than enthusiastic about the Biltmore Program for achieving Jewish statehood adopted by American Zionist organizations and later also by the Palestinians.[16]

Szold perceived the Arab–Jewish conflict in Palestine to be analogous to black–white friction in the United States; the solutions she favored were also American-made. In a 1934 article published in the United States in Yiddish on the first anniversary of the murder of Haim Arlosoroff, the Labor leader and "foreign minister" of the Jewish Agency, she remarked, that "the fulfillment of the Jewish-national ideal on the soil of Palestine is altogether bound up with the solution to the Arab problem." Two years later she wrote despairingly to her sisters of the joy and alacrity with which the residents of Tel Aviv constructed a new harbor in response to the Arabs' having closed Jaffa harbor to them. "Matters are not going to be mended," she asserted,

> if the alienation between us and the Arab population is emphasized.... It is not the way — this way of creating race-tight compartments — of healing the breach, of destroying the seeds of race-hatred.[17]

16 Henrietta Szold, letter to Edwin Samuel, 5 January 1930, quoted in Susan Lee Hattis, *The Bi-National Idea in Palestine during Mandatory Times* (Haifa: Shikmona Publishing, 1970), 171–172; Dash, *Jerusalem*, 171; Hattis, *Bi-National Idea*, 259; Anita Shapira, *Berl: The Biography of a Socialist Zionist*, tr. Haya Galai (Cambridge: Cambridge University Press, 1984), 282; M[oshe] S[hertok (later, Sharett), Jerusalem], letter to Henrietta Szold, Jerusalem, 17 September 1941, in CZA, File S25/1125; Nahum Goldmann, New York, letter to David Ben-Gurion, [Jerusalem], 26 October 1942, in CZA, File S25/237b.

17 Henrietta Szold, "Ershten Yortsayt," 15; idem, Jerusalem, letter to sisters Bertha [Levin] and Adele [Seltzer], n.p., 5 June 1936, in CZA, A125/265.

In these years she expressed the fear that "racial pride" among the Jews in Palestine would "lead to Nazi-ism." Some time later she referred to the Arab–Jewish stand-off as "a racial problem" and declared Jews "not to have stood the acid test of finding the way to [its]...solutions."[18] These were unmistakably the words of a Progressive who had experienced "the American dilemma" at first hand. Zionists of Eastern European background also deplored the fate of America's blacks. They, however, viewed it as analogous to the fate of Jews in czarist Russia and vowed to avoid being placed in such a position in Palestine. Ernst Simon noted the connection between Szold's American experience and the Palestine reality. "She, herself," Simon asserted, "had pointed to the source of her extraordinary sensitivity to the Arab problem" in the "anguish and injustice and [the] exalted efforts to free the slaves." Simon felt that Szold "erroneously (but naturally, for an immigrant from America) considered [the Arab-Jewish conflict a] 'racial problem'." He agreed with her, however, that it was "the most important of the political questions" in Palestine.[19]

Like many genteel Progressives in America, but unlike most Palestinian Jews, Szold tried to remain above politics, or at least nonpartisan,

> Not because I don't consider politics important or interesting, but because I trust my judgment on political matters even less than on others.

As overseer from 1920 to 1923 of the American Zionist Medical Unit (later, the Hadassah Medical Organization), she met considerable opposition from Laborites who assumed her to be a political foe. As a Hadassah insider described the period retrospectively, "There was then an extreme distrust of Americans, both individuals and

18 Idem, Jerusalem, letter to "dear Sisters," [United States], 22 June 1934, File A125/264; idem, Jerusalem, letter to sisters Bertha [Levin] and Adele [Seltzer], n.p., 9 July 1937, in CZA, File A125/266.

19 See Michael Brown, "Some Early Nineteenth-Century [should be Twentieth-Century] 'Travelers' to America: Sources and Contexts," in *With Eyes Toward Zion — II*, ed. Moshe Davis (New York: Praeger, 1986), 243; Simon, "Mehanekhet," 11.

institutions."[20] The Laborites, who feared that their fledgling medical institutions could not withstand what they perceived as Hadassah's colonialism and imperialism, were especially hostile.[21] Between 1927 and 1930 Szold was one of three people on the Palestine Executive of the World Zionist Organization, which was charged with making ends meet on a starvation budget. At first, she was the object of frequent "fierce denunciation[s]" by disgruntled Laborites, who felt that she and her compatriots were insensitive to the needs of working people, insufficiently Zionistic, and shortsightedly tight-fisted. (In a confrontation between the leadership of the Histadrut, the national labor union, and the Executive a short time after Szold's arrival, David Ben-Gurion accused her of stalking "the teachers and workers of Palestine dagger in hand.") They also resented her inability to extract funds from her fellow Americans, most especially the ZOA, which consistently reneged on its obligations, to her chagrin as well as that of the Laborites.[22]

20 Henrietta Szold, Jerusalem, letter to sisters Bertha [Levin] and Adele [Seltzer], n.p., 25 February 1938, in CZA, File A125/266; I. J. Kligler, "Builder and Leader of Hadassah," *Palestine Post*, 20 December 1940. Kligler's article appeared as a tribute to Szold on her 80th birthday.
21 Among other sources, see *Report* of the Activities of the American Zionist Medical Unit from July 1919 to August 1920 — Director: I. M. Rubinow, n.p., n. d; Emanuel Neumann, *Causes of the Conflict* (New York: New Maccabean, [1921]); Sophie Udin, "Henrietta Szold," *Pioneer Woman*, January 1931, 5; and contemporaneous reports in the Palestine press (*Do'ar HaYom* and *HaPo'el HaTza'ir*, for example).
22 Henrietta Szold, Jerusalem, letter to Administrative Committee, ZOA, New York, 21 December 1927, in CZA, File A125/51; Ben-Gurion, quoted in minutes of meeting between the Histadrut Executive Committee and the Palestine Zionist Executive, 12 December [1927], in the Archives of the Pinhas Lavon Institute for the Research of the Labor Movement, Tel Aviv (hereafter, LAVON), File IV–208–67bet. See also, Berl Katznelson, "Veto" (in Hebrew), and "BaKongress HaShisha-'Asar" (In the Sixteenth Congress), both in *Kitvei B. Katznelson* (Writings of B. Katznelson), vol. 4 (Tel Aviv: Hotza'at Po'alei Eretz Yisrael, 5706 [1946]), 71–75, and 79–86. These essays appeared originally in *Davar*, the first on 17 April 1929, and the second on 13 August 1929. For Szold's reactions to the ZOA, see among other sources her letter from Jerusalem to the Administrative Committee of the ZOA, New York, 21 December 1927, in CZA, File A125/51; and "Miss Szold's Message" to the recent ZOA convention in Pittsburgh, *The New Palestine*, 13–20 July 1928.

As the writer Moshe Smilansky noted, however, Szold's longstanding distrust of "'Wall Street,'...the bank trusts, and the industrial cartels that enslave peoples...to the god, Mammon" made her a natural ally of organized labor. So, too, did her idealism and her Brandeisian affinity for unions. Already during her first months in Palestine in 1921, she felt attracted to "the almost unparalleled idealism of the Haluz."[23] Despite her professed impartiality, her aversion to the militant, anti-Labor Revisionists was well known; in the 1930s she steadfastly refused to allow Youth Aliyah immigrant children to be placed in their settlements. By 1931 she could write in response to the seventieth birthday greetings of the executive committee of the Histadrut, "Happy am I, who has had the privilege of joining with you in the great task of fulfillment that lies before our generation." The men and women of the Histadrut, she said, "know from their lives and souls...the meaning of daily labor and genuine creative efforts that seek to make aspirations reality."[24]

Eventually the Laborites came to see in her a kindred spirit. An American commentator affiliated with the Palestine labor movement remarked in 1931, that because of "Miss Szold's broad sympathy and understanding...today the working element of Palestine look to her as their friend in the Palestine Zionist Executive." A few years later another observer, writing in *Davar*, the Labor daily, acknowledged that Szold's "organizational achievements had been extraordinary and that her human qualities had endeared her to the entire *yishuv*." In the internal politics of the *yishuv*, if not in religion or Arab–Jewish relations, her American experiences and vision served her well.[25]

---

23 Moshe Smilansky, "HaKedosha veHaTehora," *HaAretz*, 20 February 1945; Henrietta Szold, Jerusalem, letter to "dear Girls" [Alice and Annie Jastrow, Philadelphia], 2 May 1921, in CZA, File A125/257. The Jastrow "girls" were the sisters of Joseph Jastrow, Rachel Szold's husband, and childhood friends of Henrietta. On Szold's attraction to the *halutzim*, see Dash, "Doing Good" 104.

24 Benjamin Akzin, *MiRiga LiYerushalayim* (From Riga to Jerusalem) (Jerusalem: Hassifriya Haziyonit, 1989), 297–298; Henrietta Szold, New York, letter (in Hebrew) to Executive Committee, Histadrut, Tel Aviv, 20 February 1931, in LAVON, File IV-208-336alef.

25 Udin, "Henrietta Szold," 5; Hannah Thon, "Sheva Shanim shel Binyan" (Seven years of building), *Davar*, 6 February 1939.

III

Like Magnes, a fellow Progressive with whom she had worked
closely in the American Zionist movement, Szold went to Palestine
"because of an inexorable passion to serve, to fashion...a useful
destiny, on the pattern of the Quakers, the Social Gospelists, the
Social Reformers."[26] According to Ernst Simon, as a child she
wished nothing so much as to become "a Quaker lady," a goal
achieved in part through her dedication to pacifism and to a life of
good deeds.[27] In Palestine she devoted her energies and talents to
medical and social work and to education through the Hadassah
Medical Organization, through Youth Aliyah, which established
villages and training schools for refugee children during the Nazi
period and for local children with special needs, and through the
education and social welfare agencies of the *yishuv*. On all of these
"works" she left the mark of her American background. Here her
American experience proved capable of adaptation to Palestine, and
her American connections most useful.

Before beginning her career in Palestine, Szold had founded and
organized Hadassah, the Women's Zionist Organization of America,
an organization that exemplified in many ways the Progressive
spirit. Channeling women's activities into the areas of social work,
medicine, and child care was typical of the Progressives, who maintained "the traditional image of women as tender mothers, angels
of mercy, and keepers of the morals."[28] Brandeis and others argued
that the "supreme task" in Palestine was "the moral regeneration of
the Palestinians. That task," he asserted in 1921,

> was the reason why Miss Szold's going there was significant....
> Our meagre forces on the firing line should be strengthened by
> other women of the right calibre as soon and so far as this is
> possible.

26   Judd L. Teller, "America's Two Zionist Traditions," *Commentary* 20 (October
     1955); 351.
27   Simon, "Mehanekhet," 11.
28   Wiebe, *Order*, 122.

Brandeis feared that Szold's return to America "even for a brief visit," might endanger the Palestine work.[29]

As Carol Bosworth Kutscher has observed, Hadassah "modeled itself after...prestigious American women's organizations, rather than...Jewish religious or Zionist groups with European origins... [From the former came its] practical...emphasis on health, hygiene, and sanitation...The Hadassah leaders were ardent believers in American [methods and] institutions; they sought efficiency of operation, while enforcing strict financial accountability."[30] Szold herself was acutely conscious from the first of the differences between her women's group and the disorganized, male-dominated American and world Zionist organizations. From its founding in 1912, she remarked some years later, Hadassah was characterized by its "achievement, its trained and willing forces, [and] its tested organization."[31]

In Palestine she discovered that the ethos of the *yishuv* resembled that of Diaspora Zionist organizations. The "systemless" Eastern European immigrants "hate[d] efficiency," she wrote to her sister Adele in 1921, making it difficult for her to "accept them," at least at first. "Disorder," she declared, "nauseates me." Szold readily assumed the task of imposing "order and [the] disciplined acceptance of rules of precedence upon the workers," although she believed "a regiment of Hoovers [might be needed] for this stupendous piece of organizational work."[32] (In 1927 the future president, Herbert

---

29 Louis D. Brandeis, Woods Hole, Mass., letter to J[ulian] W[illiam] M[ack], J[acob] d[e] H[aas], S[tephen] S[amuel] W[ise], F[elix] F[rankfurter], and A[bba], H[illel] S[ilver, his minions in the ZOA], n.p., in *Letters of Louis D. Brandeis,* vol. 5, ed. Melvin I. Urofsky and David W. Levy (Albany: State University of New York Press, 1978), 8.

30 Kutscher, "Early Years," 253.

31 See, for example, her letter from Jerusalem to her family in America, 31 July 1921, in Marvin Lowenthal, *Henrietta Szold: Life and Letters* (New York: Viking Press, 1942, 185–186; and her letter of 14 March 1927 to the National Board of Hadassah, recorded in the minutes of the meeting of the ZOA Administrative Committee, 14 April 1927; Henrietta Szold, [Jerusalem], letter to the Delegates to the Convention of Hadassah, St. Louis, 4 October 1938, in CZA, File A125/58.

32 Idem, Rehovot, letter, to Adele [Seltzer], n.p., 28 April 1921, in CZA, File A125/257; idem, "The Future of Women's Work for Palestine," Jerusalem, 30 May 1930, typescript, in CZA, File A44/35 (the paper was a proposal to

Hoover, an outstanding Progressive, was still best known as the successful organizer of American relief to Belgium during World War I.)

To all of the endeavors with which she was associated in Palestine Szold brought the Progressive notions of sound financial practices, scientific management, and hard work. When anyone asked her support for a new project, her inevitable reply was, "Where is the money to come from?" She took special pride in her early days in Palestine that Hadassah paid its salaries on time, unlike other Zionist enterprises; and she implored the World Zionist Organization to manage its affairs and its funds with good sense and probity. On one occasion she lent £2,000 of her own money to the Palestine Zionist Executive so that it could meet its obligations. When Szold agreed to serve on the Executive in 1927, she did so with the conviction that "in competency it is essential at this moment that we American Zionists should attain and hold the hegemony." She had come "to the conclusion that an American system of administration must be introduced." By that she meant "a small, non-partisan Executive" similar to the city manager plans promoted by American Progressives. This was not to be "an Executive of experts, [but one]...that can supervise and manage the work of the experts."[33]

Hadassah and WIZO for the transfer of welfare activities from the Jewish Agency to the Va'ad Le'umi); and letter from *R.M.S. Caronia,* en route to Zionist Congress, to Elvira Solis, Twin Mountains, N.H., 17 August 1927, in CZA, File A125/310. Compare also, her letter from Jerusalem, to "dear Sisters," n.p., 22 June 1934, in CZA, File 125/264; and Michal Hagitti, "A Rest-Home for Agricultural Laborers in Jerusalem, 1919–1923" (in Hebrew), *Cathedra* 30 (December 1983): 99.

33   Henrietta Szold, Jerusalem, letter to Miss Pinczover, [Jerusalem], 25 May 1921, in CZA, File A 125/321; idem, Jerusalem, letter to "dear Ones" [family in the United States], 28 November 1922, in CZA, File A125/258; idem, [Jerusalem], letter to London Zionist Executive, London, 10 January 1928, in CZA, File S25/997; F[rederick] H. Kisch, [Jerusalem], memorandum to Dr. [Werner] Senator, [Jerusalem], 20 April 1930, in CZA, File S25/1594; Henrietta Szold, on board the *S.S. Amazonia* sailing from Marseille [*sic*] to Jaffa, letter to [Louis] Lipsky, [president of the ZOA, New York], 24 November 1927, in CZA, File F38/509; idem, "The Task of the Executive," address to the Cleveland Conference of the United Palestine Appeal, published in *The New Palestine*, 11 November 1927. On the Progressives and the city manager concept, see Harold

Like other American reformers of her day, she had a high regard for honesty, intelligence, and good sense, as well as expertise. She remarked to a friend in 1943 that she did not believe in courses "in administration [although]...doubtless there are techniques which [it] would be well to know and acquire." Most important for an administrator, she maintained, were "a sense of organization and, above all good common sense and interest in and knowledge of the work in hand." No less, Szold valued hard work, a concept then associated with America. In fact, she was a workaholic. At an eightieth birthday celebration for her in 1940, Laborite Moshe Shertok (later, Sharett), head of the political department of the Jewish Agency and later foreign minister of Israel, remarked upon Szold's "enormous capacity for work, her perseverance, her ability to get to the bottom of a matter, her thoroughness, [and] her concern for performance and for finishing a job." In many ways "she has enlightened us," he said, "but chiefly through" her seemingly inexhaustible energy for work.[34]

IV

Space does not permit examination here of the full range of Szold's "works" in the areas of health, education, and welfare. Rather, her contributions to medicine, her first arena of service to Palestine, will serve as an illustrative example of the way in which she successfully brought American influences to bear on the areas of *yishuv* life with which she was "professionally" involved. Public health was one of the most important concerns of American Progressives in the turn-of-the-century years;[35] and, as noted earlier, it was a field for which women were presumed to be particularly well suited. The American Red Cross was founded by Clara Barton in 1882 and

---

U. Faulkner, *Politics, Reform and Expansion 1890–1900* (New York: Harper Torch Books, 1963), 27–28; and Wiebe, *Order*, 168.

34 Henrietta Szold, Jerusalem, letter to Gisela Warburg, New York, 31 July 1943, in CZA, File A125/111; Moshe Shertok, typescript of speech (in Hebrew) given at the Jewish Agency Building, Jerusalem, 12 December 1940, on the occasion of Henrietta Szold's 80th birthday.

35 See Wiebe, *Order*, 113–117.

chartered by Congress in 1905. Other health-care organizations also came into being in these years, which saw feverish activity designed to improve the physical well-being of Americans. Influenced by the concerns of their time and place, the women of Hadassah under "the leadership of Henrietta Szold...[made] available [to Palestine] the best of American medical standards and practice."[36]

What sparked this thrust was Szold's trip to the Holy Land in 1909, during which she was struck by the widespread incidence of trachoma.[37] With the help of Nathan Straus, a New York philanthropist whose family owned Macy's Department Store, Szold and her Hadassah sisters dispatched two American nurses in 1913 to "instal [sic] a system of American District Visiting Nurses in Palestine." The guidelines for the nurses' activities were essentially those of the state of New York. Among other things the nurses would "train helpers and probationers and organize 'Little Mothers' circles" like those run by the New York City Board of Health. Shortly after the nurses began their work they were visited by Jane Addams, the settlement house pioneer from Chicago, and Rabbi Stephen S. Wise, who "heartily expressed their appreciation of the work being done." When she returned to Chicago, Addams, one of the country's foremost Progressives, held a "big luncheon" at Hull House for Szold, to whom Brandeis and others referred as "the Jane Adamms [sic] of our Jewish world." On that occasion Addams presented a copy of her memoirs to Szold.[38]

36 Irma L. Lindheim, *Parallel Quest* (New York: Thomas Yoseloff, 1962), 169. Mrs. Lindheim succeeded Szold as president of Hadassah and subsequently herself emigrated to Palestine. Among other sources that talk about "American standards," see Henrietta Szold, letters: Jerusalem, 18 August 1921, in CZA, File A125/257; Jerusalem, 1 November 1922, in CZA, File A 125/258, both to "dear Ones" [family in the United States]; and her letter from Jerusalem published as a supplement to the *Hadassah News Letter*, 13 May 1920.

37 "Mitoch Ne'umah ha-Aharon shel Henrietta Szold" ("From Henrietta Szold's Last Speech"), *HaAhot*, December, 1945. See also Dash, "Doing Good," 100.

38 Mrs. B.A. [Gertrude] Rosenblatt, Haifa, letter to Henrietta Szold, Jerusalem, 10 August 1934, including notes from Rosenblatt's diary, in CZA, File A125/18; Kutscher, "Early Years," 131; extracts from the Diary of Gertrude Goldsmith Rosenblatt, 19 May 1913, in CZA, File A125/18; Henrietta Szold, [New York], letter to Mamma, Rachel, and Joe [Jastrow, Madison, Wis.], 4 November 1913, in CZA, A125/275; and Louis D. Brandeis, Washington, letter to Alfred Brandeis, n.d. [1924], in Brandeis *Letters*, 5:107. See also Charles A. Hawley,

With war came considerable dislocation and suffering in Palestine, especially for the Jewish community, which had always depended on outside aid. At Brandeis's suggestion in 1916, Hadassah took upon itself the task of organizing the American Zionist Medical Unit (hereafter AZMU), including doctors, nurses, a field hospital, and dentists, to be sent to Palestine. Soon after the arrival there of the AZMU in August 1918, it began to revolutionize medical care with the introduction of American methods and technology. It took over the new nursing school and the Rothschild Hospital in Jerusalem, opened new clinics and hospitals elsewhere, and established a Schools Hygiene Department and an x-ray clinic in Jerusalem, dental clinics in Jerusalem and Jaffa, and infant welfare stations in a number of communities; and it mounted a Medical Sanitary Expedition "to visit all the Jewish villages and the Jewish communities in the cities." Even its hospital laundry was innovative, the first steam laundry in the country.

Between the summer of 1919 and that of 1920, when Szold arrived in Palestine to take personal charge of the Unit, the AZMU recorded almost 400,000 visits to its clinics. In 1921 with money donated by Brandeis, the Unit, now renamed the Hadassah Medical Organization (hereafter HMO), undertook a program of malaria control, "which closely resembled the methods of the International Health Board of the Rockefeller Foundation." Aside from its personnel and technology, the AZMU could be identified as a liberal American institution in the spirit of Szold, by its rule, "that no discrimination be exercised in any of its...branches of service as to race, creed, or colour" — a policy maintained to the present by the HMO.[39]

State University of Iowa, Iowa City, letter to Henrietta Szold, Jerusalem, 16 December 1935, in CZA, File A125/160. On Addams and her Progressive context, see Samuel P. Hays, *The Response to Industrialism, 1885-1914* (Chicago and London: University of Chicago Press, 1957), 76–83; and Gunther Barth, *City People* (Oxford and New York: Oxford University Press, 1980), 7–8ff. Rosenblatt was one of Szold's early compatriots in Hadassah.

39 *American Zionist Medical Unit for Palestine* (New York, 1919), 35; *Report* of Activities of the American Zionist Medical Unit from July 1919 to August 1920 (director: I. M. Rubinow) (n.p., n.d.), 7; Hadassah Medical Organization *Third Report* — September 1920–December 1921 (Jerusalem, 1922), 39–40; *Twenty Years of Medical Service to Palestine 1918–1938* (Jerusalem: Hadassah Medical

Although on several occasions she was called upon to take a more active role, after 1923 Szold served largely as a watchdog or adviser to the HMO, albeit one whose advice could not be easily ignored; and in 1925 she returned to Palestine as resident mentor to the new HMO director. The organization continued to adapt recent American medical innovations to Palestinian needs, often at her suggestion: the first hospital social service department in the country in 1934, the first medical social worker in 1937 (an idea still very new in America), and the medical center concept for the new Hadassah Hospital opened in Jerusalem in 1939. The goal of all these undertakings, as Szold told a Hadassah reception in New York in 1923, remained the "development of public health work to the same degree of efficiency attained by our [that is, American] hospitals."[40]

V

What emerges from a consideration of the faith and works of Henrietta Szold is a portrait of a woman shaped to a great degree by America, who brought with her to Palestine some American ideas that guided her most successful endeavors. One should not, however, be left with the impression that Szold was an uncritical admirer of the United States. Throughout her life she was acutely aware that "Anti-Semitism is pervasive everywhere — [the] U.S.A. not excepted." With all of her admiration for American Jews and especially for the Hadassah women, she was often quite disappointed in them. In 1931, before her return to Palestine, she wrote to her former associates in Jerusalem that she found among American Jews "no cohesion, no well-directed effort to change sentiment into

Organization, 1939), 7, 25, 27, 47; and Dash, *Jerusalem*, 116, 132. See also Henrietta Szold, Jerusalem, letters to "Family," [United States], 7 October 1921, and to Miss [Jane?] Friedenwald, [Baltimore], 4 January 1921, both in CZA, File A125/257.

40   *Twenty Years*, 17, 65, 67; Gelber, *Balm*, 103; Henrietta Szold, "Jewish Palestine in the Making," speech delivered at the Hadassah reception in her honor at the Hotel Pennsylvania, New York, 30 April 1923, typescript, in CZA, File A125/9.

action. And the young," she noted, "have been allowed to drift away." Some years later on a fund-raising tour of the United States primarily for Youth Aliyah, she remarked to Berl Katznelson that she "wanted to kill" a Hadassah woman who had boasted of having traveled from California "just for her." Already by the late 1920s she felt herself something of a stranger in America. In 1943 she wrote to a longtime Hadassah co-worker, that she had "lost touch with...[her] own Jewish America."[41]

Szold took American baggage with her to Palestine; her contributions to the country were in large measure those of American Progressivism. She did not, however, seek to make the *yishuv* into an American outpost. She could wax nostalgic about the American landscape and long for her family; but for her, from early on, Palestine was "the central Jewish undertaking, which alone" held "the promise of quickening Jewish life," as she wrote in 1929. Twenty years earlier, on her first trip to the Holy Land, she had remarked that whatever the difficulties of life in Palestine, in America Jews "could not keep the Sabbath. And," she added with prescience, "how long will America take them?" Szold acknowledged that Palestine in the inter-war period depended

> upon the Diaspora for material aid; tomorrow, [however], Palestine, resplendent intellectually, will pay back to the Diaspora its whole investment, capital and interest, in terms of spiritual succor, stimulation and strength.

For its own "salvation," she asserted in 1930, "the Diaspora...should prolong the period of its attachment to Palestine as much as possible." She conceded that there might be "disappointments in Palestine"; and she retained "optimism about the Jewish people" in general, and a conviction that they "have the greatest possibilities

41 Henrietta Szold, Jerusalem, letter to her sister Adele [Seltzer], n.p., 18 September 1934, in CZA, File A125/264; idem, New York, letter to Messrs. [Frederick] Kisch, [Arthur] Ruppin, and [Werner] Senator, Executive, Jewish Agency, Jerusalem, 6 February 1931, in CZA, File S25/1594; idem, quoted by Berl Katznelson in a letter from New York to his wife, Leah [Miron-Katznelson, Tel Aviv], 24 November 1937, in Berl Katznelson Papers, Mapai Archive, Bet Berl, File 2; idem, Jerusalem, letter to Mrs. Edward [Rose] Jacobs, New York, 7 June 1943, in CZA, File A125/35. See also, Dash, *Jerusalem*, 219-220.

of all peoples." Nonetheless, she maintained "that philosophically considered, there is nothing but Zionism for us to save us."[42]

For Szold, Palestine was to be the indisputable center of the Jewish world, not America. She devoted the last quarter-century of her life to strengthening the new center. She gave it what she had, her American connections and American notions and technology, which in the areas of health, education, and welfare were widely regarded as the most advanced available. She offered Palestine what she perceived to be the best of America. Her gift was well received.

42 Szold, en route from Trieste to Alexandria, letter to Elvira Solis, New York, 1 January 1929, in CZA, File A125/310; idem, on the Mediterranean between Alexandria and Trieste, letter to "dear Ones" [family in the United States], 28 November 1909, in CZA, File A125/276; idem, "The Future of Women's Work," 12; idem, address to special meeting of the ZOA Administrative Committee, New York, 9 June 1936, typescript, in CZA, File A125/83.

"Anu banu artza" in America:
The Americanization of the *Halutz* Ideal*

Arthur Aryeh Goren

In the course of the 1920s the image of the *halutz* and the concept *halutziut* came to represent the core ideal of Zionism. "Anu banu artza livnot u'lehibanot ba" — a folk song that became popular in Palestine about 1930 — captures the essence of that vision: "We have come to the land to build it and to rebuild ourselves in the process."[1] The *halutzim's* self-image as the vanguard of the Jewish people, totally committed to the redemption of the ancestral land, found widespread acceptance in the Zionist movement and beyond. Addressing an American audience in 1929 on the tenth anniversary of the founding of Hechalutz (the roof organization serving those preparing for *aliyah*), Chaim Arlosoroff, the labor Zionist leader in Palestine, wrote: "The name of Hechalutz has witnessed something akin to a triumphal procession around the world. ... Even those among the Jews who know little about Zionism have — somewhere and at some time — heard its magic ring." Arlosoroff went on to observe that "Hechalutz was the first word of the modern Hebrew vocabulary to gain something like international currency."[2]

In its classic formulation, *halutziut* meant above all else a return to the soil of the Land of Israel. Becoming tillers of the land in the service of the nation also required an inner metamorphosis. "To

* I would like to thank Professors Ezra Mendelsohn and Deborah Dash Moore for their critical reading of the paper and their valuable suggestions.
1 I am indebted to Professor Ezra Mendelsohn of the Hebrew University for this information.
2 *Hechalutz*, edited by Chaim Arlosoroff, Shlomo Grodzensky, and Rebecca Schmukler (New York: Zionist Labor Party Hitachduth of America and Avukah, American Student Zionist Federation, 1929), 7.

build and be rebuilt" entailed psychic no less than geographic and occupational redemption. *Hagshamah atzmit* (personal realization), the clarion call of the movement, involved the personal fulfillment of the *halutz* ideals through the instrumentality of a disciplined movement and the forging of a collective will. The most effective expression of that will was the collective settlement — the kibbutz and the *kvutza*, and some also included the cooperative moshav — where means and ends, individualism and communalism, personal conversion and national rebirth, merged. For the observer, the apparently unbounded devotion of the *halutzim* represented the first fruits of Zionist education, the creation of an army of youthful, zealous, fearless, and hardened pioneers who were conquering the land with their labor.[3]

This view did not go unchallenged. In the dense political world of European Zionism, the *halutz* movement encountered opponents on the right and the left. The Zionist right faulted the elitism of *halutziut* and its controlling collectivist temper. Furthermore, they charged, Hechalutz was a utopian movement led by fanatics who were socialist sectarians — and atheists to boot. For some Zionist idealogues on the left, class — creating a Jewish proletariat — was the imperative. Both camps argued that a select *halutz* movement offered no solution for the mass settlement of ordinary Jews, which was the overriding need of the hour. In addition, the *halutz* movement itself was riven by factional splits fed by clashes over methods, socialist theory, and ultimate goals.[4]

For the most part, America was spared the acrimony of these debates and the political jockeying they engendered. To some degree, distance and language account for this. The party debates, conducted in Yiddish and Hebrew in Poland and Palestine, were beyond the ken

3   For a perceptive semantic study of the *halutz* idea, see Henry Near, "Mihu halutz? Gilgulim semantiim shel ha-minuah ha-halutzi bitnu'at ha-avoda ha-eretz-yisraelit" (Who is a *halutz*? Semantic changes in the usage of *Halutz* in the labor movement in Eretz Israel), *Tura Bet* (Hamerkaz le-limudei yahadut, Oranim, Israel), 228–248.

4   Y. Oppenheim, *The Hechalutz Movement in Poland, 1917—1929* (in Hebrew) (Jerusalem 1982), 150–206, 323–345; Henry Near, *The Kibbutz Movement: A History*, vol. 1: *Origins and Growth, 1909*-1939 (Oxford: Oxford University Press, 1992), 97–128.

or care of most American Zionists, except for some intellectuals and the socialist Poalei Zion, who were more European than American.[5] For the overwhelming majority of American Zionists, their nonideological, philanthropic Zionism had little room for such issues as the type of settlers needed in Palestine, how they should be trained, what their ultimate purpose should be, and whether a national kibbutz or a federation of independent kibbutzim was preferable. Rather, American Zionist publicists and Jewish educators, with some exceptions, embraced the idyllic image of the *halutzim*. The communal settlements they were building were Zionism's most exalted achievement. Not only were they in the forefront of the renewal of national life; they also offered the world a singular example of a democratic, egalitarian, and just society-in-the-making. Here indeed was evidence for American Zionism's claim that the return to Zion, inspired by the universal prophetic ethic, transcended narrow nationalism.

In its pristine form, this image of the *halutz* crystallized by the mid-1920s and continued to represent for American Jewry the essence of the Zionist ideal until the establishment of the Jewish state transformed Zionism and its myths. Nevertheless, during the prestate years, the period with which we are mostly concerned, some Americans questioned the exalted place assigned to the *halutzim*. By the late 1920s, critics were commenting on the ideological rigidity of the kibbutz and the deleterious effect of collectivism on the individual. These critics questioned as well the economic viability of the kibbutz. In 1928 a commission of experts recommended withdrawing financial support from the kibbutzim, who, they declared, were wasting the limited resources of the Zionist organization in dubious social experimentation. Only through industrialization and urbanization, they argued, could the country absorb the rising tide of migration. There were others who, while admiring the idealism of

5   Both the original Hechalutz (founded in 1905) and the one established by David Ben-Gurion and Yitzhak Ben-Zvi during their stay in the United States between 1915 and 1918, were short-lived and limited by and large to the Yiddish-speaking members of the Poalei Zion. I have therefore not considered them as germane to a discussion of the Americanization of the *halutz* idea. Cf. Mark A. Raider, "The Halutz in the Mind of American Zionist Youth, 1905—1939," unpublished paper.

the kibbutzim, were uneasy over the *halutzim's* hostility to religion. However, only during the years prior to and immediately following the establishment of the State of Israel did the *aliyah* of several thousand American *halutzim* and the call from Israel for thousands more to join them provoke any compelling reappraisal of the primacy of the classical *halutz* way. This essay surveys the rise and decline of the *halutz* image, the uses American Zionists made of it, and finally its redefinition — some would say diminution — after 1948.

The figure of the *halutz*, the invention of the newly formed Zionist youth movements, made its appearance only at the end of World War I. However, in the years prior to the war, Zionists in America had adopted the precursor of the *halutz*, the *shomer*, the guard and lookout. Of course, they made much of the early Zionist colonists, of their trials, and of the stability the settlers finally achieved. And they lauded the revival of the Hebrew language.[6] But the truly heroic figure, someone who embodied the consummate change Zionism had wrought, was the *shomer*.[7]

In an address delivered shortly after his return from a visit to Palestine in 1912, the popular Zionist orator Judah Magnes captured these images for his audience. In his report, Magnes compared his stay with one four and a half years earlier. What stood out, for him, was the complete change in the spirit of the people, indicative of which was the relationship with the Arabs. On his first trip, he recalled, the "colonists" had been in constant dread of their Arab neighbors. Now, Magnes remarked, "from north to south, and from west to east, the question of the [Arab] neighbor is being looked at not with fear and trembling, but with the strong and manful gaze of young Jews and Jewesses conscious of their strength, and realizing

6   See, e.g., *Brandeis on Zionism: A Collection of Addresses and Statements by Louis D. Brandeis* (Washington, D.C.: Zionist Organization of America, 1942), 31.

7   Jonathan Frankel has analyzed the creation of a *shomer* mythology — see Frankel, "The 'Yizkor' Book of 1911 — A Note on National Myths in the Second Aliya," in *Religion, Ideology and Nationalim in Europe and America: Essays Presented in Honor of Yehoshua Arieli*, ed. H. Ben Israel et al. (Jerusalem: Historical Society of Israel and Zalman Shazar Center for Jewish History, 1986), 355–384.

the battle that is before them." These *shomrim*, "the beginnings of a Jewish militia, the beginnings of a new type of Jew, were not defending their lives alone; ...they were defending their country."[8]

The *Young Judaean*, published by the recently established Zionist youth organization, embellished the image. It described the *shomrim* as "stalwart, fearless men whose ability to shoot straight and ride like the wind has put the fear of the Lord upon would-be pilferers."[9] So exhilarating was the *shomer* figure for Henrietta Szold, Zionist leader and founder of Hadassah, that in her 1915 report on the *yishuv*'s progress she used these words, in an otherwise dry account, when discussing the *shomrim*:

> Hashomer has raised the dignity of the Jew in the eyes of his Arab neighbors. A Jew who is a good shot, and rides a horse, bareback if you will, with the same grace as the Arab, and cuts a good figure at that as he gallops 'cross country, exacts respect.

Brandeis talked of the "intrepid *shomrim*, the Jewish guards of peace, who watch the night against marauders and doers of violent deeds."[10]

For the American reader, the *shomrim* were the "minute men," as one account in the *Young Judaean* put it. In her 1916 *Course in Zionism*, Jesse Sampter, a poet and prolific contributor to Zionist journals prior to and following her immigration to Palestine in 1919, used another analogy: "They [the *shomrim*] can ride and shoot as

8   Judah L. Magnes, "A Message from Palestine: Address delivered at Cooper Union, on Saturday evening, 18 May 1912," Magnes Papers, Central Archives for the History of the Jewish People, Jerusalem, P3/1065, pp. 3–4.
9   *Young Judaean* 4(5) (February 1914):11. "Jewish Minute Men," *Young Judaean*, 3(1) (October 1912):20, a description of the *shomrim*, is apparently borrowed from Magnes's 1912 address. In that speech he described a Passover seder he had attended in Jaffa where a child asked his father to buy him a weapon in exchange for the *afikoman*, "because at times the watchmen [*shomrim*] become sick, and it is necessary for someone to take their place to take care of the houses and guard Jewish boys and girls who live in them."
10 Henrietta Szold, "Recent Progress in Palestine," *American Jewish Year Book* (Philadelphia: Jewish Publication Society, 1915), 95; *Brandeis on Zionism*, 27.

well as the Arabs or as our Western cowboys."[11] The *shomer* figure stirred up associations with the frontiersman of the American West, the solitary cowboy of the plains, and, by inference, the sheriff who imposed order on lawless country.[12] Noteworthy for understanding the changes that would take place in the 1920s, when the *shomer* image was replaced by that of the *halutz*, was the trait implicitly shared by the Palestinian Jewish hero and his American counterpart. From the American perspective, both were individualists, plucky and unyielding; but whereas the *shomrim* "prepared outlying regions, for permanent settlement to be cultivated by others," the *halutz* stood for permanency and collectivism.[13]

In his 1912 report, Magnes touched on other themes later incorporated in the *halutz* legend. One was the sheer joy of the new life. "There is one thing that I would tell as the symbol of the new life, ... singing, singing, singing everywhere." Magnes had hardly heard the voice of song during his first visit, he explained. "Today there is singing — 'Yaldah, yaldah, yaldati, Girl, girl, girl of mine; Yonah, Yonah, yonati, Dove, dove, dove of mine' — the song of the Shomer, of the watchman, to his love — the song of the Jewish guard to the girl he would take with him to Jerusalem." Hard-riding *shomrim* fell in love and courted their "girls" on horseback — all in Hebrew.

Magnes developed a second theme central to the *halutz* ideal and in full accord with the American ethos: work and self-reliance. True, there was singing everywhere, he declared, but there was also work everywhere. "Everyone is working, is trying to find work, is happy in his work, and I suppose what will appeal to an American audience, many are prosperous by reason of their work." He gave special attention to the first communal and cooperative workers' settlements, which were barely two years old. Um Juni (Deganya) and Fuleh (Merhavia) were worked by "Communist men and women." Introducing a personal note, Magnes recounted that on his visit to Kinneret, he had met an American immigrant, Eliezer Jaffe, who was probably known to many in the audience. "I have written to my

11   The quotation is from the second edition, where the title was changed to *A Guide to Zionism* (New York: Zionist Organization of America, 1920), 170.
12   For a similar profile from a European perspective, see Frankel, "National Myths," 371.
13   Szold, "Recent Progress in Palestine," 95.

friends [in America]," Jaffe told Magnes, "that here I am stronger and happier than I was there [in New York] in the press. I tell them that here I am learning to be a man, I am a full and thorough and harmonious Jew." Magnes concluded his address with a rhetorical flourish that harked back to Jaffe's message: "If you have a love of your people in your hearts and a yearning for the land of your fathers, I say to you, Go up into the land!"[14] It is unlikely that more was intended than an expression of Zionist sentiment and a word of encouragement to the handful who contemplated emigrating. And yet it is noteworthy that in this paean to the New Palestine, the proto-American *halutz* was honored.

From 1918 to 1921, new political and social developments produced the organized *halutz* movement as we know it and bred the legend of the *halutz*. The British occupation, the San Remo peace treaty giving international ratification to the national home, and the beginning of Jewish immigration on an unprecedented scale rendered the *shomer* myth nearly obsolete. Nevertheless, it did linger on. Jesse Sampter maintained that prewar Zionist idiom. In a 1920 column in the *Young Judaean*, Sampter rhapsodized: "I saw spring up, with marvelous quickness, new villages, filled with Jewish men and women, from whose lips came songs of joy and thanksgiving. I saw the *shomer*, astride his spirited steed, a mounted sentinel, guarding the frontier."[15] Sampter then went on to describe *halutzim* draining the swamps of Emek Yizre'el, the Valley of Jezreel.

How quickly the *halutzim* became a staple of Zionist propaganda can be deduced from the remarks of Reuben Brainin, the American Hebrew writer, when reporting on his 1926 visit to Palestine in the pages of the *New Palestine*: "The glorification of the *halutz* by our campaign speakers had only served to harden me, to prepare me for disillusionment." Brainin now thought differently. "Whatever you have been reading is pale, colorless, phlegmatic as compared to the spirit as expressed by the *halutzim*." The sheer willpower the *halutzim* displayed, their capacity for service and creativity, their hardihood

14   Magnes, "Report," 5–13.
15   Jessie E. Sampter, "A Vision of Redemption," *Young Judaean* 11(4) (January 1921):99. *The New Palestine* 1(22) (2 April 1920):3.

in overcoming difficult conditions were, this man of literature wrote, "beyond description." Anticipating a question about the religious beliefs of the *halutzim* — a question Americans frequently asked — Brainin responded that theirs was "the religion of labor." He asked his readers to visualize the quarry at Ein Harod in Emek Yizre'el, where the *halutzim* did the hardest of all physical work. Only then could one understand the meaning of the phrase "religion of labor." "Paid labor," Brainin wrote, "cannot break such stones with a smile and song on the lips."[16]

The single-mindedness and towering inner strength of the *halutzim* who worked the quarries and drained the swamps was magnified tenfold in the eyes of American Jews when Zionist publicists presented them as young intellectuals and professionals who had left behind promising careers for the grueling life of redeeming the land. One American Zionist official, on a mission to Palestine, described "the intense spiritual life" of the *halutzim* (a Hashomer Hatzair group in the Emek) in these words: "You can see men crushing the rocks or digging the soil, and talking about Nietzsche or Weininger, Strindberg or Ibsen, Maeterlinck or Anatole France, Wagner or Beethoven."[17] The eminent Zionist writer Maurice Samuel, in one of his dispatches from Palestine during the summer of 1924, dwelt on the same phenomenon. This was not the "plain pioneering" and "primitive determination" one found in the early history of an undeveloped country," he noted. "These are civilized and sophisticated men and women, not peasants." Here was "a paradox, if you like, the delicacy of high development combined with the ardor and resistance of the brute. They talk of books and philosophies; their shepherds go into the fields with a Bialik or Ibsen in their pockets; they have their meetings and discussions; they *know* why they suffer and endure." On another occasion Samuel explained how the *halutzim* put their intellectuality to work. He described the close on a thousand *halutzim* living near Petach Tikvah. They had been "*luftmenschen*, impractical, useless to themselves and to the world." Within a year they had learned to care for the orchards,

16   Reuben Brainin, "In the Land of Immortals," *New Palestine* 10(3) (15 January 1926):54–55.
17   Eva Leon, "With the Chalutzim," *New Palestine* 6(16) (18 April 1924):324.

to plant, sow, and reap. When you speak to them, "they startle you with their modernity. They have organized their field work as work is organized in modern factories," measured a field in hours of work, graphed out, mathematically, the amount of energy the enterprise needed. And their enterprise, their productivity, and their elan were amazing.[18] Jewish brains and Zionist idealism, Samuel's readers were expected to conclude, more than compensated for the missing brawn.

This image of the *halutz*, who sacrificed a career at home for a life of labor in the homeland, was not the property of Zionist publicists alone. In the spring of 1923, more than a year before Samuel's articles, the correspondent of the influential New York *Evening Post*, George W. Seymour, published three reports describing his impressions of Palestine.[19] Seymour's treatment of the *halutzot*, the pioneer women, who insisted on sharing the strenuous work equally with the men, was especially stirring. On the construction crew building the road to Tiberias, Seymour encountered women "lifting and carrying stones with their bare hands and devoting hours to crushing them." One of the women, who spoke English, "was a Russian Jewess, a university graduate with an M.D. degree, in a khaki skirt and peaked cap." She was the embodiment of athletic vigor and good health, and her "soft, blue eyes laughed with each stroke of her sledge hammer against the rock she was breaking. 'We are equals with the men in Palestine. We are all working for the same object: to build a nation, and we are in full accord as to the rights and privileges of each other'." In the next instant, "the steel head of the big hammer came down with a crash on the face of the huge stone, which fell apart in many pieces." Here indeed, Seymour proclaimed, was the "new feminine militancy of a newborn nation which stands unflinchingly the test of the wilderness in the old land of Israel."[20]

18 Maurice Samuel, "Outposts of the North," *New Palestine* (22 August 1924):125; *New Palestine* 7(12) (26 September 1924):205–207.
19 The articles, sent from Palestine on 5, 8, and 12 March 1923, were published in the New York *Evening Post* and reprinted in the *New Palestine*: George W. Seymour, "Triumphant Advance of Zionism: Described by a Christian Observer," *New Palestine* 5(7) (10 August 1923):134–135.
20 *New Palestine* 5(7) (10 August 1923):134, 136.

As one would expect from Henrietta Szold, her report of the *halutzim* was less dramatic and more incisive than most accounts, although no less empathetic. Szold's description was inspired by a four-day stay on Kibbutz Tel Yosef. Meticulously she explained the ideology of the Gedud-Ha'avoda (the Labor Battalion, the collectivist national organization of *halutzim*), the split with Ein Harod, the economic problems faced by the kibbutzim and agriculture in general. (She was invited to study the account books of the kibbutz.) Szold also described the rhythm of kibbutz life, how the work was organized, mealtimes in the communal dining hall, the children's homes, health care, and cultural activities. To communicate the essence of *halutziut*, Szold, with her middle-class American woman's sensibility, focused on the kibbutz women. "Do you realize," she wrote,

> what it means in the way of self-abnegation for those handsome, erect, well-proportioned, vivacious young girls to be going, week-day and Sabbath-day, not to their own trunks or closets for finery that would represent their taste and individuality, but to a common storehouse with its motley assortment of odds and ends in the way of garments?

This was not an essential feature of the commune, Szold explained, although "the zealots" desired to retain it. Nevertheless, "it was a significant illustration of the devotion of our young halutzoth."[21] It is interesting to compare Seymour's and Szold's paeans to the *halutzot* with the reactions of a young American who came to Palestine in 1925 to experience the new life. Fannie Soyer, daughter of a Hebrew writer, teacher of Hebrew literature, and Zionist, had herself studied at the Teachers Institute of the Jewish Theological Seminary. Writing to a friend in America, in Hebrew, she remarked,

> When I was in New York, I considered coming as a *halutza*. I am certain now that I would be unable to stand the [physical] work for more than a day. In a single year, the beautiful young women become old and coarse, and truly sacrifice their youth.

21 Henrietta Szold, "Jewish Palestine at Work," *New Palestine* 6(22) (6 June 1924):461–462.

As much as I am impressed by them and respect them, I would be unable to sacrifice myself as they do.[22]

The best of the reporting on the *halutzim* sought to balance the legend with the reality. Lotta Levensohn's account, "The Realities of Ein Harod," followed Szold's example. One of the founders of Hadassah, Levensohn spent a month working on the kibbutz before she undertook to chronicle her impressions. She, too, included the mundane details of kibbutz living and described her daily work assignments in the fields and the physical discomforts she encountered. Remarkably, nearly a third of the article dealt with relations between the sexes. "The gossip about the sex life in the Kvutzot," wrote Levensohn, "seems recently to have died down; but I feel bound to touch on my observations at Ein Harod in order to present publicly (for the first time, I believe) the evidence of a person who did not form a judgment *after an hour's walk about the camp while the auto was waiting*" (emphasis added).[23] The charges of immorality, Levensohn thought, derived from the fact that men and women in some kibbutzim shared the same room (almost always, Levensohn explained, when a casual visitor had to be given a bed wherever one happened to be vacant for the night), and that some couples lived together without being formally married. There were couples, she declared, who had not gone through the marriage ceremony because they opposed it in principle. Yet they "regarded themselves as much married as those who wore wedding rings," and the kibbutz made no distinction whatever. A new set of relationships between the sexes existed in the kibbutz that was vastly superior to what one found anywhere else.

> The general attitude of men and women toward each other is dignified, comradely, wholesome. There is no need or occasion for clandestine relationships. There is nothing to prevent the marriage of two young people who choose each other. In

---

22 Ezra Mendelsohn, "Morah amerikanit be-Eretz Israel: shlosha mihtavim me-fani soyer le-rivka letz (1925)," (An American teacher in Eretz Israel: Three letters from Fannie Soyer to Rivka Letz [1925]) *Katedra* 72 (June 1994):96.

23 In another context in the same article, Levensohn accused Ludwig Lewisohn of making snap judgments and misrepresenting the character of the kibbutz on the basis of a visit to Ein Harod lasting only a few hours.

the kvutza, social prestige, economic status, or ambitions of whatever kind have no place. Because all are workers, there is but one social class, one economic status, one standard of living [and] marriage is stripped of all irrelevant impediments, and restored to sheer personal attraction.

If a marriage failed, it was dissolved by mutual consent. There was no stigma. In fact, public opinion "regards it as immoral for people to live together when affection has ceased." Nor did the presence of children offer a problem, since they were all maintained and educated at the expense of the commune. The outdoor life, common occupations, common effort, and mutual confidence made for clean and normal relations between the sexes, "so that the furtiveness induced by the artificial stimulations of pandering movies and musical comedies have no place here." There were sex problems, Levensohn conceded: "the preponderance in the number of men, the subtropical climate, and the limited amount of recreation." But they were not "obscene problems of promiscuity or questionable paternity." Thus, in the wonderful world of the *halutzim*, marriage and the relations between the sexes had been elevated to a higher, more idealistic plane.[24]

Nevertherless, Levensohn's vigorous "defense" of kibbutz morality suggests that allegations of sexual promiscuity were still to be heard. Others besides Levensohn felt constrained to probe the issue. The liberal Protestant minister John Haynes Holmes, in his book on Palestine, inquired into the sexual morality of the kibbutz; and Judah Magnes in the privacy of his journal recorded a searching interview with Manya Shochet, a leader of the Gedud-Ha'avoda, over the rumors of sexual promiscuity.[25] The attention the subject evoked is understandable. Similar accusations directed at Soviet society (communism and free love going together) were commonplace in the United States. The "scandals" connected with Emma Goldman — the immigrant Jewish anarchist who was deported to Russia in 1921 — were still fresh in the public's mind. Moreover, America

24   Lotta Levensohn, "Palestine in the Making: The Realities of Ain Charod," *The New Palestine* 11(6) (20 August 1926):114–115.
25   Judah L. Magnes, [Diaries], 12 March 1925; Judah L. Magnes Papers, File 964, Central Archives for the History of the Jewish People, Jerusalem.

of the 1920s debated with unprecedented candor a set of issues connected with the New Morality and the New Woman — most of it about sex — to the dismay and chagrin of conventional middle-class America. It is not surprising, then, that some Jewish circles were troubled by this facet of the *halutz* legend, as were others by the open irreligiosity and militant secularism of the kibbutz.[26]

Two influential American Jewish figures — the writer Ludwig Lewisohn, and the philosopher and Zionist thinker Horace Kallen — were among those who visited Palestine during the 1920s and wrote books that reached a readership well beyond the Zionist community. The two praised the *halutzim* but expressed serious reservations regarding the kibbutz enterprise. In a characteristic passage, Lewisohn juxtaposed the lethargic, backward *fellah*, riding listlessly on a tired ass, his wife trudging behind, with the sudden appearance of a wagon filled with grain and fruit, "drawn by two vigorous mules." The youthful driver had "a face full of intelligence and energy. In the back of the wagon two others: bare arms and throats, taut muscles, sunbrowned by labor in the open fields despite near-sighted eyes and the foreheads of thinkers. Halutzim. These are our people."[27] (The stark contrast between the "primitive" peasant Arabs and the energetic, progressive *halutzim* was a recurring theme, as we shall see, in Zionist films.) Kallen chose to compare the *halutzim* with the earlier Biluim, the handful of pioneers who came in the 1880s. The *halutzim* possessed a "grand vision." They sought "no simple personal salvation." Their aspiration was "the prophetic one." Like the "sect" of Reform Judaism, "they believed in the mission of Israel and in Jewry's duty and destiny to be a light unto the nations." The kibbutzim and *moshavim* were "endeavors

26   Frederick Lewis Allen, *Only Yesterday: An Informal History of the Nineteen Twenties* (New York: Harper & Row, 1959; first published 1931), 73–101; William H. Chafe, *The American Woman: Her Changing Social, Economic, and Political Role, 1920–1970* (New York: Oxford University Press, 1972), 94–99; Linda Gordon, *Woman's Body, Woman's Right: A Social History of Birth Control in America* (New York: Grossman, 1976), 186–202.
27   Ludwig Lewisohn, *Israel* (New York: Boni & Liveright, 1925), 150.

to kindle that light," and the *halutzim* were "the pathfinders and the renewers."[28]

Along with the glorification of the *halutz* legend came unflattering descriptions of their life that called into question not the intentions of the *halutzim* but their fundamental philosophy. Lewisohn described the dinner hour at Ein Harod. "In the huge eating shed several hundred people were eating at the rude tables. The benches had no backs. The dishes and utensils were of the coarsest. There was clatter and noise. There were flies. There was a sense of haste, of improvisation." And yet, to Lewisohn's distress, the young men and women were "quite satisifed with this hubbub, this...messiness." In the children's home, he observed parents who "snatched what seemed to us a pitiful and again crowded glimpse of both the children and each other before, the dinner hour being over, each had to return to his or her appointed task." For Lewisohn, the liberal American intellectual, the spirit of their "communist austerity" violated the "aim, fruit, goal, meaning of human life — the creative individual." The "large kvutzah" was "a contamination of our life by the supineness, the mass-life, the morbid and dangerous submersion of personality that seems to mark the Russian character whether under Czar or Soviet." True, Lewisohn hastened to add, he found "magnificent self-sacrifice, magnificent fortitude, magnificent singleness of purpose." The kibbutzim were agricultural and industrial triumphs; but as social experiments "they fill my Western mind with misgiving and dismay."[29] Not so the *moshavim*! Each family with its home, gardens, fields, had its privacy and flexibility yet benefited from the cooperative endeavor. Wandering through the gardens and farmyards of Nahalal was "an unforgettable experience." Flowers were all about. The admirable union of harmony and convenience found its expression in the physical layout of the village, which "seemed to coincide with the temper of the men and women who live and labor here." No land was held as private property, no hired

28   Horace M. Kallen, *Frontiers of Hope* (New York: Horace Liveright, 1929), 91–92.
29   Lewisohn, *Israel*, 178–181.

labor was employed. "Here, too, the social ideals of the Prophets shall prevail."[30]

Kallen's observations were based on a longstanding strategy for the economic development of the national home. One of the formulators of the Pittsburgh Program adopted by the Zionist Organization of America in 1918, he insisted that considerations of ideology and politics had no place in building the Zionist homeland. That task required "business acumen and technical skill," not party functionaries who wrote for journals and swayed audiences. For Kallen, the increase in Jewish population from 10 percent in 1920 to 18 percent in 1926 was "testimony to the place of the Holy Land in the deep heart of Jewry rather than to the abilities of the Zionist administration." The concentration on agricultural colonization in "a country beautiful but barren" was foolish, more a matter of ideology than nation building. The large-scale settlement that European Jewry required could be achieved only by industrializing the country.[31]

Nevertheless, Kallen took the grand tour of Emek Yizre'el with its kibbutzim and *moshavim*. He, too, found the *halutzim* heroes and the kibbutzim insufferable. This was Ein Harod: "A straggling village; military housing without military tidiness; machinery rusting on the ground; sanitary arrangements a stench and a menace; omnipresent flies over everything; a thick, black, buzzing, beating layer of life on freshly baked bread set out to cool." Here is the Friday night meal at Ein Harod: "The food is being brought in pails and bowls from the kitchen and passed from hand to hand, badly cooked, without nourishment to the eye, unalluring to the palate. But how quickly consumed! While the everlasting doctrinal argument flows high, and the flies buzz."[32] (Why, one might ask, did the middle-class,

---

30 Ibid., 181–185.
31 Kallen, *Frontiers of Hope*, 108–114, 117–118. Emanuel Neumann described being "torn between admiration for the *halutzim* in the Jezreel Valley, and the impressive reality of the rapidly growing town of Tel Aviv. ... In the light of our ultimate goals, which of the two carried the greater appeal?" What convinced him that urban, industrial development was preferable was a conversation (in 1925) with members of a kibbutz who did not believe in the possibility of a Jewish majority in Palestine. Emanuel Neumann, *In the Arena: An Autobiographical Memoir* (New York: Herzl Press, 1976), 82.
32 Kallen, *Frontiers of Hope*, 85–86.

American-born women of genteel German pedigree — Henrietta Szold, Lotta Levensohn, and Jesse Sampter — show forbearance and humility in their visits to Ein Harod while Lewisohn, and Kallen, the renowned scholars and moralists, failed to see much beyond the flies?)

Legends and myths are for the believers. By the beginning of the 1930s, American Zionists and their sympathizers had embraced the *halutz* legend and Americanized it to fit their needs. *Halutzim* were educated young idealists who had volunteered to reclaim desert and swamp. No less important, they had dedicated themselves to creating a moral society where equality, fellowship, and the common good reigned. (The critics' words, since they praised as much as they damned, could be filtered to support the legend.) If the *halutzim* were the ultimate Zionists, they were also the ultimate Jews, and the prophetic ethic that inspired them made them Americans in spirit. One could now literally sing the praises of the *halutzim* by learning their songs and dances and, in this way participate vicariously in building the land and being rebuilt. At Zionist gatherings, in the concert hall, among youth groups, even at a conference of Jewish social workers, the folk songs and the hora of the pioneers, reputedly sung and danced into the night after a hard day's work draining swamps, uplifted the participants. As early as 1919, the musicologist Joseph Reider, writing on the "Revival of Jewish Music," noted the influence of the "folksong of the New Palestine." One example that had reached America was the popular "Po ba'aretz" (here in the land). "In Zionist circles," Reider declared, "it vies with Hatikvah in popularity." The song was "firm and manly, joyous and hopeful, brimful of verve and resilience, elasticity and sinuosity, and buoyancy and warmth."[33]

For some time the *Young Judaean* had been offering a song a month from Palestine. Local and national Zionist organizations published song booklets, which were used at meetings and by the Zionist choirs that were established. In 1926 a handsomely published

---

33   Joseph Reider, "A Revival of Jewish Music," *Menorah Journal* 5(4) (August 1919): 225. The song, entitled "Nitzanim," was composed in 1910, the music by Herman Ehrlich and the lyrics by Yisrael Dushman. The opening lines are: "Po be'eretz hemdat avot/titgashemna kol ha-tikvot." I am grateful to Dr. Natan Shachar for this information.

collection of Palestinian folksongs appeared that was intended for a wide audience. Selected, arranged and annotated by the composer and musicologist Abraham W. Binder, after a visit to Palestine, the book went through a second edition in 1929, and in 1933 "Book II" appeared. The song book was used extensively in religious schools. One Jewish educator recalls that "many youngsters made their first contact with Zionist ideas through the new Palestinian music."[34]

In 1926, the *halutz* theme reached the realm of serious music. Jacob Weinberger's full-length folk opera "The Pioneers (Hechalutz)" won first prize at the international music competition held at the Sesquicentennial Exposition in Philadelphia. Drawing on Yemenite folk themes Weinberger's *halutzim* abandoned the backwardness and anti-Semitism of their Polish town for the freedom and rapture of their kibbutz in the Galilee. Eight years later the opera had its world premiere in New York City, with choreography by Dvora Lapson, who began popularizing Palestinian folkdances in Hebrew schools and Jewish centers. In the triumphant final scene of Weinberger's opera, when love conquers all (mostly the objection of the bride's wealthy parents, who follow their errant daughter to the wilds of Palestine with a proper groom in tow), Leah and Zev are about to be married (under a *huppah*!) in their kibbutz. A "l'chayim" is raised to the young couple, but Leah is not to be found. Then a comrade finds her in the cowshed:

> Leah: Why are you celebrating already?
> Nahum: Leah, enough. It is late enough. Time you stopped working.
> Leah: And what about the cattle! They must have water as well. Soon all my work will be finished.

Those assembled wait for Leah to finish caring for the cattle.[35]

---

34 Abraham Wolf Binder, *New Palestinian Folk Songs* (New York: Bloch Publishing, 1926, 1929); *Book II* (New York: Bloch Publishing, 1933); Irene Heskes, "A Biographical Sketch of Abraham Wolf Binder," in *A. W. Binder: His Life and Work* (New York: National Jewish Music Council, 1965), 4.

35 *New York Times*, 3 November 1956, 26 November 1934. The opera was given in a concert version in Carnegie Hall in 1946. See A. W. Binder, "Jacob Weinberg, 1875-1956: A Tribute," *Jewish Music Notes*, Spring issue, 1957, 3. The published libretto and music can be found at the Jewish Theological Seminary. Ayalah Goren's research on Binder and Weinberg were most helpful, as was her

During the 1920s, and more so during the 1930s, pageants, exhibitions, and especially films became the main vehicles for carrying the *halutz* legend to mass audiences. Zionist films, usually commissioned and financed by Keren Hayesod (the Palestine Foundation Fund), were distributed throughout the Jewish world.

The film that received extraordinary notice, the feature-length *Land of Promise*, opened at New York's Astor Theater on 20 November 1935 to the acclaim of New York's leading critics. The *Times* praised the "noble, excellently photographed and skillfully edited film record of the rebuilding of the Jewish homeland in Palestine." The *Times* critic was especially captivated by the powerful contrast between the Arabs in their medieval marketplaces and the "sad-faced" *fellahin* in the fields flailing wheat. ("This was Palestine, says the camera, before the Jews flocked back to the homeland.")

> Then, suddenly, the lens is opened wide upon a dancing, singing group of young men and women [*halutzim*] on the foredeck of a liner, coming to give new life to the century old city, coming to water its fields, run its factories, build its homes. The effect upon the audience is electric."[36]

Although scenes of Tel Aviv, Jerusalem, and Haifa present bustling urban life in a positive light — construction work, industry, relaxing at the beach, a concert in the Hebrew University's amphitheater on Mt. Scopus, the Technion of Haifa — the heroic figures of the film are the *halutzim*, the tillers of the soil. Water is the leitmotif: *halutzim*

---

interview with Dvora Lapson in March 1993. John Martin of the *New York Times* wrote: "[Lapson's] ballet, based on the Palestinian Hora, spirited and well composed, was quite the brightest spot of the entire production." *Jewish Frontier* 2(6) (April 1935):29.

36 *New York Times*, 21 November 1935, 2. See also reviews in the New York *Evening Journal, World Telegram*, and *American*, of the same date. For an account of the making of *Land of Promise*, see Hillel Tryster, "Anatomy of an Epic Film," *Jerusalem Post Magazine*, 30 October 1992, 16–18; and idem "'The Land of Promise': A Case Study in Zionist Film Proganda," *Historical Journal of Film, Radio and Television* 15 (2) (1995): 187—217. See also Ayelet Kohn, "Reyshit ha-kolnoa ha-eretz-yisraeli kimshakef rayonot ha-tekufa" (The cinema of Eretz Israel in the 1930s: A reflection of the ideas of an era) *Katedra* 61 (September 1991):141-155.

drilling for it, directing its flow to the fields, spraying groves; then reaping the harvest and celebrating in a harvest festival and grand parade. Women work alongside men in construction, in field work, in feeding and milking the cows. And there is singing in the dining hall of the kibbutz led by the composer Daniel Sambursky teaching his "Emek Song" (the theme song of the film), and more singing on the way to the fields. The success of *Land of Promise* represented the accumulated experience of fifteen years of Zionist film making in Palestine, a spirited producer, a gifted director, and a superb cameraman on loan from Fox-Movietone films.[37]

The Zionists also took full advantage of the public relations possibilities of the New York première. A distinguished list of guests, headed by Albert Einstein, attended, and the opening ceremonies were broadcast by radio. The *New Palestine* described the "thrilling scene" when a group of "American halutzim" arrived from their training farm for the première. Dressed in white shirts with pitchforks and rakes on their shoulders, they entered the lobby as "hundreds of people cheered and camermen eagerly sought to photograph them." The blue and white banner strung across Broadway advertising the film gave "poignant evidence to all who pass that Palestine has become a vital reality in Jewish life."

The opening of the Palestine Pavilion at the New York World's Fair (1939) was another landmark mass event. The pavilion ran for nearly two years, and over 2 million saw it. Visitors entered a "Hall of Transformation," ascending stairs that symbolized Jewish immigration to Palestine. Dominating the staircase was "a heroic statue of a *halutz*," and behind the statue a sweeping photomural depicted "the march of the *halutzim*." On the right was a mural showing a huge map of Palestine; opposite were wall photos that "depicted the transformation of swamps into healthful settlements, of rocky hills into a thriving colony, and sand dunes into the modern metropolis of Tel Aviv."[38]

---

37 Tryster, "Anatomy"; and idem, work-in-progress.
38 Meyer Weisgal ...*So Far; An Autobiography* (New York: Random House, 1971), 110–121, 130–139; 149–151; 161–163. *New Palestine* 29(18) (12 May 1939):8; *New Palestine* 29(19) (19 May 1939):8–10.

Viewed from afar — through the lenses of the movie camera, the visit to the exhibit hall, the Zionist rally — the "heroic *halutz*," as we have seen, became a stirring myth and slogan for American Zionists. What then happened when young men and women considered becoming *halutzim* themselves? Ironically, when a native American *halutz* movement appeared in the 1930s, it made little impression on the American Zionist public, although it won the approbation of no less a personage than Louis Brandeis. Nevertheless, the endeavors "to make *halutzim* in America," meager as the results were, shed much light on the Americanization of the *halutz* ideal.

As early as 1926, Jesse Sampter articulated the reasoning and motivation behind the call for an American *halutz* movement. Writing in the *New Palestine*, she criticized the existing Zionist youth organizations, with their thousands of members, for "calmly preaching and teaching and collecting and selling, oblivious of those who rebel against the agony of being Zionists — at long distance." Some Americans had settled in Palestine, but they had done so as individuals and had encountered difficulties in adjusting. Needed were groups — "nuclei" — of "several hundred pioneers," who after preparations would join an existing farm commune in Palestine. Clearly, Sampter was proposing the European *halutz* model: group agricultural training (*hachsharah*) directed to collective settlement in Palestine. Interestingly, she dismissed as inconsequential "the very small though devoted nucleus [of *halutzim*] on the East Side of New York, most of whom cannot properly be called American youth at all but are a temporarily transplanted branch of the large and heroic Zionist youth movement of eastern Europe."[39]

The Zionist youth organizations of the 1930s were, in fact, either transplants from Europe or American inventions. In the first case, *shelihim*, emissaries from Eretz Israel, almost always sent by a particular kibbutz movement, collaborated with handfuls of immigrants who brought their *halutz* movement affiliations with them from Europe and established Hashomer Hatzair, Gordonia,

---

39   Jessie E. Sampter, "Youth and Palestine," *New Palestine* 10(23) (18 June 1926): 564–568. As early as 1921, "A Message from our Palestinian Young Judeans," signed by a distinguished list of sixteen, called on America to send "ideas and men." Eleven of the sixteen were women. *Young Judaean* 9 (8) (May-June 1921):220–221.

the Orthodox Hashomer Hadati, Hechalutz, and several training farms. These *halutz* movements were "exclusivist" in the sense that educating their members for kibbutz living was their sole purpose. Their Zionism was embedded in the notion of *shelilat ha'galut* (negation of the Galut) — rejection of the possibility or desirability of creative Jewish living in the Diaspora. Hashomer Hatzair (the Young Guard), for example, dropped those members who did not begin their *hachshara* training at the designated age (usually eighteen) in preparation for *aliyah* to the kibbutz.[40] Young Judaea represented the American prototype. The oldest and largest of the Zionist youth organizations, it maintained a nonpartisan Zionist posture that enabled it to reach out to a broad stratum of Jewish youth. This was in keeping with the outlook of its sponsors, the Zionist Organization of America (ZOA) and Hadassah. In many places, Young Judaea clubs provided the sole locale for Jewish teenagers to meet in an informal social setting.[41]

In the typology of Zionist youth organizations, the Young Poalei Zion Alliance (YPZA), the youth arm of the Labor Zionists, occupied an intermediate position. Immigrant in its origins, the movement's increasingly American-born or American-educated leadership searched for ways to attract an acculturated generation of American Jewish youth to its program. To that end it established a satellite organization, Habonim (the builders), which by 1940 had supplanted the YPZA. Through recreational club work, a children's magazine, young adult activities, a network of summer camps modeled after the kibbutz, and leaders drawn from its own ranks who served as role models, YPZA—Habonim endeavored to impart an interest in Jewish culture, contemporary affairs, socialist Zionism, and the *halutz* ideal. *Aliyah* and *halutziut* were the most important educational goals of the movement, but not the exclusive ones. Unlike the European *halutz* movements and their American affiliates, Habonim defined itself as "halutz centered and halutziut inspired." It offered, in a somewhat ambiguous formulation, "a

40 Samuel Grand, "A History of Zionist Youth Organizations in the United States from Their Inception to 1940," (Ph.D. dissertation, Columbia University, 1958), 240–241, 248–292, 310–331.
41 Ibid., 43–67.

synthesis (not a compromise) between halutziut and a program for America." (The *halutz*-weighted duality inherent in the Habonim approach, it should be noted in passing, did in fact create tensions within the movement with its calls for true parity between the two goals.)[42]

How did Young Judaea, the most American of the Zionist youth organizations, and YPZA-Habonim, with its European–Eretz Israel socialist Zionist ties and American orientation, respond to the *halutz* ideal?

Halutziut first appeared on the agenda of Young Judaea when the 1933 annual convention resolved that "the spirit of *halutz* youth be incorporated in the ideology of Young Judaea and that Young Judaeans be urged to join Hechalutz with a view to ultimately settling in Palestine."[43] In 1935 a national leader of the organization on his return from a visit to Palestine declared that Young Judaea's task was "transmitting the current of Jewish life in Palestine to the future halutzim of America." At the convention that year Maurice Samuel, one of American Zionism's foremost intellectuals, spoke about "reorienting" the Young Judaean program "to prepare Jewish youth for such a time as they may have to emigrate to Palestine."[44] However, these sentiments led to little else. When Young Judaea published an ambitious educational program, "The Chalutzim Series," its content reflected the organization's own equivocations. The introduction to the program declared: "We are taking our clubs through a movement from beginning to end, inviting our members actually to live through, rather than to talk about it, or to play at it." The program was to be as realistic an act of simulation as possible. The authors continued:

> We have chosen the liveliest, most vital phase of Zionism, and of all modern Jewish life, for that matter, as we say to our

---

42   Ibid. 200–240; Akiva Skidell, "The Year Ahead," *YPZA News and Views* 3(6) (29 March 1938); Herman Finkel, "Galut Chalutzim," *YPZA New and Views* 4 (12 April 1930): 9–10; Herman Finkel, "Wanted: A Program for America," *YPZA News and Views* 6 (26 December 1940): 4. See also *Arise and Build: The Story of American Habonim*, ed. David Breslau (New York: Ichud Habonim Labor Zionist Youth, 1961), 8–26, 31–37.

43   *Young Judaean*, 21(8) (September 1933):10.

44   *Young Judaean* 23(7) (May 1935):6–7; 23(10) (October 1935):12.

Young Judaeans, 'This year BE CHALUTZIM! Go to Eretz Israel, found your colony.'... We hope that many of them will be challenged and inspired with the dynamic urge to go to Palestine and to become builders. But we need Chalutzim here, too.[45]

Apparently the *halutz* enthusiasts among the *Young Judaean* leadership were sufficiently aggressive for a Young Judaean editorial, "The Spirit of Young Judaea," to reassert the organization's traditional position. Some maintained, the editorial declared, that Young Judaea should "make a narrower but more militant appeal to the "chosen few," [and send] a few score of youngsters to kibbutzim in Eretz Yisrael." The editorial rejected the elitist, *halutz* approach and reaffirmed its "all-Jewish programme," which it addressed to "the tens of thousands of America's Jewish youth." Besides, the editorial added, there were Young Judaeans in Palestine "consecrating themselves to the enrichment of Jewish life in Eretz Yisrael," playing important roles in education, in industry and culture, and in "commanding posts" in the Zionist executive. They were also to be found, the editorial concluded, serving the cause of Zionism in Zionist districts and Hadassah chapters, in fund-raising campaigns, and in the fields of education and religion. Thus the *halutz* legend could be stretched to become the "spirit of halutziut," defined as devotion to the cause of Jewish survival anywhere. One could be a *halutz* in America! For Young Judaeans, the Americanization of the *halutz* ideal provided uplift and inspiration for the here and now of Jewish living in America.[46]

At first sight, Habonim's "halutz-centered" approach resembled Young Judaea's "spirit of halutziut." But the resemblance was at best superficial. For Habonim, *halutziut* carried far greater ideological weight. It not only equated *halutziut* with building a socialist society

---

45   *The Chalutzim Series*, n.d. [1935?], Central Zionist Archives, E25/330. Among the members of the committee that prepared the series were Ben M. Ediden and Joshua Trachtenberg.

46   *Young Judaean* 24(7) (May 1936):2. As a youngster, I recall one of my Habonim leaders, a former Jewish educator, saying that he once thought standing up in front of a Hebrew school class was true *halutziut*. It was surely more difficult than draining swamps.

in Eretz Israel, but it pursued that end by allying itself organization-
ally with the Poalei Zion party, the world-wide Hechalutz organization, and the kibbutz movements in Palestine. Yet, in important
ways, Habonim spoke with a distinctly American voice. It respected
individual choice: the decision to become a *halutz* was a private
one, to be reached without coercion and for "positive" reasons. The
movement taught love of Zion, not rejection of America. Eager to
reach out to the widest circles of Jewish youth, Habonim stressed its
openness and tolerance. There was place within its ranks for those
who chose to remain in America. Striving to maintain Jewish life in
America was not to be disdained. In fact, educating for *halutziut*,
Habonim argued, made those who chose to remain in America better
Jews, committed Labor Zionists, and activists in the communal life
of American Jews.

This permissiveness, or pluralism, ran counter to European notions of "party discipline" or "kibbutz discipline" or "ideological
collectivism"; in the European movements ambivalence was unacceptable. But for the founders of Habonim, the dogmatic and
doctrinaire were unacceptable, even though that stand resulted in a
less demanding, possibly less effective movement than its European
or Eretz Israel prototypes.[47]

American Hashomer Hatzair criticized Habonim because it had
"seriously modified its standards as a *halutz* movement by forgoing
its *halutz* exclusiveness and by introducing into its atmosphere various attributes of American life, with the assertion that an adjustment
to the American scene is necessary in order to create a large *halutz*
youth movement."[48]

It was a valid enough observation. However, the truth was that
Habonim's "reach out" program — its declared "nonexclusive-
ness" — had only limited success. It was stymied by the inherent

---

47   Arthur A. Goren, "Ben Halpern: 'At Home in Exile'," in *The Other New
York Jewish Intellectuals*, ed. Carole Kessner (New York: New York University
Press, 1994), 82–85. Mark A. Raider, "From Yugnt to Haluzim: The American
Labor Zionist Youth Movement between the First and Second World Wars,"
forthcoming, *Jewish Frontier* 62 (6) (November-December 1995).

48   From *Youth and Nation* [Hashomer Hatzair] (February 1947), as quoted in
Furrows 5(3) (March 1947). Although the quote is some ten years after the
period discussed here, the position holds for the earlier period.

elitism of the movement's core leadership. At a 1937 conference of YPZA–Habonim leaders, Ben Halpern, at the time the secretary of Hechalutz, who in the 1940s became the managing editor of the *Jewish Frontier* and one of Labor Zionism's leading intellectuals, enumerated the qualifications an American *halutz* needed to succeed. One had to know Hebrew. One had to have acquired a knowledge of the philosophy of the *halutz* movement through the writings of such socialist Zionist thinkers as A. D. Gordon, Yosef Hayim Brenner, and Berl Katznelson. Only then was a member ready for the physical and psychological rigors of *hachsharah*, the final stage before the kibbutz. There were no short cuts.[49]

During the 1930s, some two hundred members of the youth organizations affiliated with Hechalutz completed their training and settled in Palestine. They generally joined kibbutzim associated with their American movement. But the attrition rate was high. As many as half were unable to make the adjustment to physical labor and communal living, and returned to America. The outbreak of war ended even this modest trickle.

One should note that YPZA's and Habonim's nonexclusivity did produce some results. During the 1930s and 1940s, "graduates" of the movement who chose to remain in America began playing a role of some significance in Jewish communal service — in Jewish education, the rabbinate, and social work — and in uplifting Zionist discourse. One conduit for their activity was the League for Labor Palestine, a creation of the Labor Zionist organization, whose purpose was to gain the support of the acculturated generation of Jewish intellectuals, professionals and communal activists. Through its efforts, the Rabbinical Assembly of America endorsed the labor movement in Palestine in 1934, and a year later 231 Reform Rabbis followed suit. In 1936, the League called a conference of social workers, educators, and rabbis to discuss the occupational maldistribution of American Jews and in particular the future of "the young men and women who today are attending high schools and colleges and tomorrow will be seeking employment." The purpose

49 *YPZA News and Views* 3 (1, October 1937): 2–4; Ben Halpern, "Habonim and American Zionism," *Jewish Frontier* 26 (December 1959):16–18; Hayim Stopak, "Our Approach to Chalutziut," *Furrows* 10(4) (June-July 1949):27–29, 32–35.

of the sponsors was transparent enough — namely, the application of the classic Zionist analysis to the American situation: economic crisis, anti-Semitism, and upwardly mobile Jewish youth thwarted in their ambitions. *The Reconstructionist* commented that the only significant idea to emerge from the discussion was "the need for encouraging and supporting the Hechalutz movement in the United States."[50] At the annual conference of Jewish educators held the same year, an evening was devoted to a symposium on "Program and Educational Implications of *Halutziut* and *Hachsharah*." The featured speakers were Enzo Sereni of Kibbutz Giv'at Brenner, an emissary to Hechalutz, and Moshe Furmansky of Kibbutz Mishmar Ha'emek, an emissary to Hashomer Hatzair. The subject appeared on the agenda once again at the 1936 conference of Jewish social workers and center executives, when Golda Meyerson [Meir] spoke to a "vast crowd" on "*halutziut.*" During the summers, the League for Labor Palestine sponsored work-study programs at the Cream Ridge, New Jersey, *hachsharah* farm. These activities, and others like them, created some pro-*halutz* sentiment and modest local funding for the Zionist youth organizations. But by and large, American *halutziut* remained an esoteric presence on the fringes of American Zionism.[51]

Some changes in attitude began to occur in 1946. With attention focused on the embattled *yishuv* and its efforts to smuggle the survivors of the Nazi horror through the British blockade into Palestine, Zionist organizations, mobilized to the hilt for political and fund-raising campaigns, passed tepid resolutions approving of American *halutziut.* Tenuous as these resolutions were, they

---

50   *The Reconstructionist* 2(3) (20 March 1936):4–5; Zalman Rubashow, "Remaking Jewish Youth," *Jewish Frontier* 3(4) (April 1936):19–23. The young Conservative rabbi Ira Eisenstein believed the conference was contrived to get promises "to raise some money for hakhshara." Yet it was "a success as it brought to the attention of these men the existence of such organizations as Hashomer Hatzair and Hechalutz." "Labor Zionism in America," *Jewish Frontier* 3(8) (August 1936):146–147.

51   "Proceedings of the Eleventh Annual Conference of the National Council for Jewish Education," 29 May–2 June 1936, *Jewish Education* 8 (1936): 146–147; *The Reconstructionist* 2(10) (26 June 1936):5; *Labor Zionist Handbook* (New York: Poale Zion Zeire Zion of America, 1939), 131–133.

legitimized the notion that some form of voluntary service in Eretz Israel by American Jewish youth was praiseworthy.[52]

The period 1946-1952 was the American *halutz* movement's finest hour. The backlog of those who had been unable to go on *aliyah* during the war years (many because of service in the armed forces), the fruits of persevering educational work, and the dramatic events connected with the struggle for Jewish statehood produced a fivefold increase in *halutz aliyah*. For the first time, Young Judaea and Junior Hadassah alumni, members of the Intercollegiate Zionist Federation of America, formed *halutz* groups together with returned soldiers — often to the discomfort, if not outright opposition, of their ZOA and Hadassah sponsors. The number of *hachsharah* farms rose from two to eight. Five kibbutzim with substantial numbers of Americans were founded during these years. Moreover, members of the American *halutz* movement played key roles in the covert operations conducted by the Haganah (the underground military force of the Jewish Agency) in the United States. They organized and manned the ships purchased in the United States for transporting the "displaced persons" from Europe to Palestine, aided in procuring arms for the Haganah, and helped recruit volunteers to serve in the fledgling Israel Defense Force.[53]

Nevertheless, for the leaders of the State of Israel, all this was not enough. To their mind, the thousand or so *halutzim* and volunteers who had settled in Palestine between 1945 and 1948 or had participated in Israel's War of Independence were harbingers of the many times that number who would join in the enormous task

52 Murray Weingarten, "Great Expectations, Meager Results," *Furrows* 5(10) (November 1947):12–15; "Declaration of the National Assembly for Labor Palestine," *Jewish Frontier* 16(7) (July 1949): 21–22; Daniel Frisch, *On the Road to Zion* (New York: Zionist Organization of America, 1950), 46, 76. Cf. *The State of the Organization; Report Rendered by Daniel Frisch, President of the Zionist Organization of America*, New York, 13 November 1949, pp. 9–10.

53 Naomi Cohen, *American Jews and the Zionist Idea* (New York: Ktav, 1975), 114–119; Leonard Slater, *The Pledge* (1970); Shmuel Ben-Zevi, "The Halutz Movement Develops: 1934–1948," in *Pioneers from America: 75 Years of Hehalutz, 1905–1980* (Tel Aviv: Bogrei Hehalutz of America, 1981), 83–88; Moshe [of Kibbutz Barkai], "The Zionist T.N.T. Ring," in ibid., 103–104; Akiva Skidell, "Aliya Bet Ships," in ibid., 124–127; Avraham Schenker, "Restrospect and Outlook," in ibid., 189–194.

of absorbing the tens of thousands of physically and emotionally injured immigrants pouring into the country.

The times demanded extraordinary measures. For David Ben-Gurion, who had led the *yishuv* to statehood, as well as for his close political associates, American Jewry had to provide not only political and financial aid but *aliyah* as well. Themselves the founders and mentors of the *halutz* movements in Poland and then Eretz Israel, they now argued that the traditional approach of the *halutz* purists was too narrow and restrictive. Raising an elite vanguard through youth movement education was too slow a process. Moreover, the kibbutz, although still important, was no longer the premier instrument of nation building that it had been for thirty years. Consequently, the doctrine of *halutziut* had to be broadened. The old way should not be abandoned, but the emphasis should be on summoning American Jewish youth in their thousands to provide desperately needed American know-how.[54] The call had to go out that the young state required engineers, scientists, teachers, and administrators — in fact, trained personnel of all kinds. This, too, was *halutziut*. At a closed meeting that Ben-Gurion called in July 1950 to discuss "Our Approach to American Jewry," Abba Eban, at the time Israel's ambassador to the United Nations, put the matter this way:

> One should not identify the concept *halutziut* with "agricultural settlement." One must free this concept *halutz* from its confining framework.... The physician who immigrates to the country is a *halutz*; also the pilot who joins the air force is a *halutz*; and also a nurse who comes to the country to work in a hospital is a *halutza*; and yes, also one who comes to teach at the university.[55]

54 Shortly before the creation of the state, Pinkhas Lubianker (later Lavon), while touring the United States to evaluate the work of American Hechalutz, appealed for a "Congress of Jewish Youth for Eretz Israel...that would accomplish in three days what your methods take three years to accomplish." Artie Gorenstein, "Balance-Sheet of American Chalutziut," *Furrows* 8(2) (October 1950):8. See also Lubianker, "Call to Jewish Youth," *Furrows* 7(1) (February 1949).

55 Zvi Ganin, "New York ve-yerushalayim be-perspectiva historit" (New York and Jerusalem in historical perspective) [with appended document]: "Al haperek:

It is beyond the scope of this study to consider the bitter controvery that Ben-Gurion's reinterpretation of *halutziut* stirred in Israel, most of all within the kibbutz movement; nor is it possible to consider here his dispute with American Zionists, especially the Zionist leadership, over their failure to settle in Israel. Along with his call to American Jewish youth — whom he assumed were not organizational Zionists but "just good Jews" — to come to Israel, Ben-Gurion and other leaders of Israel's Labor movement insisted that Zionism required its adherents to make *aliyah*. Not to take that step meant ceasing to be Zionists. Crucial for our discussion is the fact that these debates over principle and definition, both in Israel and in America, drained the *halutz* idea of its ideological and organizational specificity. Israel's genuine need for Western *aliyah*, on the one hand, and American Zionism's defensiveness, on the other hand, spawned a host of programs under the rubric "service for Israel." Typical was Arthur Hertzberg's suggestion of "limited *halutziut*." Summer camps should be established in Israel, study programs for college students organized, and a central bureau opened to match professionals with job openings in Israel. Young American Jews should also be asked to volunteer for a year or two of service in kibbutzim and immigrant reception centers.[56] Eban's vision of the *halutz* — physician, pilot, nurse and professor — and

gishatenu le-yahdut amerika, protocol p'gisha be-misrad rosh ha-memshala David Ben-Gurion, 25 July 1950," (Our approach to American Jewry) *Kivunim* (April 1993):59. In the above discussion, and elsewhere, Ben-Gurion differentiated between *olim* (immigrants) and *halutzim*. The latter would settle in agricultural settlements especially in the Negev. He also envisioned the required military training as giving recruits "military capacity and the capacity to pioneer" — i.e., agricultural training in addition to their military training.

56 For the debate over *halutziut*, see Henry Near's illuminating "Halutzim ve-halutziut be-mdinat yisrael: hebetim semantiim ve-historiim, 1948–1956" (*Halutzim* and *halutziut* in the State of Israel) *Iyunim bitkumat Yisrael* 2 (1992):116–140. For Ben-Gurion's thinking, the most important text is his introduction to *Government Yearbook*, 5712 (1951/52), which in the English version, is entitled "The Call of Spirit in Israel." In the Hebrew edition, the introduction is entitled, "Y'udei ha-ruah ve-ha-halutziut be-yisrael" (The call of the spirit and *halutziut* in Israel). On the criticism of American Zionism and the movement's reaction, see Melvin I. Urofsky, *We Are One! American Jewry and Israel* (Garden City, NY: Anchor Press, 1978):193–195, 258–277, 287–297;

Hertzberg's "limited *halutziut*" were a far cry from the heroic model of unconditional *halutziut*, and far less threatening for American Jews.

Severe as Israeli leaders were with American Zionists, they were no less laudatory of young American Jews. The superb training of Americans and their professionalism were unmatched, which was why they were so needed, Israeli officials told their audiences. Moreover, Americans possessed traits and attitudes that were needed as much as knowledge and efficiency for the development of the state. In a message read to an assembly of American Zionist youth organizations in 1946, Chaim Weizmann wrote that American *halutzim*

> reared in freedom, nurtured by the pioneering traditions of the New World, and equipped by the skills and experience which America alone can offer,...will be a factor of inspiring vigor and guidance in the building of Eretz Israel and the resettlement of the remnants of European Jewry.[57]

This notion that American Jews *qua* Americans had a unique contribution to make was given its most striking formulation in the pages of *The Reconstructionist*. Early in the debate, an editorial in that publication (11 January 1946) echoed Weizmann's statement: "Trained and healthy young people who can introduce American techniques and 'know-how' and assume leadership among the thousands of refugees who will bring to Palestine only their own broken and starved bodies" was a noble undertaking. "The emphasis will be placed on *experts*, available nowhere in the world at present except in our country." Bearing in mind no doubt the American Jewish Committee's denunciation of any move to initiate a drive for *halutzim* in the United States, the editorial continued: "American *halutzim* will not be unique in this role. American Christians have traveled and settled in all parts of the world, as missionaries either of Christian religion or American medicine." Many Americans spend years among the "natives."[58] On another occasion, in January 1948,

and Arthur Hertzberg, "New Horizons for the ZOA," *New Palestine* 39(18) (27 May 1949):12.

57   *Pioneers from America*, 55.
58   *The Reconstructionist* 11(17) (11 January 1946):6–7.

THE AMERICANIZATION OF THE HALUTZ IDEAL

The Reconstructionist discussed the role the American immigrant should play in Israel as an emissary from America. The American *halutz* should be trained not only to adjust to conditions in Israel but also "to bring to Eretz Yisrael the values of his American experience of which the Yishuv stands in need." How to apply "American democratic principles to the specific conditions of life in Eretz Yisrael should be studied and discussed."[59]

In America, aside from the *halutz* movements themselves, few challenged this American mission concept of *halutziut*. Five years after the establishment of Israel, at an ideological conference on Zionism and the State of Israel sponsored by the World Zionist Organization, Ben Halpern challenged it in the name of classical *halutziut*. However, his point of departure was the emphasis Ben-Gurion had given to the power of the state to promote *halutziut* — *halutziut* in the broad sense of devotion and service to the nation. (More than any other American Zionist, Halpern's understanding of American Jewry resembled Ben-Gurion's: America was the *Galut* — a benign one, but spiritually still *Galut*.) One could claim, Halpern remarked, that Israeli citizens living under the government's austerity program, soldiers ordered to work in a frontier kibbutz, or immigrants assigned to development towns in the Negev were all *halutzim*. But this approach could not of course be applied to enlist American Jewish youth. The only way American Jews would emigrate to Israel Halpern declared, was by "personal conversion, the sense of calling of the *halutz*." Still holding to views expressed many years earlier, he explained that the passage to *halutziut* began when a Zionism that was taken seriously instilled a sense of the inadequacy of American Jewish life and bred an unwillingness to accept compromises and the path of least resistance. This was the "push." The "pull" sprang from the expectations of building an ideal Zion. However, the *halutz* types — the rebels, "devotees of the absolute," Halpern called them — who found it insufferable to accept "inane compromises" in America would surely find the

---

59 *The Reconstructionist* 13(19) (23 January 1948):4–6. For an essay that reconciles *halutziut* with "reconstructionism," see Jack Cohen, "*Halutziut* for American Jews," *The Reconstructionist* 12(17) (27 December 1946):10–16, where Cohen expands *halutziut* to include Jewish communal work in America.

reality of Israel difficult to accept as well. "Only if contemporary Israel is seen through and accepted as a society in embryo and a community with potentialities for building toward the envisioned ideal, can the chalutz movement hope to bring American Jews to Israel and help them strike roots there."[60]

Of course one could remain a Zionist in America and still subscribe to Halpern's views. This had been the case since the legend of the *halutzim* had come to dominate the American Zionist imagination, since the time, in Ben-Gurion's words, when "a new phenomenon appeared which changed the course of Jewish history: the phenomenon which we call *halutziut* — the creative and revolutionary capacity for action which brings into play the human faculties for the realization of the ideal without recoiling from any difficulty or danger." A score of young American Zionists took the ideal seriously and endeavored "livnot u'lehibanot ba." And for a while, around the time of the establishment of the state, their personal actions confronted American Zionism with the fundamental moral questions it had hitherto avoided.[61]

In America, the legend of the *halutzim* was adapted and popularized to appeal to American sentiments. But the true Americanizers of the *halutz* ideal were the Israelis. Struggling to win the battle for the state, and then facing the floods of immigrants, Israeli leaders extended the *halutz* ideal to include anyone who would volunteer to come to the aid of the nation or, living in Israel, labor with devotion in his or her station in life. The title *halutz* was easily awarded. *Halutzim* were no longer the elect, and *halutziut* became a conventional slogan. Speaking on "the true mission of Zionism" in 1949, Ben-Gurion declared that "in the forefront of the Zionist movement [was] the promotion of the independent sovereign and *halutzic* State of Israel."[62] The independent sovereign state — *mamlakhtiyut* — became the determining force shaping the structure and ethos of the

60   Ben Halpern, "The Problem of the American Chalutz," *Forum for the Problems of Zionism: World Jewry and the State of Israel* 1 (December 1953):50–51.
61   David Ben-Gurion, "Vision and Redemption," *Forum* 4 (Spring 1959):116.
62   *Jewish Frontier* 17(1) (January 1950):22. I hope sometime to trace the changing perception of the *halutz* ideal through the commercial and propaganda films produced between 1946 and 1960.

society, and it replaced *halutziut* as the source of moral strength and expression of the collective will. American Jews followed this lead and transferred their idealization of the *halutz* to the state.

Part II

Religious Vision
and Education

Envisioning Israel in the Liturgies
of North American Liberal Judaism

David Ellenson

Shimon Rawidowicz, in a seminal essay, "Israel's Two Beginnings," observed that Jewish history has two points of origin, two sources of genesis — a "first house" and a "second house."[1] The first house, Rawidowicz maintained, "is based on prophet-seer, and the Urim and the Thummim, king, sanctuary, and prophet." Its venue is the Land of Israel alone and its history, from Solomon through the destruction of the Temple in 586 B.C.E., is marked by Jewish political sovereignty. The Judaism of the second house, that Judaism initiated by Ezra whose loci were in both Israel and Babylon, "has a sanctuary, priests engaged in worship, and Levites singing and chanting." However, Rawidowicz pointed out, "Its heart is turned to the Torah and not to the sanctuary."[2]

"The first house struggled with the difficulties of tribe and state." In the second, the house became "stronger than the state."[3] The second house provided a second beginning for the Jewish people, one in which an "eternal teaching" was "planted in the heart of Israel." The "unbreakable condition" of the first house — "If you are not a people with a state, you will finally pass away from the world" — was abandoned. Jewry in the Diaspora was no longer compelled to view itself — as it would have in the first house — as "driven out from being joined to the inheritance of God."[4] To be

---

1 Simon Rawidowicz, "Israel's Two Beginnings: The First and the Second 'Houses'," in *Studies in Jewish Thought*, ed. Nahum Glatzer (Philadelphia: Jewish Publication Society of America, 1974).
2 All quotations in this paragraph are taken from ibid., 104.
3 Ibid., 105.
4 Ibid., 106.

sure, the second house continued to express a "yearning" for a return to the Land and for the reestablishment there of Jewish political sovereignty. However, this "yearning," Rawidowicz observed, was "connected with a vision of the future,... not something which existed as a contemporary] reality."[5] The second house "discovered the secret of settling down in the Diaspora" and "refused to let [itself] depend on land and state" as an indispensable prerequisite for Jewish existence.[6] In simple terms, "The establishment of the second house did not cause the Diaspora to disappear."[7] Instead, the second house established a foundation for Jewish life outside of the Land. Israel, in the period of the second house, became "freed from the land." As Rawidowicz perceptively phrased it, "[The second house] conceded territorial centralization as a condition for the existence of the nation."[8]

Modern Zionism, to employ Rawidowicz's typology, sought "a return to the genesis of Israel."[9] It reflected the desire of the Jewish people "to acquire a house for the nation."[10] Zionism, when it arose at the end of the nineteenth century, "intended to solve the question of Israel in the Diaspora," Rawidowicz wrote, "by taking Israel out of the world of the Diaspora." In so doing, it turned "toward the first house."[11]

Rawidowicz's adumbration of the two houses and his assertion that modern Zionism is linked principally to the first and not the second house is echoed in the work of Jacob Neusner. Neusner, in *The Enchandtments of Judaism,* proclaims, "Zionism...declares that Jews who do not live in the State of Israel must aspire to migrate to that nation... . Zionism holds, moreover, that all Jews must concede — indeed, affirm — the centrality of Jerusalem, and of the State of Israel, in the life of Jews throughout the world. Zionism draws the necessary consequences that Jews who live outside the State of

---

5   Ibid., 108.
6   Ibid., 109.
7   Ibid., 108.
8   Ibid., 106.
9   Ibid., 169.
10   Ibid., 170.
11   Ibid., 171.

Israel are in significant ways less 'good Jews' than the ones who live there."[12]

The thrust of this analysis is undoubtedly correct. The classical political Zionism of Herzl negated the viability and worth of Jewish life in the Diaspora, and the legacy of this position remains strong in Israel today. Yet, as Rawidowicz conceded, there are "different kinds of Zionism." More specifically, there is not only "a Zionism of the first house." There is also "a Zionism of the second house." For the Zionist adherents of the second house, Jewish tradition and history are one. Religion and state, devotion and land, complement one another. Modern day religious Jews "praise the first house" and the territoriality and sovereignty it promises. At the same time, "the camps of religious tradition have neither the will nor the strength to give up the second house at all."[13]

For North American Jews, Rawidowicz's analysis is particularly appropriate for illuminating the nature of Zionism and the vision of Israel that has emerged in the Jewish community of this continent. Jews in America feel, correctly or incorrectly, that they have found a home, not just a haven, on America's shores. Furthermore, Jews in the United States are accorded status, as Ben Halpern observed, "as a religious community."[14] Their Judaism is principally one of religion, not ethnicity. Hence Jewish religion, not nationality, provides the chief lens through which Zionism and the Jewish state have been and are envisioned. These characteristics distinguished American Zionism historically from Zionist strains that dominated in Europe, and they continue to inform the Zionist vision in present-day America.

These proclivities, as Jacob Neusner has pointed out, lead America's Jews to affirm a Zionism that "chokes" on the notion that Jews "who do not live in the Jewish state are in exile. ... Their Judaism makes no concession on this point."[15] At the same time,

---

12   Jacob Neusner, *The Enchantments of Judaism* (New York: Basic Books, 1987), 126.
13   All quotations in this paragraph are taken from Rawidowicz, *Studies in Jewish Thought*, 176.
14   Ben Halpern, "The Americanization of Zionism," *American Jewish History* 69 (1979):32–33.
15   Neusner, *The Enchantments of Judaism*, 26.

American Jewry identifies "with the State of Israel" and regards "its welfare as more than a secular good." Indeed, it sees the state "as a metaphysical necessity, as the other chapter of the Holocaust."[16] Contemporary American Jewry finds its bearings, as Neusner points out, through the "Myth of Holocaust and Redemption," the murder of 6 million Jewish people and the birth and establishment of the State of Israel. Indeed, this "myth" often supersedes and at times complements the classic "myth" of the second house that gave birth to normative rabbinic Judaism — the "'myth' of the Dual Torah," a Written and Oral Law revealed by God to the people of Israel through Moses at Mount Sinai — as an orienting vision for the public life of the Jewish people in America.[17]

It is in the prayerbooks of the community that all these ideas and tendencies of the North American Jewish community coalesce. A description and analysis of how the State of Israel, as both a religious ideal and a modern nation, is presented in the contemporary prayerbooks of the major liberal denominations — Reconstructionist, Reform, and Conservative — of American Jewish life provide significant insight into both the nature of the American Jewish community today and the way in which that community perceives and envisions Israel.[18] The prayerbooks, on one level, are classical religious documents. They are products of the rabbinic

---

16   Ibid.

17   Ibid.

18   The primary Reconstructionist prayerbook employed in this paper is David A. Teutsch, ed., *Kol Haneshamah* (Wyncote, Pa.: The Reconstructionist Press, 1989). In addition, reference is made to *Sabbath Prayer Book* (New York: Jewish Reconstructionist Foundation, 1945); *Festival Prayer Book* (New York: Jewish Reconstructionist Foundation, 1958); and *Daily Prayer Book* (New York: Reconstructionist Press, 1963). The principal Conservative source used in this essay is Jules Harlow, ed., *Siddur Sim Shalom: A Prayerbook for Shabbat, Festivals and Weekdays* (New York: The Rabbinical Assembly and the United Synagogue of America, 1985). Reference is also made to *Sabbath and Festival Prayerbook* (New York: The Rabbinical Assembly and the United Synagogue of America, 1946) and *Weekday Prayer Book* (New York: The Rabbinical Assembly, 1961). *Gates of Prayer* (New York: Central Conference of American Rabbis, 1975) and Chaim Stern, ed., *Gates of Repentance* (New York: Central Conference of American Rabbis, 1978) constitute the major Reform liturgies cited in this paper. Citations of Hebrew texts are interspersed through the paper and are faithful to the source. However, I have elected to use spellings of God's

imagination, an imagination initially unleashed by the second house. Their structure and much of their content harkens back to tannaitic, amoraic, and geonic structures, sensibilities, and sources. For the authors of these *siddurim*, Judaism is a whole cloth, a unified and evolving religious tradition that stretches from Abraham and Sarah to Ezra and Nehemiah, and from Ezra and Nehemiah to Bialik and Heschel. They view the incarnation of the Zionist vision — the State of Israel which, as Rawidowicz maintained, looked for its symbolic genesis to the first house — through the eyes of the second house.

These prayerbooks, like all prayerbooks, are also particularistic documents. They reflect the time and place of the persons who composed them. In this instance, these works reflect more than the inherited categories of Jewish religious tradition. They bespeak the sentiments and opinions of North American Jewry in the latter part of the twentieth century. They reflect a peculiarly American variant of Zionism, a Zionism far removed from the political variety that derives its inspiration from the first house.

The liturgies of the Reconstructionist, Reform, and Conservative movements in North America are ideal sources for examining how the State of Israel is envisioned by many modern American Jews. As religious documents, they incorporate the religious myths and symbolic language that provide the framework for how most American Jews view and understand Israel. In addition, as liberal liturgies, these works embody a self-conscious attempt on the part of their framers to adapt and reform the manifest content, the actual wording, of the prayers to contemporary perceptions and realities. The major Orthodox liturgies of the North American Jewish community — de Sola Pool, Art Scroll, and Birnbaum — which, with the exception of a prayer for the State of Israel that has been included in the Birnbaum *siddur* and one edition of the Art Scroll, have not been altered to reflect the existence and reality of the Jewish State. In contrast, these liberal prayerbooks have reformed and adapted the manifest content of their liturgies to affirm the existence of the State of Israel and its contemporary meaning for liberal Jews.[19]

---

names in the Hebrew quotations that are consonant with certain traditional Jewish religious sensibilities. The reader should be aware that these names are spelled differently in the original text.

19   The failure of Orthodox liturgies to take cognizance of the Jewish state is hardly

Reconstructionist Innovations

In 1989, the Reconstructionist movement published *Kol Hane-shamah*, a Sabbath evening prayerbook. It was the first official Sabbath liturgy to be produced and sanctioned by the Reconstructionist movement in several decades. In his introduction, the editor, Rabbi David Teutsch, indicated that *Kol Haneshamah* would self-consciously reflect a "cognizance of contemporary problems and aspirations" and, in light of such "cognizance," "produce new liturgy and edit the traditional liturgy in order to be true to contemporary Jewish sensibilities and moral vision" (xiv). These "contemporary Jewish sensibilities" mandated the creation of a new Reconstructionist liturgy; for "the situation of North American Jewry," Teutsch wrote, "has changed remarkably since the 1940s" (xiv–xv). Foremost among these changes were those epic events in the history of contemporary Jewry — the Holocaust and the establishment of Israel. As Teutsch observed, "In the 1940s the horror of the Holocaust and the emergence of the State of Israel had not yet redefined the Jewish sense of self" (xv). The newly composed texts in *Kol Haneshamah* were purposefully designed "to include suitable references to the Holocaust and the founding of the State of Israel" (xvii).

Earlier editions of Reconstructionist liturgy had already displayed comparable sensibilities. In the *Sabbath Prayer Book (Seder tefillot l'shabbat)* of 1945 (116) and the *Festival Prayer Book (Mahzor l'shalosh regalim)* of 1958 (106–108), the traditional expression of hope for a Jewish return to the Land of Israel in the *Ahavah Rabbah* prayer immediately prior to the recitation of the *Sh'ma* — וַהֲבִיאֵנוּ לְשָׁלוֹם מֵאַרְבַּע כַּנְפוֹת הָאָרֶץ וְתוֹלִיכֵנוּ קוֹמְמִיּוּת לְאַרְצֵנוּ. "O bring us peace from the four corners of the earth, and enable us to march erect into

---

a reflection of Orthodox disinterest in or indifference to the Jewish state. It rather reflects an Orthodox reluctance to tamper with the received liturgy. See Philip Birnbaum, *Daily Prayer Book* (New York: Hebrew Publishing Company, 1949); David de Sola Pool, *The Traditional Prayer Book for Sabbaths and Festivals* (New York: Behrman House and The Rabbinical Council of America, 1960); and Nosson Scherman and Meir Zlotowitz, *The Complete Art Scroll Siddur* (New York: Mesorah Publications, 1985).

our land" — was retained. However, in a foreshadowing of liturgical change to come, the 1963 edition of the *Daily Prayer Book (Seder tefillot l'ymot hahol)* altered the words of this supplication to read: וְקַבֵּץ אֶת־נִדְחֵינוּ מֵאַרְבַּע כַּנְפוֹת הָאָרֶץ וְתוֹלִיכֵם קוֹמְמִיּוּת לְאַרְצֵנוּ. "O *gather the homeless of our people* from the four corners of the earth and enable them to march erect into our land" (18, emphasis added). The manifest content of the prayer has been transformed. The Land of Israel still remains a central element of Jewish concern and hope. Nevertheless, this prayer now expresses the view, as Justice Brandeis phrased it almost fifty years earlier, that "neither [the American Jew] nor his descendants will ever live there." Instead, the land "may well become a focus for [the American Jew's] declassé kinsmen in other parts of the world."[20] As Neusner has pointed out, most American Jews "do not have the remotest thought of emigrating from America to the State of Israel,"[21] and this emendation in the liturgy reflects the benign formulation of the Zionist message that has long dominated the movement in America.

The framework of the *siddur* and the unique manner in which religion shaped the contours of American Zionism found expression in other parts of post-World War II Reconstructionist liturgy. In the *Musaf* service on both the Sabbath and the pilgrimage festivals (372), the traditional prayer for the restoration of the sacrificial cult in a rebuilt Temple in Jerusalem was removed. In its place, the following prayer was inserted. The relevant part in Hebrew, with its call for "renewal" and "sanctification" of the land to be directed in God's service, was obviously inspired by the writings of Rav Abraham Isaac Kook and religious Zionism. The prayer reads.

[אלקינו ואלקי] אֲבוֹתֵינוּ. יְהִי רָצוֹן מִלְּפָנֶיךָ שֶׁיֶּעֱרֶה עָלֵינוּ רוּחַ מִמָּרוֹם בְּיוֹם הַקָּדוֹשׁ הַזֶּה לְכוֹנֵן אֶת־אֶרֶץ יִשְׂרָאֵל. לְחַדֵּשׁ וּלְקַדֵּשׁ אוֹתָהּ לַעֲבוֹדָתֶךָ. וְשָׁכַן בָּאָרֶץ שָׁלוֹם חֹפֶשׁ צֶדֶק וּמִשְׁפָּט. כַּכָּתוּב עַל־יַד נְבִיאֶךָ. כִּי מִצִּיּוֹן תֵּצֵא תוֹרָה וּדְבַר[ה׳] מִירוּשָׁלָיִם. וְנֶאֱמַר. לֹא־יָרֵעוּ וְלֹא־יַשְׁחִיתוּ בְּכָל־הַר קָדְשִׁי כִּי־מָלְאָה הָאָרֶץ דֵּעָה אֶת־[ה׳] כַּמַּיִם לַיָּם מְכַסִּים:

---

20   Louis Brandeis, "The Jewish Problem and How to Solve It," in *The Zionist Idea: A Historical Analysis and Reader*, ed. Arthur Hertzberg, (New York: Atheneum, 1959), 520.
21   Neusner, *The Enchantments of Judaism*, 26.

The English translation is: "O Lord our God and God of our Fathers, may the observance of this festive season inspire us to rebuild the homeland of Israel and rededicate it to Thy service. May peace and freedom, justice and loving kindness abide in Zion and make Thy presence manifest to all mankind. In the words of Thy Prophet: From Zion shall go forth the Law, and the word of the Lord from Jerusalem."[22]

One last change in the Sabbath liturgy is of particular note. Immediately after the reading of the *haftarah* and its benedictions (162), an "Invocation of Blessing on All Who Share in The Spiritual Life of Israel" includes:

וְכָל־מִי שֶׁעוֹסְקִים בַּתּוֹרָה בְּצָרְכֵי צִבּוּר וּבְבִנְיַן אֶרֶץ יִשְׂרָאֵל בֶּאֱמוּנָה. הַקָּדוֹשׁ הוּא יְשַׁלֵּם שְׂכָרָם and וְיִזְכּוּ לִרְאוֹת בְּשׁוּב [ה'] אֶת־שִׁיבַת צִיּוֹן.

May those who sincerely occupy themselves with the needs of the community, and with the upbuilding of Eretz Yisrael be rewarded by the Holy One. ... May they be privileged to behold Zion restored by God's grace." This rewording of the traditional *Yekum purkan* prayer reflected the Reconstructionist movement's early desire to acknowledge the importance of the newly established Jewish state through the medium of Jewish liturgy. Yet this very medium dictated that the State would be viewed in religious terms as *"Eretz Yisrael —* The Land of Israel," not *"Medinat Yisrael —* The State of Israel." The secular national elements that informed the Zionist movement in Europe and that played such a crucial role in the formation of the state are simply ignored within the framework of the prayerbook. However, a vision of Zion and the Jewish homeland emerges that is compatible with and reflective of the reality of an American Jewish community defined principally by religion and committed to a spiritual-cultural vision of the Zionist message.

Kol Haneshamah is heir to this Reconstructionist tradition. The changes it introduces into its text bespeak the evolving and more explicitly self-conscious recognition of what the State of Israel means to this segment of American Jewry. Bialik, who is identified as "the great poet of the Hebrew national revival," and his poem *"Shabbat*

22   The translation of the prayer is taken from the Festival and not the Sabbath prayerbook — hence the reference to "festive season" in the translation.

Hamalkah / The Shabbat Queen" are accorded canonical status
in the Kabbalat Shabbat service (12–13). In the second blessing of
the *Amidah, Gevurot* (Divine Power), two traditional and seasonally
related phrases are inserted. One, מוֹרִיד הַטָּל — "You send down
the dew," is recited "in summer," while, "You make the wind blow
and the rain fall מַשִּׁיב הָרוּחַ וּמוֹרִיד הַגָּשֶׁם — is included "in winter"
(103). The commentary notes, "We acknowledge the presence of
God in the natural rhythms of passing seasons. ... The mention of
rain or dew follows the two-season climate of *Eretz Yisra'el*" (102).
These observations stem from Judaism itself. Their significance
nevertheless extends beyond the tradition from which they draw. The
balance they reflect between the particularity of Jewish tradition and
the universality of God is compatible with the ethos of the American
nation and very much characteristic of the way in which American
Jews interpret and understand their religion.

The attempt to strike such a balance, and what this reveals about
the sensibilities of Reconstructionist visions of Israel, is evidenced in
the *Hashkivenu* prayer in the evening service (88–91). The *hatimah*
of the blessing,

בָּרוּךְ אַתָּה [ה׳] הַפּוֹרֵשׂ סֻכַּת שָׁלוֹם עָלֵינוּ וְעַל כָּל־עַמּוֹ יִשְׂרָאֵל וְעַל יְרוּשָׁלָיִם

is translated as, "Blessed are you, Yah/The Compassionate who
spreads your harmonious canopy over all your people Israel and over
Jerusalem" (90). The commentary acknowledges the contemporary
struggles Israel must confront and asserts, "We pray that real and
complete peace be the lot of Israel and Jerusalem, so torn by strife
in recent memory" (91). However, it quickly goes on to supplement
and balance the particularity of this sentiment by noting, "For our
ancestors, the future of Jerusalem was not just about the future of
the Jewish people. Jerusalem, in the biblical vision, will become the
capital of the whole world. Praying for the peace of Jerusalem is the
same as praying for the unity of all humanity and peace throughout
the world" (90). As Rabbi Arthur Green explains, "Our tradition
sees Jerusalem as the center of the world. Creation began there,
according to the rabbis. So may the peace that begins there radiate
forth and bless all earth's peoples. The peace of Jerusalem, the "heart
of the world," is also the peace of every human heart" (91). Even
when the territoriality of Jewish existence in the state is recalled

and the presence of the Jewish people in the Land is acknowledged, the universal elements in the tradition remain highlighted. Such calibration between the universal and the particular means that even when the latter is affirmed, the former is not neglected.

This emphasis, as well as the linkage American Jews make between the tragedy of the Holocaust and the redemption provided by the State of Israel, finds its clearest expression in the text of *Emet Ve'emunah*/Redemption, "the blessing immediately following the Shema" (83). This prayer, which "deals with the theme of divine redemption," has been rewritten to include "reference to the Holocaust, from which there was no redemption, and the return to Zion, a fulfillment of Israel's ancient dream. The same divine spirit that gave Israel the courage to seek freedom from Egypt in ancient times inspired those who fought for Israel's freedom in our own day" (83). The relevant portion, in English, states: "From one generation to the next, God is our guarantor, and even on a day that turned to night, God stayed with us even when death's shadows fell. And even in our age of orphans and survivors, God's loving acts have not abandoned us, and God has brought together our scattered kin from the distant corners of the earth" (82). The Hebrew (83–85) reads:

מִדּוֹר לְדוֹר הוּא גוֹאֲלֵנוּ:
וּבַיּוֹם שֶׁהָפַךְ לְלַיְלָה עִמָּנוּ הָיָה בְּגֵיא צַלְמָוֶת:

גַּם בְּדוֹר יְתוֹמִים לֹא עֲזָבוּנוּ חֲסָדָיו וַיְקַבֵּץ נִדָּחֵינוּ מִקְצוֹת תֵּבֵל : כְּאָז גַּם עַתָּה
מוֹצִיא אֶת עַמּוֹ יִשְׂרָאֵל מִכַּף כָּל אוֹיְבָיו לְחֵרוּת עוֹלָם .

At the same time that such passages are added, the prayer is also edited to omit "those portions of the [traditional] text that glory in the enemy's fall or see in God a force for vengeance. All humans are God's beloved children, as were the Egyptians who drowned at the sea" (83).

In this prayer the State of Israel is seen, as Neusner phrased it, "as a metaphysical necessity, as the other chapter of the Holocaust." The connection between these two events in the consciousness of the American Jewish community could not be more palpable. The state provides a type of "moral-religious compensation" for the atrocity of the *Shoah*. This view is undoubtedly not exclusively held by American Jews. Significant numbers of Israelis also link the two in a comparable manner. However, as the commentary indicates, this linkage is complemented by a "moralism" that marks American Judaism.[23] The reality of the State of Israel is refracted specifically through the prism of a universalistic ethos. This tendency, as we shall see, is not confined to the Reconstructionist movement. It typifies Reform and Conservative liturgy as well.

In an age when the State of Israel is a political reality, and not simply a religious hope, this has profound implications for the way in which American Jews envision the Jewish state. The State of Israel, from such a perspective, expresses more than the fulfillment of an age-old dream of national restoration for the Jewish people. It reflects a just payment made to the Jewish people for the crimes committed against the people Israel in Europe during World War II. The state, in such a vision, is not comprehended in political terms. Nor is it approached in exclusively religious-spiritual ones. Rather, it is ultimately justified in moral categories. This means that American Jews have a propensity to view the state from a moral vantage point. It should hardly be surprising that American Jews are particularly critical of Israel when its actions are perceived to be morally wanting. Such a tendency, as alluded to above, is not the exclusive province of American Jews. Indeed, there is some justification for it within Jewish religious tradition. However, the liberal ethos of the Jewish community in the United States allows it to find a particular intensity of expression that manifests itself in a prayerbook such as *Kol Haneshamah*. I now turn to look at how this idea is expressed in the prayerbooks of the Conservative and Reform movements.

Conservative Revisions

Rabbi Jules Harlow has noted that liturgical renewal in the Conservative movement since the late 1950s has been marked by a conscious effort to affirm the significance of the State of Israel

23 On this point, see the discussion in Joseph Blau, *Judaism in American* (Chicago: University of Chicago Press, 1976), 9–10.

in Conservative prayer.[24] In the *Weekday Prayer Book* of 1961, prepared for the movement under the direction of a committee chaired by Rabbi Gershon Hadas, a passage, based on the '*Al hanissim* (For the miracles) prayers that are traditionally recited on Purim and Hanukkah to express gratitude to God for deliverance, was inserted (64–65) for Yom Ha'atzmaut, Israel's Independence Day. The significance of the modern State of Israel has thereby given official liturgical sanction by the Conservative movement.

Another innovation of particular note was also introduced. In the *Festival Prayer Book* of 1927, as well as in the *Sabbath and Festival Prayer Book* of 1946 (141), the petition in the *Musaf* service for the restoration of animal sacrifice in a rebuilt Temple in Jerusalem had been transformed into a prayer of "recollection." As Harlow summarizes the change, "Conservative liturgy continues to pray for the restoration of the Jewish people to the Land of Israel and for the experience of worship there, particularly in Jerusalem, but the liturgy merely recalls with reverence the sacrificial ritual of our ancestors; it does not petition for its restoration."[25]

The 1961 *Weekday Prayer Book* maintained this approach in one text of the *Musaf* services for Rosh Hodesh, the New Month, and for the intermediate days of the three pilgrimage festivals. In an alternative text for this service, a different vision, containing distinct ideological nuances, was also provided. The text petitioned: "Lead us with song to Zion, Your City, and with everlasting joy to Jerusalem, Your sanctuary. There, as in days of old, we shall worship You with reverence and with love" (186). The "Israel-centrism" of the traditional text was thereby affirmed even while the manifest content of the traditional service, with its call for a restoration of the temple cult, was, in keeping with Conservative religious hopes, abjured. However, the exclusive emphasis on the centrality of Israel in this petition was muted by the addition of a phrase calling on God to bless "Your people Israel, wherever they dwell" (186).

24   On this point, as well as for an extended discussion of other features of Conservative liturgy, see Harlow's excellent and straightforward essay "Revising the Liturgy for Conservative Jews," in *The Changing Face of Jewish and Christian Worship in North America*, ed. Paul F. Bradshaw and Lawrence A. Hoffman, (Notre Dame, Ind.: Notre Dame University Press, 1991), 125–140.
25   Ibid., 126.

This prayer, *in toto*, provides great insight into the nature and beliefs of Conservative Judaism and the attitudes it takes toward not only the Land of Israel but the State — the contemporary embodiment of the traditional religious hope for Jewish sovereignty on the Land — as well. The state embodies a religious hope that is central to Judaism and the Jewish people. Hence the prayer asks that the Jewish people worship God in Zion "with reverence and love." Such hope is fully consistent with the tenets of a religious-cultural Zionism nurtured by the inhabitants, to use Rawidowicz's phrase, of the "second house." Equally significant for an appreciation of the character of American Zionism is the addition of the final blessing, which asks God to bless Israel in all their places of habitation. It reflects an affirmation of the Diaspora that does not view territoriality, land and state, as the exclusive venue, an indispensable prerequisite, for Jewish existence. Israel is central in such concerns. Modern-day American Jews "praise the first house." The hopes it engenders are "more than a secular good." At the same time the prayer bespeaks the determination of American Jewry to assert that Jews "who do not live in the Jewish State are [not] in exile." This prayer, a product of the "second house," provides a telling insight into the nature of American Zionism and American Judaism. It is a Judaism and a Zionism that views the relationship between Israel and the Diaspora through the metaphor of an ellipsis, in which the importance and significance of Jewish life in both places are equally affirmed. The image of an Israeli center, with the Diaspora orbiting around it as the planets revolve around the sun, is discarded. This emphasis on the importance and religious significance of Jewish life in both Israel and the Diaspora is maintained in the most contemporary Conservative liturgy, *Siddur Sim Shalom: A Prayerbook for Shabbat, Festivals, and Weekdays* (1985), and this idea finds prominent and consistent expression in its pages.

Sim Shalom's affirmation of the religious significance of the modern State of Israel and its inclusion of the state in its liturgy is one of the most prominent characteristics of this Conservative prayerbook. As Harlow observes,

> For centuries Jews have prayed for the restoration of Jerusalem and for the reestablishment of a Jewish State in the Land of

Israel. Those prayers have been answered, thank God, and the liturgy should not remain unaltered, as if nothing has changed in this regard.[26]

An investigation of *Sim Shalom* reveals that the Conservative movement has responded to the modern birth of the Jewish state as an epoch-making event and has celebrated its reality as one of religious significance and import. Israel's Independence Day is defined as a holiday along with "special occasions such as Hanukkah, Purim, Rosh Hodesh, Festivals,... Fast Days,... and the ten days between Rosh Hashanah and Yom Kippur" (xv).

On Yom Ha'atzmaut, *Hallel* — the traditional psalms of praise and thanksgiving recited on Hanukkah, Purim, the pilgrimage festivals, and Rosh Hodesh — is said (378ff). Furthermore, a Torah reading from Deuteronomy 7:12–8:18 is assigned to mark this holiday and Isaiah 10:32–12:6 is chanted as the haftarah (prophetic reading) following the Torah reading (872). In the Yom Ha'atzmaut *Musaf* service, "additional passages were added that reflect the reality of the State of Israel in the Land of Israel" (xxiii). Finally, *tahanun*, the traditional prayers of supplication, and Psalm 20 are omitted from the liturgy on Yom Ha'atzmaut, as they are on all other Jewish holidays (128). These liturgical prescriptions and changes elevate Israeli Independence Day to the status of a festival and bespeak the religious significance the Conservative movement assigns the Jewish state.

The devotion and commitment *Sim Shalom* displays toward the Land of Israel as a religious ideal, and the manner in which this fuses into this prayerbook's vision of the state, is displayed in other parts of this *siddur* as well. In the well-known passage in the *Ahavah Rabbah* prayer prior to the *Sh'ma,* the line reading

וַהֲבִיאֵנוּ לְשָׁלוֹם מֵאַרְבַּע כַּנְפוֹת הָאָרֶץ וְתוֹלִיכֵנוּ קוֹמְמִיּוּת לְאַרְצֵנוּ

is rendered in English as "Bring us safely from the ends of the earth, and lead us in dignity to our holy land" (347). The rendering of לְאַרְצֵנוּ as "our holy land," and not simply "our land," indicates that Israel is to be viewed as more than a mere nationalistic yearning

26   Ibid., 131.

of the Jewish people. Instead, the land now embodies a "spiritual" hope consonant with the religious vision of American Jewry.[27] This view of Israel as both modern state and religious ideal is echoed in a passage of explanation found in *Sim Shalom* prior to *Sefirat Ha-'omer*, the tradition of "counting the omer" — a daily offering brought from the new barley crop to the ancient Temple from the eve of the second day of Passover until the first night of Shavuot (236). The prayerbook explains,

> "By counting the days of this period, we recall the events with which these days connect in the Jewish calendar: the liberation from enslavement, commemorated by Pesah, and the gift of the Revelation of Torah, commemorated by Shavuot. These events took place during the journey of our people to the Promised Land. ... On our personal journeys in life, we each have our own enslavements and liberations, revelations and promised lands. As we often count the days leading to significant events in our personal lives, so we count such days in the life of our people.... We also call to mind the close connection with the soil of the Land during centuries past, as well as in modern Israel. ..." (236)

National memory and personal spiritual quest, religious festivals and the contemporary vitality of the land, are all integrated into a single vision. The ideals of the second house and those of the first meld together in the crucible of a twentieth-century American present.

Prior to the recitation of *Yekum purkan, Sim Shalom* — like the Reconstructionist prayerbooks discussed above — retains a change introduced into earlier versions of Conservative liturgy. As Harlow

---

27   One should note that *Sim Shalom* is not unique among modern prayerbooks in translating references to Israel in this way. Isaac Noa Mannheimer, the *Religionslehrer und Prediger* of the *israelitischen Bethause zu Wien* who officiated at the Vienna *Stadttempel*, in his traditional 1843 *Tefillot Yisrael — Gebete der Israeliten*, translated all passages concerned with the land of Israel in exactly the same manner, always rendering "the land" as "holy land." It may be that the redactor of *Sim Shalom* had this paradigm in mind here. It is possible that the contours imposed on Jewish liturgy by a modern Western ideology led both Mannheimer and the authors of *Sim Shalom* to respond in comparable ways to the spiritual—religious ideals of Israel in Western consciousness and religion.

points out, "a prayer for the welfare of the community, recited following the Torah service on Shabbat, was modified to include a phrase commending those who are devoted to rebuilding the Land of Israel" (xxii). The text, instead of reading, "May God who blessed our ancestors...bless...all who devote themselves faithfully to the needs of the community."

וְכָל מִי שֶׁעוֹסְקִים בְּצָרְכֵי צִבּוּר בֶּאֱמוּנָה.

— is amended to state, 'May God who blessed our ancestors...bless... all who devotedly involve themselves with the needs of this community and the Land of Israel"—

וְכָל־מִי שֶׁעוֹסְקִים בְּצָרְכֵי צִבּוּר וּבְבִנְיַן אֶרֶץ יִשְׂרָאֵל בֶּאֱמוּנָה.

(414). The priority assigned to the task of rebuilding the land, and the determination to define that task as religious-communal, not simply national, is apparent.

The full scope of the Conservative movement's vision of Israel as contained in this most contemporary expression of Conservative liturgy is found in those passages that "were added [or deleted] that reflect the reality of the State of Israel," as *Sim Shalom* states, "in the Land of Israel" (xxiii). An acknowledgment of the reality of the contemporary state is expressed through the omission of those lines and passages in the *tahanun* that "contain references to the destruction of Jerusalem." They have "been deleted, abridged, or adapted" so as to make the prayer "closer to us in spirit" (xxv). Furthermore, in the afternoon service of Tisha B'av there is "a basic change in the text of the traditional prayer (*Nahem*) which is distinctive for that service. This change was made to reflect the contemporary reality of Jerusalem restored and our hopes for its future, not only the sense of grief over its destruction in ancient times" (xxii).

The traditional prayer for *Minha* on Tisha B'av, as contained in Hebrew and English in the Birnbaum *Siddur* (167–168), reads:

נַחֵם, [ה' אלקינו] אֶת אֲבֵלֵי צִיוֹן וְאֶת אֲבֵלֵי יְרוּשָׁלָיִם, וְאֶת הָעִיר הָאֲבֵלָה וְהַחֲרֵבָה, וְהַבְּזוּיָה וְהַשּׁוֹמֵמָה: הָאֲבֵלָה מִבְּלִי בָנֶיהָ, וְהַחֲרֵבָה מִמְּעוֹנוֹתֶיהָ, וְהַבְּזוּיָה מִכְּבוֹדָהּ, וְהַשּׁוֹמֵמָה מֵאֵין יוֹשֵׁב. וְהִיא יוֹשֶׁבֶת וְרֹאשָׁהּ חָפוּי, כְּאִשָּׁה עֲקָרָה שֶׁלֹּא יָלָדָה; וַיְבַלְּעוּהָ לִגְיוֹנוֹת, וַיִּירָשׁוּהָ עוֹבְדֵי פְסִילִים, וַיָּטִילוּ אֶת

עַמְּךָ יִשְׂרָאֵל לֶחָרֶב, וַיַּהַרְגוּ בְזָדוֹן חֲסִידֵי עֶלְיוֹן. עַל כֵּן צִיּוֹן בְּמַר תִּבְכֶּה, וִירוּשָׁלַיִם תִּתֵּן קוֹלָהּ. לִבִּי לִבִּי עַל חַלְלֵיהֶם, מֵעַי מֵעַי עַל חַלְלֵיהֶם. כִּי אַתָּה [ה'], בָּאֵשׁ הִצַּתָּהּ, וּבָאֵשׁ אַתָּה עָתִיד לִבְנוֹתָהּ, כָּאָמוּר: וַאֲנִי אֶהְיֶה לָהּ, נְאֻם [ה'] חוֹמַת אֵשׁ סָבִיב, וּלְכָבוֹד אֶהְיֶה בְתוֹכָהּ. בָּרוּךְ אַתָּה, [ה'] מְנַחֵם צִיּוֹן וּבוֹנֵה יְרוּשָׁלָיִם.

Comfort, Lord our God, the mourners of Zion, the mourners of Jerusalem, and the city that is in mourning, laid waste, despised and desolate. She is in mourning because she is without her children; she is laid waste as to her homes; she is despised in the downfall of her glory; she is desolate through the loss of her inhabitants. She sits with her head covered like a barren, childless woman. Legions devoured her; idolaters took possession of her; they put thy people Israel to the sword, and killed wantonly the faithful followers of the Most High. Because of that, Zion weeps bitterly; Jerusalem raises her voice. How my heart grieves for the slain! How my heart years for the slain! Thou, O Lord, didst consume her with fire, and with fire thou wilt in future rebuild her, as it is said: "I will be to her, says the Lord, a wall of fire round about; and for glory — I will be in the midst of her." Blessed art thou, O Lord, Comforter of Zion and Builder of Jerusalem.

Sim Shalom, in contrast, alters the liturgy in both English and Hebrew (176–177). The revised text, in Hebrew, states:

נַחֵם, [ה'] אלקינו, אֶת־אֲבֵלֵי צִיּוֹן וְאֶת־אֲבֵלֵי יְרוּשָׁלַיִם, וְאֶת־הָעִיר שֶׁחֲרֵבָה הָיְתָה, וַאֲבֵלָה מִבְּלִי בָנֶיהָ. עַל עַמְּךָ יִשְׂרָאֵל שֶׁהוּטַל לֶחָרֶב וְעַל בָּנֶיהָ אֲשֶׁר מָסְרוּ נַפְשָׁם עָלֶיהָ, צִיּוֹן בְּמַר תִּבְכֶּה וִירוּשָׁלַיִם תִּתֵּן קוֹלָהּ: לִבִּי לִבִּי עַל חַלְלֵיהֶם, מֵעַי מֵעַי עַל חַלְלֵיהֶם. רַחֵם [ה'] אֱלֹהֵינוּ, בְּרַחֲמֶיךָ הָרַבִּים, עָלֵינוּ וְעַל יְרוּשָׁלַיִם עִירְךָ הַנִּבְנֵית מֵחָרְבָּנָהּ וְהַמְיֻשֶּׁבֶת מִשּׁוֹמְמוּתָהּ. יְהִי רָצוֹן מִלְּפָנֶיךָ, מְשַׂמֵּחַ צִיּוֹן בְּבָנֶיהָ, שֶׁיִשְׂמְחוּ אֶת־יְרוּשָׁלַיִם כָּל־אוֹהֲבֶיהָ וְיָשִׂישׂוּ אִתָּהּ כָּל־הַמִּתְאַבְּלִים עָלֶיהָ, וְיִשְׁמְעוּ בְּעָרֵי יְהוּדָה וּבְחוּצוֹת יְרוּשָׁלַיִם קוֹל שָׂשׂוֹן וְקוֹל שִׂמְחָה, קוֹל חָתָן וְקוֹל כַּלָּה. תֵּן שָׁלוֹם לְעִירְךָ אֲשֶׁר פָּדִיתָ וְהָגֵן עָלֶיהָ, כָּאָמוּר: וַאֲנִי אֶהְיֶה לָהּ, נְאֻם [ה'], חוֹמַת אֵשׁ סָבִיב וּלְכָבוֹד אֶהְיֶה בְתוֹכָהּ. בָּרוּךְ אַתָּה. [ה'] מְנַחֵם צִיּוֹן וּבוֹנֵה יְרוּשָׁלָיִם.

The English reads:

Comfort, Lord our God, the mourners of Zion and those who

grieve for Jerusalem, the city which once was so desolate in mourning, like a woman bereft of her children. For Your people Israel, smitten by the sword, and for her children who gave their lives for her, Zion cries with bitter tears, Jerusalem voices her anguish: "My heart, my heart goes out for the slain; my entire being mourns for the slain." Have mercy, Lord our God, in Your great compassion for us and for Your city, Jerusalem, rebuilt from destruction and restored from desolation. Lord who causes Zion to rejoice at her children's return, may all who love Jerusalem exult in her, may all who mourn Jerusalem of old rejoice with her now. May they hear in the cities of Judah and in the streets of Jerusalem sounds of joy and gladness, voices of bride and groom. Grant peace to the city which You have redeemed, and protect her, as proclaimed by Your prophet: "'I will surround her,' says the Lord, 'as a wall of fire, and I will be the glory in her midst.'" Praised are You, Lord who comforts Zion and rebuilds Jerusalem.

The changes here are significant and bespeak the Conservative movement's commitment to the reality of the modern state and its affirmation of the state's religious significance. The State of Israel is possessed of religious meaning. The altered version of this prayer, in which the tense is changed from present to past, asserts that Jerusalem is no longer "despised and desolate in mourning." The Jewish people have returned to Zion and this is cause for celebration. While, as Harlow puts it, "we...nonetheless continue mourning for the ancient devastation that remains an ineradicable fact of history," the words of Jeremiah and Isaiah referring to Jerusalem as "rebuilt from destruction and restored from desolation" and praying that "all who mourn Jerusalem of old rejoice with her now" are added "to reflect a Jerusalem partially restored to greatness."[28] Jewish sovereignty is once again restored in the Jewish people's ancestral homeland, and the capital of ancient Israel, Jerusalem, is once again reunited. These events, in the minds and hearts of the framers of contemporary Conservative liturgy, demand liturgical recognition. To ignore and fail to acknowledge these developments in the prayers

28   Harlow, "Revising the Liturgy for Conservative Jews," 132.

of the Jewish people would be dissonant with the "metaphysical necessity" Israel represents to the Jewish people in America. The inclusion of modern Israel in the texts of *Sim Shalom* is a sign of the religious significance contemporary American Jews assign to the Jewish state.

The religious vision that *Sim Shalom* embraces of the Jewish state is more fully revealed in the *'Al Hanissim* prayer included for Yom Ha'atzmaut. This prayer, taken from the *Weekday Prayer Book* of 1961, celebrates Israel's Independence Day with a prayer of gratitude based on the traditional formula employed on Purim and Hanukkah. "The style and language of the prayer of gratitude," Harlow observes, "were adapted to produce a passage appropriate for commemorating liturgically Israel's Independence Day."[29] The prayer reads, in the Hebrew and English versions (182–183), as follows:

בִּימֵי שִׁיבַת בָּנִים לִגְבוּלָם, בְּעֵת תְּקוּמַת עַם בְּאַרְצוֹ כִּימֵי קֶדֶם, נִסְגְּרוּ שַׁעֲרֵי אֶרֶץ אָבוֹת בִּפְנֵי אַחֵינוּ פְּלִיטֵי חֶרֶב, וְאוֹיְבִים בָּאָרֶץ וְשִׁבְעָה עֲמָמִים בַּעֲלֵי בְרִיתָם קָמוּ לְהַכְרִית עַמְּךָ יִשְׂרָאֵל, וְאַתָּה בְּרַחֲמֶיךָ הָרַבִּים עָמַדְתָּ לָהֶם בְּעֵת צָרָתָם, רַבְתָּ אֶת־רִיבָם, דַּנְתָּ אֶת־דִּינָם, חִזַּקְתָּ אֶת־לִבָּם לַעֲמוֹד בַּשַּׁעַר, וְלִפְתֹּחַ שְׁעָרִים לַנִּרְדָּפִים וּלְגָרֵשׁ אֶת־צִבְאוֹת הָאוֹיֵב מִן הָאָרֶץ. מָסַרְתָּ רַבִּים בְּיַד מְעַטִּים, וּרְשָׁעִים בְּיַד צַדִּיקִים, וּלְךָ עָשִׂיתָ שֵׁם גָּדוֹל וְקָדוֹשׁ בְּעוֹלָמֶךָ, וּלְעַמְּךָ יִשְׂרָאֵל עָשִׂיתָ תְּשׁוּעָה גְדוֹלָה וּפֻרְקָן כְּהַיּוֹם הַזֶּה.

In the days when Your children were returning to their borders, at the time of a people revived in its land as in days of old, the gates to the land of our ancestors were closed before those who were fleeing the sword. When enemies from within the land together with seven neighboring nations sought to annihilate Your people, You, in Your great mercy, stood by them in time of trouble. You defended them and vindicated them. You gave them the courage to meet their foes, to open the gates to those seeking refuge, and to free the land of its armed invaders. You delivered the many into the hands of the few, the guilty into the hands of the innocent. You have wrought great victories and miraculous deliverance for Your people Israel to this day, revealing Your glory and Your holiness to all the world.

29   Ibid., 129.

Israel's successful battle for independence is accorded canonical status in the liturgy of *Sim Shalom*. However, an alteration in the introductory lines of the prayer is particularly telling for assessing the attitudes of this liturgy toward modern Israel. This sentence, which states: עַל הַנִּסִּים וְעַל הַפֻּרְקָן, וְעַל הַגְּבוּרוֹת, וְעַל הַתְּשׁוּעוֹת, וְעַל הַמִּלְחָמוֹת שֶׁעָשִׂיתָ לַאֲבוֹתֵינוּ בַּיָּמִים הָהֵם וּבַזְּמַן הַזֶּה. is translated in English as "We thank you for the miraculous deliverance, for the heroism, and for the triumphs in battle of our ancestors in other days, and in our time" (182–183). As Harlow points out, *Sim Shalom* "follows the text of Rav Amram Gaon's *'Al ha-nissim*, amending the introductory formula which expresses gratitude for miracles 'in other times, at this season,' to read 'in other times and in our day'" (xxvii). While the warrant for this innovation is derived from the received liturgical corpus of Judaism, its adoption by the authors of this prayerbook bespeaks their choice to view the establishment of the state as a "contemporary miracle." This vision of the state, while not at odds with a Mizrachi-style religious Zionism, is certainly distinct from a view that a more secular version of the Zionist idea would promote. The prayers of *Sim Shalom* indicate the manner in which American Judaism promotes an affinity with a particular stream of cultural-spiritual Zionist thought.

There are several other prayers in *Sim Shalom* that allow a complete picture of this prayerbook's approach to the State of Israel to emerge. "A Prayer for the State of Israel," based on a text written by the Chief Rabbinate of Israel, is included on pages 416–417 of the prayerbook. Interestingly, this addition to the Conservative prayerbook is mirrored in the Birnbaum Orthodox *siddur* as well. In the back of the *Birnbaum Siddur*, attached as an appendix on pages 789–790, is the prayer in Hebrew taht begins: אָבִינוּ שֶׁבַּשָּׁמַיִם, צוּר יִשְׂרָאֵל וְגוֹאֲלוֹ, בָּרֵךְ אֶת מְדִינַת יִשְׂרָאֵל, רֵאשִׁית צְמִיחַת גְּאֻלָּתֵנוּ.

Birnbaum renders the phrase רֵאשִׁית צְמִיחַת גְּאֻלָּתֵנוּ as "which marks the dawn of our deliverance." In contrast, *Sim Shalom* offers a more restrained translation. It asserts, "with its promise of redemption," that the State of Israel embodies the religious hopes of the Jewish people. However, the messianic affirmation of the Hebrew prayer contained in the Birnbaum translation is eschewed by the translators of the Conservative prayerbook, and the state is viewed as embodying a redemptive wish, a "promise of redemption." Israel's religious significance is affirmed through the inclusion of this prayer. Yet as this translation suggests, no nation, not even the modern Jewish state, should be seen as the incarnation of a messianic dream.

Another difference in how *Sim Shalom* treats this prayer offers particular insight into the Conservative movement's vision of Israel and its religious meaning. In Birnbaum, the text reproduces all four paragraphs of the original Israeli text composed by the Chief Rabbinate. In *Sim Shalom* only the first two paragraphs are included. The third paragraph, which asks that God "remember our brethren, the whole house of Israel, in all the lands of their dispersion, [and] speedily let them walk upright to Zion," is omitted in *Sim Shalom*. American Jewry asks that God "shield" Israel with love. It does not affirm a vision that beseeches God to end Jewish life in the Diaspora and "gather and fetch" all Jews "dispersed in the uttermost parts of the world" back to the Jewish state. *Sim Shalom* insists that Israel is of the utmost religious importance. Simultaneously, it refuses to concede that Jewish life outside of Israel ought to be regarded as "exile."

Sim Shalom's vision of the Jewish state, as manifest in this last prayer, is consistent with changes introduced by the authors of this liturgy into the *Musaf* service for the Sabbath and all Jewish holidays. The religious significance of the modern state is once more acknowledged. While the traditional *siddur* makes no mention of the State of Israel as a contemporary reality, and asks only that God replant the Jewish people at some future date in the Land so that the sacrificial order can once again be renewed, *Sim Shalom* gives thanks to God, "who restores His children to their land — הַמֵּשִׁיב בָּנִים לִגְבוּלָם (434). The inclusion of this phrase into the *Musaf* service of every holiday reflects the Conservative conviction that "The reestablishment of the Jewish State in the Land of Israel" represents a divine answer to the millennia-old prayers of the Jewish people. Israel is a "metaphysical necessity" that demands acknowledgment and recognition in the prayers bequeathed the Jewish people by the second house.

At the same time, each of these services, like the *Musaf* services in the 1961 *Weekday Prayer Book*, includes the sentence,

וּתְקַבֵּל בְּרַחֲמִים אֶת־תְּפִלַּת עַמְּךָ יִשְׂרָאֵל בְּכָל־מְקוֹמוֹת מוֹשְׁבוֹתֵיהֶם.

Compassionate King, accept with compassion the prayer of Your people Israel, wherever they dwell" (434–435). This phrase has ample biblical precedent. However, it represents, as discussed above, a noticeable departure from the traditional manifest content of the liturgy for this service. The text is no longer centered exclusively on Israel. The Jewish people dwell in the Diaspora as well, and this presence in the lands of dispersion is not regarded as a *malum* (an evil) from which the Jewish people seek release. The metaphor of the ellipsis as the appropriate model for understanding the relationship between Israel and the Diaspora, and the rejection of a vision that affirms Israel as the exclusive center of Jewish life, is once more affirmed.[30]

Sim Shalom, as this analysis has shown, accords the State of Israel sanctified status. The particularity of this prayerbook on this point is striking and unapologetic. On the other hand, *Sim Shalom* will not surrender its claim that religious life in the Diaspora is of religious import as well. It is a work, as Rawidowicz would have it, of the second house that "praises the first house" and views present-day Jewish territoriality and sovereignty in the Land of Israel as an absolute *bonum* (a good) endowed with religious significance. Yet, precisely because it is a work of the second house, it refuses to concede "territorial centralization as a condition for the existence of the nation." *Sim Shalom*, like *Kol Haneshamah*, speaks to the reality of American Jewish visions of the State of Israel. Refractions of these visions abound in the pages of contemporary American Reform liturgy as well. A description of them will provide additional insight into how American Israel envisions the contemporary Jewish State.

---

30   It is also interesting to note that other modern liturgists have made comparable changes in parts of their liturgy. Abraham Geiger, for example, in the 1870 edition of his *Seder Tefilah D'var Yom B'Yomo*, changed the phrasing of the seventh wedding benediction to include reference to *"chal moshvot yisrael —* all Israel's dwelling places" (xv). Geiger, however, unlike Harlow, purged this blessing of all nationalistic references.

Reform Transformations

The twin events of Holocaust and Israel, given the mythical resonance they provide for American Jewish self-understanding and consciousness, find prominent expression in the contemporary liturgy
of the Reform movement in North America. With the appearance of
a revised Reform liturgy, *Sha'arei Tefillah — Gates of Prayer* in
1975, and in the subsequent publication of over a half-dozen other
liturgies and liturgical commentaries in the 1980s, Reform Judaism
has borne witness to the seminal role this myth plays in the life of
present-day American Jewry. Commentator after commentator has
made note of this in the publications issued by the Reform movement
during the past twenty years.

"The events of the Holocaust and the birth of modern Israel,"
observes Rabbi Lawrence A. Hoffman, "stand foremost in [the
American Jews'] minds."[31] This led the Central Conference of
American Rabbis to establish Yom Ha-Shoah as a day of commem-
oration and Yom Ha'atzmaut as a permanent annual festival in the
religious calendar of Judaism. The State of Israel, in Reform as in
Conservative Judaism, is accorded sacred status. Furthermore, in
Reform writings on the subject, it is tied, directly to the Holocaust.
In *Gates of the Seasons: A Guide to the Jewish Year* published by the
CCAR in 1983, the text states, "The celebration of Yom ha-Atzma'ut
recognizes that a new era has dawned in the life of the Jewish
people. It attests to the essential unity of the whole household of
Israel and marks the cultural and spiritual renaissance which draws
strength from the symbiotic relationship between Israel and world
Jewry. The rebirth of Israel from the ashes of the *Sho'ah* is a symbol
of hope against despair, of redemption against devastation" (102).
After the first night of Passover, "we count seven weeks to Shavuot.
During this period on Yom ha-Sho'ah, we mourn the death of six
million Jews, but our grief gives way to rejoicing when we join in the
celebration of Israel's rebirth on Yom ha-Atzma'ut" (6). The linkage

31 Lawrence A. Hoffman, "The Liturgical Message," in *Gates of Understanding: A
Companion Volume to Sha'arei Tefillah*, ed. Lawrence A. Hoffman (New York:
Central Conference of American Rabbis and the Union of American Hebrew
Congregations, 1977), 162.

between the genocidal fury of the Holocaust and the redemption offered by the establishment of the State of Israel in the minds of American Jewry could not be more strongly or directly expressed.

These days are defined as "holidays" in the religious life of American Judaism. The commemoration and celebration of each of them is elevated to the status of "commandment" for contemporary Reform Jews. As Rabbi Simeon J. Maslin, then Chairman of the Committee on Reform Jewish Practice, in his "Foreword" to *Gates of the Seasons*, wrote, "Certain *new* practices are also recommended as *mitzvot* — ...the observance of Yom ha-Sho'ah and Yom ha-Atzma'ut come readily to mind" (viii). Hence, of Israeli Independence Day, Rabbi Peter Knobel, editor of *Gates of the Seasons*, states,

> It is a *mitzvah* for every Jew to mark Yom Ha'atzmaut by participation in public worship services and/or celebration which affirm the bond between Jews living in the Land of Israel and those living outside. Furthermore, a special act of Tzedakah to an organization or institution which helps to strengthen the State of Israel would be a significant way of affirming the unity of the Jewish people. One may wish to have a festive meal on Yom ha-Atzma'ut at which one serves food from Israel and sings Israeli songs. (102)

In light of this, it hardly comes as a surprise, as Rabbi A. Stanley Dreyfus, chairman of the Liturgy Committee of the CCAR put it, when *Gates of Prayer* initially appeared, "The enormity of the Holocaust on the one hand, and, on the other, the establishment of the State of Israel, brought a reawakening of faith and commitment and, for Reform Jewry, mandated a complete revision of the liturgy."[32] *Gates of Prayer*, like both *Kol Haneshama* and *Sim Shalom*, observes in its "Introduction" that "in the liturgy of the synagogue the Jewish people has written its spiritual autobiography. ... As Jews have done since the the twilight of the days of the Second Temple, we have sought, in our own way, to express our people's soul" (xi). That "soul" today has been marked by the events of our century, "and we Jews have also experienced the Holocaust and the rebirth of the

---

32 A. Stanley Dreyfus, "Reform Judaism's Worship," in *The Changing Face of Jewish and Christian Worship in North America*, 146.

State of Israel — events that loom large in our consciousness. To these, in particular, have we attempted a response" (xii).

The link between the Holocaust and the establishment of the State, as well as the significance the contemporary Reform movement attaches to the State, are manifest in the treatment accorded Tisha be-Av in *Gates of Prayer*. "The martyrdom of European Jewry under the Nazis has given a renewed impetus," states one Reform commentary, "to the commemoration of Israel's sufferings generally."[33] As a result, for the first time in the twentieth century, a service for Tisha be-Av is included in an American Reform liturgy.[34] It had been omitted from the *Union Prayerbook, Gates of Prayer's* predecessor precisely because the authors of that liturgy did not regard the destruction of the Temple and the subsequent dispersion of the Jewish people into the Diaspora as an occasion for lament. The power of the Holocaust as a guiding myth for American Jewry was such that this assessment was reversed. However, Tisha be-Av no longer possesses the mythic power to stand alone and, instead, is collapsed into a service for Yom ha-Sho'ah (573–589). While the date for observing the latter has been proclaimed by the CCAR as the twenty-seventh day of Nissan, "the anniversary of the Warsaw Ghetto Uprising,"[35] and the date for the observance of the former remains the traditional ninth day of Av, the service commemorating each event is one and the same. One Reform source notes that some Reform Jews "continue to observe [Tisha be-Av] by attending special services and/or by fasting"; but that same source asserts that "many [Reform] Jews have abandoned Tisha be-Av, in part, because of the re-establishment of the State of Israel."[36]

---

33   Chaim Stern and A. Stanley Dreyfus, "Notes to *Shaarei Tefillah*," in *Gates of Understanding*, 246.

34   Most nineteenth-century European Liberal prayerbooks, as well as David Einhorn's *Olath Tamid* (1858), included services for Tisha be-Av. As Jakob J. Petuchowski observed in his *Prayerbook Reform in Europe* (New York: World Union for Progressive Judaism, 1968), 291, "Notwithstanding Geiger's extremely negative views on the subject of Zion, neither Geiger himself nor the vast majority of the European Liberal and Reform liturgists did away with the services for the Ninth of Ab."

35   Ibid.

36   Peter S. Knobel, ed., *Gates of the Season: A Guide to the Jewish Year* (New York: Central Conference of American Rabbis, 1983), 104.

The Reform treatment of Tisha B'av reveals that modern day Reform displays a "commitment to Zionism."[37] It is a commitment so strong that it may, for some Reform Jews, obviate the observance of Tisha B'av for reasons entirely distinct from those put forth by their nineteenth- and twentieth-century forebears. Yet precisely because that commitment is linked so indissolubly in the minds of many of those same Reform Jews to the tragedy of the Holocaust, it becomes unthinkable that Tisha B'av not be observed. Failure to observe the holiday would be tantamount to a rejection of the historical memories that bind all generations of Jews together. As Hoffman observes of this rather complex development in the evolution of Reform Judaism, "To what do we owe the rediscovery of ourselves as a people, not just a religion? Israel's birth certainly, but also the Holocaust preceding it, which tragically underscored the Zionist argument."[38]

In *Gates of Repentance*, the High Holiday *mahazor* of the Reform movement, the attachment between the Holocaust and the establishment of the state finds the same type of manifest expression that was apparent in *Kol Haneshama*. One prayer in the morning service for Rosh Hashanah states, "Life's harsh winds uproot the weak, its hard rains beat down upon our kin. ... How good to redeem the pledge, for joy to blossom in arid soil" (175). It is in the afternoon service of Yom Kippur that this linkage between destruction and redemption, Holocaust and Israel, reaches its apogee. In the *Eileh ezkara* (For the Ten Martyrs) prayer, the martyrdom that has beset the Jewish people throughout history is recounted, climaxing with the Holocaust. "Now the lifeless skulls/ Add up to millions. ... Silence. Where in the Holocaust is the word of God?... The world was silent; the world was still" (437).

For that act, the congregation, in the *'Al het*, now confesses, "For the sin of silence, For the sin of indifference,... For the crime of indifference,... For all that was done, For all that was not done, Let there be no forgetfulness before the Throne of Glory" (439). Yet "despite the suffering" the Jewish people did not die. The vision of Ezekiel 37 came to be realized. The "dry bones" of the Jewish

37   Hoffman, "The Liturgical Message," 152.
38   Ibid., 153–154.

people took on renewed life in the Land of Israel (443). As *Gates of Repentance* proclaims, "In one land especially we glimpsed the rays of a new dawn: the land of Zion, made ready for habitation by generations of pioneers. The great day came: Israel independent at last, the millenial dream, a dream no more! Drawn by its brightness, her children flocked to Israel from distant lands of despair, and found hope. Though bent in mourning, they ploughed the earth deep, so that grain would grow tall. And as they restored the land to its fruitfulness, they began themselves to be restored. Israel lives: a people at home again, rooted in its soil, its way of life, its ancient faith" (442–443). Jewish nationalism is here affirmed. Israel is portrayed as a beacon of refuge for the dispossessed of the Jewish people ("her children flocked to her from distant lands of despair") and defended in religious terms ("a people... again... rooted in its ancient faith"). The vision of the pioneers' productivity ("they restored the land to its fruitfulness") is also not neglected. All these elements are undoubtedly a legitimate part of the Zionist enterprise and message. However, it is equally clear that such emphases are congenial to the spirit of American culture and religiosity. They reflect the manner in which Israel is envisioned by America's Jews.

The connection to Israel finds expression in other ways as well. Quotations from Israeli and Zionist poets and authors — among them Bialik, Berdechewski, Ahad Ha'am, Amir Gilboa, and Joseph Zvi Rimmon — frequently appear in the pages of these Reform liturgies. Furthermore, "A Prayer for the State of Israel" is included for every Sabbath and holiday morning service. This prayer does not adopt the prayer of the Israeli Chief Rabbinate. Instead, it states, "We pray for the land of Israel and its people. May its borders know peace, its inhabitants tranquillity. And may the bonds of faith and fate which unite the Jews of all lands be a source of strength to Israel and to us all. God of all lands and ages, answer our constant prayer with a Zion once more aglow with light for us and all the world, and let us say: Amen" (452). The prayer, as does the rest of the prayerbook, totally abjures the notion of "Ingathering of the Exiles." Furthermore, even though this prayer's inclusion in the liturgy takes cognizance of the Land and, in effect, expresses a hope for the State, it refuses to forsake a traditional Reform emphasis on the universal mission of Israel. In so doing, it indicates that even when the Jewish particularity of land and state is underscored, it is still tied to the moral task of the Jewish people.

Gates of Prayer has also "readmitted" the traditional *hatimah* of the seventeenth benediction of the *Amidah*, "Who has caused the divine presence to return to Zion — הַמַּחֲזִיר שְׁכִינָתוֹ לְצִיּוֹן —" with which previous editions of Reform liturgy had such difficulty. However, as Hoffman notes, *Gates of Prayer*, even though it elected to include the traditional Hebrew, "rephrased the English to read, 'Blessed is the Lord whose presence gives life to Zion and all Israel'."[39] This translation, which Rabbi Chaim Stern, the editor of *Gates of Prayer*, and Rabbi Dreyfus, in their "Notes" to the prayerbook, characterize as "rather broad," is offered "to carry out the more universal theme we wish to convey, i.e., God's presence in Zion and wherever our people worships Him in truth."[40] The particularity of the prayer, as well as its nationalistic overtones, is thereby seriously muted. This confirms Neusner's observation that Jews in the United States will not cede centrality to the Jewish state.

The most significant liturgical innovations reflecting the Reform attitude to Israel are found in the "special service for the Sabbath before Israel's Independence Day and another service for Independence Day itself." The prayers in these services, Hoffman continues, employ fragments of "Palestinian prayers which history had consigned to desuetude. ... As world Jewry has redeemed the physical heritage of our land, so Reform Judaism now reclaims our spiritual legacy. ... When Israel's Independence Day fell in 1976, Reform Jews prayed from reconstituted prayer texts which had not been part of official public worship for centuries! This very undertaking of reclaiming our roots and planting ourselves firmly amidst an eternal people of cosmic significance is part of our new Jewish vision of ourselves."[41] Thus the exclusively territorial vision of the first house is again rejected, and the state, even as it is affirmed, is viewed through the religious lens of the second house.

In the service for the "Sabbath before Yom ha-Atzma'ut" as well as in the service for Yom ha-Atzma'ut itself the linkage between the

39   Ibid., 153.
40   Stern and Dreyfus, "Notes to *Shaarei Tefillah*," 192.
41   Hoffman, "The Liturgical Message," 153.

Holocaust and the establishment of the state is prominent. In both services, Hannah Szenes's "Blessed is the match ..." is included (413 and 590). In the former service, following the recitation of passages from Psalm 137, "If I forget you, O Jerusalem," a prayer proclaims,

> Blessed are the eyes that behold Israel reborn in its ancient land of promise! Blessed the age that has seen our people outlive death's kingdom! With gratitude we recall the devotion of Israel's builders and the valor of its defenders. We give thanks for this example of courage, this expression of our creative will. For every anguished yesterday, let there be a joyful tomorrow (412).

This is paralleled by the treatment accorded the *Gevurot* benediction in the *Amidah* for the Yom Ha'atzmaut service. The prayer, in Hebrew and English (599), reads:

אַתָּה גִּבּוֹר, מַשְׁפִּיל גַּאִים; חָזָק וּמֵדִין עָרִיצִים; חֵי עוֹלָמִים. מְקַיֵּם מֵתִים, מַשִּׁיב הָרוּחַ וּמוֹרִיד הַטָּל, מְכַלְכֵּל חַיִּים, מְחַיֶּה הַמֵּתִים. כְּהֶרֶף עַיִן יְשׁוּעָה לָנוּ תַצְמִיחַ. בָּרוּךְ אַתָּה, [ה'] מְחַיֶּה הַמֵּתִים.

> Life of the universe, Your greatness humbles the proud, Your power brings judgment upon tyrants. By Your might the dead live, the winds blow, the dew descends. You sustain the living and give life to the dead; You are the Source of our deliverance. Blessed is the Lord, who gives life to the dead.

Particularly striking is the decision by the authors of this liturgy to include the traditional *hatimah* to this blessing, בָּרוּךְ אַתָּה [ה'] מְחַיֶּה הַמֵּתִים — "who gives life to the dead" — as well as the phrases מְקַיֵּם מֵתִים — By Your might the dead live — and מְחַיֶּה הַמֵּתִים — You...give life to the dead" — inasmuch as the idea of bodily resurrection they express is rejected elsewhere in *Gates of Prayer*. In view of the editors' inclusion of Ezekiel 37 in another part of this service (597), and in light of the many references to God's might in humbling "the proud" and bringing "judgment upon tyrants," the attention paid to the Holocaust in these prayers of thanksgiving and gratitude for the establishment of the state is noteworthy. These services canonize the linked myth of Holocaust and Redemption in the liturgical life of the Jewish people in America.

Universal themes, even in these services that celebrate the particularity of the Jewish state, find prominent expression. There is an absence of any prayers for "normalization." The desire to be "like all the other nations," so characteristic of large segments of political Zionism, is totally absent in these liturgies. The creation of the state will cause God to allow "the plant of justice to spring up soon — אֶת־צֶמַח צְדָקָה מְהֵרָה תַצְמִיחַ (601).

Zion, it is hoped, "may become a light to the nations" whose people will "build a land in which the vision of justice and mercy shall be fulfilled for the good of all" (414). The wish is articulated that "Israel, and all peoples, [shall] know peace for ever" and that "the great shofar of freedom [will] be sounded for us and all peoples. ... Let every wanderer come home from the bitterness of exile" (602). The religious thrust and universalistic hopes attached to Zionism and the Jewish national idea are made preeminent, and this expresses the ideal of Israel held by many Jews in the North American Diaspora.

Rabbi Hoffman himself offers a concise and insightful summary of what these Reform liturgical innovations reveal about present-day American Reform visions of Israel and Zionism. "We Reform Jews today," he writes, "still agree with the pioneers of our movement in insisting that we are not in exile. ... We are also the generation blessed in sharing in the miraculous rebirth of the State of Israel. The idea that God's presence returns to Zion after centuries of the Land's virtual demise, reflects the reality of our love for Zion. But Zionism within Reform ideology differs from secular Zionism in that, for us, any state — even a Jewish one — is incomplete without the guiding hand of God." *Gates of Prayer*, like *Sim Shalom*, provides a consistent "'affirmation of Jewish life in Israel." However, it affirms Jewish life in "the Diaspora equally. ... God is present in Zion and in Jewish life everywhere." This liturgy will not concede "territorial centralization" to Zion, even as it celebrates the birth and existence of the state as a miraculous rebirth after the destruction of the Holocaust.[42]

42   Lawrence A. Hoffman, ed., *Gates of Understanding 2: Appreciating the Days of Awe* (New York: Central Conference of American Rabbis, 1984), 22–23.

Conclusion

Evyatar Friesel has observed, "It is justified to speak about a Zionized American Jewry represented in large measure by its religious movements."[43] Friesel's observation, in a land where Jews have principally been portrayed "as a religious community," is a reminder that the manner in which the State of Israel is envisioned in the prayerbooks of the community is crucial for both grasping American Jewish self-understanding of the state and appreciating the manner in which the state is presented to Americans — Jews and non-Jews alike. As we have seen, there is a remarkable confluence of vision among the present-day prayerbooks of Reform, Conservative, and Reconstructionist Judaism. Israel is seen primarily in religious, not national, categories in the prayerbooks of all the movements. This means that the present-day reality of a secular Israel, as well as the non-religious ideas that initially motivated the founders of the Zionist movement, are far removed from the vision of the Jewish state presented in these liturgies. Simply put, the State of Israel embodies a religious, not a secular nationalistic, reality for the adherents of these American Jewish religious denominations. In addition the linkage myth of Holocaust and Redemption informs them all, particularly the *siddurim* of the Reform and Reconstructionist denominations. Finally none of them will depart from the notion that Jewish life in the *Diaspora* is as viable and legitimate as Jewish life in the state. The idea of "*shelilat hagolah — the Negation of the Diaspora*" that informed so much of classical political Zionism is totally rejected. It is also significant to see the role that universalism plays in shaping the vision the prayerbooks of especially the Reform and Reconstructionist movements have of the Jewish state. It is a vision totally compatible with the liberal ethos that dominates and informs the overwhelming majority of American Jews.[44] It is an ideology which asserts, as Charles Liebman has phrased it, "that the Jewish tradition has a message for all people." The meaning of

---

43 Evyatar Friesel, "American Jewry as Bearer of Contemporary Jewish Tasks," *American Jewish History* 78 (1989): 491.

44 Charles S. Liebman, "Ritual, Ceremony, and the Reconstruction of Judaism in the United States," in *Studies in Contemporary Jewry: An Annual* (1990): 278.

institutions, practices, and rituals in Jewish life, in view of this ideology, is reinterpreted and given meaning in light of universal moral categories. "Jewish symbols," Liebman explains, "are retained in their particularistic form, but the referent or meaning is explained as a moral or ethical imperative."

Liebman's observation provides insight into the manner in which prayerbooks of these most liberal religious denominations of American Judaism envision the Jewish state. The exclusively nationalistic or secular elements of the Zionist dream and the contemporary incarnation of those political elements in the state are downplayed, if not completely rejected. Israel, though a refuge for Jews in a time of persecution, is seen instead as an ultimate expression of the religious and moral hopes of the Jewish people. Universalism informs and animates this vision of the Jewish state, a vision that is highly consonant with the American and diasporan context that inspired it.

Israel as Symbol and as Reality:
The Perception of Israel among
Reconstructionist Jews in the United States*

Stephen Sharot and Nurit Zaidman

American Jews and Israel

After 1967 a common statement among observers of American Jewry
was that Israel had become an important element in the religion of
American Jews. Some even suggested that Israel had become *the*
religion of American Jews. There are many definitions and meanings
of religion, but there has been little clarification of the "religious"
meanings attributed by American Jews to Israel. We may ask if Israel
has a religious meaning for American Jews in the sense of providing a
focus or symbol of transcendent values or concerns. Is Israel central
to the most frequent religious actions or behaviors of American
Jews? Or is Israel of religious significance to American Jews in
terms of a functional meaning of religion that does not necessarily
imply transcendental meanings? In this functional sense, support for
Israel may be said to unite American Jews despite their different
religious views, practices, and affiliations. The unifying function of
Israel would appear to be the basis of Jonathan Woocher's statement
that denial of support for the State of Israel is the only heresy of
American Judaism.[1]

Few studies of American Jewish religion and identity have considered the possible multidimensional nature of the attitudes and
behaviors of American Jews toward Israel. Most have limited their
inquiries to asking general questions on how important American

* This study was supported by a grant to Stephen Sharot from the Center for the
  Study of North American Jewry, Ben-Gurion University of the Negev.
1 Jonathan S. Woocher, *Sacred Survival: The Civil Religion of American Jews*
  (Bloomington: Indiana University Press, 1986), 77.

Jews consider support for Israel, if they have visited Israel, and if they have considered making *aliyah*. The 1990 National Survey of American Jews found that the percentage of American Jews who had visited Israel was somewhat less than had been thought on the basis of data from previous, less encompassing surveys. Just over one-quarter of respondents who identified as Jewish had visited Israel: 15 percent had been once, and 12 percent had been twice or more. A little more than 30 percent of those born-Jewish respondents who identified with one of the Jewish denominations had visited Israel, compared with 10.9 percent of those who identified as secular Jews and 11.4 percent of those who had not been born Jewish but had "chosen" Judaism.[2] Another recent large survey found that American Jews who identified as Orthodox were the most likely to have visited Israel, followed by Conservative Jews, Reform Jews, and lastly, those who identified themselves as "just Jewish."[3]

Other surveys, especially those conducted by Steven M. Cohen, have provided more information on American Jewish orientations toward Israel; but the empirical focus of most of these surveys has been on the question of American Jewish identity, with the rather general questions on Israel providing just one dimension among many. We have tried to probe more deeply into the multiple meanings of Israel by conducting in-depth interviews with twenty-five Reconstructionists: six faculty members and rabbis of the Reconstructionist seminary, eight students of the seminary, and eleven members of Reconstructionist congregations. This is, of course, a small and unrepresentative sample, but we will argue that the particular nature of its unrepresentativeness can provide us with a deeper understanding of the complexity of American Jewish orientations toward Israel.

Investigations of the place of Israel in the identities and religious life of larger and denominationally heterogeneous samples of American Jewry provide a framework for an evaluation of our findings

2   Sidney Goldstein, "Profiles of American Jewry: Insights from the 1990 National Jewish Population Survey," *American Jewish Year Book* 92 (1992), 139–140, 173.

3   Peter Y. Medding, Gary A. Tobin, Sylvia Barack-Fishman, and Mordechai Rimor, "Jewish Identity in Conversionary and Mixed Marriages," *American Jewish Year Book* 92 (1992), 27–28, 61.

with respect to Reconstructionists. These investigations indicate that although a large proportion of American Jews call themselves Zionists, their meanings of Zionism are closer to what some investigators have called pro-Israelism. According to the still common Israeli definition of a Zionist as one who views the Diaspora negatively and considers the settlement of Jews in Israel as essential, the vast majority of American Jews would not be considered Zionists.[4] Gilboa defines a Zionist as one who views Israel as his or her spiritual and cultural center and for whom Israel plays a central role in personal life and identity. Pro-Israelism better describes the majority of American Jews but the strength of this orientation varies considerably.

Cohen summarized the findings of a survey undertaken in 1986 by reporting that one-third of Amercian Jews were relatively indifferent toward Israel, one-third were moderately pro-Israel, and one-third were passionately pro-Israel. He wrote that pro-Israelism was not part of the core identity of most American Jews. Although Israel has an important place in the public sphere of American Judaism, in the massive philanthropic and political lobbying apparatus, it has few consequences for Jewish identity in the private sphere. On those occasions when Judaism enters the private lives of American Jews — such as the rites of passage and the important religious holidays — Israel as society, culture, state, language, or sacred concept has little meaning.[5]

In the introduction to their book, Liebman and Cohen wrote that almost everything that Israelis do tends to be understood by American Jews as deriving from, and having consequences for, an authentic Judaism;[6] yet their discussion in the body of the book indicates that although Israel serves to express and reinforce the Jewish identity of American Jews, it has little relevance for their religion. They write, for example, that hardly any American Jews

---

4   Eytan Gilboa, "Attitudes of American Jews toward Israel: Trends over Time," *American Jewish Year Book* 86 (1986), 110–125.

5   Steven M. Cohen, "Israel in the Jewish Identity of American Jews: A Study in Dualities and Contrasts," in *Jewish Identity in America*, ed. David M. Gordis and Yoav Ben-Horin (Los Angeles: University of Judaism, 1991), 119–138.

6   Charles S. Liebman and Steven M. Cohen, *Two Worlds of Judaism; The Israeli and American Experiences* (New Haven: Yale University Press, 1990), 8.

realize that the Land of Israel played an important part in traditional Judaism, and few worshipers pay serious attention to the passages in the liturgy that express a yearning for the physical ingathering of Jews in the Holy Land.[7] Israel is more likely to have religious meanings among Orthodox Jews, but for most American Jews "Israel" is a symbol with a functional significance that makes it unnecessary to distinguish the Israeli people from the Land of Israel and State of Israel. Thus although Israel as a symbol may substitute for Judaism in the sense of its functioning as a means of Jewish ethnic survival in the United States, its substantive religious meanings for most American Jews are minimal or nonexistent.

A similar argument can be made in somewhat different terms by noting that Israel has an important place in the civil religion of American Jews and a minor place in their traditional religion. In his book on the civil religion of American Jews, Woocher wrote that Israel is the central theme in the fund-raising campaigns of the Jewish federations and provides the symbolic center of civil Judaism. The survival of the Jews is one of the principal themes of the American Jewish civil religion, and Israel, as a symbol of both Jewish insecurity and strength, is the most important focus of that theme. The civil religion does not present Israel as standing alone; it is in "partnership" with the Diaspora, and it is the combined strength of Jews in the Diaspora and Israel that insures the destiny of the Jewish people. The centrality of Israel is integrated by the civil religion within the broader framework of the Jewish people, and, as an all-important symbol, Israel has multiple meanings for civil religion. Woocher writes that in addition to being a symbol of Jewish survival, Israel is also a focus of a sense of peoplehood and an exemplifier of the fundamental values of Judaism.[8] These latter meanings are not, however, explored by Woocher, and they may be regarded as more problematic for American Jews than Israel as a symbol of survival.

Israel is not just a symbol. It is also, as Woocher notes, a real place, and the question arises of the implications of events in the real Israel on Israel as a focus of American Jewish identity and

7   Ibid., 94, 86.
8   Woocher, *Sacred Survival*, 76–80, 100–101, 114–115.

as a symbol of Jewish survival, peoplehood, and the fundamental values of Judaism. Liebman and Cohen may be correct when they write that most American Jews are ignorant of even the most elementary features of Israeli life; but even if the information received by American Jews on Israel is confined to the American news media, events in Israel are likely to be conveyed to them fairly regularly. American Jews have commonly perceived a consonance between their support for Israeli society and policies and their "Americanness." Israel is frequently presented as the only true democracy in the Middle East, and until the mid-1970s concern for Israel was virtually synonymous with support for its leaders' policies. However, since the 1970s an increasing number of American Jews have expressed their reservations or opposition, from a dovish viewpoint, to certain policies of Israeli governments. American Jewry is known for its relative liberalism within the American political spectrum, and Cohen found a correlation between liberalism, which was found especially among younger and more educated American Jews, and less support for the policies of Israel's governments.[9]

The opposition of some American Jews to the policies of Israeli governments has not been confined to questions of war and peace. When the last Likud government appeared to be on the verge of accepting its religious coalition partners' definition of "Who is a Jew?" American Jewish pressure groups mobilized their forces to persuade the government that for the majority of Diaspora Jews this was not an acceptable position. As Cohen has noted, the far greater concern of American Jews with the "Who is a Jew" affair than with the *Intifada* highlights the powerful symbolic role of Israel for American Jews. The initiative of the Orthodox political parties in Israel to define a Jew in a way that would exclude conversions performed by Conservative and Reform rabbis was perceived by many American Jews, most of whom identify with Conservative and Reform Judaism, as a delegitimization of their ties to Israel.[10] This

9   Steven M. Cohen, *American Modernity and Jewish Identity; The Israeli and American Experiences* (New York: Tavistock Publications, 1986), 164–167.

10 Cohen, "Israel in the Jewish Identity of American Jews," in *Jewish Identity*, ed. Gordis and Ben-Horin."

was an issue where the symbolic value of Israel for American Jews was being threatened by the political action of Israelis.

Reconstructionism: Size, Ideology, and Official Positions

The survey data, based on large, heterogeneous samples, have provided the broad contours of the orientations of American Jews toward Israel, but their format imposes limitations. The risk of obtaining only "socially acceptable" answers is especially acute when interviews are highly formalized; and the possibilities of probing multiple meanings, some of which may be in tension with one another, is limited by the replies being dependent on closed, forced-choice questions. The lengthy interviews with Reconstructionist Jews conducted for our study were based on both forced-choice and open-ended questions, and respondents were encouraged to give reasons for their answers and to follow through on their train of thought. Our intention was not to provide a representative sample of the views of Reconstructionist Jews — let alone of American Jews in general — but to probe the understandings and meanings of a small sample that included articulate Jews likely to have thought about and discussed at least some of the issues covered by our study. A relatively intense involvement with Israel was thought to be especially likely among the rabbis, rabbinical students, and teachers of the seminary, nearly all of whom had studied in Israel for at least one year.

The Reconstructionist movement has grown in recent years. By the end of the 1960s — by which time Reconstructionism had become the fourth Jewish denomination in the United States, with its own congregational organization, seminary, and rabbinical organization — there were ten member congregations. A modest growth occurred in the 1970s, and by 1983 there were forty-six member units.[11] Today, there are sixty-nine congregations and *havurot* affiliates. The movement remains, however, by far the smallest of the American

11   Charles S. Liebman, "Reconstructionism in American Jewish Life," *American Jewish Year Book* 71 (1970), 39; Marc Lee Raphael, *Profiles in American Judaism* (San Francisco: Harper & Row, 1984), 185, 188–194.

Jewish denominations; the 1990 National Jewish Population Survey found that just over 1 percent of American Jews identify with Reconstructionism.[12]

Despite the small size of the movement, its ideology makes it a sociologically interesting phenomenon, and the orientations of Reconstructionist Jews toward Israel may be especially illuminating. One point of interest is that the arguments of its founder, Mordecai M. Kaplan (1881–1983), were influenced by sociological interpretations of religion and, in particular, by the writings of Emile Durkheim. Following Durkheim, Kaplan understood religion as a group rather than an individual phenomenon, and this emphasis led him to redefine Jewishness in terms of belonging rather than believing. Jews linked themselves to the Jewish people in diverse ways, but it was belonging and the sense of a shared past and destiny that united them. Judaism was the "evolving religious civilization of the Jewish people," and the term "civilization" implied a totality that included all elements of group life and not just those elements conventionally understood as religion.[13] This definition of Judaism encompasses what would normally be considered secularist perspectives, and it allows for the legitimation of Jewish practices, such as lighting Hanukkah candles, as expressions of Jewish identity and belongingness rather than as religious observances.[14]

The sociological arguments for the special significance of Reconstructionism, which Charles Liebman expounded in an important paper published in 1970, are still relevant today and are especially relevant to the subject of American Jews and Israel. In brief, Liebman argued that it was the very explicitness of Reconstructionism in its articulation of the major values and attitudes of American Jews which explained its small size. He contended that American folk Judaism is oriented to the survival of the ethnic group, but that most American Jews would not join a synagogue which made this the cornerstone of its ideology. In America religious separatism

12   Goldstein, "Profiles," 127.
13   Mordecai M. Kaplan, *Judaism as a Civilization: Toward a Reconstruction of American-Jewish Life* (Philadelphia: Jewish Publication Society of America, Reconstructionist Press, [1934] 1981).
14   Rebecca T. Alpert and Jacob J. Staub, *Exploring Judaism: A Reconstructionist Approach* (Wyncote, Penn.: The Reconstructionist Press, 1985), 8–18.

is seen as more legitimate than ethnic separation, and American Jews had accommodated to this situation by stating their differences with non-Jews in religious rather than ethnic terms. American Jews would feel uncomfortable if they had to admit that their religious observances focused around ethnic rather than specifically religious concerns.[15] Since Liebman wrote his article, ethnic pluralism has achieved greater legitimacy in the United States, but there is still a tendency to make a differentiation between religious and ethnic identities, and to legitimate religion by ethnic separation is still an unappealing stance.

The position of Mordecai Kaplan, the founder of Reconstructionism, toward Israel became the typical position of American Jewry. Kaplan and his early followers supported the campaign for a Jewish state from the 1920s. Kaplan wrote that the establishment of a national home in Palestine was essential for the "corporate life" of Jews and that the Jews had a right to possess the Land of Israel because of its essential connection to the Jewish past. Israel was to be the center of a Jewish renaissance, and as Israel was the spiritual center of the world Jewish community, Judaism was unlikely to survive without it.[16] Kaplans's Zionism did not extend, however, to the need for American Jews to make *aliyah* or to the negation of the Diaspora. In fact, Kaplan articulated at an early date the theme of "partnership" between Israel and the Diaspora that has become, according to Woocher, an important theme of the American Jewish civil religion. Kaplan wrote: "World Jewry without Eretz Yisrael is like a soul without a body; Eretz Yisrael without World Jewry is like a body without a soul."[17] In an address before the Rabbinical Assembly of the Conservative movement in 1949, Kaplan said that the Zionist ideal should be extended into a "Greater Zionism" based on the concept of a "transnational" Jewish community whose core is Eretz Israel but whose branches extend throughout the world.[18]

---

15   Liebman, *Reconstructionism,* 3–99.
16   Kaplan, *Judaism*, chap. 20.
17   Quoted by Gilbert S. Rosenthal, *Contemporary Judaism: Patterns of Survival,* 2nd ed. (New York: Human Sciences Press, 1986), 246.
18   David Rudavsky, *Modern Jewish Religious Movements; Attitudes of Emancipation and Adjustment* (New York: Behrman House, [1967] 1979), 359.

Kaplan did not believe that support for Israel should take precedence over loyalty to the United States. American Jews could be Zionists only if they found their Jewish life in America to be of significance, and a meaningful and rich Jewish life was possible in the United States because of its separation of church and state, its democratic pluralism, and its tolerance of diverse cultural expressions. There was no need to choose between Jewish and American identities; American Jews were able to live in two civilizations and to integrate the democratic values of an open society into a reconstructed Jewish civilization.[19]

In many respects the approach to Israel among Reconstructionists has not changed since Kaplan. The by-laws of the Federation of Reconstructionist Congregations and Havurot include the proviso that an affiliate will have a "commitment to the support of the State of Israel." A document detailing the official platform of the movement includes the following positions on Israel, Zionism, and the Diaspora:

> Reconstructionists are deeply attached historically and emotionally both to *Eretz Yisrael* and to the survival there of a secure, prospering, and democratic state.
>
> While recognizing that *Eretz Yisrael* is central to the spiritual life of the Jewish people, Reconstructionists affirm that a satisfying, authentic and creative Judaism can also flourish in the Diaspora, nurtured under conditions of political, social, and economic freedom.
>
> Reconstructionists advocate acceptance of religious and cultural pluralism in Jewish life in Israel.
>
> Reconstructionists are committed to furthering the dynamic relationship between Diaspora and Israeli Jewry, recognizing that only through mutual respect, cooperation and moral dialogue can Zionism become a means for the revitalization of Jewish civilization.[20]

19 Albert and Staub, *Exploring Judaism*, 38–40; David Klatzker, "Renewing the New Zionism: Notes toward the 1985 Rearticulation of Reconstructionist Principle," *Reconstructionist* 50 (5) (March 1985), 10–14, 34.

20 Rebecca T. Alpert and Jacob J. Staub, *The Activity/Discussion Guide to Exploring Judaism: A Reconstructionist Approach* (Wyncote, Penn.: The Re-

The importance attributed to Israel in the movement's central organizations is demonstrated by the requirement that students of the Reconstructionist Rabbinical College spend a year in Israel as part of their study program. However, central members of the staff of the Rabbinical College, such as Arthur Green, who was the college president, have not hesitated to criticize the policies of Israeli governments, and a resolution passed by the Reconstructionist Rabbinical Association at its convention in 1988 expressed the dovish views of the majority of Reconstructionist rabbis. The resolution supported "direct negotiations with the representatives of the Palestinian people," deplored the "excesses which have been perpetrated by all sides," and expressed the belief "that the Jewish people's own experience with historical persecution and homelessness should make us especially sensitive to the frustrated sense of national fulfillment felt by the Palestinians."[21] There are, however, limits to the criticisms of Israel that are permitted within the movement. A member of the seminary teaching staff, who identified himself as spokesperson of the seminary, lost his position after he wrote a piece in a local newspaper comparing the activities of the Israeli army within the Occupied Territories with those of Nazis.

The critical view of Israeli government policies among the Reconstructionist rabbis and seminary staff does not appear to be shared by many Reconstructionist laypeople. When the president and executive director of the Federation of Reconstructionist Congregations and Havurot sought to introduce a dovish resolution to the Federation's convention, proposing that the Palestinians be allowed to establish their own form of government in the territories occupied by Israel since 1967, its withdrawal was requested. It was argued that such a resolution would give rise to a divisive debate within the convention.[22]

We have noted that in Reconstructionist ideology it is the sense of

---

constructionist Press, 1987), See also Arthur Green, "Where We Stand: Theory and Practice of Contemporary Reconstructionism," *Reconstructionist* 56 (1) (Autumn 1990), 12–17.

21   "On the Current Conflict in Gaza and the West Bank." Resolution adopted by the Fourteenth Annual Convention of the Reconstructionist Rabbinical Association, 1988.

22   "Israel Resolution" Memo to Board of FRCH (Federation of Reconstructionist

Jewish peoplehood that is most basic to Judaism as a civilization. If Israel has become the focus of the sense of Jewish peoplehood among American Jews, it can be said, in Reconstructionist terms, to have become a religious object. The influence of Durkheim is evident in Kaplan's statement that "whatever is an object of collective concern necessarily takes on all the traits of a religion."[23] Although Kaplan did not explicitly apply this analysis to Israel, his sociologically informed philosophy justifies the position that Israel is a core element of the religion of American Jews. This position would not be affected by the recognition of Israel as a basically secular society with a predominantly secular population, but in fact few American Jews are likely to admit that a secular Israel has become their central religious focus. Liebman's conclusions in his 1970 article, based on a survey of American Jewry, are of relevance here. He wrote that, although the majority of lay American Jews agreed with the Reconstructionist position on the primacy of the Jewish people rather than its religion, they still required their Judaism to be defined in terms of religion rather than peoplehood.[24] Thus the fact of collective concern might be sufficient for some sociologists to refer to Israel as the religion of American Jews, but it would not be a sufficient criterion for most American Jews who prefer to define their religion as one resembling Protestantism or Catholicism.

Our evidence suggests that Reconstructionist Jews do not differ from other American Jews in defining their Judaism in terms of religion rather than in terms of ethnicity or peoplehood. American Jews join Reconstructionist synagogues for all kinds of reasons (one respondent told us that she joined because Reconstructionists are interested in ecology and protecting animals), but Kaplan's characterization of Judaism in terms of peoplehood does not appear to be one of them.

Congregations and Havurot), 11 February 1988. FRCH Archives, Wyncote, Penn.

23   Kaplan, *Judaism*, 216.
24   Liebman, "Reconstructionism," 95–97.

Reconstructionists and Israel: Data from the Interviews

Whether Israel is regarded as the focus of the Jewish sense of peoplehood was one of the questions asked in the interviews with twenty-five Reconstructionists. This question was preceded by asking whether respondents agreed with the statements that "Caring for Israel is a very important part of being Jewish" and "Israel is the most important spiritual homeland for all Jews." All respondents demonstrated their pro-Israelism by agreeing with the first statement (although one qualified this by saying "not necessarily"). All but one of the eleven congregational members agreed with the second statement, and six of the eight seminary students did so; the religious professionals were even less unanimous (of the three asked this question, one said yes, another was not sure, and a third hesitated and then said no). Few of the respondents, in all three categories, gave an unqualified yes when asked if Israel was the focus of the Jewish sense of peoplehood; they emphasized that there were other centers or that the world-wide Jewish community in its entirety should be considered the center.

The answers to these questions indicate the importance of Israel as a focus of collective concern and an important symbol for respondents, but as respondents answered other questions it became clear that an agreement with such statements did not imply that they believed Israel to be central to their religion. The Reconstructionist prayerbooks, like the prayerbooks of the major Jewish denominations in America, present a religious and moral vision of Israel that is consistent with the self-definition of American Jewry as a religious community.[25] The prayers make no reference to the secular and national elements of Zionism and Israel; but outside the specific context of the synagogue, American Jews think of Israel in these terms and do not, therefore, relate to Israel in religious terms. Thus when respondents were asked if Israel was important in the religion of the American Jews and in their own religion, the answers, even if positive, demonstrated that Israel was of little relevance to their religion. Those who said it was important expressed a concern with

---

25   David Ellenson, "Envisioning Israel in the Liturgies of North American Liberal Judaism," chap. 5 in this volume.

the existence of the Israeli state and people or the importance of
Israel as part of Jewish ethnic identity and did not try to relate Israel
to their religious beliefs and behaviors. Those who said Israel was
not important in their religion said they did not connect Israel with
being religious, or they pointed out that Israelis were not religious.
One student distinguished between Israel as symbol and the real
Israel, and expressed enormous disappointment with Israel for not
upholding the values of Zionism. A rabbi made a similar distinction
between the image of Israel and the political reality, and expressed
how Israel troubled her politically.

Few respondents answered with explicit religious references when
asked about the importance of the land or territory of Israel in the
religion of American Jews and in their own religion. One student
said that the land was the birthplace of the religion and of the Jewish
ancestors, and one congregant said that the origins of the religious
holidays were tied to the land. Many respondents emphasized the
importance of Jerusalem, and the students in particular emphasized
the sacredness of the city. However, there appeared to be little
conception of sacred land apart from Jerusalem and its immediate
environs, and some respondents were quite explicit in saying that
the land was not important. One congregant said that the land was
of minimal importance for her because she cared about Jews for
political reasons, not religious ones. Another said that if Israel shifted
to Egypt it would be all right with her as long as the people living
there were safe. Many answers related not to the land as such but to
the events going on within it. The absence of differentiation between
land and people tended to confirm one congregant's observation
that American Jews see the land and people as one package. A rabbi
observed that Israel's disappearance tomorrow would not have a
dramatic effect on the religion of American Jews; it would certainly
be less traumatic than the closing of synagogues.

It is clear from the answers reported so far that, however important
Israel may be in the Jewish identification of respondents, Israel has
not taken on the traits of religion in the sense that most of the
respondents understand religion. They have not adopted Kaplan's
conception of the centrality of Israel in a Judaism whose essence is
peoplehood. There were exceptions among the students whose year
in Israel had strengthened their feelings of involvement with the

Israeli culture and people. A year in Israel was an obligatory part of their program, but it was evident from the interviews and from letters sent by students in Israel and printed in the student newspaper that they felt their stay in Israel had provided them with an important "intellectual and emotional experience" and contributed to their "spiritual growth." Some students adopted Israeli names, clothing styles, and food, wrote poems or articles in Hebrew, and became actively involved in such Israeli social movements as Peace Now and Women in Black. The assumption that Israel is a cultural center of Jews and a center of Judaism justified their involvement, as non-citizens, in the country's political and social problems. A few declared that they now had a divided identity, part American and part Israeli.

Some students stated that Israel was more important to them than it was to the majority of the faculty members, and they felt that modern Israel was not given sufficient emphasis in the curriculum and activities of the college. After their return to America, students find that their stay and experiences in Israel are of little relevance to their prospective or actual occupations in the American rabbinate. The length of time they have spent in Israel and their attitudes toward Israel are not among the factors considered by congregations when appointing a rabbi.

The question now to be asked is how important Israel is, and what place it has in the "Jewish-American" or "American-Jewish" identity. We asked a number of questions that shed light on this subject. We asked respondents if they would define themselves as Zionists and, if so, what they meant by that. Four congregants said they were not Zionists because they did not believe that Israel was their homeland or that every Jew should live in Israel or that the full expression of being Jewish was living in Israel. All other respondents said that they were Zionists, and most defined their Zionism in such terms as supporting the right of Israel to exist as a Jewish homeland, as a Jewish state, as a cultural center of Jews, and as a focus of Jewish identity. Two congregants and one religious professional commented that although they conceive of themselves as Zionists, they would not be Zionists according to the meaning of one who makes or intends to make *aliyah*. Two students assumed that being a Zionist implies support for the political policies of the

Israeli government. One said that he was not sure how far he would go politically in supporting the right of Jews to the land, and the other, a convert, said that she was a Zionist because she did not agree that the Arabs should have equal rights.

Most respondents said that they talked about Israel with friends occasionally or often; all except three congregants had visited Israel, but hardly any had seriously considered settling in Israel. A few of the students and rabbis said that they had thought about settling in Israel when they were teenagers but were no longer seriously considering *aliyah* because of the absence of non-Orthodox rabbinical career opportunities in Israel, especially for women. One congregant said he was tempted to make *aliyah* each time he visited Israel, and another was thinking about retiring in Israel.

Four of the congregants but none of the students or professionals agreed with the statement: "American Jews place too much emphasis on Israel and not enough on strengthening Jewish life in the United States." One of the congregants who agreed with the statement said that she had had an unsettling experience on the day of the interview. She had gone on behalf of her mother to a Federation of Jewish Charities in Atlantic City to ask about programs for older people. She had been told that money for such programs was not available because it was being sent to Israel. She felt that the federations should give first priority to the people at home.

Further indications of differences between Jewish leadership, including rabbis, and lay congregants over the relative importance of Israel came out in the responses of rabbis. One rabbi reported on the lack of interest among her congregants in a ceremony for Israel's Independence Day. Out of a congregation of about two hundred, only ten to fifteen came to the ceremony. This contrasted with a Hanukkah ceremony to which nearly all the congregants came. When the rabbi asked her congregants why they did not come to the Independence Day ceremony, some said that they could not see what purpose the ceremony served, and others said that they did not agree with Israel's policies or that Israel did not stand up to normative standards. Another rabbi also reported that there was a low turnout for Israel's Independence Day. She said that she did not receive requests from congregants to talk about Israel, and that a program for sending children to Israel got little response. She commented that although Israel is central in the movement's beliefs, it is peripheral to the lives of the majority of congregants.

Respondents were asked to rank the following goals of the American Jewish community in order of importance: to provide financial support for Israel, to provide political support for Israel, to provide Jewish education for American Jews, to support Jewish religious activities and institutions in America, to promote civil rights and social justice in American society. All except five respondents put the provision of Jewish education for American Jews as their first priority (two respondents gave it first priority along with some other goal). No respondent put support for Israel, financial or political, as his or her first priority, and more than two-thirds put support for Jewish religious activities and institutions in America in second place, before support for Israel options. One student said that whereas in the past Israel would have had first priority, there had been a change among American Jews in recent years. Some justified their choice by noting the importance of supporting Jewish education in order to combat assimilation among American Jews. More than two-thirds put at least one of the support for Israel options before the promotion of civil rights and social justice in American society; but some qualified this by saying that their choice might be different if there was a crisis in civil rights and social justice and two congregants put this option as their first priority. Financial support for Israel tended to take precedence over political support for Israel. One respondent said that there should not be any political support for Israel in the sense of supporting the policies of the Israeli government.

Further information on the place of Israel in the identity of American Jews was sought by asking respondents to rank three loyalties in order of importance: loyalty to the United States and their fellow citizens, loyalty to Israel and its Jewish population, and loyalty to world Jewry. Only two respondents, a teacher in the seminary of Israeli origin and a congregant, put loyalty to Israel and its Jewish population unequivocally in first place. Two respondents put loyalty to Israel in first place along with another loyalty. Most respondents, however, were divided between putting loyalty to American or world Jewry in first place. The director of the Federation of Reconstructionist Congregations was convinced that most Reconstructionist members would put the American loyalty first, and a rabbi said that just about all her congregants would put the American loyalty first. In stating their loyalties, two respondents separated country and people. One said that the United States would come first but without fellow Americans, followed by Israel, world Jewry, and lastly fellow Americans. Another said Israel without its Jewish population would come first, followed by the United States and fellow Americans, the Jewish population of Israel, and lastly world Jewry.

In their answers to some of the foregoing questions, a few respondents indicated that although Israel did have a place in their Jewish identity, they felt uncomfortable with certain features, especially the political policies, of Israel. We now turn to the answers to questions that were intended to discover what respondents felt about the real Israel in relationship to their Judaism and religious values. One set of questions sought to discover the views of respondents on the religious scene in Israel in relationship to their own religious values and what they believed the religious scene should be in Israel. Another set of questions probed the views of respondents, from the perspective of their religious values, on political issues of territory and policies toward Arabs in Israel.

As proponents of a liberal form of religion, most respondents supported religious pluralism and a personalistic orientation toward the religious life. These values influenced their perceptions and evaluations of Judaism in Israel. All respondents agreed with the statement that "Orthodox, Conservative, Reform and Reconstructionist Judaism are all legitimate forms of Judaism," although one student qualified this by saying that Orthodox Judaism was the least legitimate because it did not respond to the modern world and that the Orthodox were still living in the nineteenth century. When asked if religious Jews in Israel would agree with the statement, all respondents answered no — apart from one congregant who said that he did not know. In answering this question, some respondents compared the situation in Israel unfavorably with the American situation. One student said that the image of progressive Judaism in Israel was a caricature. Another said that Israelis lacked the American premise that there was no way in which the Jewish law could be enforced.

166 STEPHEN SHAROT AND NURIT ZAIDMAN

The value of personalism was expressed in respondents' agreement with the statement that "all Jews should be free to decide which religious practices they should observe according to the personal meanings that the practices have for them." All respondents said that Jews had that freedom in the United States. Most believed that Jews also had this freedom in Israel, but some qualified their answers by saying that it is harder to practice religious freedom in Israel, or that the freedom does not extend to all areas of life. One said that Israeli Jews have the freedom but do not practice it. Similar points were made in answers to the question of whether respondents believed they could live a fuller Jewish life in Israel than in the United States. Most respondents in all three categories either said no or said that in some ways yes but in other ways no. On the one hand, it was remarked that the Israeli environment provided greater support for religious observance and that religious observances, such as the building of succot, were more visible. On the other hand, it was emphasized that there were fewer possibilities of religious choice and experimentation in Israel. The difficulties of being a progressive Jew in Israel were pointed out, and some of the students and religious professionals said that there was no possibility of a rabbinical career for them in Israel. Congregational members, including those who had not been to Israel, emphasized that the majority of Israelis were not religious. One said that the friends she had in Israel were far less observant than her friends in the United States.

Respondents differed, however, in the extent to which they applied to Israel the religious principles they supported unequivocally in the United States. The image and support of Israel as a Jewish state leads some respondents to apply a different set of standards to the two societies. All respondents said that there should be no relationship between religion and state in the United States, but the answers to the question of the relationship between religion and state in Israel were more varied. Just over half applied the same rule and said there should be no relationship between religion and state in Israel. Some pointed to the excessive power of the Orthodox in Israel. Most of the other respondents gave ambiguous replies. One said that it was impossible to avoid some relationship, particularly because of the centrality of the Jewish calendar. Another said that her head told her there should be separation but her heart felt otherwise. Others envisaged some sort of vaguely formulated relationship but emphasized that it should be different from the present situation, in which the Orthodox had too much power. One suggestion was that there should be a separation of public and private domains; food in public contexts should be kosher, but there should not be any control over marriage and conversion.

Mixed feelings were also expressed when respondents were asked what they thought about religious restrictions on public services in Israel, such as the law forbidding public transport on Shabbat. Half of the respondents objected to the restrictions and the inconvenience they cause, but the other half were either ready to accept the restrictions or felt they had positive as well as negative implications. A number said that the restrictions produced the feeling of a Shabbat, of a quieter day in which one could feel more Jewish. Some minimized the problem by stating that it was possible to drive or by noting that in the United States there was less public transport on Sunday.

Most respondents took more definite positions when it came to considering Israeli policies toward Arabs and land in the light of Jewish religious principles. Respondents were asked if they believed that Judaism contains values of social justice that are relevant to all mankind. Nearly all said yes, but the Dean of the Seminary qualified his answer by saying "Judaism as interpreted in modern times"; and a student said that one can find in Judaism what one wants to find, including ethnocentric views. Respondents were then asked if, according to their knowledge, Israeli government policy toward Arabs living in Israel was in accord with the Jewish religious values of social justice. Nearly all respondents said no, and many were critical of the Israeli governments or expressed discomfort with their actions. Some congregants excused Israel's policies by emphasizing problems of security and survival. One congregant said that the Israelis try to maintain moral and ethical values, but one cannot know the difficulties without being there. He would always support Israel no matter what it did, and whereas he would argue about Israel with other Jews, he would not condemn Israel in public. Another said that he did not want to see bad things about Israel.

The only student to express support for Israeli government policies toward Arabs was a convert, who said that the values of social justice are irrelevant with respect to those who do not play fair. According to her, justification for the nonapplication of religious principles to nonrighteous people was also supported by Buddha and Confucius. This view was quite different from the views of other students and the religious professionals. A particularly harsh version of the majority critical view was expressed by a student who said: "Arabs in Israel are second-rate citizens. There is discrimination and bigotry against Arabs. Israeli society as a whole does not operate according to the principle of social justice." Another student represented the somewhat more common moderate critical approach to Israeli policies: "The impression is that of injustice. I do not know if the government desires to be unjust or it is because of the political realities. The situation is sad, difficult and more complex than the principles of social justice. There have been sad mistakes made. I do not necessarily value the Jewish claims over the Arab or Palestinian claims." Another student who clearly felt uncomfortable with the question said: "If I was a young Palestinian woman I would be militant. There are many developments that are anti-Arab. We do not really have the right as Americans living in our luxurious world to make judgments. If my son was in the army, I would want him to defend himself. Golda Meir said that Arabs had put Jews into the situation that they have to fight in this way."

All but two students and three congregants agreed with the statement that "Israel should withdraw from most or all of the occupied territories (West Bank and Gaza) in exchange for peace." In their replies a number emphasized that Jerusalem should be excluded from any land settlement. The importance of Jerusalem was raised by respondents at a number of points in the interviews, particularly by the students who had spent a year in Israel as part of their rabbinical training. The respondents who had a conception of sacred land or place appeared to confine this to Jerusalem and its immediate environs. Nearly all respondents disagreed with the view that Israel should resist territorial concessions because the West Bank (Judea and Samaria) is sacred land for the Jews. Some said that peace is more important than sacred land, and one respondent said that the sacredness of land does not mean that one has to live there. Two congregants expressed agreement with the statement.

One of these had never been to Israel and had not heard of Gush Emunim.

Finally, an attempt was made to probe respondents' images of religious differences between American and Israeli Jews and their social contexts by asking them two questions. We asked respondents if they believed that Reconstructionism was more suited to American than to Israeli Jews or if it was equally suited. In addition, we asked if respondents believed that Reconstructionism had a special message for Jews living in Israel. Several respondents commented that Reconstructionism had emerged in response to specific conditions in America. A student said that Reconstructionism provided a way to live in a non-Jewish society and remain Jewish, and that this emphasis on living in two civilizations was not relevant to Israel. Another view was that the Reconstructionist model of living in two civilizations was also a useful model for Israelis; "Israelis should appreciate that there was truth both within and outside their tradition." One respondent said that the rationale of Reconstructionism had a lot to do with peoplehood, and this was of little relevance in Israel because they did not need to create a Jewish community. However, most respondents, including those who emphasized the American roots of Reconstructionism, believed that it was also suited to Israel. One said that Reconstructionism was "suited wonderfully for all disenchanted Jews wherever they are; for those who had lost their Jewish roots or had become disappointed with the Judaism that they had grown up in."

In reflecting on the suitability of Reconstructionism for Israel and its special message for Israeli Jews, respondents developed further their criticisms of the religious situation in Israel. Among the comments were the following:

> Many Israelis know little about what it is to be Jewish. Israel will lose its identity if it loses its relationship to Judaism. Reform Judaism in Israel is more like Reconstructionism, and Reform in Israel makes religion accessible to Israelis, as Reconstructionism did in the States.

> There is a lack of religious options in Israel, and Reconstructionism could take off there. I would never wish to raise a daughter in Israel because of the religious context. There

is little [gender] egalitarianism. There is a religious-secular divide.

The Israeli mentality does not see the legitimacy of other forms of Judaism. If it did, Reconstructionism would be just as suitable.

Reconstructionism would be very good in Israel. Many Israelis are Reconstructionist in their thinking, but they do not know it. They need to understand that they can be religious and non-Orthodox. Many Israelis do not observe anything; they lack spiritual substance.

[The Reconstructionist message for Israel is that] you can lead a rich, observant life without being Orthodox.

You can be religious without being *halachic*. You can be religious without selling your soul to the rabbinate.

Conclusions

Our sample was not meant to be representative of Reconstructionist Jews in the United States. The leadership of the movement and its rabbis and seminary students, all of whom had spent at least a year in Israel, were overrepresented, and laypeople were underrepresented. There were some indications that the importance attributed to Israel was greater among the movement's leadership and rabbis than it was among a large section of their congregations. A finding from a survey conducted by the movement reinforces this impression. The participants in the study, who represented fourteen Reconstructionist congregations in nine different states, were asked to react to two brochures published by the movement in 1991. The participants expressed their views on many of the themes discussed in the brochures, but they did not initiate discussion about Israel, which was extensively covered in the brochure. In answer to the question, "What could be eliminated from the brochure?" participants said that Israel did not require such extensive discussion.[26] Although the leaders and

26 Bonnie Lee Leavy, *Overview of Focus Group Findings*. Report presented to the Board of Governors of FRCH, 11 October 1991, containing an overview

rabbis were aware of the lower level of consciousness with respect to Israel among the majority of laypeople, they were still surprised by the lack of response to programs centered on Israel. The executive director of the Federation of Reconstructionist Congregations was disappointed when he received no response whatsoever to a letter he sent to the congregations outlining a special program in Israel with special rates in a kibbutz with a Reconstructionist approach to Judaism.

Some of our respondents expressed the view, without any prompting, that Israel had become a less important focus among American Jews and that Reconstructionists were like other American Jews in this respect. Comparisons were made between the years following the Six-Day War and recent years. It would appear that, in some cases at least, reservations about the events and policies of the real Israel had lessened the symbolic importance of Israel for American Jews. One student believed that disappointment with Israel had had a negative effect on the extent of commitment to Judaism. He said: "The confusion among some about how to relate to Israel politically has had an effect on how they relate to Judaism. Liberal Jews have been frustrated with the Israel political scene. Part of this frustration has been converted into a frustration with Judaism."

Three dimensions of the attitudes and behaviors of American Jews were distinguished in our study: its importance as a symbolic focus of the Jewish people and its concerns; its importance in the "Jewish-American" identity; and the perceptions and opinions of the religion and politics of Israeli society and state. Although the Reconstructionist ideology provided a clear rationale for regarding Israel as a symbolic focus of Judaism, most respondents appeared to think about Israel in ways that were divorced from what they regarded as their religious concerns. Reconstructionist prayerbooks, like Conservative and Reform prayerbooks, present Israel in religious terms; but the prayerbook image of Israel appears to have little influence on how American Jews perceive the "real" Israel in relation to their religion.

---

of information presented to the FRCH Public Relations Commission on 2 October. FRCH Archives, Wyncote, Penn. Reference to Israel on p. 5.

Orthodox American Jews, with the exception of certain ultra-Orthodox groups, are more likely to attribute more traditional religious meanings to Israel. However, we would expect that for the majority of Reform and Conservative as well as Reconstructionist Jews, Israel is not an important religious symbol. Israel symbolizes the survival of the Jewish people, and the Jewish people was the most focal element in Kaplan's philosophy; but Reconstructionist Jews, like most other American Jews, express themselves and act according to more conventional definitions of religion. In the context of modern discourse, in which Jewish ethnicity is differentiated from the Jewish religion and Jewishness from Judaism, Israel can be regarded principally as a symbol of Jewish ethnicity rather than as a symbol of the Jewish religion.

Israel is an important element in the ethnic identity of American Jews, but material support for Israel and identity with the Israeli Jewish population take second place to the specific concerns of American Jewry and identity with the United States. The indications are that there has been some decline in the importance of Israel among American Jews in recent years. This may be partly because the perceptions of Israel as a real place have somewhat damaged its symbolic qualities. The problem is felt most acutely by those liberal religious American Jews who take their religion seriously, such as the religious professionals and the seminary students in the Reconstructionist movement. Their liberal and dovish political views and their understanding of Judaism as a universalistic, personalistic religion of social justice lead them to take a highly critical stance toward religion in Israel and Israeli politics. We should be careful, however, not to exaggerate the effects of such criticisms on the symbolic value of Israel among American Jews. Even the most critical of our respondents continue to express an identity with and affection for Israel, and negotiations toward a peaceful settlement are likely to temper the criticisms with respect to political issues. It is, perhaps, still too early to speculate about the symbolic value for American Jews of an Israel that lives in peace with its Arab neighbors.

Israel in American Jewish Education

Walter Ackerman

I doubt that there is anyone of my generation of Americans who attended a Jewish school or was a member of a Jewish youth movement that did not see the film *A House in the Desert*.[1] A prototype of its genre, the movie tells the story of a group of *halutzim*, a mixture of handsome, confident sabras and wan-looking but determined "refugees" from the displaced persons camps in Europe, who joined together to establish a kibbutz in the Arava. Against all odds they produced their first crop and managed to secure a foothold in that "wild of sand."

It later became fashionable to make fun of these "UJA movies." Whatever their technical quality, they were offered as evidence by those who claimed that "propagandists" and other interested parties created an image of the *yishuv*, and later of the state itself, that was far removed from a less romantic reality and raised expectations beyond any possibility of realization. All that is probably true, but I have never forgotten the last frame of that movie — a fragile sliver of white bud bursting through the dry and dusty brown of desert waste.

* * *

What young people in the United States once learned about the *yishuv* in Palestine and know today about the State of Israel depends very much on the setting that is the source of their information. Those who were members of *halutzic* youth movements in the years immediately before World War II — largely the children of

---

1   *A House in the Desert (Ba'it ba-Arava)*, produced by Norman Lurie and distributed by Keren Hayesod, 1948.

immigrant parents whose adolescence knew the Depression and
Father Coughlin — learned about the kibbutz and even simulated
behaviors that were meant to be preparation for life in a collective
settlement. Members of *Hashomer Hatzair* — the most radical and
perhaps also the most disciplined and demanding of the youth
movements, and more than any other controlled by an ideology
developed in the cruel circumstances of Europe — read Marx and
learned about Borochov, tithed to their *shevet* (tribe, the smallest
organizational unit); and those who did not have to work spent their
summers — or part of them — not at camp but on *hachsharah.* The
girls did not wear lipstick or any other make-up, and the boys did not
smoke; and only folk dancing was permitted. Soccer, however, was
the most powerful symbol of the rejection of the American *Golah*
that the organization proclaimed. *Shomrim* did not play baseball,
only "Palestinian football," and then without keeping score. Two
generations of American Jewish youth, never very many but always
a significant factor among youth movements, grew up in an imagined
community.

The beginnings of Zionist education in the United States, as a
matter of fact, were in clubs and other autonomous youth groups
rather than in schools. Young Judaea, the only indigenous American
Zionist youth organization, was founded in 1909 by the Federation
of American Zionists "to popularize Jewish study, to arouse enthusiasm for learning Jewish history, Jewish literature and Hebrew, to
secure respect for Jewish tradition and observance, and to instill
loyalty for the Jewish race and devotion to Palestine as the Jewish
homeland."[2] This rather generalized stance, so unlike the ideologically driven movements of Europe, is of a piece with the character
of American Zionism and the purposes of the organization's adult
sponsors, Hadassah and the Zionist Organization of America. The
activities sponsored over the years of its existence by Young Judaea
— clubs, conferences, publications, summer camps, and programs in
Israel — have been the avenue to Jewish involvement for thousands
of youngsters.

Jewish schools, the medium that more than any other exposes

2   Alexander Dushkin, *Jewish Education in New York City* (New York: Bureau of
Jewish Education, 1918), 86.

Jewish children to Zionism and Israel, do not generally elicit the behaviors nurtured by youth movements. Learning is rarely experiential and almost always mediated by textbooks. These, no less than movies, contribute to the idealization of Jewish efforts in Palestine and then Israel. A history book for elementary schoolchildren brings its readers to Tel Aviv and a circle of "Jewish young men and women dancing and singing freely in the streets. They sang of their joy in rebuilding Eretz Yisroel, they sang of the glory of labor, of the brotherhood of Israel. Their voices were clear and unafraid. There was grace and freedom in their motion.... Ben David joined a group that was dancing the Hora. The circle opened at once to receive him. Friendly arms were entwined around his shoulders. He was one of them." "I did not dream that Jewish life could be like this."[3] Of all the symbols of the developing myth of the "miraculous achievements of our halutzim [and] the miracle of the rebirth of our people,"[4] none was more pervasive, and perhaps more powerful, than the picture of the "*matmid [yeshivah* student] who became a watchman on horseback [and] the Yeshiva student a road builder" whose

> Hands join in circle, feet begin to beat
> The circle sways, the feet and hands
> And heads and bodies sing and dance
> the Hora turns, now right, now left.

Several generations of children were taught that a new kind of Jew "built cities on desert lands, planted fields and vineyards on wasted soil, forested bare hills, irrigated dry soil and dried malaria ridden marshes."[5] There is hardly a textbook which also does not emphasize that the Arabs, invariably portrayed as backward and exploited by rich landlords among their own people, would also benefit from these heroic efforts.

The details of Zionist endeavor in Palestine are embedded in motifs particularly attractive to young people, Jewish and others. There is, first of all, the contrast between the old and the new; the charms

3   Dorothy Zeligs, *History of Jewish Life in Modern Times* (New York: Bloch, 1943), 320–321.
4   Azriel Eisenberg, *Modern Jewish Life in Literature* (New York: United Synagogue Commission on Jewish Education, 1952), 149.
5   Ibid.

of ancient Yaffo pale alongside the "new and modern buildings and wide boulevards" of Tel Aviv. Palestine is a place of young men and women, easily accessible, and not of the old people who live in the old-fashioned *shtetlach* of Europe. These young people make things happen; they do not sit around waiting for someone to help them. Most of the Jews in Palestine, it would appear, live in the country, away from crowded and dirty cities. And in the new country developing in the old homeland everyone is treated fairly and justly without any of the discrimination and inequality found by Jews almost everywhere. Palestine thus presented is worthy of our support and allegiance because it embodies the principles of liberal American progressivism. All this, however, does not produce even the slightest suggestion that the young readers of these texts might themselves someday want to live in this wonderful place.

The hyperbole was not altogether unfamiliar. The text books of American history that these children used in their public schools portrayed a country that was perfect, "the greatest nation in the world and the embodiment of democracy, freedom and technological progress."[6] Few schools of that time taught pupils to question or led their charges along the road to discovery; there seemed "no point in comparing the visions [of the textbooks] with reality, since they were the public truth and were thus quite irrelevant to what existed and to what anyone privately believed."[7] Textbooks and other instructional materials, it should be borne in mind, are designed by adults with a particular purpose in mind. They present children with material their elders think they ought to know; in a very real sense they are handbooks of the ideas one generation values sufficiently to consider worthy of transmission to another.

Zionism and its practical expression in Palestine, and later in the State of Israel, has been one of the formative factors in the development of modern American Jewish education.[8] Nowhere was this more true than in the case of the *Talmud Torah*, the much maligned Hebrew school. The national Hebrew afternoon school,

6   Frances Fitzgerald, *America Revised* (New York: Random House, 1980), 10.
7   Ibid.
8   Barry Chazan, "Israel in American Jewish Schools Revisited," *Jewish Education* 47 (2) (Summer 1979): 7–8.

and to some degree the Conservative congregational school and some day schools, drew its inspiration from Ahad Ha'am's conviction that the Hebrew language and its literature, more than anything else, was the medium that would tie children with bonds of love and reverence to their people and its land and "awaken in them the desire to dedicate themselves to the service of their people and to contribute to the national rebirth."[9] The justification of Jewish education in the United States drawn from the democratic convention of cultural pluralism, stressed that "even the possibility of maintaining a vital ethnic culture in the Diaspora is dependent on the existence of a cultural center to serve as a source of spiritual replenishment and to prevent the ethnic spirit from becoming the petrified relic of an ancient grandeur."[10] The best teachers in these schools made their pupils feel that the mastery of Hebrew was as important to the national rebirth as reclaiming a dunam of land in the homeland.

Theodore White, a graduate of such an institution, has wonderfully captured the atmosphere and spirit of those schools dedicated to Hebrew and the national renaissance of which it was a symbol.

> The Beth-El Hebrew School captured me.... Most of our teachers were then newly arrived young immigrant scholars, who had come from post World War I Europe to seek a secular education in Boston's universities; they taught Hebrew in the evenings to earn their living. They despised Yiddish, a language I knew from home, for to despise Yiddish was their form of snobbery; and as a matter of principle they would speak no English in class, for their cardinal political principle was Zionism. They were about to revive the Hebrew language and make it a living tongue; after a little pampering with English in the first and second year, as we learned the ancient alphabet and pronunciation, we were into the Bible in Hebrew — it was

9   Ahad Haam, "Emet Me-Eretz Yisrael" *Kol Kitvei Ahad Haam*, (Tel Aviv: Dvir, 1977), 33.

10   Isaac Berkson, *Theories of Americanization* (New York: Columbia University Press, 1920), 109.

explained to us in Hebrew, pounded into us in Hebrew, and we were forced to explain it to one another in Hebrew.[11]

The spirit of Hebraism and the concomitant attachment to Israel was one of the foundations of the Hebrew-speaking camps that once flourished in the United States.[12] The first such camp, Achvah, was established in 1927, to be followed by Massad (1941), Yavneh (1944), and the Ramah network (1947). Only Yavneh and the Ramah camps are in existence today; they no longer are Hebrew-speaking. While each of the camps had different purposes and different educational styles, they all had certain "Zionist" characteristics in common. Formal and informal educational activities — classes, discussion groups, special events, and the like — were often based on questions and issues related to Israel; the Maccabiah was the major athletic event of the season, the alternative to "color war"; bunks carried Israeli place names, as did paths and lanes; only Hebrew songs, "imported" from Israel, were sung in community song sessions; the flag of the state flew beneath the Stars and Stripes; and campers were given the opportunity to work in the vegetable garden, invariably directed by a *shaliach*. There can be no doubt that Israel, in all its varied possibilities, was a significant element in shaping the atmosphere and spirit of these camps.

Eretz Israel in these camps, like in the Zionist youth groups and their camps, was a country of the mind. These islands of separation, possible only in closed settings, created moments of transcendence that connected young people to something larger than themselves, particularly in the days immediately following World War II and during the events leading to the establishment of the state. In that time the facts of life in the real country were almost irrelevant.

This climate was an expression of the claim that "Palestine [should] become the dynamic, integrating force of our primary curriculum. It is Palestine, or Palestinianism that gives meaning to our ceremonial observances, to our worship and prayers, to

11   Theodore White, *In Search of History* (New York: Harper & Row, 1978), 21–22.
12   Walter Ackerman, "A World Apart: Hebrew Teachers College and Hebrew Speaking Camps," in *Hebrew in America,* ed. Alan Mintz (Detroit: Wayne State University Press, 1993), 105–128.

our language and literature, as well as to much of our present environment. Why then not make the introduction of Palestine the first step in the process of integrating the child into Jewish life?"[13]

Even those educators who sensed a need for careful consideration of the place of Palestine in American Jewish schools were not altogether free of an enthusiasm that strained the reserve of their caution, "Before my very eyes Palestine is again becoming the central sanctuary of the Jewish people, the new *Beth Hamikdash*, in which are preserved and developed those things most sacred to us: our literature, classic and modern, religious and secular; our Hebrew language; our perennial festivals and customs; our way of life. We must put our best thought to analyze a true relation to Palestine and to devise methods for teaching it effectively, with sanity and with truth."[14] Almost two decades later this same writer, one of America's foremost Jewish educators, hailed the establishment of the Jewish state because "the modern Zionist saga is a demonstration of a miracle.... All the marvels in the making of the new Jewish state will enable us to teach Jewish history, Bible and poetry with greater significance for us moderns." The existence of the state will be a source of "new events, new heroes, new stories, poems, songs, dances.... They will have in them the quality of earthiness and fullness of living in the land of the Bible."[15]

The contents of textbooks and the pronouncements of administrators several steps removed from schools do not always provide an accurate picture of what actually goes on in classrooms. A study published in 1959, the first of its kind, disclosed that

> out of over a thousand teacher reports in the sample communities, only 48 teachers reported teaching Israel as a subject of study.... Some teachers report specifically using storybooks

13   William Chomsky, "The Curriculum for the New Jewish Weekday School," *Jewish Education* 5 (1) (Jan. 1933): 22–26.
14   Alexander Dushkin, "Sanity in the Teaching of Palestine," *Jewish Education* 2 (2), (June 1930): 65–67.
15   Ibid.

and texts, JNF and similar materials; but few make this live and significant subject a focal point in teaching.[16]

Over the years a significant change has taken place; the most recent study, the third of its kind, reports that in the early 1980s 98 percent of the responding schools "included Israel/Zionism in some form or another as part of the curriculum."[17] Formal classroom instruction about Israel is reinforced by iconography — posters, art objects, the Israeli flag; and other decorative items related to Israel line the walls of corridors and classrooms. The overwhelming majority of schools today observe Yom Ha'atzmaut in one way or another. Most important of all, an increasing number of teenagers from Jewish schools participate in programs in Israel for periods that range in time from a few weeks to an entire school year. In some communities youngsters are enrolled in Israel Experience Saving Plans, concurrent with their entrance to the first grade. Participation in an Israel program is more and more becoming an integral aspect of the Jewish educational experience. The investment of time, effort, and money in guaranteeing a stay in Israel for as many youngsters as possible rests on the assumption that the experience contributes to Jewish identity and identification with the Jewish people in a way that cannot be matched by the school and other settings in the Diaspora. Surprisingly, or perhaps not, there is little evidence available from research which either supports or questions the assumption.

A new generation of textbooks on Israel, published by the educational arms of synagogal and other religious organizations and by commercial firms, exposes its readers to a somewhat more realistic picture of Israel, its history and growth. The new books are like their predecessors in conforming to current techniques in children's literature and regnant conceptions of childhood and children's abilities and interests. They are clearly influenced by the style of American social studies textbooks spawned by the conflicts that rocked the United States during the decade of the 1960s. They

16 Alexander Dushkin and Uriah Engelman, *Jewish Education in the United States* (New York: American Association for Jewish Education, 1959), 194.
17 George Pollack, "Israel in American Jewish Schools in the 1980's," *Jewish Education* 52(4) (Winter 1984–1985), 12–14.

are more attractive in design than their forerunners and more elaborately illustrated. Some of them surround the running text with a variety of explanatory material, much of it drawn from original sources. The more recent publications also reflect an understanding of children's intellective capacities drawn from the work of Piaget and his American interpreters. In one respect, however, the new books are just the same as the old: they too are "selling" a product.

The insistent "promotion" of Israel, which characterizes all the books, may stem from the realization that today's pupils are already several generations removed from the immigrant experience and the sequence of proximate events that led to the establishment of the state. Jewish youngsters in America today do not know a world without Israel and are rooted in the country of their birth in a way unprecedented in the Diaspora. The erosion of traditional attachments to Eretz Israel coupled with a reality somewhat removed from the utopian commonwealth envisioned in the ideology of national rebirth may explain the strained quality of the justifications for learning about Israel. The new state is interesting and important because "the Jewish people has special qualities and so does the Jewish state. Our problems are like no other people's problems. Neither are the solutions we are working out for them. We have ideals of our own in a country of our own."[18]

> Israel's story is full of adventure...there are many similarities between America and Israel's history.... Both required pioneering under great hardship, a sharp break with the past, an open mind toward the future. Israel's founders in many ways repeated the struggles of America's pilgrims, colonial settlers, western pioneers.... [Israel] is a model, a pilot for other undeveloped lands trying to become modern and independent.[19]

[It is] a country which has been through so many wars and terrorist

---

18 Helen Fine, *Behold the Land* (New York: Union of American Hebrew Congregations, 1977).
19 Harry Essrig and Abraham Segal, *Israel Today* (New York: Union of American Hebrew Congregations, 1977), 4–5.

attacks...has built so dramatically and achieved so much...has ob-
sorbed so many poor and downtrodden people and given so many
shamed outcasts a new sense of dignity."[20]

Even though noted earlier in connection with the older texts, the
imagery of the excerpts cited above warrants additional comment.
It is replete with themes central to the creed of American liberalism:
humanitarianism and social justice, modernism, progress, support
for the underdog, uniqueness, and example. The resort to a moral
fervor drawn from the vocabulary of the American ethos suggests a
locus of legitimacy that conditions the terms of interest, identification, and support. Israel is worthy of our loyalties as much for its
affinity with the values of American idealism as for its place in the
Jewish heritage. The appeal to Americanism in our texts is of a piece
with the posture of American Zionism, which even as it celebrates
the pluralism that protects the promise of Jewish life in the United
States feels constrained to stress the compatibility between Jewish
nationalism and American virtue.

As might be expected, the new books are like earlier volumes
in the extensive treatment of the *halutzim*. This time around the
approach is somewhat less hagiographic. One of the books, Amos
Elon's *Understanding Israel*, in many senses the most interesting
of them all, calls the students' attention to some important but
often neglected aspects of life in the early days of the modern
yishuv: "Totally committed to politics, the leaders often displayed
an amazing lack of personal sentimentality. Ben-Gurion met and
married a young nurse in New York...only to abandon her almost
penniless and in the sixth month of her pregnancy in order to
volunteer for the Jewish legion." The people of the Third Aliyah
were

> passionately anti-authoritarian...[but] were sometimes so in-
> tolerant of minority views that people holding even slightly
> different opinions often found it impossible to live in the same
> settlement...the dreamers of Bittania were, by any measure,
> fanatics; some of their practices bordered on the bizarre...they

20   Amos Elon, *Understanding Israel* (New York: Berman House, 1976), 93, 95,
107.

viewed their leaders as a combination guru and father confessor.

An imaginative insight led this same author to compare the *halutzim* of the Second Aliyah to "the hippies who make their appearance more that half a century later in the industrial societies of the West." They both

> came from middle class backgrounds and deliberately left established society in pursuit of a new life based on a seemingly impossible dream...[they] sought a community in which their own identities could be redefined and where social and personal relationships would be based on love.

Another analogy cites the similarities between the members of the mythic Labor Brigade and American cowboys: "Both groups broke away from established centers of civilization. Both had a desire for adventure, a willingness to endure hardships and danger, a need to explore unchartered territory, and the hope of taming a wilderness. Both cowboys and Chalutzim became folk heroes of their respective cultures." Sensing perhaps that the comparison might be somewhat overdrawn, Elon quickly adds a caveat:

> But for all their similarities, there were crucial differences. The American pioneers were essentially loners, their basic drive was to cut loose from all organized society.... The Chalutzim on the other hand were interested in new forms of community life, forms that would express their new principles..., [they] were the nucleus of a new culture.

The didactic technique of this particular book is interesting because of the demands it makes on students. Each chapter is followed by an exercise, *Issues and Values*, which asks the reader to consider the implications of various matters. Some of the nettlesome questions raised by the treatment of the *halutzim* are considered under the heading "Individual and Community." The thrust of the questions matches the portrayal of the *halutz* as, among other things, a rebel against the established order. Readers are asked to define "doing your own thing" and whether "personal fulfillment [is] strictly a private affair." This query is followed by

If you had to define the Jewish "establishment" of today, who or what do you think it is? Do you feel that you are a rebel against the Jewish establishment in any way? Do you think you are leading basically the same kind of life as your parents or do you try to make space for changes?[21]

For all the good intentions of the author, the personalization of the issue, sensible from a pedagogic point of view, cannot mask the absence of a conceptual framework, which alone transforms rebellion from an act of individual idiosyncrasy to a statement of social significance. The student is nowhere led to the intellectual ground in which the values of *halutziut* were rooted.

The texts to which we have referred support the view which holds that schools rarely deny or contradict the norms or values of the society that sponsors them. Students of American Jewry are in agreement that the establishment of the State of Israel was a watershed in the history of the American Jewish community, as it was for Jews everywhere. It was "a wondrous event, a kind of recompense for ages of persecution"[22] which provided "great self-confidence, self-reliance, courage...viability of spirit [and] shored up grace for an entire people."[23] There is also general agreement among scholars that the way in which American Zionists perceived and understood the idea of a Jewish state differed substantially from the conception of nationalism that guided the European founders of the movement. The American version of Zionism reflects the deep attachment of Jews to their country; it speaks in a vocabulary and uses an imagery which is rooted in American ideals and values. A deep belief in the promise of America has led Jews in the United States to view Zionism and Israel as a philanthropic effort in behalf of their less fortunate brethren in other parts of the world rather than as an instance of personal and national redemption.[24]

The texts and other materials that were examined, all produced in the United States, are of a similar posture. In one way or another the

21   Ibid., 93, 95, 107.
22   Marshall Sklare, *American Jews* (New York: Random House, 1971), 215.
23   Naomi Cohen, *American Jews and the Zionist Idea* (New York: Ktav Publishing, 1975), 12,
24   Ibid., 147

message is that "American Jews do not believe we are in exile — the United States is our safe and happy home."[25] The youngster who has learned his lessons well will acquire a great deal of information about Israel, no matter the text. The very detail of description, because it rests on the assumption that Israel is really a place for other Jews, obscures the essential meaning of Jewish sovereignty and does little to satisfy the reader's need to know how the existence of a Jewish state affects his/her life in Boston, New York, or Los Angeles. What indeed can be the importance of a place of which our elders can say:

> Under fair, friendly treatment we were naturally not as eager to go back to Eretz Yisroel as we were under cruelty and persecution. In the modern world Jews became rich, powerful, important... most of us, in a democracy, consider our homes and communities permanent. We like it where we are and do not tend to emigrate."[26]

Empirical data drawn from a study conducted in 1974,[27] a replication of a similar study conducted six years earlier after the Six-Day War,[28] corroborates the contention that Israel as taught in American Jewish schools does not confront the student with existential questions. Inquiries as to the goals and purposes of teaching Israel elicited the following responses:

25 Essrig and Segal, *Israel Today*, 349.
26 Elias Charry and Abraham Segal, *The Eternal People: The Story of Judaism and Jewish Thought through the Ages* (New York: United Synagogue Commission on Jewish Education, 1967).
27 Chazan, "Israel in American Jewish Schools."
28 Alvin Schiff, "Israel in American Jewish Schools," *Jewish Education* 38(4) (October 1968): 6–24.

Goal	Total %	Schools		
		Orthodox	Conserv.	Reform
To create positive attitudes towards Israel	47	41	49	46
To tie us to the Jewish people	43	33	39	53
To teach us about our history and heritage	37	35	34	40
To teach us about the contemporary state and current events	13	18	32	28
To teach us about Israel as a religious Holy Land	7	37	16	7
To make us better Jews	9	12	18	22
To encourage *aliya*	3	12	9	5.4

As we can see, the major goals of teaching about Israel were the creation of positive attitudes, the strengthening of ties with the Jewish people, and the enrichment of the students' knowledge of Jewish history and of the heritage of the Jewish people. The author's conclusions are important to our theme: "All three goals are low-level and ambiguous... they reflect no ideological principles beyond the assumption that Israel is important, nor do they delineate any clear sense of [the] meaning of Israel for Jewish life. The two...positions which do reflect a hint of some explicit ideological perspective — *aliyah* and religion are low on the list."[29]

This absence of an ideology of commitment is very often a source of tension between American Jewish educators and the plethora of Israeli agencies active in the United States. *Shelihim* to youth movements, teachers in schools, counselors in summer camps, lecturers who travel the country, and scholars in residence dot the

29   Chazan, "Israel in American Jewish Schools," 7–8.

continent and guarantee an Israeli presence in every imaginable educational setting. An unending stream of books, pamphlets, brochures, posters, videos, tapes, Hebrew courses, and the like place Israeli-centered educational materials within easy reach of any interested party. In some places, particularly smaller communities, Israel-based activity is the sole guarantor of Jewish life. Its ultimate goal everywhere, no matter how veiled, is *aliyah*.

It is difficult to know exactly how all the efforts described have affected the intended audience. We know that the overwhelming majority of the Jewish children in the United States who are exposed to Jewish schooling — at any given moment approximately 40–45 percent of all the Jewish children of school age — attend part-time Jewish schools.[30] We also know that they learn very little in those afternoon and one-day-a-week schools. Recent efforts to increase exponentially the number of youngsters who experience Israel firsthand through any one of a bewildering array of travel and study programs attest to a lack of confidence in the effectiveness of formal schooling and an increased commitment to the idea that Israel is central to the identity of Jews growing up in America.[31]

Children, however, encounter Israel in ways beyond the control of textbook writers, designers of curricula, and planners of

30 *Jewish Supplementary Schooling: An Educational System in Need of Change* (New York: Bureau of Jewish Education, 1988).

31 The following is an example of this approach: "Despite these differences, in my view, Israel offers the greatest potential for inspiring the younger generation of American Jews. This cannot be accomplished if Israel is merely an abstraction to be contemplated from afar. It requires a program of long-term visits and full exposure to Israeli cultural and intellectual achievements. For our youth, the Jewish state can be a place to return to our roots, a source of pride of accomplishment and a demonstration of a glorious commitment to our 2000-year history, our heritage and our religion. The enormous progress achieved by Israel in building a country out of the desert in just 45 years, and doing it in the face of Arab wars and threats which required the allocation of so much of its resources to defence must be a source of great pride. Certainly, Israel's willingness to welcome endangered Jews from all over the world at great sacrifice to its own people is inspirational. And Israel's scientific contributions and educational accomplishments which increasingly are being recognized elsewhere in the world must make us all feel good to be Jews." Robert Lifton, Occasional Letter 36, *American Jewish Congress*, March 1993. Lifton is president of the American Jewish Congress.

summer programs. An important example is provided by *yordim*, who increasingly staff classrooms and administrative positions in schools and other educational agencies. As early as 1959, one-third of the teachers placed by the placement committee of the United Synagogue Commission on Jewish Education, the educational arm of the Conservative movement, were Israelis in the country for personal reasons.[32] Comparable statistics were soon reported by similar agencies in other movements. Today it is doubtful that Jewish education in the United States could function without Israelis. They are in many ways the counterparts of the Eastern European immigrant Hebrew schoolteachers of several generations ago. These teachers and principals also create an image of Israel. They, like all other people, should be free to choose where they want to live. The presence of *yordim* in a school, symbolically different from Israelis who are official representatives of the state, must, however, certainly mitigate the impact of teaching attachment to a country that they themselves have rejected.

Recent events create a quandary of a different kind. What children learned about Israel in schools and other places hardly prepared them for the sights and sounds to which they were exposed during the war in Lebanon and later the Intifada. Questions of politics and the objectivity of media coverage aside, much of what they saw (and still see) on television often seems to violate American notions of fair play and the ideals of prophetic justice that they have been taught are hallmarks of Israel's social ethic. Loyalties, if at all existing, are strained.[33]

A symposium organized after the beginning of the Intifada by

---

32   Hyman Chanover, "Israelis Teaching in American Jewish Schools," in *The Education of American Jewish Teachers,* ed. O. Janowsky (Boston: Beacon Press, 1967), 231.

33   "There are areas of Israeli life that are hard for American Jewish youth to admire. One of these, of course, is the control in the territories of a rebellious Palestinian population accompanied by continued flare-ups of violence and counter-violence and the concomitant breach of civil rights, even if required for security. Another area is the lack of broad-based acceptance of American values of pluralism and tolerance. This is reflected in the disproportionate power of the ultra-Orthodox parties because of the nature of the Israeli political structure and the discrimination against conservative and reform elements. Moreover, one must recognize that there are significant differences in Israeli mores derived

the editor of *Jewish Education*, the major journal in the field, asked educators "What should be the role of the Jewish school in transmitting knowledge and perceptions about Israel to Jewish students and their families?" The responses are quite predictable: make a trip to Israel an integral part of every child's educational career in order to learn Israel's problems firsthand; help students understand the complexities of the current situation; design courses that provide a more realistic picture of life in Israel. The characteristic common to all these suggestions, and others not mentioned, is the belief in the power of explication and the reliance on *telling*. Even though many of the proposals are conceptually alike, two assumptions significantly different in their implications are apparent: one views Israel instrumentally, as a means of enhancing Jewish identity; the other believes that Israel can be significant only in the context of some broad sense of Jewishness and Judaism. Neither, however, suggest that Jewish schools in the United States might reexamine the purpose of teaching about Israel and the meaning of a young person's relationship to the country.

The study of Israel in Jewish schools and other educational settings in the United States may be likened to a trip abroad. The sociological study of tourism teaches that trips to foreign countries or visits to historical sites may be thought of as voyages of self-discovery; we turn to other cultures, places, and times to affirm our own identity and authenticity. This idea is prominent in much of the material that reaches pupils — they often suggest that to grow up in America without a knowledge of Israel and some acquaintance with life there is to be somewhat less than complete as a person and lacking in authenticity. As with a trip to a foreign country, no one suggests moving there.

The attention paid Israel in American Jewish education is an exercise in "symbolic ethnicity."[34] The stated goals of instruction and other forms of experience — "positive attitudes" and some sense

---

from its peoples' backgrounds as compared to the Anglo-Saxon mores which influence American Jewish youth." Lifton, *Occasional Letter*.

34   Herbert Gans, "Symbolic Ethnicity: The Future of Ethnic Groups and Cultures in America," *Ethnic and Racial Studies* 2(1) (January 1979): 1–20.

of identification with the country — even when achieved require very little in the way of behavior. They permit a sense of affiliation and attachment without in any way interfering with life in America's mainstream. How long such a form of ethnic identity can persist is a moot question.

Part III

Fund Raising
and Jewish Commitment

American Experts in the Design of Zionist Society: The Reports of Elwood Mead and Robert Nathan

S. Ilan Troen

European colonization has been characterized since its beginnings by a conscious effort on the part of the mother country to control the course of colonial development. Whether through governmental policies or those of companies established by government patent, European states were actively engaged in the social, physical, and economic design of their colonies. This effort at control was also true of Zionist settlement even though there was no "mother country" in the conventional sense. From the end of the nineteenth century, both Zionists and sympathetic non-Jews from throughout Europe formulated designs for Zionist colonization. After World War, I, Americans became increasingly involved in this process.[1] Although Europeans and Americans shared a fund of social ideas that were common to Western culture, there were important distinctions that can be attributed to discrete national characteristics. The advice given by French, German, or American experts bore the imprint of distinctive national experiences.

This paper will suggest how the ideas put forward by American experts reflected an attempt to export a quintessential American ethos of capitalism, efficiency, and individualism into the Zionist

---

1   The best study of the pre-World War I period is Derek Penslar, *Zionism and Technocracy: The Engineering of Jewish Settlement in Palestine, 1870–1918* (Bloomington: Indiana University Press, 1991). For a discussion of the phenomenon of cultural transfer and control in the context of European colonization, see Benedict Anderson, *Imagined Communities: Reflections on the Origin and Spread of Nationalism*, rev. 2nd ed. (London: Verso Press, 1991). For a recent application of Anderson's ideas to Israeli society, see S. Ilan Troen, "The Discovery of America in the Israeli University: Historical, Cultural and Methodological Perspectives," *Journal of American History*, June 1994.

enterprise. The phenomenon is illustrated by examining the work
of two American experts, Elwood Mead and Robert Nathan, on a
continuing problem that required different solutions at two different
periods — the 1920s and 1940s. Both were concerned with how to
develop Zionist society on a basis sufficiently sound to contribute to
the rapid and sustained development of the country.[2] In the 1920s,
Mead operated in a framework that envisioned Palestine largely in
pastoral terms. In the 1940s, Nathan worked in a political context
that urgently required enlarging the *yishuv* into a technologically
advanced urban/industrial society with a flourishing if secondary
agricultural sector. Both Mead and Nathan rooted their reports in
the understanding that the *yishuv* must be organized on the basis
of a capitalistic economy and that Jews, in the *yishuv* and in the
Diaspora, would have to learn that modern societies ought to be
created and supported by capitalist means. This contention was not
merely based on abstract economic theory. It was anchored in a
moral vision that suggested changes not only in the organization
of the *yishuv* but in how American Jews relate to it. In both cases,
their views were clearly informed by interpretations of the American
national experience.

I. Designing Zionist Rural Society: The 1920s

Background
Toward the end of World War I, the Zionist movement undertook
to transform the underdeveloped region of Palestine into the Jewish
National Homeland. In the light of past difficulties it was clear that
such an effort required careful planning. Monetary resources were
few, and the task was immense. Moreover, many of the achievements
of the previous decades had been lost due to the dislocations caused
by war. Nevertheless, the Balfour Declaration and the prospect of
the British replacing the Ottomans generated great expectations.
Since the beginning of the First Aliyah and the outbreak of World

2   S. Ilan Troen, "Calculating the 'Economic Absorptive Capacity' of Palestine:
     A Study of the Political Uses of Scientific Research," *Contemporary Jewry* 10
     (2) (1989):19–38.

War I, the Jewish population in Palestine had approximately doubled, reaching about 65,000, about 9,500 of them in thirty new *moshavot*.[3] The moment seemed propitious for finally realizing the dream of massive colonization, particularly the settling of masses of Jews on the land. In the estimate of two young Zionist leaders, David Ben-Gurion and Yitzhak Ben-Zvi, who in 1918 published an extensive guide for Jewish colonization, 10 million Jews could be placed in historic Eretz Israel, or the Palestine on both sides of the Jordan River. In their calculations, Palestine was "a country without a people," and the land could be redeemed and populated by industrious Jews.[4]

With the fighting over, the international Zionist organization moved to realize such ambitions. At Zionist headquarters in London, officials began systematically to seek the best advice they could find, and by the spring of 1919 the files in London were replete with discussions and memoranda on establishing proper planning procedures. Seven areas were identified as requiring the advice of experts: (1) irrigation — to contend with the desert that covered much of the country; (2) agriculture — to discover the most suitable crops for Palestine and the most efficient methods to cultivate them; (3) electricity — particularly hydroelectric power, since they believed that the Jordan might produce energy; (4) law — to formulate a legal code and a structure of government that could aid development; (5) sanitation and medicine — to treat diseases that were rampant in this underdeveloped region; (6) physical development — especially the civil engineering that was necessary for designing roads and other elements of the country's infrastructure; and (7) architecture or planning — to design communities that would be aesthetic and efficient. The greatest number of potential recruits were from Britain and America.[5]

---

3   The data derive from Yossi Ben-Artzi, *Hamoshava Ha-Ivrit benof Eretz Israel, 1882–1914* (The Hebrew *moshava* in the landscape of Eretz-Israel, 1882–1914) (Jerusalem: Yad Ben-Zvi, 1988), 46–7, Table 1.

4   David Ben-Gurion, and Itzhak Ben-Zvi, *Eretz Israel in the Past and in the Present* (in Hebrew), trans. from Yiddish by D. Niv (Jerusalem: Yad Ben-Zvi, 1979), 227. The book was first published in Yiddish in New York in 1918 by the Poalei Zion Palestine Committee.

5   Y. Wilkansky to J. Simon, 9 July 1919, and Memorandum on the Sending

The United States appeared to be an excellent source of expertise, particularly in areas related to agriculture. Unlike Europe, Palestine required solutions to the problems of cultivation in the kinds of arid or semi-arid conditions found in many parts of the American West. American agricultural experts and engineers familiar with irrigation and the building of water projects had developed new technologies to make America's deserts bloom. A corps of experts with a rich experience in transforming large sections of the West, particularly southern California, into fabulously successful oases has also made their careers in reclaiming deserts, from China to the Middle East. With this in mind, American Zionist leaders like Louis Brandeis urged Weizmann to invite leading American experts to Palestine.

In February 1920, for example, Brandeis suggested to Weizmann that H. T. Cory, a recognized expert in irrigation and water power be sent to Palestine. Brandeis wrote that Cory was "one of the most eminent civil and hydraulic engineers in the United States; and...his present work in Egypt will place him among the foremost of his profession in the world." In addition to working in the Aswan region along the Nile, he had worked on controlling the Colorado River and in bringing irrigation to the Imperial valley in southern California.

Cory was more than willing to go. Like other gentiles well disposed to the Zionist effort, he employed friends to present himself to prominent Zionist leaders in order to participate in what he and other planners of his generation perceived as one of the great, historic planning missions of his time. Zionist leaders recognized that there was an advantage in inviting non-Jewish experts like Cory. A Zionist sponsor wrote that in addition to good technical advice,

> upon his return to the United States you will find him [Cory] ready to cooperate with you in arousing and extending the interest in the Zionist movement — speaking not as a Jew, but as a great engineer who has studied the problems of Palestine in precisely the same spirit that he is now studying the problems of

---

of Experts to Palestine by Mr. L. Robison, London, Central Zionist Archives (CZA), File 8002, Z4/1741.

the Nile. Might he not be very influential in augmenting popular interest and support for the cause which strongly appeals alike to his mind and his heart?[6]

Cory's invitation was but a forerunner of those extended to experts — Jews and non-Jews — who during the Mandate carried out research on Palestine. Among the more widely circulated studies were those produced by two gentiles: Elwood Mead, an agricultural specialist, and Walter Clay Lowdermilk, an irrigation expert. Both provided estimates on the number of people who could be supported by the land, suggestions as to the kinds of technologies that ought to be employed, and proposals for the form of social and political organization best suited to implementing these technologies. Mead argued for the transfer of the American experience in homesteading. Lowdermilk pressed for a Palestinian equivalent of the TVA — a Jordan Valley Authority. Such studies are important not only for what they indicate about Palestine's problems and prospects but for what they reflect of their authors' experiences and on American society. American experts were exporting not merely socially neutral technologies but the social and economic experience of America's development of its own frontiers. I shall concentrate here on perhaps the most far-ranging American model put forward as an alternative to the Labor Zionist conception of colonization — the report of Elwood Mead and his associates.

Report of the Experts

The *Report of the Experts* was officially a joint British and American effort initiated by Chaim Weizmann, president of the World Zionist Organization(WZO), and Mark Schwartz, director of the Palestine Department of the Zionist Organization of America, who proposed the creation of joint Anglo-American study dealing with changes in agricultural colonization since 1923. The significance of 1923 stemmed from reservations regarding the proliferation of the kibbutz as the chosen instrument of Zionist colonization during the mid-1920s. As a consequence, the WZO created an Anglo-American

6   William E. Smythe to Louis D. Brandeis, 28 February 1920, Washington, D.C., Department of the Interior, CZA, File 8002. See, too, Jacob De Haas to Zionist Organization, London; 3 March 1920, New York, CZA, File 8002.

commission of professionals, most of whom were American.[7] Dr. Elwood Mead, a former professor at the University of California and then Commissioner of Reclamation in the Department of the Interior in Washington, was the commission's chairman and leading figure. He had previously conducted research on Palestine in 1923 at the behest of the Zionist Organization and, as prefigured in the discussion concerning Cory, his positive findings on the potential of the *yishuv* were hailed before American audiences as the judgment of "the best living authority on agricultural colonization."[8]

Most of the 1928 report is appropriately technical. It is concerned with the identification of good soils, an assessment of water resources, the evaluation of suitable crops, and suggestions for the kinds of modern technologies required to make farming not only possible but profitable. The report is only tangentially political with regard to Arab-Jewish tensions. The authors address the economic implications of a situation where many landholders are Arabs opposed to Jewish settlement. They observe that there are numerous difficulties in acquiring land and that when available its price is exaggerated relative to productive value. Written prior to the disturbances of 1929 and the consequent White Papers, the authors are hopeful for relations sufficiently amicable to permit Jewish agriculture to expand.

7   Elwood Mead et al., *Report of the Experts Submitted to the Joint Palestine Survey Commission*, Boston, October 1928, 13–15. In addition to Mead, the commission members were J. G. Lipman, director of the Agricultural Experiment Station of the New Jersey College of Agriculture, A. T. Strayhorn, soil technologist with the U.S. Department of Agriculture, Frank Adams, an irrigation specialist at the University of California, Knowles Ryerson, an American serving in the Agricultural Experiment Station in Haiti, and C. Q. Henriques, irrigation engineer of the Zionist Organization in Palestine.

8   In an address to the American Palestine Conference in New York on 17 February 1924 by Arthur Ruppin, who was in charge of planning in Palestine for the World Zionist Organization, Ruppin observed: "Elwood Mead, Professor at the University of California, who is regarded as the best living authority on agricultural colonization has, at the request of the Zionist Organization, inspected the Jewish agricultural settlements in Palestine, a few months ago. Prof. Mead compared Palestine with California." A. Ruppin, "The Economic Development of Palestine," *Zionist Review*, 7 (May 1924): 9–10.

The remainder of the report is concerned with the cultural, political, and economic problems of transforming European Jews into farmers. Viewing the challenge of Zionist settlement in Palestine through the prism of the experience of farming elsewhere, although particularly in the United States, Mead and his collaborators argued that Jewish colonists, like farmers everywhere, had to become secure and independent owners of their lands. In addition to vocational preparation and technical assistance, an essential precondition was removing financial obstacles that hindered private ownership. In a brief review of assistance programs, from Germany to Australia, they observed that the common strategy had been to find a mechanism that would enable individuals to settle and remain on their own land. This of course is what had occurred in the United States. American agriculture was based on the ideal of independent homesteaders who had title to their own farms. The American experts believed that this had to be replicated by Jews in Palestine if they expected to establish a viable homeland.

The commission's proposals for Palestine derived from their perception of what afflicted American agriculture. They knew that from the Greenbackers of the 1870s to the Populists of the 1890s to the agricultural crisis of the 1920s, farmers had sought technical, political, and economic assistance to enable them to remain on the land. It had been a losing struggle. The 1920 census officially announced that the United States was an urban nation and confirmed the diminishing proportions of Americans living on the land. They believed that technical expertise, legislation, and economic assistance could retard the tide, but they were not certain it could stem emigration to the cities.[9]

Mead and his commission understood that to achieve in Palestine what was difficult in the United States was an even more daunting challenge. In the United States, which began and expanded as an agricultural nation, the primary problem was holding people to the land. In Palestine, Jews had yet to settle as farmers. Moreover, Jews had little experience with farming before arriving in the country.

9 *Report of the Experts*, 13–20.

Instruction prior to settlement and continuing education could compensate for technical ignorance, but in the American view the most serious problem was cultural:

> Another intangible, but serious difficulty, in the creation of a solvent Jewish agriculture is the appeal this [agricultural settlement] movement makes to emotional people — poets, reformers, labor and social leaders, men with keen minds and lively imaginations, but lacking the rural traditions, practical experience and balanced judgment so necessary to success in farming. The tendency of people so equipped is to try experiments.[10]

Indeed, it was the social experimentalism of the Zionist farmers that the American observers viewed as the biggest obstacle to widespread private ownership. Beyond the technical aspects of the report, countering the socialist alternatives to capitalist agriculture was the most important item on the agenda. On the basis of the American experience, Mead and his associates urged the transplantation of homesteading as the key to establishing an agricultural society.

In essence, the report may be read as a brief against the growing commitment of Zionist settlement authorities to the kibbutz. As such, the report argued for the maintenance of the dominant tradition of Zionist colonization — settlement by independent farmers who owned their own land. Nearly all the settlements established between the 1880s and World War I had been designed as villages composed of independent farmers. This is what was envisaged in the plans of most of the *moshavot*. It was the difficulties of achieving this goal that had brought about the interventions of Baron Rothschild and his officials during the 1880s and 1890s and the establishment of the Palestinian Office of the World Zionist Organization under Arthur Ruppin in 1907.

Unlike the American experience, Zionist colonization had never meant isolated farms. Settlement had usually been initiated and carried out by companies or societies that sought to organize individuals into groups who would establish villages. The models were

10   Ibid., 28

invariably European, primarily German and Russian. German Templars, for example, who settled in mid-nineteenth-century Palestine provided an influential model. Around World War I, the southern Italian experience was invoked as the most worthy of emulation. Yitzhak Wilkansky (Elazari-Volcani), its leading proponent, envisioned Palestine as based primarily on intensive agriculture that produces dense rural settlement. Without industrial cities, Palestine would have a culture of towns; but these would be intended primarily to serve the countryside and to share in its values.[11] Such a conception found its way into the 1918 plan for developing the country that was authored by Ben-Gurion and Ben-Zvi.[12]

From the early 1920s, Labor Zionism actively and successfully pushed the village idea away from long-held bourgeois conceptions. Small groups of Jewish pioneers of the Second Aliyah began to experiment with cooperative and collectivist ideas just prior to the outbreak of World War I. Moreover, bourgeois Central-European philanthropists and experts decided to support these experiments, if only because they had come to understand that middle-class Jews were not coming to Palestine in sufficiently large numbers; and of those who did come, few were willing to invest their capital in the countryside. Experience and necessity, rather than theory, had been pointing toward a radical shift in the orientation of Zionist colonization prior to the Mandate. During the 1920s, these beginnings became the starting point for various forms of socialist agricultural colonization. In the view of a growing lobby within the Zionist movement, particularly among colonists already in Palestine, these experiments offered the best hope for organizing the massive settlement of the country.[13]

The American experts, for whom socialist colonization was both impractical and incompatible with American values, pointed to alternatives. In their view, the Templars provided the most successful example of colonization since the 1870s:

These [Templar settlements] are not merely self-sustaining,

11 Y. Wilkansky, article in *BaDerech* (1918); 417–425.
12 Ben-Zvi and Ben-Gurion, *Eretz Israel,* 208–228.
13 Margalit Shilo, "The Settlement Policy of the Palestine Office, 1908–1914" (in Hebrew) (Ph.D. dissertation, Hebrew University, 1985).

they are decidedly prosperous. The neat two-story stone houses, their large barns usually of stone and their plantations, livestock and equipment make a pleasing rural picture which is enhanced by closer examination. ... In one of their colonies not a single farmer is in debt...they are educating their children and living in better homes than the average farmer in Europe or America. This shows that farming in Palestine carried on by Europeans who are both good workers and good managers can be made profitable.[14]

The other useful model was that of the PICA (Palestine Jewish Colonization Association) colonies founded by the Rothschilds:

Those in charge of PICA colonies realize that enduring agricultural success in Palestine calls for industry, thrift and good management, as in other countries. They pay no attention to social theories, or to claims that the Jew has a peculiar temperament that places him outside the influence of economic and business facts which prevail elsewhere. They have had a trying experience in substituting business for philanthropy. ... What is important, is that they have made progress in the direction that Zionist colonization must travel. ... There is a complete absence of the peculiar social experiments so conspicuous in the Zionist colonies.[15]

They also believed that the homestead model was viable. As evidence, the commission cited the personal experience of a Mr. Broza, who came to Palestine around 1890 and pioneered in the hill country outside Jerusalem:

That a Jewish farmer can, without outside help, overcome all local obstacles, acquire a farm and prosper in its cultivation in direct competition with Arabs is shown by the case of Mr. Broza. ... Mr. Broza has prospered because he exercises all the faculties with which his race is so richly endowed. He is a worker, an organizer and a business man.[16]

14   *Report of the Experts*, 33.
15   Ibid., 35.
16   Ibid., 36.

American experts believed that Broza's experience could be replicated if Zionism would remain faithful to what had motivated colonizers in other places in the world: "As a rule, the governing motive in colonization is to build up a permanent and prosperous rural life with broad opportunities for qualified people of small means to become home owners." Unfortunately, the commission concluded, Zionist authorities were subordinating success in colonization "to the creation of a new economic and social order, with a strong antagonism to Capital." The villain was the Histadrut, the Jewish Federation of Labor: "It is the view of the Commission that...the influence of the Jewish Federation of Labor is giving these colonies a character not in harmony with the ideals and aspirations of the Jewish race." The report then uses scientific arguments to support the vision of a Jewish homeland based on independent farms and free of the corruptions of socialism.[17]

The report failed to change the direction of Jewish settlement. In 1929 planners from the Jewish Agency, including Levi Shkolnik (Eshkol) and Yitzhak Wilkanski reacted to it by formulating a set of principles that negated individualistic and capitalistic agricultural colonization. They envisioned the multiplication of clusters of co-operative villages with about 80 to 100 family units in each, based on an agricultural system — mixed farming — that would support them. This plan was justified for political and security as well as economic reasons. They maintained it could secure Jewish lands by creating population densities necessary for assuring the Jewish presence in a contested country.[18] This concept was repeatedly affirmed in the experience of "stockade and tower" at the end of the 1930s and during the period of mass immigration in the decade after independence. By the end of the first decade of the state, when the agricultural colonization of the country was nearly complete, hundreds of socialist colonies in the form of *moshavim* and kibbutzim had been established.[19]

Thus while Zionist authorities in Palestine eagerly sought the

17 Ibid., 36.
18 *Key for the Settlement of Various Zones in Palestine; Reports of the Preparatory Commissions, submitted to the Department of Colonisation of the Palestine Zionist Executive, Jerusalem/Tel Aviv, May 1929,* 109–110.
19 S. Ilan Troen, "Spearheads of the Zionist Frontier: Historical Perspectives on

technical advice and experience of American agricultural experts, they rejected the social philosophy on which it was based. Israel did not become — like so much of the United States beyond the Appalachians — an expanse of privately owned homesteads separately and neatly placed in the continental geometric grid. Rather, the countryside of Palestine remained true to the village conception of early European immigrants, although its social form was significantly modified by the economic, political, and security exigencies of Zionist settlement.[20]

II. Designing and Supporting a Modern Capitalist Society: The 1940s

Robert Nathan and His Report

If in the mid-1920s the *yishuv's* leadership supported the kibbutz and the *moshav* at the expense of individualistic forms of agricultural organization, twenty years later they were actively exploring a radical change in orientation. Beginning in 1943, they began to develop plans for transforming the *yishuv* from an agricultural into a modern, urban-indusrial society. Experts form abroad were again called in and once again from America. The most important foreign consultant was Robert Nathan, and it is to an evaluation of his work that we now turn.

The international debate over the future of Palestinian society after World War II was the immediate context of the invitation. In March 1943, the British government initiated an official study on postwar reconstruction which, from the outset, promised that Palestine would continue to be regarded as primarily an agricultural country. It was immediately understood by the *yishuv's* leadership that if Palestine remained predominantly agricultural then the immigration of large numbers of Jews could not be accommodated without pushing Arabs off their land. The only practical way to absorb large-scale *aliyah* was

---

Post-1967 Settlement Planning in Judea and Samaria," *Planning Perspectives* 7 (January 1992): 81–100.

20   Shilo, "Settlement Policy," 290ff.

to create a modern urban economy that could absorb immigrants. Only on this basis could leaders of the *yishuv* argue against the limitations of White Paper policies, reach out to the survivors of the war that was raging, and ensure that those who emigrated could find work and be absorbed.[21]

Yishuv experts mobilized to address the problems posed by the British action. As in the past, they knew that it would be advantageous to find outside experts of unquestioned reputation who could provide the required scientific sanction to Zionist claims. They therefore welcomed the unprecedented decision of a group of American Zionists and anti-Zionists to collaborate in organizing a study demonstrably free from the taint of partisanship and special pleading. Robert Nathan was the choice to conduct that study, and it is through this work that he became an ardent advocate for Zionist aspirations.

Nathan had come to public attention as director of the National Income Division of the U.S. Department of Commerce from 1934 to 1940.[22] During World War II, his reputation grew as he advanced through various posts in government wartime planning, obtaining in 1945 the post of deputy director of the Office of War Mobilization and Reconversion. Nathan was widely recognized as one of the outstanding young economists of the New Deal and, given his areas of expertise, was an excellent choice to direct the study of Palestine's potentialities.

Together with two other economists, Oscar Gass and Daniel Creamer, Nathan undertook in 1944 to study the economic absorptive capacity of Palestine in the context of detailed proposals for the development of the country. The project was funded by the American Palestine Institute, a nonpartisan research organization, which raised about $100,000 — a sum it claimed was the largest that

---

21 On the role of foreign social scientists in developing the social sciences in Palestine, see Troen, "Calculating the 'Economic Absorptive Capacity' of Palestine."

22 His first major publication was *National Income, 1929–36* (Washington, D.C.: U. S. Government Printing Office, 1937). Much of the material on Robert Nathan is from oral interviews and materials from his files, designated here as the Nathan Papers, which are in the possession of the authors (Nathan, Gass, and Creamer) and in the Ben-Gurion Archives in Sede Boqer.

had hitherto been committed to examine an issue of public policy through social science research. Nathan's report, *Palestine: Problem and Promise*, was published in 1946. It contributed to the debate preceding the UN vote on partition in November 1947 and became an important part of the testimony marshaled by supporters of a Jewish state before international forums.[23]

Nathan and his associates provided data and assessments that confirmed and buttressed internal Jewish Agency studies. Their study had both an immediate and a long-term impact. After independence, their research was incorporated into the economic and development assumptions that shaped Israel's first national plan — the Sharon Plan of 1950. Two decades earlier, Mead and his associates had urged that Palestine be settled by independent farmers; the Sharon Plan provided that Israel should become at least 80 percent urban and only 20 percent rural. In fact the rural component never reached its target figure, and Israel, like the United States and most other modern societies, has relied on a much smaller proportion of its people working the land.[24]

In formulating a new model of Zionist society, Nathan recognized that unprecedented amounts of capital would be required for realizing it. He also appreciated that American Jewry was an important potential source for these funds. This led him to evaluate what could be collected through traditional fund raising and to explore new methods for raising additional monies. This investigation was so sensitive that, unlike the public attention accorded the earlier study, it had to be carried out clandestinely. Through his work in Palestine and his official responsibilities in Washington, Nathan developed a wide range of contacts with the leadership of the *yishuv*, Jewish organizations, and the American government. This made him a good candidate to carry out a confidential analysis of the financial support American Jews could provide for Israel.

23 Robert Nathan, Oscar Gass, and Daniel Creamer, *Palestine: Problem and Promise; An Economic Study* (Washington D.C.: 1946), v-vi; and interview with Nathan, Washington D.C., June 1986.

24 S. Ilan Troen, "The Transformation of Zionist Planning Policy: From Agricultural Settlements to an Urban Network, *Planning Perspectives* 3 (January 1988):3–23.

Survey Research and the Origins of Israel Bonds

Nathan and the *yishuv*'s leadership anticipated that friendly foreign governments would help a new, Jewish state with grants and loans. They also expected reparations from Germany. And they knew they could rely on the continuing philanthropy of world Jewry — primarily American Jews, who after the Holocaust constituted the largest and wealthiest Jewish Diaspora. But given the enormous amount of money needed for national development, more was required than these sources could provide. Israel Bonds were created to supplement these resources.

It is difficult to fix a date and an author to the idea of Israel Bonds. Nathan was clearly involved in the early stage of the process that produced the concept and in formulating the strategy of the early bond campaigns. At about the same time that *Palestine: Problem and Promise* was published, Nathan became involved in the first of his extensive surveys of the American Jewish community. The surveys were designed to develop data on the following questions: How much money could American Jewry make available to the Jewish state? What were the best ways to raise money for Israel? Would greater sums be transmitted to Israel if they were to arrive in the form of investments as well as charitable contributions? These were highly sensitive issues, equally important for Israel's new government and for Americans raising funds for Israel. Addressing these questions required developing information that only surveys could provide.

It is useful to remember that survey research was a relatively new tool of applied social science. Methods for divining popular attitudes on a systematic and scientific basis were still being developed. The first primitive, and often inaccurate, polls to predict election results were not conducted until the 1930s; statistical sampling techniques were being transferred from genetics and animal studies to research on human populations; "Gallup poll" inquiries into popular attitudes were increasingly frequent but lacked sophistication; and questionnaire-based research on psychological adjustment and a host of social issues had only recently been conducted on a wide scale by the psychological measurement branch of the American army during World War II. The product of this latter research — the four-volume *American Soldier* series, authored by a team headed by Samuel Stouffer — would become widely available only through publication by an academic press in 1949-1950. Thus the research on American Jews discussed below may be considered a pioneering effort in the growing attempt to apply social analysis techniques to the formulation of policy. Specifically, survey research was employed to give scientific information on how American Jews envisioned the *yishuv* and Israel, with the ultimate purpose of using those data in devising fund-raising strategies.[25]

Nathan was not the first social scientist recruited by an American Jewish organization to assist in its operations. Perhaps the first use of commissioned scientific advice for that purpose was sponsored by the United Jewish Appeal in 1941. The context was a disagreement between Jewish communal organizations and the UJA over the proportion of the funds raised from the Jewish community to be sent to the *yishuv* and how those funds should be distributed among the agencies active in Palestine's development. To address these issues, the UJA hired a well-known Columbia University economist, Dr. Eli Ginzberg, to study the giving patterns and the rationale of the allocation system. His report is a pioneering analysis of the earning power of American Jewry and the portion of income that might be contributed to Zionist causes. Moreover, Ginzberg examined the division of contributions according to the community, and according to the relative wealth of individuals — i.e., big givers versus smaller givers. The study alone did not resolve outstanding issues surrounding Zionist fund-raising, but it did provide the basis for more rational argument. Ginzberg also recommended that the UJA establish a permanent research bureau to study fund raising and allocation. Although this was not immediately done, his work became a precedent for further studies including those that Nathan would carry out after the war.[26]

25   For the wider context of the history of survey research from which some material in this paper is drawn, see Russell Stone and S. Ilan Troen, "Early Social Survey Research in and on Israel," in *Israel; The First Decade of Independence*, ed. S. I. Troen and Noah Lucas (Albany: State University of New York Press, forthcoming).

26   Eli Ginzberg, *Report to the Allotment Committee of the United Jewish Appeal for 1941* (New York: United Jewish Appeal, 1941); Ernest Stock, *Partners and Pursestrings: A History of the United Israel Appeal* (Lanham, Md.: University Press of America, 1987), 119–121.

In 1946, Robert R. Nathan Associates, the firm Nathan established on leaving government service, received a large contract from the United Jewish Appeal "to undertake a comprehensive statistical and economic study of the basis for setting proper relative quotas for United Jewish Appeal contributions throughout the United States." This involved building on Ginzberg's original efforts as well as applying survey research to highly sensitive organizational and policy issues on a national scale. The project, funded at $50,000, gathered data in seventy-five communities through conventional methods as well as the relatively new instrument of survey research, which required field workers throughout the country to conduct interviews according to carefully prepared questionnaires.[27]

The carrying out of such a task was sometimes subject to opposition. Many community professionals and lay leaders did not want to expose themselves to even a discreet survey. Indeed, Nathan advised his "field men" that they might "get a runaround" and concluded his instructions with the advice: "The main thing is not to be discouraged." While there was some resistance in the field, important sectors of the United Jewish Appeal leadership were deeply committed to the research.[28]

This 1946 study preceded a far more ambitious survey in 1948 on a matter of even greater sensitivity. The issue was whether or not American Jews would donate money for the development of the Jewish national home and also invest in it. In present-day terms, the question was: Would American Jews make contributions to the UJA and, in addition, purchase Israel Bonds? Both in the *yishuv* and in the United States, there was a growing recognition that there was a limit to funds available from charitable contributions. At the same time there was uncertainty about whether Jews would invest at all, or if their investments would be at the expense of contributions. Survey research was employed to assess attitudes on these issues.

Among American Jews, a significant tradition of investing in the development of the *yishuv* had existed since the beginning of

---

27 Memorandum to Field Men from Robert R. Nathan, 11 July 1946, and Letter from Robert Nathan to the United Jewish Appeal, 19 June 1946, Nathan Papers.

28 Memorandum to Field Men from Nathan.

the century. In the 1920s Meir Dizengoff, mayor of Tel Aviv, had successfully solicited money from New York Jewry in the form of bonds for the development of the new city. However, most investments were connected with the development of agricultural land and settlement. In many cases investors purchased shares in projects or tracts of land with the intention that at some time they would themselves immigrate to Israel. There were also a small number of companies devoted to developing industries. What had not been tried was a mass solicitation of American Jewry inviting them to participate in rebuilding Palestine through the purchase of interest-bearing loans, much as the United States government had raised money from its citizens during the world wars. Zionist fund raising had remained firmly rooted in charitable contributions rather than investments.[29]

However, traditional methods were inadequate to meet the needs of the *yishuv*. Immense funds were needed for absorbing immigrants, building a national economy, and defending the country. There was great concern that with the ebbing of the passions generated by the tragedy of European Jewry and the euphoria of independence, contributions would diminish. This in fact happened. After Kristall-nacht in 1938, the UJA collected an unprecedented $14 million. And from 1945 the amount rose dramatically, reaching a peak of $150 million during the War of Independence in 1948 and $104 million in 1949. Thereafter the funds declined steadily to $88 million, $80 million, and $64 million in subsequent years.[30]

29   See discussion on Dizengoff's attempt to raise money in the United States in S. I. Troen, "Establishing a Zionist Metropolis; Alternative Approaches to Building Tel-Aviv," *Journal of Urban History* 18 (1) (November 1991):10–36. The commitment of an important segment of the leadership of American Jewry to investment rather than charity is clearly expressed in the conflict of the Zionist Organization of America headed by the Brandeis group versus Weizmann and the Europeans. See Statement to the Delegates of the Twelfth Zionist Congress on Behalf of the Former Administration of the Zionist Organization of America, Carlsbad, June 1921; and *Report of Activities of the Palestine Economic Corporation Presented to the Palestine Royal Commission* (New York: Palestine Economic Corporation, 1936).

30   See Nathan's "highly secret" study, "Fund-Raising for Israel in the United States: A Study, May 1952," Nathan Papers, 3–4; Stock, *Partners and Purse-strings,* 145.

Their sense of the provisional nature of these contributions in the face of Israel's great needs troubled the leaders of the UJA — Henry Montor, the wonder-working professional head of the organization, and Henry Morgenthau, Jr., Secretary of the Treasury during World War II and president of the UJA during Israel's War of Independence.[31] They recognized that the flow of charitable contributions also depended on potentially reversible and politically motivated interpretations of the tax exemption granted the UJA. They appreciated that the Israeli government would want to be totally independent in determining the purposes for which overseas funds would be employed — as, for example, in realizing settlement or defense policies. In fact the tax-exempt status of UJA contributions was suspended during April–May 1948, and it required, among other actions, Morgenthau's personal intervention with former colleagues to reverse the ruling.[32]

With these concerns in mind, they approached Robert Nathan for assistance in January 1948, shortly after the UN vote for partition. Nathan, in turn, contacted on behalf of the UJA the most important organizations for survey research in America — the Survey Research Center at the University of Michigan, the National Opinion Research Center at the University of Chicago, and Elmo Roper and Louis Harris in New York. In the letter of invitation for submitting bids, Nathan clearly stated the objectives of the proposed survey:

> One of the proposals which is being given serious attention is that of floating a bond issue in the United States for the new State. Many uncertainties must be cleared up if such a loan is to be undertaken. There are questions as to the magnitude of

31   Charles E. Schulman, "Fund-Raiser par Excellence," in *Understanding American Jewish Philanthropy*, ed. Marc Lee Raphael (New York: Ktav, 1979), 91–101.

32   Henry Morgenthau was among the most steadfast supporter of bonds — even to the point of wanting to diminish the UJA, which he headed, although he hesitated to say so publicly. One major reason, according to Nathan, is that Morgenthau "felt that the presentation to the American public of the picture of Israel as a dependent people, coming to the United States for charitable funds, must seriously affect Israel's capacity to float public loans and to stimulate private investment." See Nathan, "Fund-Raising for Israel," Study, 21; and Stock, *Partners and Pursestrings*, 127–130.

212 S. ILAN TROEN

the loan, its duration, its interest rates, its denominations and similar matters. In order to answer these and other questions it has been suggested that a survey be made of samples of Jewish families. The task of submitting an estimate of cost of such a survey and of advising on the matter has been turned over to us...

Information should be sought as to the willingness of people to participate in such a loan; what some of the inducements might be; how it would affect their UJA contributions; what kind of investments they now hold in Palestine; what experience they have had in Palestine investments; whether they would invest immediately or would wish to spread their investment over time; whether they would prefer investments relating to specific projects, such as irrigation or housing; and the like.[33]

The bid from Rensis Lickert of the University of Michigan was accepted, and the contract was signed on 12 May, 1948 — two days before Israel became a state. Not yet knowing what the name of the state would be, the contract carried the heading "Survey to Determine Attitude toward Bond Drive for the Jewish State in Palestine."[34]

The initiative for the 1948 survey was American — primarily Montor and Morgenthau. They were in constant contact with Ben-Gurion and his advisers about the difficulties the UJA was having in meeting the demands of the *yishuv*, and they shared their suggestions for exploring additional ways to raise funds. Encouraged by the results of the survey, Morgenthau went to Israel in October 1948 to meet with Ben-Gurion and in extensive conversations made the argument for going beyond the organization he headed, the UJA, and beyond Abba Hillel Silver and Emmanuel Neuman, the leaders of the American Zionist establishment, which Morgenthau considered marginal and of very limited financial potential. At the same time,

---

33 Robert R. Nathan to Louis Harris and Elmo Roper, New York, 14 January 1948, Nathan Papers.
34 See in the Nathan Papers the contract for a "Survey to Determine Attitude toward Bond Drive for the Jewish State in Palestine," signed 12 May, 1948 by Robert Nathan for Robert R. Nathan Associates and by R. P. Briggs, vice-president of the Regents of the University of Michigan.

Nathan communicated directly with Ben-Gurion to urge by-passing the American Zionist leadership, and invited the direct intervention by Israel's leadership, particularly Finance Minister Eliezer Kaplan, whom Nathan had come to know and admire since his work on *Palestine: Problem and Promise*.[35]

Ben-Gurion did not yet want to make such a radical departure. During that first year of statehood, he was still unwilling to upset the existing network of fund raising, despite the fact that he and his advisers were aware from the earliest stages of the war that new sources of revenue had to be developed. Moreover, he hoped that with the establishment of the state many of the country's needs could be met by loans and grants from the American government and other international bodies.[36]

It took about two years for Israel to make the radical shift Nathan had proposed in the way it mobilized funds from American Jews. Relations between Israel and the Zionist organizations in America were complicated by tradition, personal ties and rivalries, and uncertainties over the effectiveness of alternatives. The first campaign for Israel bonds was launched only in September 1950. By then, the role of the UJA as a source of funds had considerably diminished and there had been a break with the traditional Zionist leadership. There

---

35 There are numerous entries in Ben-Gurion's diaries from this period on contacts, particularly with Morgenthau, when the two discussed the problems of organizing American Jewry. See G. Rivlin and E. Orren, eds., *The War of Independence: Ben-Gurion's Diary* (in Hebrew) (Tel Aviv: Ministry of Defense, 1982), 3: 725, 757, 769-772, 780, 784.

36 Rivlin and Orren, *The War of Independence*, 2:652. Abe Feinberg, another leader of American Jewry who enjoyed close relations with Ben-Gurion, invoked Morgenthau to criticize the establishment of the ZOA for pushing aside the majority of American Jews who would have liked to be generous toward the Jewish state. For internal problems in American Jewish fund raising and particularly the proposal "to get rid of the 'Tammany Hall' of the leaders of the ZOA," especially Abba Hillel Silver, see in Vol. 3, 26 January 1949, 963. Perhaps especially significant was the extensive discussion with Morgenthau on American Jewish community, see entry for 25 October 1948 (ibid., 3:770–772). Finally, the relationship between Ben-Gurion and Morgenthau was especially warm. Appreciation for Morgenthau's services led to the naming of a settlement for him during the war — Tal Shachar — which is the Hebrew equivalent of Morgenthau.

was, then, the need, the opportunity and an available rationale for a change in fund raising.

The justifications for inaugurating bonds were well articulated by Nathan in a 1950 confidential report entitled "Notes on Republic of Israel Loan."[37] Much of the content of this document had clearly been formulated in connection with the 1948 survey, and it was communicated to Morgenthau, who shared it with Ben-Gurion in their October 1948 meeting. The report also provided a blueprint for structuring and organizing the sale of Israel Bonds.

Nathan's proposals were based on a mixture of economic analysis and interpretation of attitudes. He first estimated the income of American Jews and how much of it was available for bonds. He then analyzed the kinds of bonds that could be marketed, their rates of interest and dates of maturity. He proposed the denominations in which bonds should be issued in order to reach the optimal proportion of potential purchasers in the different income brackets. That is, how many bonds could be sold to small investors and how many to wealthy Jews. By-passing the established fund-raising network, Nathan suggested that the bonds should "be sold by an organization of volunteers organized in city offices." Moreover, experience with the American Jewish community as well as the survey suggested to him that it was not

> either necessary or advisable to tie the loan to specific projects or to offer specific guarantees or security. It seems obvious that success or failure of the loan will be determined primarily by the willingness of the Jewish community to help in the development of Israel, and not by technical considerations of security, or for that matter of yield, which most of the potential buyers of the bonds could not even understand.[38]

Nathan's proposals informed the government's decision to launch Israel Bonds, and he was a key participant in the two public events

37   R. Nathan, "Notes on Republic of Israel Loan," 31 October 1950, Nathan Papers.
38   See in the Nathan Papers: Robert Nathan to Henry Montor, 15 September 1949; "Notes on Republic of Israel Loan, 31 October 1950"; "Fund-Raising for Israel in the United States: A Study, May 1952"; and Robert Nathan, "Some Notes on Fund Raising in the United States for Jewish Purposes, 20 April 1955."

that inaugurated them. The first was a three-day conference of influential and wealthy American Jews in Jerusalem on 3–6 September 1950, where Ben-Gurion announced an Israel Bond issue of $1.5 billion over a three-year period. This conference was followed by a similar one in Washington, D.C., on 29 October 1950 to advance the project further.

In his speech at the inauguration of the bonds in 1950, Nathan succinctly expressed the public rationale for this form of investment. In so doing he contended that philanthropy was necessary and legitimate but should be directed at such social problems as transporting immigrants and providing for their initial adjustment. Financing the development of the country was another matter. In Nathan's view, building an infrastructure, erecting and outfitting factories, purchasing agricultural equipment and developing tourism should be based on investment, not charity. Moreover, the participation of American Jews in these areas was not merely a matter of Jewish loyalty but also in the American national interest, since "Israel can be a bulwark for the forces of freedom and the democratic process in the vulnerable Middle East. A strong Israel economy is certainly in the best interests of the free world." This appeal drew on a perception that American Jews would respond favorably to Israel Bonds if they could envision support for Israel in American terms.[39]

The "Americanness" of purchasing bonds derived from an understanding that "American citizens have given and loaned abroad well over thirty billions of dollars since the end of World War II." Such funds had "arrested the parade of communism in many parts of the world" and "strengthened democracies that need to be strengthened." In Nathan's view, such support was particularly necessary in the vulnerable Middle East. In this vein he could claim that if Israel can become "the forerunner of economic development in the Middle East," then the Middle East "will be saved for the democracies by Israel." He went on to link American patriotism with Jewish loyalty: "Therefore I say that as an American citizen investment over there is consistent with our whole program of overseas aid and overseas grants; ...And I say it is time for the individual American citizen to get in line with the American Government."[40]

39   "Summary of Remarks of Robert R. Nathan, 26 October 1950," Nathan Papers.
40   Text of Address by Robert R. Nathan, National Economic Conference for

Israel Bonds immediately proved their importance, and their very success led to frictions with the UJA. Whereas previously the UJA had been in competition with local federations, the threat of bonds forced cooperation, as the federations came to recognize that they needed the appeal of the UJA's connection with Israel to generate enough funds for local needs. This new competition, the UJA and the federations versus the Bonds, generated continued research on fund raising. Montor, who left the UJA to direct the Bonds, continued to seek Nathan's services for further surveys, which Nathan conducted in 1949, 1952, and 1955. The proven value of research generated demand for more research.[41]

While survey research was carried out by American Jews on their own community, it was always clear that in addition to American Jewish organizations, an ultimate consumer of the data was the Israeli government. This was true of the initial study during the War of Independence, as it was of later ones. For example, in the 1952 report entitled, "Fund-Raising for Israel in the United States: A Study" and classified "HIGHLY SECRET," Nathan's first sentence explained the purpose of his research: "For the sake of its financial and moral position in the United States, the State of Israel should examine the manner in which funds are now obtained for Israel." He went on to review how the current pattern of fund-raising had developed and suggested what Israel could do to shape the organizational structure of American Jewish fund-raising.

Here, as throughout his relationship with the *yishuv* and the Israeli government, Nathan was the sympathetic outside consultant, offering advice with the hope of shaping policies that were based on American models, on what had worked, and on what he believed could succeed in America. From an outsider, unaffiliated with Zionism and Israel, Nathan had become the discrete insider valued by leaders of American Jewry and of the Jewish state.

Israel, Washington, D.C., 21 September 1951, Nathan Papers. See, too; Robert R. Nathan, "Israel and Point Four," *Annals of the American Academy of Political and Social Science*, July 1950, 140–149.

41   See in the Nathan Papers: Nathan's confidential notes of 31 October 1950; Nathan, "Fund-Raising for Israel in the United States: A Study, May 1952"; and Nathan to Montor 10 September 1949.

He enthusiastically served both communities, since he believed they shared common values. In traversing this course, Nathan saw neither contradictions nor conflict. He saw his efforts to involve American Jews in the realization of a grand design for Israel appropriate for and worthy of him — both as an American expert and as a Jew.

Conclusion

Mead and Nathan were part of a growing modern profession — planners who use scientific research for formulating social policy. Both were highly trained specialists and professional civil servants who had held important positions in the United States government. This visibility opened to them international careers in which they were invited to export American experience and technologies. In particular, their work was but a part of the large body of research on developing the *yishuv* undertaken by American experts on behalf of Zionist and non-Zionist organizations.

Despite these similarities, the reception given their proposals was substantially different. It is not clear if Mead understood the extent to which intra-Zionist conflict motivated one faction to issue an invitation to him and his colleagues. In the face of the greater strength of an opposing camp, his proposals for Zionist homesteading were rejected. Nathan's proposals on the other hand were welcomed. The questions of whether and how to redirect the *yishuv*'s public resources away from the near-exclusive support of agriculture toward developing an industrial base had been examined by Jewish Agency experts in Palestine during the year prior to Nathan's study. His conclusion that Palestine could absorb a massive immigration only if reorientation took place was one that leading Zionist planners in Palestine had already reached. Nathan's report served to legitimate the idea that the *yishuv* had to emulate the United States and other modern industrialized societies. There was, then, an identity of vision between outside and local experts on the need for change and its direction.

For all the differences in the context, focus, and fate of their work, Mead and Nathan shared a common commitment to the principle of individual responsibility. While recognizing the accomplishments of farmers on collective farms, Mead could not abide their dependence on outside support. His report concluded that the building of kibbutzim should be immediately terminated, since they were a burden on the Zionist organization. Although he recognized the need for grants in the short term, he argued that it was inefficient, unproductive, and contrary to sound business principles to create a system that encouraged or tolerated charity. Moreover, he believed that philanthropy was corrupting the settlers. His analysis derived from his understanding of the significance of individual initiative and responsibility in developing the United States.[42]

Nathan's conception of bonds was similarly grounded. Israeli economic independence could not be achieved if Jews inside and outside the country viewed the new state as dependent on charity. America's Jews, like other citizens, supported their country in a time of crisis through investing in bonds. This American experience had shown that sentiment, patriotism, loyalty, and proper economic behavior could be complementary. Research suggested this pattern could be replicated in the relationship between American Jews and the Jewish state.

Mead and Nathan were, in sum, exporters not only of development strategies but of social ideas that were shaped by the society in which they had matured and gained their professional experience. Generalizations based on American society informed the models they created for what the Zionist experience could and ought to be. Imported concepts, however, could not be readily transplanted or imposed. The relationship between American Jewry and its experts was not like that between a mother country and its colonies. The reception accorded to American visions of Zionist society depended ultimately on how well such visions conformed to local concepts and interests.

---

42   Mead concluded the report with the advice that "from now on settlement shall only proceed in accordance with sound business methods...only such new settlements should be started as can be made self-supporting from the thrift and industry and good management of the settlers." *Report of the Experts*, 64–65.

Envisaging Israel:
The Case of the United Jewish Appeal

Menahem Kaufman

Introduction

The in-house report of the UJA Long Range Planning Committee, issued in March 1982, defined the formal role of the organization as (a) "to facilitate and enhance the fund-raising efforts of the American Jewish communities by actively providing services to Federations and non-federated communities, so that through joint efforts maximum funds may be raised for local, national and overseas needs"; and (b) "to be an advocate for overseas needs."[1]

It may be said, however, that the UJA is not just a service and fund-raising organization of the American Jewish community and its federations. Since 1948 it has been a living link between the American Jewish community and Israel. A service organization simply accommodates requests; the UJA sets its own agenda and acts in accordance with it. The main focus of the UJA's activity has been the rescue of Jews, the organization of immigration to Israel and its absorption there, and the strengthening of the State of Israel. While actively engaged on special progams and projects, the UJA has developed variegated ideological approaches and attitudes toward the State of Israel, its economy and society. Some federation leaders asserted in the late 1970s that it would be more efficient to incorporate the UJA into the machinery of the CJF (Council of Jewish Federations). Had this proposal been accepted, overseas needs — and those of Israel in particular — would have suffered. The proposal was rejected. When the proponents of incorporation

---

1   Peter Golden, *Quiet Diplomat: A Biography of Max Fisher* (New York–London–Toronto, 1992), pp. 76, 80.

backed down, the CJF opted for cooperation between the two organizations. The UJA still champions the interests of Israel.[2]

UJA leaders have always been proud of Israel, the only real democracy in the Middle East. Yet American Jewry itself has not established an ongoing system of elected representation. The two elected "parliaments" in the past — the American Jewish Congress at the close of World War I and the American Jewish Conference that was elected in 1943 — served as representative bodies of the entire American Jewish community for only short periods. American Jewry functions through its organizations. UJA leaders believe that they speak for a million contributors from 800 communities. These Jews express their commitment through contributions and by participating as representatives at meetings and on special missions; this is a participatory relationship. UJA leaders claimed to represent Jewish public opinion and to have established contact with more American Jews than any other Jewish organization. In this sense the UJA has to some extent become a democratic representation of American Jewry. Since the end of the 1960s the UJA has been the primary agent and most common denominator of identification with Israel and the Jewish people.[3]

The UJA leaders who have created the image of Israel have not been limited to the volunteer lay and professional national leadership. Creators of opinion with respect to Israel go all the way down the ranks. Active volunteer workers operate in the various "cabinets," which were established *inter alia* in order to carry the message into every corner of the American Jewish community. The most important of these are the regional cabinets, the women's

---

2   Interview with Irving Bernstein, 28 October 1992, 2–3 (Oral History Collection, Institute for Contemporary Jewry, Hebrew University, Jeursalem — hereafter OH–ICJ); Golden, *Quiet Diplomat,* 80–81; interview with Irving Bernstein, 1 September 1981, 2–3 (OH–ICJ); Statement at General Assembly of CJF, 10 November 1978, quoted in Abraham J. Karp, *To Give Life: The UJA in the Shaping of the American Jewish Community* (New York, 1981), 166.

3   Interview with Irving Bernstein, 29 April 1980, 21–22; (OH–ICJ). About "big givers" see interviews with Herbert Friedman, 1975–1976, 164 (OH–ICJ). See also Marc Lee Raphael, *A History of the United Jewish Appeal, 1939-1982* (Providence, R.I., 1982), 74; interviews: with Abraham Harman, 3 April 1980; with Frank Lautenberg and Irving Bernstein, 19 June 1975, 11; (OH–ICJ).

division cabinets, the young leadership cabinets, the rabbinical cabinets, the faculty cabinets, the student cabinets and the young women leadership cabinets. The UJA professional field workers have also done their share in transmitting information on Israel and on Diaspora Jewish communities in distress. However, the central policy of the UJA is determined by the organization's national leadership.[4]

The attitudes of the UJA leadership were always grounded in American and Jewish values. One important influence on this development was Louis Brandeis's approach to American Zionism. He claimed that there is no contradiction between the American ethos of a free democratic nation and the age-old Jewish values immortalized by the ancient prophets. On the contrary, American Jews are bound to support the revival of the Jewish people and its national entity in Eretz Israel and thus help restore ancient Jewish values in a modern, free, and democratic state. Even though the federations did not allocate sufficient funds to Israel during the "lean fifties," the Council of Jewish Federations and Welfare Funds (CJFWF) General Assembly's resolutions of 1957 did include the statement that the State of Israel is a bulwark of democracy, a salvation for refugees seeking freedom and security, and a haven for the oppressed. According to Jonathan Woocher, federation leaders could identify with Israel because they saw in it a reflection of their own American-bred ideals.[5]

Such attitudes were all the more characteristic of UJA leaders. In 1981 Irving Bernstein admitted that money was being raised as a basic tenet of Jewish tradition and that the secular Jew was donating money to *kelal Israel*, the spiritual Jerusalem, because it is a Jewish value to do so, especially in times of emergency for Israel and of distress in Jewish communities throughout the world. The welfare of Jewish brethren demanded unity. Oddly enough, a "thorough union" was always created when the American Jewish community

4   Interviews: with Irving Bernstein, 28 October 1992, 5–6; with Edward Ginsberg, 9 March 1976, 26 (OH–ICJ).

5   Menahem Kaufman, "The Influence of American Society on American Zionism in the USA in the Second Decade of the Twentieth Century" (in Hebrew), *Yahadut Zemanenu* 6 (1990): 252–270; Jonathan S. Woocher, *Sacred Survival: The Civil Religion of American Jews* (Bloomington–Indianapolis, 1986), 57.

was challenged to respond to crises abroad, rather than to domestic needs. This trend helps explain the unifying power of the UJA, despite the pluralistic character of the American Jewish community. During the Kishinev pogroms, World War I, and the immediate post war years, American Jewry promptly extended its material aid to the impoverished and ravished Jewish communities of the Old World. Thus one of the basic norms of American Jewish fund raising, one of the pillars of UJA ideology, was established. The other pillar of the UJA value system was support of the Jewish community in Eretz Israel. UJA leaders thought that Israel represented a consummation of American values of democracy and justice, American ideals, and the American ethos.[6]

Many students of civil religion have, in one way or another, expressed agreement with the concept that the UJA is, through Israel, America's Jewish religion. Norman Podhoretz, editor of *Commentary*, believes that in 1967 American Jews went through a kind of mass conversion to Zionism. Israel truly became the "religion of American Jews." In the early 1970s, Max Fisher believed that the vanguard of support for Israel in the free world was the American Jewish community, which by and large was rapidly becoming secularized, and that Israel was now the cornerstone of Jewish identity. On the same subject, Irving Bernstein said in 1980:

> How do we practice Judaism today? Not by prayer but through philanthropy. Not by standing before the *aron hakodesh*, but by standing in front of Israel — for Israel.... Where do you make your Jewish commitment, where do you get a lesson in Jewish values? You get it through your philanthropic work.[7]

Discussing a UJA conference, Jonathan S. Woocher concludes that the participants

> had come [*inter alia*] to express their identity and faith as Jews. The fact that they were gathered under the banner of UJA — probably the most visible symbol of that polity — was no

6   Interview with Irving Bernstein, 18 November 1981, 4 (OH–ICJ); Karp, *To Give Life*, 11–12, 33ff.
7   Raphael, *History*, 115; quoted in Golden, *Quiet Diplomat*, 130. See also interview with Irving Bernstein, 29 April 1980, 11–12 (OH–ICJ).

coincidence, because the Jewish commitment that they had come to manifest was first and foremost to the polity's civil religion.[8]

In his eloquent opening speech at that conference, Edward Robin, chairman of the Young Leadership Cabinet, suggested that history had put Jews "in the forefront of every decent human movement and the cutting edge of every crisis." He pointed to the Holocaust and stressed that if American Jews wanted to avoid "the abyss of despair fearfulness and insecurity," they could draw on a reservoir of strength: the State of Israel.[9] Robin's address was a virtual catechism for the civil religious faith of the American Jewish polity.

The UJA Image of Israel between the War of Independence and the Six-Day War

The way in which UJA leaders have envisaged Israel since 1948 has political and ideological roots. Ben-Gurion supported choosing a UJA leadership that was not part of the organized Zionist movement in America. Faced by a choice between Zionist leaders Abba Hillel Silver and Emanuel Neumann on the one hand and Henry Morgenthau and Henry Montor on the other, he preferred the latter two. Thus American non-Zionists, assisted by pro-Israel professionals, were installed as the permanent elite of the UJA, and their attitude toward Israeli society and its government has determined the view of that organization for the last forty-five years.[10] Ben-Gurion believed that leadership of the UJA must not become a partisan issue but should represent the American Jewish consensus. Raising hundreds of millions of dollars entailed great political power, and he was unwilling to place this power in the hands of the American General Zionists, the allies of the main opposition party to his Mapai (labor)-controlled government in Israel.

After a short struggle late in 1948 and early in 1949, between Henry Montor, executive vice chairman of the UJA and executive

8 Woocher, *Sacred Survival*, 63ff.
9 Ibid., 64.
10 Interview with Abraham Harman, 3 April 1980, 7–9 (OH–ICJ).

vice president of the United Palestine Appeal (UPA), who was supported by Ben-Gurion, and the Jewish Agency in Jerusalem as well as the ZOA leaders, Montor was reappointed as the chief professional person of both the UPA and the UJA after the Jewish Agency had asked Morgenthau to serve again as general chairman of the UJA. Silver and Neumann resigned from the Executive of the Jewish Agency. The outcome of this conflict had a long-lasting impact on the relationship between the UJA and Israel.[11]

In September 1950 Montor predicted the UJA's decline, estimating that in the following years it would not raise even $25 million annually. While Montor did not accurately predict the figures, he nonetheless correctly discerned the trend. From a high of $150 million in 1948, the pledges dropped from year to year, reaching a low of $60 million in 1955.[12]

From 1949 to 1967 there was certainly a substantial depreciation in the image of Israel as perceived by the leadership — and probably also by rank-and-file members — in the Jewish communities and their federations. Local needs were afforded priority over those of Israel. The 1948 War of Independence was now over, and the Arab aggressors had been defeated. The state had been established and recognized by the United States. The displaced persons (DP) problem had been solved. There was no immediate military threat to the existence of the Jewish state. There was also no direct involvement of high-ranking federation officials, or even of the UJA leaders, in the Israeli economy or in the absorption of hundreds of thousands of new immigrants. The slow process of building up the State of Israel and the needs of the Jews in the Muslim countries were not as dramatic an issue as the postwar DP camps and the armed struggle of the *yishuv* against seven Arab states.[13]

In 1959 110,000 immigrants still lived in *ma'abarot*, transit camps of wooden and tin shacks and huts. The argument that "while the requirements of the local community organizations were relatively

11   Ernest Stock, *Partners and Pursestrings: A History of United Israel Appeal* (Lanham, N.Y. — London, 1987) xiii, 133–141; Raphael, *History*, 35–37.
12   Interviews with Herbert Friedman, 1975–1976, 4 (OH–ICJ); Stock, *Partners*, 145; Raphael, *History*, 137 (tables); interview with Edward Ginsberg, 9 March 1976, 13 (OH–ICJ).
13   Interviews with Herbert Friedman, 1975–1976, 70–71 (OH–ICJ).

static, those of the UJA's Israeli beneficiaries were open ended" did not convince the keepers of the pursestrings in the federations in the early 1950s.[14]

Every year was marked by a struggle, with UJA executives having to negotiate fiercely with many of the federations and expend great efforts just to preserve the status quo. The greatest decline in UJA income occurred between 1950 and 1955, when the UJA was headed by well-meaning but lukewarm non-Zionists who tried to organize campaigns but failed to create a unified community working for Israel and Jews overseas. The general chairman during these years was Edward M. Warburg. His view was

> that the people of Israel will hold their frontiers...those spiritual frontiers...free education, freedom of religion, just courts, the right to vote — the right of men to try to make the world a little better than they found it.

He was not the person to lead the UJA into a more aggressive fund-raising campaign for Israel or to convince the federations to allocate a greater part of their income to the needs of Israel and of Jews in countries of distress. The incumbent executive director was Joseph (Joe) Schwartz. He was kind, warm-hearted Jew, but in the day-to-day conflict over how much money should be allocated to the UJA and how much the federations should keep for local needs, Schwartz lost every battle.[15]

Other circumstances contributed to the decline of support for Israel in the local communities. One of the major deficiencies of the UJA at the time was its lack of local and national opinion leadership groups. These '"cabinets" were created only after 1955 by Herbert Friedman, the new, aggressive executive vice chairman, in order to intensify identification with Israel of the rank–and–file members of the communities through the UJA. Special funds designated to serve the needs of Israel were created to halt the erosion of

---

14 Raphael, *History*, 64; Ernest Stock, *Beyond Partnership: The Jewish Agency and the Diaspora 1959–1971* (New York — Jerusalem, 1992), 207.

15 Interview with Abraham Harman, 13 November 1980, 6–7 (OH–ICJ); Karp, *To Give Life*, quotation on p. 112; Edward M. Warburg's address to the annual conference of the UJA, 12 December 1953, quoted in ibid.; interviews with Herbert Friedman, 1975–1976, 9 (OH–ICJ).

income.[16] William Rosenwald, perhaps the most efficient fund raiser in American Jewish history, was called on to act as general chairman.

Rosenwald and Friedman saved the UJA in the mid-1950s, putting an end to the decline in fund-raising; but they were unable to increase the annual income to any great extent. In his disputes with the federations Friedman tried to convince them to raise the target sum of the entire campaign, not only the percentage given to Israel, but the local communities did not respond. They continued not to focus their interest on Israel. Even high-ranking UJA officials, busy fighting for every dollar, could not devote much time to dealing with the image of Israel as a democracy or to such issues as the relationship between religion and state, Israeli internal party politics, and so forth. The great need for funds left Friedman with no alternative but to confront the federations.[17]

In June 1958 Friedman tried to transmit to the communities the message about a "large group waiting to be resettled from the mountains of Sahara to the mountains of Judea...the villages of Lachish." Two or three years later he tried to make American Jews in the local communities aware of the problems of development towns and the need to close social gaps. Due to the lack of money in the 1950s, these gaps still exist four decades later.

Without a voice as to how funds raised by the federations should be spent in Israel, it was difficult by the beginning of the 1960s to expect greater involvement of American Jewish communities in specific economic and social problems and projects of Israeli society. Only in a very limited manner were they involved in the changes that the Israeli occupational structure was undergoing, as the country developed its industrial and service sectors. Lack of funds slowed down this development.[18]

In the past, the UPA had created the so-called Constructive Enterprise Funds for Israeli political parties, which in fact became beneficiaries of the UJA. This money could also be put to use

16   Karp, *To Give Life*, 121, 126–127.
17   Ibid., 123–125; interviews with Herbert Friedman, 1975–1976, 12–13, 18, 49, 121 (OH–ICJ). The annual income of the UJA in the period 1955-1966 fluctuated between $60 and $80 million. See Raphael, *History*, 141 (tables); interview with Irving Bernstein, 18 November 1980, 17 (OH–ICJ).
18   Interview with Irving Bernstein, 68, 77; Stock, *Partners*, 167.

in political conflicts between the Israeli parties. Non-Zionists and philanthropists particularly disliked the Israeli multi-party system, characterized by permanent struggles between political groups and the tendency to politicize every aspect of Israeli life. They opposed the "historical" practice of allocating public monies to the parties for their election campaigns. In 1960, and again in 1966, the Jewish Agency in Jerusalem tried to find ways to prevent allocations of funds by the UJA to political bodies in Israel. But the parties represented on the Executive of the Jewish Agency were unwilling to be deprived of these funds. Before such allocations could be prevented, however, the Six-Day War broke out and the resolution of this issue was postponed.[19]

Wars and emergencies in Israel have always had a strong impact on fund raising in the United States. The Sinai Campaign had been no exception; the UJA campaign income in 1957 was $85 million, the highest sum raised during the fifties. A year later, however, there was already a drop in donations. Compared with the Six-Day War and the Yom Kippur War, the Sinai Campaign did not greatly impress American Jewry and the UJA. Even Friedman could not fathom the urgency of the Sinai Campaign to the security of Israel and its population. Though the 1957 campaign brought in more money, American Jews were still unable to understand Israel's security problems clearly.[20]

The Sixties: From Pure Philanthropy to a Neo-Zionist Movement

During the three decades between 1950 and 1980 the UJA was transformed from a purely philanthropic fund-raising organization into a movement that Fisher called "neo-Zionism."[21]

Irving Bernstein claimed that the UJA, under his leadership and that of Herbert Friedman, had become not only a movement but

19   Interview with Irving Bernstein, 149–151; Raphael, *History*, 74–76.
20   Interview with Irving Bernstein, 141; interviews with Abraham Harman, 20 May 1980, 1, 13 November 1980, 6 (OH–ICJ); interviews with Herbert Friedman, 1975–1976, 70, 94, 92 (OH–ICJ).
21   Interview with Irving Bernstein, 27 February 1980, 33 (OH–ICJ).

an educational process. He believed in Zionism with a small *z*, but thought that no Jew in America could deny being a Zionist. Abraham Harman considered the UJA to be a surrogate for the Zionist mass movement that had preceded the establishment of Israel. We should probably accept Bernstein's judgment that the ZOA played a critical role in history, "but young America is not with the ZOA...it is with the UJA. So to young Americans the UJA represents the area in which they can express their commitment to all that Israel stands for in its most spiritual sense." The basis for this new UJA of young America was created by the UJA leadership of the sixties.[22]

One of Friedman's most important initiatives was the inception of the UJA Young Leadership program in 1960. The first Young Leadership Cabinet, which created a body of senior opinion makers, was established three years later.[23] This program was a way to educate young potential leaders about their secular Judaism and to make them aware of their duties to contemporary Jewry and Israel.

The Young Leadership program was an important method of transforming the UJA into a movement. In the 1960s a new generation of Jewish leaders had to be trained and motivated. The new generation differed from its predecessor. Friedman believed that "If you talked to their fathers who were born in Minsk, Pinsk or Trinsk, then all you had to do was something like the Pavlov conditioned reflex... [and] he would give 20 dollars." Friedman decided to teach the future leaders contemporary Jewish history, because they lacked a Jewish education. Intellectual involvement, however, was not enough.

Israel was the focus of Friedman's efforts: "What I tried to do was to make them proud of being Jews and of being connected to Israel.... I left them...with the feeling that they had a big responsibility."[24]

During the summer of 1961 the first Young Leadership Mission visited Israel. This new approach provided an opportunity to look at Israel not as an abstract image but as a reality; it created interest

---

22   Ibid., 3, 8, 28–29, 33; interview with Abraham Harman, 13 November 1980, 3 (OH–ICJ).

23   Interviews with Herbert Friedman, 1975–1976, 183 (OH–ICJ).

24   Raphael, *History*, 67–68; Karp, *To Give Life*, 129–130; interviews: with Abraham Harman, 20 May 1980, 4, with Herbert Friedman, 1975–1976, 200–211 (OH–ICJ).

by getting people involved not only in the fund-raising process in America but also with the details of Israel's daily life and struggles. The very fact that it was the UJA Young Leadership cabinets that in 1982 organized the biennial conference on "Civil Jewish Faith" is evidence of the important role of the UJA Young Leadership program as the "reservoir of strength of the American Jew."[25]

Leonard Bell, the third chairman of the National Young Leadership Cabinet, gives us an insight into the impact of the Young Leadership program:

> The mission in the early sixties of the Young Leadership Cabinet was to raise the level of involvement of young people. How was it done?... Friedman got up for three hours and told you the greatest historical story ever told.... I think he convinced us that we are going to really deal with the destiny of our people...at times I thought I was Moses.... Herb Garon, the next one, thought he was Moses.... Gordon Zacks, who followed Garon, still thinks he's Moses.[26]

During their encounter with the hard facts of Israeli life, particularly after the Six-Day War, young leaders formed their own opinion. When Bell was asked, in a 1977 interview: "Do you believe today that Israel is a democratic country?" he replied: "I believe today that my people has a right to survive.... Don't tell me the Golan Heights shouldn't belong to Israel. I saw Rabin when he just came back from the Heights...."[27] Such opinions show that these young leaders became deeply involved with the basic — even controversial — issues of Israel as a state and a society.

An important group activated by Friedman in the lean years before the Six-Day War was composed of rabbis of Orthodox, Conservative and Reform congregations. It was no simple matter to convince rabbis of the three religious denominations to cooperate. There was also antagonism between the religious congregations and the secular federations. Friedman's slogan was: "We want 100% of the synagogue members to become contributors to Israel." After

25   Woocher, *Sacred Survival*, 63–64.
26   Interview with Leonard Bell, 10 July 1977 (OH–ICJ).
27   Ibid.

fifteen years he could conclude: "You can work together, reformed and orthodox people, on anything which has to do with Israel...that's *kadosh, kadosh*." The rabbis and their council became very effective during the Six-Day War, and even more so at the time of the Yom Kippur War. Israel was attacked at the very moment when many American Jews were at prayer in the synagogues, and rabbis called on their congregants from the pulpit to make the greatest possible effort to support Israel through the UJA.[28]

UJA missions to Israel were another method of creating a closer relationship between American Jews and the new state. The first mission had been organized by Henry Montor in February 1948. After their return to the USA, the participants of this mission became campaign organizers and canvassers.[29]

The major objective of most pre-Six-Day War missions was to convince the participants to increase their own contributions. The program emphasized exposing the participants to the achievements and accomplishments of Israel. It was almost impossible for them to establish personal contact with Israelis at large, those involved in the day-to-day process of building a democracy despite military and economic pressures, a society torn by internal political and religious controversies.[30]

Instead the Young Leadership missions were planned as educational visits. They began with visits to Auschwitz and other Nazi death camps; from there the participants continued to Israel to study Jewish revival and the Israeli experience. Such visits increased their understanding of successes and failures.[31]

The Six-Day War changed the character of UJA missions. In June 1967 UJA leaders, together with members of the UJA cabinets, arrived on a study mission. This was the beginning of mass missions. "Tens of thousands, mainly consisting of compact community units," came to Israel during the 1970s. The encounter with daily life in Israel during and after the Six-Day War created not only

28   Karp, *To Give Life*, 132–135; Raphael, *History*, 69–72; interviews: with Herbert Friedman, 1975–1976, 181–185, with Jacob Feldman, Dallas, 13 March 1976 (OH–ICJ).

29   Raphael, *History*, 34–35, 41.

30   Karp, *To Give Life*, 134–135.

31   Interview with Leonard Bell, 10 July 1977, 4 (OH–ICJ).

a solid basis for unprecedented fund raising but also an affinity between American and Israeli Jews. The slogan "We are one!" gained credence.[32]

In an interview, Herbert Friedman stated: "In the middle of the sixties, in 1964, I started the 'Keren Hahinuch' (the Israel Education Fund — IEF)." Through the efforts of three Israelis — Arieh [Louis] Pincus, Pinchas Sapir, and Teddy Kollek — the project was "sold" to the UJA.[33]

It was very difficult to involve the UJA in practical work in Israeli communities. Since the law did not obligate the Israeli government to provide fully free secondary education, the development towns settled by recent immigrants — mostly from the Middle Eastern countries — lacked facilities for advanced education. Construction costs of new schools presented an almost insurmountable obstacle. In response to a request by the government of Israel, the Executive of the Jewish Agency became involved in education and recommended special fund-raising for this purpose. The minimum contribution to be solicited was set at $100,000. The UJA leadership was not keen to accept direct responsibility for specifically defined objectives and projects in Israel — due no doubt in some degree to the Israeli governmental and bureaucratic system which was unable to measure up to American standards of efficiency.[34]

At last, the IEF was established. Its first task was the construction of comprehensive high schools in development towns. The first of these, built in Dimona, began functioning in 1966. After comprehensive high schools, the IEF placed emphasis on constructing prekindergartens and day nurseries to provide culturally deprived immigrant children with a vitally needed headstart in education. By 1 April 1988, 696 projects financed by American donors through the UJA had been completed or were under construction.[35]

This kind of activity contributed to the solution of a difficult

32 Interview with Edward Ginsberg, 9 March 1976, 7 (OH–ICJ); Karp, *To Give Life*, 135.
33 Interviews with Herbert Friedman, 1975–1976, 183 (OH–ICJ).
34 Interview with Irving Bernstein, 28 October 1992, 21 (OH–ICJ); Stock, *Beyond*, 104ff.; minutes of the Executive of the Jewish Agency, quoted in Stock, *Beyond*, 108.
35 Stock, *Beyond*, 108.

problem for development towns and other underprivileged neighborhoods. A great number of donors regularly visited their projects, proud that their gifts had helped bridge the culture gap, and supported the intellectual and social development of second-generation immigrants from the Oriental countries and their integration into Israeli society.

The Impact of the Six-Day War on the UJA-Israel Relationship

A general malaise characterized Israeli society during 1966 and the first half of 1967. It resulted from an economic recession, a low level of immigration coupled with a high rate of *yerida* (Jewish emigration), and a continuous state of violent hostilities, though none of these was an especially dramatic event. The UJA had to make great efforts in order to raise the same sums as in the previous year. In the tense weeks of May 1967, UJA leaders did not believe that war was imminent.[36]

Prior to June 1967 the UJA had tried every means possible, often in vain, to alert the communities to Israel's situation. The outbreak of the Six-Day War had a completely unanticipated and unpredictable impact on the Jews of America. Through the critical weeks of June 1967 the UJA was in the unique position of collecting money rather than of fund-raising. Abraham Harman remembered: "We had an administrative problem how to handle the flow of money." There are thousands of stories of how Jews who had contributed to the UJA in the past now gave sums ten times or more than their regular contributions, while others who had never donated a penny in the past sent checks for and pledged enormous amounts. Jake Feldman, of Dallas, gave $250,000, saying: "If that isn't enough, you guys tell me what I ought to do, because you can have everything I own, for if anything happened to Israel what I had left would be meaningless." He donated from his principal, not from his income, later explaining

---

36 Stock, *Beyond*, 123–124; interviews: with Abraham Harman, 13 November 1980, 7, with Edward Ginsberg, 9 March 1976, 3, with Herbert Friedman, 1975–1976, 133, 149 (OH–ICJ).

that since the Holocaust he had felt a guilt complex that he would never overcome. The threat to Israel aroused the fear of another Holocaust and awakened a strong will for survival.[37]

There was a very substantial difference between the manner in which American Jews reacted during earlier emergencies and after the Israeli victory in the Six-Day War. In June 1967 they donated as never before. "Jews now feel their Jewish identity more intensely than they have for at least a generation." The swift victory marked the end of passive acceptance of persecution. As Rose Halprin phrased it: 'There was no Jew who did not stand more erect." This radical transformation in the attitude of the American Jewish community was reflected in the success of the UJA emergency campaign. Funds collected by the UJA jumped from $64 million in 1966 to $241 million in 1967. One of the major tasks of the UJA was to maintain annual income at its new plateau ($146 million was collected in 1968 and $167 million in 1969).[38]

The struggle for UJA recognition of the needs of Israel had not come to an end, but the situation had altered. The amounts raised never dropped again to the low levels of the lean years between 1949 and 1966. The war and the shock of 1967 created the UJA that we know today. It was the instrument with which Israel reached out to American Jews and became their main link to the Jewish state. The relationship with the federations improved. There were — and still are — very serious differences of opinion as to how much money should be used for local needs, but UJA leaders and federation executives tried to work together to solve problems. The distinction between Zionists and non-Zionists lost its relevance.[39]

To protect its tax-exempt status under American law, the UJA

---

37 Chaim I. Waxman, *America's Jews in Transition* (Philadelphia, 1983), 112–114; interviews: with Abraham Harman, 13 November 1980, 7; with Herbert Friedman, 1975–1976, 129, with Edward Ginsberg, 9 March 1976, 5, with J. Feldman, 13 March 1976, 4–5 (OH–ICJ); Waxman, *America's Jews,* 114; interviews: with Pinchas Sapir, 11 June 1976, with Irving Bernstein, 18 July 1976 (OH–ICJ).

38 Arthur Herzberg, "Israel and American Jewry," *Commentary* 44 (2), (August 1967): 72; minutes of the Executive of the Jewish Agency, 29 July 1967, quoted by Stock, *Beyond,* 128; Raphael, *History,* 141 (tables).

39 Interview with Irving Bernstein, 27 February 1980, 14–18 (OH–ICJ); Stock, *Partners,* 189.

made it clear to its contributors that their money would not be used for arms. Since the Israeli government needed all of its resources for the war effort, world Jewry, through the Jewish Agency, assumed partial financial responsibility for social welfare — including health services and care of the aged — for educational needs, settlement programs, and the costs of immigration and its absorption. Edward Ginsberg, the acting national chairman at that time, stated: "So we became the main support of Israel's morale during this period."[40] On 19 June, Minister of Finance Pinchas Sapir wrote to Arieh Pincus, chairman of the Jewish Agency:

> In the last few years, the government and the taxpayer had to bear the major part of the expenses for immigrant housing, rural settlement, higher education and welfare services, including support of the old and infirm.... As of July 1, 1967, the government will no longer have the means to participate in any form whatever in the programs of the Jewish Agency for immmigrant absorption and rehabilitation...in education, health, culture and welfare, which it planned to support in the current year.[41]

Since the income of the UJA was not sufficient to achieve all these objectives, the United Israel Appeal was forced to borrow $65 million from American banks to maintain the services in Israel. Major contributors to the UJA used their contacts, and the loans were speedily granted.[42]

The Six-Day War also marked the end of forceful opposition to Israel, and even to the UJA, on the part of the American Council for Judaism (ACJ). Some of its leaders even made substantial contributions, sensing that it was not Israel alone but Jews in general who were threatened. There were members of the ACJ who retained

40 Interview with Edward Ginsberg, 9 March 1976, 12–13 (OH–ICJ); Raphael, *History*, 77.
41 Text of Finance Minister Sapir's letter to Chairman Pincus, Jerusalem, 19 June 67, quoted by Stock, *Beyond*, Appendix C, 216–217. For programs financed by the UIA, 1967–1968, see "Jewish Communal Services: Programs and Finances," *American Jewish Yearbook* 69 (1968): 309.
42 Interviews: with Irving Bernstein 27 February 1980, 14, with E. Ginsberg, 9 March 1976, 24–25 (OH–ICJ).

their ideological opposition to Zionism yet supported Israel. When six years later, on 6 October 1973, Arab armies attacked Israel from the south and the north, Jews felt that everything was at stake. Donations to the UJA campaign reached $504.7 million in 1974 — the highest annual sum received by the UJA during the forty-year period 1940–1980.[43]

Involvement of the Federations through the UJA: The Conference on Human Needs and "Project Renewal"

After the Six-Day War, Arieh Pincus tried to involve the CJF directly in the solution of the social problems facing Israel. One result of this effort was the Conference on Human Needs (COHN) held in Jerusalem in June 1969 under the joint auspices of the government of Israel and the Jewish Agency. This was the first time that federation leaders had participated in the discussion of a major project dealing with the Israeli economy and society: housing, agriculture, education, welfare, health, and — last but not least — the problem of financing immigration absorption. The object of the Israeli participants was to involve Diaspora Jewry in the practical implementation of projects, not just in their financing. This was possible only with the active participation of the UJA.[44]

The conference itself dealt with the "re-appraisal of human needs in Israel, which transcend the limited potential of the state." In its concluding statement the conference took note of the difficulties related to the absorption of mass immigration from the Muslim countries. We find there a remark about the low level of these immigrants' education and professional training. The participants gained a better understanding of the Israeli economy, in which 75 percent of the income from taxes was expended on military and

43   Waxman, *America's Jews*, 113; Melvin I. Urofsky, *We Are One! American Jewry and Israel* (Garden City, N.Y., 1978), 355. For details on the UJA during the Yom Kippur War, see interview with Paul Zuckerman, 11 March 1976, 6ff. (OH–ICJ); Karp, *To Give Life*, 131–134; Raphael, *History*, 155 (tables).

44   Interview with Philip Bernstein, 3 March 1976, 26 (OH–ICJ); Stock, *Partners*, 190; Stock, *Beyond*, 150–156; interview with Irving Bernstein, 28 October 1992, 43–45 (OH–ICJ).

security requirements, leaving little for social services. They agreed that those dependent on the state should be raised to a level of self-dependence and enabled to live a life of dignity and decency.[45]

Federation leaders, however, did not forget their own local interests. They stressed that if Israel needed more funds from the Diaspora these should come only through increased contributions to the campaigns. COHN was important because, after 1967, it provided federation leaders with the challenge of finding ways to improve the quality of life in Israel in order to create a better society. Though COHN did not bring about direct work in the field by American Jewish communities in Israeli slum areas, it was a significant step toward a real partnership and toward the reconstitution of the Enlarged Jewish Agency in 1971.

Some ten years later — after the trauma of the Yom Kippur War, the difficulties created by the absorption of the first wave of Russian immigrants in the 1970s, and the change of government in Israel after the 1977 elections — Jewish communities from abroad for the first time agreed to become directly involved in communal work in Israel. Through the UJA, the American Jewish community participated in "Project Renewal." After winning the 1977 elections, Prime Minister Menachem Begin presented the Jewish Agency with a program for renovating the homes of some 45,000 families, mostly of Oriental origin and residents of overcrowded neighborhoods, who still belonged to the lower strata of Israeli society. It was their protest vote, in response to Begin's campaign propaganda, that had made the Likud victory possible. The prime minister proposed a $2 billion campaign for housing. Negotiations were held with the UJA, not with the CJF. But the UJA rejected the concept proposed by the Israeli government.[46]

From the outset, UJA leaders visualized a comprehensive program that included housing as well as improvement of the social and physical infrastruture for the benefit of neighborhood residents — community centers, youth clubs, etc. They preferred to deal with

---

45 "An Introduction to the Issues before the Conference on Human Needs in Israel — Purpose and Promise," 16–19 June 1969, quoted in Stock, *Beyond*, 155; interview with Irving Bernstein, 28 October 1992, 45 (OH–ICJ).

46 Interview with Irving Bernstein 22–45; Raphael, *History*, 101–110; interview with Irving Bernstein, 28 October 1992, 22–23 (OH–ICJ).

the problems, as in America, by calling on various agencies with expertise in different fields to tackle them under one coordinating organization. The comprehensive approach of the Americans created much friction. The UJA personnel simply could not fathom the complicated decision-making process in Israel, where every minister refused to surrender any of his authority.[47]

The process of working through coordinating committees was very burdensome for people who came to Israel with the intention of providing solutions to the economic and social problems of slum neighborhoods by means of expertise and professional efficiency in accordance with American norms. As they came to know Israel through "Project Renewal," UJA leaders probably became aware more than ever before that in the Israeli system of government all fields of action dealt with by the cabinet and the ministries are subject to politicization — further complicated by the necessity to form coalition governments.

Yigael Yadin, deputy prime minister in Begin's first government, defined "Project Renewal" as follows "It is a common ground of activity between American Jewry and Israel in which American Jews have a legitimate right to interfere and to have 'a say'."[48] A few days before he left the government, he declared that he considered "Project Renewal" to be "the biggest social problem the Jewish people have ever tried to overcome in this country...the only joint program of the government and the Jewish people." He claimed that the project was active in seventeen neighborhoods, influencing the lives of some 400,000 people.[49]

From the American (UJA) point of view, a very important achievement of "Project Renewal" was that many American Jews now became personally involved. Diaspora lawyers, contractors, millionaires, and professionals sat down with the local neighborhood steering committee, composed of a housewife, a small retail businessman, a machine worker, the local mayor, and a social worker, to talk about the future of the community. They discussed

---

47 Interview with Irvin Field, 4 May 1979, 9ff. (OH–ICJ).
48 Ibid., 14–15; interviews: with Irving Bernstein, 28 October 1992, 25, with Yigael Yadin, 28 July 1981, 39 (OH–ICJ).
49 Interview with Yigael Yadin, 21–22.

how to overcome the drug problem.[50] This was not a case in which contributors came, asked questions, and took notes. They met real people in the slums and development towns, contacts they considered to have a great potential for future relationships.

Prior to 1978–1979, UJA fund-raisers were aware of the socio-economic gap in Israeli society, but it was thought preferable not to include visits to slum dwellings on the agenda of campaign missions. "Project Renewal" changed this approach, trying to give the poor the means for self-rehabilitation. American Jews who came to Israel on UJA "Project Renewal" missions understood the need to build viable communities. The project was a success in that it provided American Jews with firsthand knowledge of Israel and also because it was bringing about some changes in Israeli society, even though it did not solve its physical and social problems. Whereas neighborhood steering committees believed in their partners from overseas, they lacked confidence in the Israeli government bureaucracy. The aim of "Project Renewal" was to give the communities not only what the governmental agencies believed they needed but what the recipients felt they needed, and to have them participate in the decision-making process. This could not be easily achieved under conditions prevalent in Israel — which probably explains why, after about fifteen years, the project could show only modest achievements.[51]

From the outset, the UJA leadership was not enthusiastic regarding the prospects of direct personal involvement by contributors and fund-raisers in the solution of social problems. Irving Bernstein was skeptical of success because of

> the structure we have here [in Israel], whether in the Agency or in the government — leadership based on political entities, and not on merit.... Too many things get accepted without our awareness that they can never be achieved.[52]

It was not easy for UJA leaders to explain to their donors a situation in which bureaucracy and political infighting wore down good

50   Interview with Irving Bernstein, 3 July 1980, 45–46 (OH–ICJ).
51   Raphael, *History*, 102–103; interviews with Irving Bernstein, 3 July 1980, 4, 28 October, 1992, 43–44 (OH–ICJ).
52   Interview with Irving Bernstein, 3 July 1980, 9–10 (OH–ICJ).

intentions and at the same time to ask for an increase in contributions for the project.[53]

In 1981 Yigael Yadin still believed that "Project Renewal" was no longer a vision and had become a reality. But under the impact of such political and military events, as the war in Lebanon, the government of Israel did not give the project a high priority; this was probably true also of the UJA leadership. However, during the last decade "Project Renewal" has remained the only program in which UJA leaders and rank-and-file American community members have tried to participate in the solution of social problems in Israel by field work.[54]

UJA Leadership Views on Israeli Society and Polity

As an organization outside the Israeli polity, the UJA could not criticize Israel's democracy and its political system. Its leaders, however, especially through their increasing involvement during the last three decades, have shaped their own opinions concerning many aspects of Israel's public life. There is a rather long history of critical attitudes in these decades. After the establishment of Israel, UJA leaders continued to visualize Israel as a free, democratic, and pluralistic society. The leaders never raised questions regarding its democratic nature,[55] but they were not always happy about the manner in which these concepts were actually applied in Israel.

Direct involvement by the UJA in specific social activities in Israel increased its criticism of the influence of political parties on the system of government. UJA leaders felt that, unlike in America — or even in Britain — in Israel every minister represented a party or even just an interest group within the leading party of the coalition government. UJA officials had to deal with a minister (David Levy) who, early in 1979, had forbidden his staff to speak either with the

53   Interview with Yigael Yadin, 18 July 1981, 12–13 (OH–ICJ).
54   Ibid., 13; Raphael, History, 110.
55   Interview with Irving Bernstein, 28 October 1992, 7 (OH–ICJ); Karp, To Give Life, 112–113 (address of E. Warburg, 12 December 1953).

deputy prime minister or the deputy director general of "Project Renewal."[56]

UJA professionals were willing to concede that every organization needs an effective administration, of which bureaucracy is an essential element. But bureaucracy in its negative sense hampered many of the operations in Israel. The Americans at first had patience and some understanding for this troublesome system of administration and government, believing it to be a heritage from the Ottoman and British periods of rule in Palestine and the Zionist congresses, when the *yishuv* had to conduct its affairs without the authority of a sovereign state. However, they became critical of an Israeli society that failed to overcome these faults and deficiencies. They considered their own system of government, with its checks and balances, to be more effective than the complex Israeli parliamentary democracy.[57]

With the reconstitution of the Jewish Agency, appointing the officers and heads of departments became a bone of contention between the Israeli political machinery and American fund raisers. It is customary for Israeli political parties, when in power, to appoint people to the Jewish Agency and other frameworks on the basis not of ability but of political affiliation. In the late 1970s, representatives of the CJF in the UJA tried to put a stop to the extension of Israeli politics into the Jewish Agency. When Begin told Max Fisher: "I want you to meet the next treasurer of the Agency, Yoram Aridor," Fisher replied: "That's not how we're going to do things anymore." Begin was quite upset, insisting that appointments were the prerogative of the ruling party in Israel and the WZO. Aridor was rejected by the American community leaders, who also vetoed Begin's second choice for the post, Raphael Kotlowitz. Jerold C. Hoffberger, who replaced Fisher in 1983 as chairman of the Board of Governors, was also very impatient with the "overlapping implementation systems" in Israel, which created considerable bureaucratic inefficiency. Fierce arguments of a similar nature between Labor party politicians and Mendel Kaplan of South Africa, the incumbent chairman of the

---

56   Interview with Irving Bernstein, 27 February 1980, 42; (OH–ICJ); Raphael, *History,* 105.

57   Raphael, *History,* 106; interviews with Irving Bernstein, 28 October 1992, 53, 1 September 1980 (OH–ICJ).

Board of Governors in 1992–1995, is further evidence of the fact that no Israeli political party likes to surrender power and make appointments on the basis of ability and professional qualification.[58]

CJF and UJA leaders always opposed the allocation of UJA funds to Israeli political parties — a practice that finally came to a stop shortly after the reconstitution of the Jewish Agency. UJA leaders argued that the system which had made these allocations possible contradicted the basic principle of depoliticization to which the UJA adhered. The intricacies of the Israeli political system later gave rise to a negative attitude on the part of UJA contributors regarding their own investment policy in Israel. In the 1980s they became bewildered over what was happening to the Israeli economy. To their very great surprise, the government that was responsible for the deteriorating economic situation was reelected by a democratic vote. Their reaction was to concentrate their efforts on philanthropy and the purchase of Israel Bonds, and not direct investment in private enterprises. Investors want to make a profit. In the light of their experience, many American Jews preferred to contribute money to the UJA, rather than to invest it unprofitably.[59]

Currently, Israeli entrepreneurs and businessmen have begun to create a new reality. Israeli government policy today, is more attuned to attract investments by Jews from abroad, but UJA leaders are still of the opinion that in 1995 it continues to lag behind the advances of the business world in the Diaspora, and even in Israel. UJA personnel have made many efforts to set before the governments of Israel those conditions that they believe would stimulate investment. Israeli governments have in principle been willing to sell off "socialist" or state enterprises that were developed over several decades, but the process of privatizing such enterprises, which the American partners strongly advise, is a slow one. It is intimately connected with ideologies, traditions, and the heritage and vested interests of labor unions and political parties. That is the norm. COHN, followed by "Operation Independence" and "Project Opportunity,"

58   Interview with Irving Bernstein, 28 October 1992, 35; Golden, *Quiet Diplomat*, 225–228.

59   Interviews with Irving Bernstein, 28 October 1992, 13–14, 1 September 1981, 34 (OH–ICJ); See also Stock, *Partners*, 149–150.

only partially achieved their goals. All this has had its impact on the image of Israeli society held by the leadership of American Jewish communities represented by the CJF and the UJA.[60]

It has been difficult for UJA officials to become deeply involved in the internal life of Israeli society. UJA leaders often lacked detailed information on Israeli domestic issues. They found the Israeli press to be rather parochial. UJA officials did not wish to become too deeply involved in controversial domestic social or ideological issues, though there were exceptions. One issue that from the outset has had very important implications for the development of Israeli society is the relationship between religion and state. UJA leaders always expected Israel to be a nonclerical state; but as long as the issue had no impact on American Jewry, they did not adopt any position on "religious legislation" initiated because of coalition considerations. Americans who visited Israel often failed to understand why it seemed that in Israel one could only be either Orthodox or totally secular.[61]

However when, in the 1980s, the religious parties tried to force the Likud government to amend the "Law of Return" and to redefine legally the concept "Who is a Jew?" even the leaders of the "nonpolitical" UJA had to express clearly and defend the strong reaction and opposition of American Jews. When the Orthodox religious parties in Israel questioned the Jewishness of many American Jews, this led to strong protests. Thus the UJA was unable to invite Dr. Josef Burg, the eloquent leader of the National Religious party, for a campaign speaking tour.[62]

For UJA leaders, "Who is a Jew?" was not an internal Israeli issue. Furthermore, they believed that the government of Israel was not authorized to rule on this issue. When, late in the eighties, Prime Minister-elect Yitzhak Shamir courted four Orthodox parties during difficult coalition negotiations and they demanded that anyone who converted to Judaism without strictly complying with the letter of the *halakha* (Jewish religious law) not be considered Jewish, Max Fisher and a host of Jewish leaders flew to Israel and warned

60 Interview with Irving Bernstein, 28 October 1992, 19–20, 31–32, 86 (OH–ICJ).
61 Ibid., 3, 51, 1 September 1981, 12, 23 February 1982, 18 (OH–ICJ).
62 Ibid., 11 November 1981, 25–26.

Shamir not to alienate American Jewry. Shamir did finally manage to create a government without promising amendment of the Law of Return. Americans expected that Israel, being a pluralistic society, should practice separation of religion and state. UJA leaders also unreservedly supported equality of opportunity for women in Israeli society, an issue that was related to religious legislation. Israeli women were invited to conduct lecture tours in America, while the women in the UJA itself were held up as role models for Israeli women.[63]

Visiting members of UJA missions often have several preconceptions of Israeli society. They expect to see a country with open frontiers and a populace imbued with the pioneering spirit. At one and the same time they want the Israeli to be Ari Ben-Canaan, the hero of Leon Uris's epic novel *Exodus*, or Yoni Netanyahu, the hero and commander of the Entebbe rescue operation, but also to be a leading scholar, an entrepreneur in modern industry and a sophisticated, modern, high-tech scientist. In real-life situations, these images sometimes contradict. Americans expect to find in Israeli society the ideal qualities of the American ethos — freedom, democracy, and a sense of mission — which have been extolled as the vision and meaning of America. It is certainly not easy to satisfy all these expectations. The image of the *halutz* has faded to some degree. Moreover, this image of the pioneer did not always make an impact on potential UJA contributors. American Jews who come in contact with Israel through the UJA understand that in the present decade it is still a haven for oppressed Jews, the means for historic rescue missions — such as of Jews from the former Soviet Union and from Ethiopia. To fulfill its many objectives, Israel must still have its historical pioneering spirit but must, at the same time, function as a modern, high-tech industrial society.[64]

63   Ibid., 28 October 1992, 4, 10, 11, 18, 36; Golden, *Quiet Diplomat*, 450–451.
64   Interviews with Irving Bernstein, 18 November 1981, 36; 23 February 1982, 17; 28 October 1992, 51–52 (OH–ICJ); Karp, *To Give Life*, 114; Golden, *Quiet Diplomat*, 217.

UJA Involvement in Israeli Politics

The UJA is expected to remain neutral on controversial issues of the Israeli body politic. In reality, however, UJA leaders hold their own opinions and attitudes on many political issues. The UJA tends to defend publicly the policy of every Israeli government on issues in which there is a consensus of opinion between Israel and the American Jewish community.

Irving Bernstein said in October 1992:

> There was never a sense of antagonism toward a government because it either was Labor or Likud, socialist or non-socialist. There was rarely an objection to Likud for its philosophy of government — except for 'Who is a Jew' and the West Bank.[65]

Despite this declared attitude, there has long been a closer relationship between leading contributors to the UJA and the Labor party. Some American Jewish capitalists continued to support Labor even after Begin's victory in 1977.[66] Prior to the 1977 elections there were almost no personal relations at the highest level between Herut (later the Likud) and the UJA; Menachem Begin was the only member of the opposition then known to the UJA's leading professionals. Thus for a long time the UJA did not invite members of the opposition to its campaign meetings in the United States, the excuse being that it could only avail itself of the services of leading personalities who could interest potential donors, and these were to be found in the parties that formed the government. UJA professionals admit, however, that the Likud is justified in believing that the UJA was Labor-oriented.

UJA leaders had great difficulty establishing close relations with the cabinet members of the first Likud government formed in 1977, who preferred to deal with the American Jewish community through political channels. Likud ministers believed that the Conference of Presidents of Major Jewish Organizations (COJO) best represented American Jewry. One probable reason for this inclination was the historic ideological preference of the Revisionst movement for "the

---

65 Interview with Irving Bernstein, 28 October 1992, 11–12 (OH–ICJ).
66 Stock, *Partners*, xiii.

political approach. During the prestate period, Revisionists had been rather antagonistic to fund-raising agencies. Begin's formalism induced him to give priority to what he considered to be "the political forces," and these — he believed — did not include the UJA. In 1981 Begin made an unfortunate remark to the effect that "not every contributor in the United States is a Jewish leader," creating tension between the Likud government and important lay leaders of the UJA and the federations, a rather harmful situation. However, a good relationship was finally established between Begin and UJA leaders. "Project Renewal" and the prime minister's missions created an atmosphere of improved understanding.[67]

Relations with other Likud leaders such as David Levy and Ariel Sharon were also, for a while, problematic. In November 1981, Irving Bernstein recalled: 'We brought over many younger [Likud] members of the Knesset.... I don't believe they understood the American [Jewish] mentality. Labor understood it better because they grew up with it.... This group hasn't."[68]

When members of the Labor party came into contact with Americans within the framework of the UJA, they could invoke an understanding of Israel and its problems. When Likud members such as David Levy met with UJA senior officials, the latter "wanted him to get some understanding of the American Jewish community." Furthermore, senior Likud personalities such as Ariel Sharon and Moshe Arens represented points of view that were difficult for the Americans to accept. Arens, for example, opposed the Camp David accords. In 1981 the highest UJA officials even questioned whether he should be invited to America. On the whole, however, such political considerations were not the norm.[69]

The established practice of UJA leaders was to refrain from adopting a position in matters of Israel's foreign affairs or security policy. Though the West Bank issue was an exception, they did not make their position public. The UJA's constituency was divided on the subject. However, it would seem that in the past decade the

---

67 Interviews: with Irving Bernstein, 29 April 1980, 17–18, with Yigael Yadin, 28 July 1981, 37–38 (OH–ICJ).

68 Interview with Irving Bernstein, 18 November 1981, 25–28 (OH–ICJ).

69 Ibid., 24, 27.

majority of the UJA's contributors, canvassers, and professionals, in their individual capacities, were more sympathetic toward peace efforts than to the stance that posited no territorial concessions, even in exchange for peace.[70]

Financial noninvolvement by the UJA in the West Bank and the Gaza Strip, however, was mainly on account of its legal status in the United States. Most persons connected with the UJA differentiated between the West Bank and the Golan Heights. It was widely accepted that the West Bank had become a religious, rather than a security or political issue, but that the settlers of the Golan Heights were there to develop the land. UJA missions visited the Golan, their members returning with the impression of Israel's vulnerability in that region. A positive attitude prevailed in the American Jewish communities regarding Israeli control of the Golan Heights.[71]

The legal status of the UJA precluded the adoption of an official stance on such issues as the Israeli–Arab conflict. But in private conversations, its members were prepared to give expression to what they believed was the prevailing opinion among both the leadership and the rank and file: that a greater effort should be made to reach an understanding with the Palestinians and the Arab world. Israel should encourage dialogue, but at the same time not relinquish territory for peace except beyond the "green line" in the West Bank. It was also their opinion that Israel was making a mistake by not providing its Arab minority with greater equality in the fields of education, political rights, and economic opportunities, and that if the situation was not soon rectified, Israel would face grave trouble in the future.[72]

In their official capacity, UJA personnel could not be very effective advocates of Israeli policy when it clashed with that adopted by the American administration. When on 20 December 1974 President Ford welcomed nineteen Jewish leaders, Frank Lautenberg, chairman of the UJA, and Mel Dubinsky, chairman of the UIA, were among those invited to the White House who heard the president

70   Ibid., 28 October 1992, 16–17, 27–28.
71   Ibid., 1 September 1981, 7, 9–10; Golden, *Quiet Diplomat*, 362, 366, 448; interview with Leonard Bell, 10 July 1977, 16 (OH–ICJ).
72   Interview with Irving Bernstein, 28 October 1992, 15–16 (OH–ICJ).

promise continued American support for Israel. In that same year, Lautenberg and Irving Bernstein created opportunities for Israeli cabinet members to meet with American policymakers. The person who more than anyone else became a nonofficial intermediary during the period of "reassessment," when the Ford administration was pressuring Israel, was Max Fisher. His activities might be indicative of what Jewish leaders closely affiliated with the UJA can do for Israel in Washington — and for the United States in Jerusalem — during difficult times. In 1975, when President Ford and Secretary Kissinger were unable to convince the Rabin government to withdraw from the Mitla and Gidi passes in Sinai without a formal renunciation of belligerency by the Egyptians, the Ford administration placed a partial curb on U.S. military and financial support for Israel.

American Jewish reaction was a nationwide campaign of support for Israel. Fisher was invited to the Oval Office, and was prepared to make great efforts to find a solution. Fisher's final note on the meeting in the White House was: "I settled the President down." In Jerusalem, Rabin concluded his final meeting with Fisher by saying: "Max, tell Kissinger and Ford not to worry — the process will continue. The talks will be resumed."[73]

In 1975 and again in 1981, during what was known as the AWACS crisis between the Begin government and the Reagan administration on issues between the two governments, Fisher saw himself as a builder of bridges and not as a spokesman of the American Jewish community in its support of Israel. In 1975 Fisher stated: "My fundamental responsibilty was as an American. Then as an American Jewish leader. And finally I had my love for Israel." There was no question of dual loyalty.[74]

When Israel was under attack in the international arena, and the United Nations adopted the infamous "Zionism equals racism" resolution, the UJA leadership, headed by Frank Lautenberg and Irving Bernstein, reacted by organizing a supermission of more than 3,000 Jews from hundreds of American communities. Named "This

---

73   Interview with Frank Lautenberg, 19 June 1975, 7ff (OH–ICJ); Golden, *Quiet Diplomat*, 310–312, 326.
74   Golden, *Quiet Diplomat*, 426–430; 322–323.

Year in Jerusalem," it turned into a demonstration of political solidarity that heartened even the most skeptical of Israelis.[75]

"No Taxation without Representation" — the UJA Demands a Say

The desire of American Jewish fund raisers to be somehow involved in decisions as to how the money they raised should be spent is an old story.

After the establishment of Israel, the CJFWF increased its pressure to have a say in the allocation of funds raised by the federations under the auspices of the UJA. Philip Bernstein, executive vice president of the federation movement since 1954, explained:

> The Federations obligated the CJF to help carry out the trusteeship of their funds sent to national and international organizations outside of their communities — to ensure that they would be spent more effectively.[76]

In order to get more information, the CJF sent study missions to Israel. One of those missions, in 1958, proposed instituting a more effective framework for cooperation and the exchange of views with the Jewish Agengy. Irving Kane, who chaired a special committee, reported to the General Assembly of the CJFWF in November 1958 that 10 percent of the funds contributed by world Jewry were used to finance WZO activities, even in the United States. A resolution was adopted demanding reorganization that would ensure ultimate *American* responsibility and control of the expenditure of the funds and that they would not be used for any kind of political activity or for cultural or educational projects in the United States.[77]

Also, under pressure of a threat that in view of a new ruling by the U.S. Internal Revenue Service the UJA was in danger of

---

75   Karp, *To Give Life*, 156.
76   Stock, *Partners*, 168; Philip Bernstein, *To Dwell in Unity: The Jewish Federation Movement in America since 1960* (Philadelphia, 1983), 8–9.
77   Stock, *Partners*, 170–171; CJFWF, Assembly Paper, Twenty-Eighth General Assembly — Report by Irving Kane, 14 November 1959, quoted in Stock, *Partners*, 170.

losing its tax-exempt status unless full control of expenditure was transferred to an *American* organization, the Jewish Agency agreed to the reorganization. The Jewish Agency for Israel, Inc. (JAFI Inc.), which had been incorporated in New York already in 1949, would be responsible for disbursement of all funds raised by the UJA, while the Jewish Agency in Jerusalem would become its agent. Members of the JAFI Board of Directors had to be American citizens, some of them representatives of the federations. Thus in the early 1960s, UJA contributors received a certain voice in the disbursement of UJA funds. Allocations were no longer made to Israeli political parties.[78]

In 1966 JAFI Inc. merged with the UIA after the latter had invited 100 leaders of the federations to serve on its Board of Trustees. Though still called the United Israel Appeal after the merger, it was no longer a Zionist organization. America's Jewish communities, "the grass roots" to use Max Fisher's term, had a sizable share in it. The renewed UIA took over supervison of the budgeting of funds raised by the UJA and the way they were to be spent by the Jewish Agency in Jerusalem. This was a very important step toward the reconstitution of the Enlarged Jewish Agency in 1971, in which the UIA would participate in the decision-making processes of the Jewish Agency itself.[79]

After the unprecedented rise in the status of the UJA and the CJF as contributors to the State of Israel during and after the Six-Day War, American fund raisers, dissatisfied with only formal membership in the UIA in New York, repeated their demand to become equal partners in the Jewish Agency in Jerusalem. Negotiations toward the reconstitution of the Jewish Agency entered their final phase.[80]

Abraham Harman considered the constitution of an expanded Jewish Agency as

---

78 Stock, *Partners,* 173; interview with Philip Bernstein, 21 March 1976, 40–41 (OH–ICJ).

79 Interview with P. Bernstein, 21 March 1976, 42–43; (OH–ICJ); Stock, *Partners,* 186–187.

80 Formulation of Mel Dubinsky, who succeeded Max Fisher as chairman of the UIA in 1971. See Golden, *Quiet Diplomat,* 218; Stock, *Partners,* 191.

a combination of three factors: firstly of wanting to know what was happening here [in Israel] and having a voice in it; secondly the legal aspect... [complying with American law]; thirdly — and not less important — an increasing feeling here, in the Agency, *that without reform the thing* [i.e., fund raising in the U.S.] *would collapse.*[81]

A comparison of the processes of establishing the Jewish Agency in 1929 with its reconstitution in 1971 illuminates more than anything else the major historical change in how American Jewish philanthropists visualized Eretz Israel. In the negotiations that preceded the conclusion of the "Pact of Glory" (1929), the non-Zionist partners were not even asked to recognize the priority of Eretz Israel in future fund-raising efforts. After the Six-Day War, the centrality of Israel had become one of the most important pillars of the forthcoming renewed Jewish Agency.[82]

Conditions after the Six-Day War were obviously different from those that prevailed in 1929. The UJA–CJF had become partners in major efforts to provide partial financial backing for the smooth functioning of many Israeli social, cutural, and educational services as well as the financing of the immigration and absorption process. The Jewish Agency, which received funds from the UJA–UIA, was a full partner in this historic development.[83]

Legally the reconstitution was a question of revival, but essentially it was a new creation. On the Israeli side there was some suspicion that at least some of the community leaders were bent on taking over the Jewish Agency, and that they might be tempted to use their financial clout to neutralize the WZO. The Herut party (later the leading component of the Likud) rejected *in toto* the idea of reconstitution. The General Zionists had reservations about letting professionals serve on the Executive of the Enlarged Jewish Agency.

---

81   Interview with A. Harman, 20 and 29 May 1980, 19–20 (OH–ICJ).
82   Menahem Kaufman, "Louis Marshall, Chaim Weizmann and the Establishment of the Enlarged Jewish Agency," *Studies in the History of Zionism Presented to Israel Goldstein*, ed. Y. Bauer, M. Davis, and I. Kolatt (Jerusalem, 1976), 38–95; idem, *Ambiguous Partnership*, (Jerusalem: Magnes Press, 1991), 26–28.
83   Interview with Philip Bernstein, 23 June 1976, 41 (OH–ICJ).

The negative image of Baron Rothschild's administrators in the First Aliyah colonies had not yet been forgotten.[84]

In July 1969 the Zionist General Council adopted the plan for the reconstituted Enlarged Jewish Agency. On 21 June 1971 the Founding Assembly of the reconstituted Jewish Agency approved the agreement between the partners and stipulated that the WZO would bear responsibility for Zionist programs such as Zionist-oriented education, and the Jewish Agency for immigration and its absorption.[85]

In the late 1980s and early 1990s, however, the overseas fund-raising agencies were unable to provide the Jewish Agency with all the funds necessary to finance the wave of mass immigration. Simultaneously, the UJA–CJF's influence in decisions concerning expenditures, which it had received through the reconstitution of the Jewish Agency, now decreased.[86]

The impact of the American Jewish model on Israeli society, then, was probably less than that expected by the initiators of the agreement of 1971. But American fund raisers would have liked to see a higher priority given to social planning, better housing, and education for immigrants, as well as greater coordination of immigrant absorption — not only between the Jewish Agency and the government but also between the many governmental agencies dealing with those issues. Last but not least, they would have preferred greater investment in the commercial and industrial sectors.[87]

Epilogue

The image of Israel held by UJA–CJF opinion leaders during the 1990s is made up of various components. There is now a rather greater similarity in the views of the leadership of the federations'

84 Interview with A. Harman, 20 and 29 May 1980, 20 (OH–ICJ); Stock, *Beyond*, 192; Stock, *Partners*, 193.
85 Stock, *Beyond*, 179–180; interview with Philip Bernstein, 21 March 1976, 42 (OH–ICJ); Agreement for the Reconstitution of the Jewish Agency for Israel, quoted in Stock, *Beyond*, Appendix D, 221–229.
86 Stock, *Beyond*, 194–195.
87 Interview with Irving Bernstein, 28 October 1992, 30, 51–52 (OH–ICJ).

roof organization and those of the central fund-raising agency than before the reconstitution of the Enlarged Jewish Agency. For most of these American Jewish leaders, Israel of the nineties is the focus of Jewish identity and identification. It is the spiritual homeland of the Jewish people, a kind of "old country" for American Jews. There is no major problem of dual loyalty because, as American citizens, they feel they are an integral part of the American nation. They still envisage Israel today as a land that has played the historic role of a haven, a place of refuge for Jews in times of crisis, and they see themselves as partners in the drama of Jewish revival and survival, in which Israelis play the key roles.

American Jewish fund raisers have never been passive observers of Israel. They have always been actively involved, and there has been a constant pattern of mutual give and take. The American Jewish communities gave money; Israel received the funds and in return provided American Jews with a civil religion, new pride in their Jewishness and a haven for their oppressed brethren. Nevertheless, there have been ups and downs in this partnership.

Under the impact of the Holocaust and guilt on the part of many American Jews, the security of Israel and its survival have always had first priority. Pinchas Sapir said in 1975: "When Jewish blood is running in the streets people make a bigger effort than in 'normal' days."[88]

Jewish immigration to Israel has been the second important issue that has molded the relationship between the UJA–CJF and Israel. But the financial response of American Jewish communities to the needs of immigration and its absorption was not so self-evident. Even the substantial financial contribution of the UJA to "Operation Exodus" for Jews from the former USSR during the early 1990s has not come up to Israel's expectations.

Levi Eshkol succeeded in explaining to Max Fisher the meaning of mass immigration. When Fisher suggested: "Because you are short on money, wouldn't it make sense for Israel to shut down immigration for a while?" Eshkol replied: "Even if you don't give us a dime, no Jew is ever going to add to the six million.... Israel exists

88   Karp, *To Give Life*, 153; interviews: with Herbert Friedman, 1975–1976, 9–15, with Pinchas Sapir, 6 June 1975 (OH–ICJ).

so Jews may exist." Irving Bernstein said that the UJA has opposed any planning of *aliyah* and that "the UJA's reaction is to rescue in the whole sense of rescue. I'm not sure there would be the same response if we said we're going to take a limited number." In periods of mass immigration the UJA leadership has had to reactivate its machinery of rescue and rehabilitation.[89]

Full success has depended on the response in the communities. After the Six-Day War and the increased personal involvement of the UJA rank and file in the daily life of Israeli communities, the UJA became more and more concerned with the provision of a better life in the development towns and the underprivileged quarters of Israeli cities.[90]

Before the establishment of Israel the centrality of Eretz Israel was, for non-Zionists, limited to its religious and probably also to its cultural aspects. The first change occurred after the Holocaust, but the War of Independence was the main turning point. Between 1948 and 1967 the federations accepted the central role of Israel as a haven for Jews in distress, but it was not always the focal point when the distribution of funds raised in the campaigns was on the agenda. The Six-Day War was the second turning point. It was then that the centrality of Israel became a matter of American Jewish consensus and the focus of Jewish fund raising. The opposite is also true. The State of Israel has recognized the importance of the UJA "as a major instrument for Jewish unity centering on Israel, as probably the most popular and encompassing instrument for Jewish identification with Israel."[91]

89   Golden, *Quiet Diplomat*, 63; interview with Irving Bernstein, 28 October 1992, 31 (OH–ICJ); Karp, *To Give Life*, 151.
90   Interview with Irving Bernstein, 1 September 1981, 20 (OH–ICJ).
91   Interview with A. Harman, 13 November 1980, 5 (OH–ICJ).

Bonding Images:
Miami Jews and the Campaign for Israel Bonds

Deborah Dash Moore

How did American Jews initially envision the first Jewish state in almost two millennia? Is there some way to delve beneath the pronouncements of American Jewish leaders and the politics of American Jewish organizations to glimpse images that ordinary Jews might have found appealing? Scholars have paid attention to Israel's significance for American Jews usually by focusing on the national organizations headquartered in New York City.[1] But there is something to be learned from viewing local responses to the Jewish state.

This essay explores aspects of the convergence of world Jewish events and local Jewish perceptions: specifically, how Israel came to be part of the consciousness of American Jews, taking Miami as a case study. My choice of Miami reflects research I did on that city as a new, postwar American Jewish community.[2] In 1948, most American Jews lived in a rather parochial society, so one must look at that milieu to understand how they came to terms with the rapidly changing Jewish world in the aftermath of the Holocaust. Such a local perspective potentially can balance or correct analyses of Israel's meaning for American Jews emphasizing national trends.

Looking backward from a distance of almost half a century, it

---

1 See, for example, Melvin I. Urofsky, *American Zionism from Herzl to the Holocaust* (Garden City, N.Y.: Doubleday, 1976); idem, *We Are One! American Jewry and Israel* (Garden City, N.Y.: Doubleday, 1978); and Aaron Berman, *Nazism, the Jews and American Zionism, 1933–1948* (Detroit: Wayne State University Press, 1990), 13, 156–158.

2 Deborah Dash Moore, *To the Golden Cities: Pursuing the American Jewish Dream in Miami and L.A.* (New York: Free Press, 1994).

appears that Jews took Jewish political sovereignty in stride. There was much less anguish and hand wringing than one might have expected, given the controversies Zionism provoked during World War II and the interwar years. Yet the process of integrating Israel into American Jewish consciousness — of finding and securing a place for the new state — involved struggles and choices. The outcome we recognize today — an Israel that is an integral part of American Jewish life, affirmed and celebrated as a crucial component of Jewish identity — was not inevitable.[3]

Along with a local focus on Miami Jews, I look closely at the meanings attached to Israel Bond campaigns in the 1950s. Israeli leaders asked American Jews to contribute funds to support the fledgling state, and during the early years of statehood hundreds of thousands of American Jews responded to those appeals. Wherein lay the power of these requests for aid? Surely their rhetoric, which reached many American Jews, produced compelling imagery that helped American Jews envision Israel. Israel Bond drives took selected themes, along with personnel, from postwar United Jewish Appeal (UJA) fund-raising efforts. These interpretations of Israel evoked powerful emotions and helped shape a myth around the state that integrated it into the consciousness of Miami Jews. Ironically, this process ultimately involved by-passing Zionism, especially Zionist politics, and allowing an unmediated vision of the meaning of the state to form.

Miami Jews treated the political realities of the postwar world as raw material for their vision of Israel and its creation. According to their perceptions, the major players on the Jewish stage of world politics included: Palestinian Jews, settlers and pioneers living in the land of Israel; the British, mandatory power and ruler over the Palestinians; and refugees, European survivors of the Nazi death camps. Important but minor players included: the United States, influential observer and power in the free world; American Jews, less influential observers but economically secure; and Arabs, fellow residents of Palestine who opposed Jewish immigration to the land.

---

3   On current views, see Charles S. Liebman and Steven M. Cohen, *Two Worlds of Judaism: The Israeli and American Experiences* (New Haven, Conn.: Yale University Press, 1990).

In the drama of the creation of the State of Israel, Palestinian Jews were heroes, seeking to rescue refugees from the displaced persons (DP) camps and bring them to their homeland through illegal immigration. The British emerged as villains, trying to thwart illegal immigration and prevent the establishment of a Jewish state. DPs were objects of pity and suffering, who yet possessed a spark that could be kindled into a flame in their homeland. American Jews were helpful supporters (as were all freedom-loving peoples), Arabs were harmful opponents (but not as serious an enemy as the British), and the United States was to be wooed and enlisted on the side of liberation.

As a drama, this vision of the creation of Israel paralleled the American experience. It combined elements of the American revolution against the British with frontier settlement and the fight against Native Americans. Reduced to melodrama, this reading of postwar Jewish politics ignored the bitter, fratricidal struggles among Zionist parties, especially between Labor Zionists and Revisionists, and their respective military arms, the Haganah and Irgun. Its themes were liberation and redemption, reenactment in secular terms of a religious message. Although rooted in Zionist understanding of recent Jewish history, transformation of newspaper headlines into frontier visions ultimately eclipsed American Zionist politics. American Zionists played no role, not even a supporting one, in this interpretation of Israel's creation. They appeared neither as important intermediaries with American leaders nor as vital Jewish figures rallying American Jews to support their brethren fighting the front-line battles. The vision departed significantly from historical reality.

During the first precarious months of Israel's existence, as it fought a war against Arab armies on all fronts, American Zionists were, indeed, best prepared to throw themselves into the fateful task of helping Israel survive the Arab onslaught. Zealously, Zionists raised funds, lobbied for political support, purchased arms and materiel and secretly shipped them to Israel, staged enthusiastic receptions for the first Israeli representatives to arrive in the United States, and gloried in symbols of statehood. Yet by the time Israel Bond campaigns commenced in 1951, Zionists found their hegemony as interpreters of Israel to Americans and American Jews undermined by their very success. As American Jews rallied to Israel's cause, they also grasped the power to project their own visions on historical reality, forming an attractive image of the meaning of the Jewish state that ignored any role for American Zionists.[4]

Israel's feisty prime minister, David Ben-Gurion, on the other hand, made it clear that Zionists belonged in Zion. The task of winning the American diaspora to the support of Israel, he argued, could best be accomplished by Israelis. Zionists could not easily ignore the prime minister's call to American Jews to come to Israel, or at least to send their sons and daughters to settle and build the new state. Nor could they summarily reject Ben-Gurion's appeal for *aliyah*, as did the anti-Zionists.[5] What it meant to be an American Zionist became increasingly vague. Although Zionists intensified and expanded their political roles within the American Jewish community, they found themselves gradually displaced by other, less politically committed interpreters of Israel, especially the fund raisers. These manipulators of symbols contributed to the Zionist loss of control over Israeli myth making.[6]

Miami Jews projected their fantasies of Israel on visiting Israeli emissaries and endowed them with the virtues of the Jewish state. These individuals acquired heroic proportions as creators of Jewish sovereignty. They came to Miami to ask American Jews for money, encouraging a vision of partnership in the great task of state building. Yet even in Miami the Zionist leadership lost its hegemony as guardians of Israeli myth. A more independent Israel, freed of American Zionist entanglements, drew on wider circles of support. The decision to establish Israel Bonds allowed Miami Jews to invent an Israel they adored. Cabinet ministers, ambassadors, and military men graced the numerous bond rallies, dinners, meetings, and receptions and presented a vision of Israel with heroic dimensions. Bond drives similarly transformed the realities of Zionist politics into cultural rhetoric that appealed to Miami Jews and addressed their desire for a homeland to redeem Jews. The State of Israel loomed

---

4   Henry Morgenthau III, *Mostly Morgenthaus: A Family History* (New York: Ticknor & Fields, 1991), 411, 418.

5   Urofsky, *American Zionism*, 259, 266–270.

6   See the essay in this volume by S. Ilan Troen, "American Experts in the Design of Zionist Society: The Reports of Elwood Mead and Robert Nathan," where he details Nathan's influential role in initiating the idea of Israel Bonds.

above all of the petty political intrigue and ideological debates that plagued Zionism. Through the purchase of bonds in a public forum designed to stimulate support for Israel, Miami Jews simultaneously invested in a vision and signified their identification with the heroes and heroines who appealed to them.

Unlike the United Jewish Appeal's plea for tax-deductible contributions, only part of which went to the faction-ridden Jewish Agency, Israel bonds were sold as direct investments in the state. No intermediaries stood between the state and American Jewish investors. Bondholders received interest on their investments from the State of Israel. "I moved over to Bonds because everybody moved over," Lou Boyar recalled.

> We weren't fighting local — local didn't have Bonds. We honestly believed that the future of the Jewish people in Israel meant they have to be self-supporting. They have to earn enough money, and they can't earn it unless they get investments.[7]

Support for bonds translated into exclusive support for Israel, not shared with local Miami Jewish organizations.

A series of exceptionally effective speakers delivered the message and delineated the role of Miami Jews in fulfilling its terms, beginning in the months following the U.N. vote for partition. They spoke, logically, as Palestinian Zionists and appealed to Miami Jews to support them in their struggle for independence. Among the most effective was Golda Meir (Meyerson), who visited Miami in February 1948. Walking into a meeting room of the White House Hotel where forty hotel owners were holding their Central Jewish Appeal breakfast, she generated "a sudden fever of excitement." "As if instructed by an invisible courier, the entire assemblage was on its feet, applauding."[8] Meir's unexpected visit — she was in Miami to attend a national meeting of the United Jewish Appeal, not to speak

---

7   Louis Boyar, Oral History Interview, 14 March 1976, 5–6, Oral History of the United Jewish Appeal, Oral History Archives, Institute of Contemporary Jewry, Hebrew University (OH–ICJ).

8   *Jewish Floridian*, 13 February 1948. The dramatic article was written by Milton Malakoff, the public relations person for the UJA in Miami.

to local givers — allowed those Miami Jews assembled to hear her message.

"Miami Beach reminds me of Tel Aviv," she began, "except that here one doesn't hear any shooting by day and by night." She went on to explain that the war had begun; it was not a war the Jews had chosen, "but the Mufti, friend and co-worker of Hitler during the World War, has refused to permit us to live in peace.... Great Britain is neutral — neutral between the attacker and the attacked." Jews could not even legally possess weapons to defend themselves under Britain's policy, she explained. "This is your war, too," Meir concluded. "But we do not ask you to guard the convoy. If there is any blood to be spilled, let it be ours. Remember, though, that how long this blood will be shed depends upon you."[9] Meir's message of collective responsibility, of the continuing war against Hitler's minions now in Arab dress, and of Britain's betrayal sparked Miami Jews to raise unprecedented sums to help secure the Jewish state.

Meir remembered Miami as "a good example" of what she did. "[We] started off with a breakfast meeting; then there was a luncheon in a nightclub, and in the evening we flew from Miami to Miami Beach for another meeting in the big hotel there." She explained that "the breakfast meeting was for the local community while the luncheon was arranged for Jews who were spending their vacation in Miami. At both we did very, very well." But the dinner meeting was another matter. "At that hotel, although it was owned by a Jew, fund-raising was forbidden." But the pressing needs of the fledgling Jewish state could not defer to such rules. If wealthy Jews on vacation were willing to come to a dinner, Meir had to appeal to them for their financial support. Although she did not necessarily expect an invitation to fund-raise, Meir nonetheless found the situation daunting. "I remember coming down to the patio, which was so beautiful, and thinking that this I couldn't take." As she looked at the audience,

> I was sure they couldn't care less. I didn't eat a thing. I drank black coffee and smoked my cigarettes with tears in my eyes. I thought 'How can I, in this beautiful atmosphere, speak about

9   Ibid.

what's happening at home.'... I was sure that when I got up to talk, they would all walk out.

But Henry Morgenthau, Jr., reassured her, though it was his first visit to Miami. The former secretary of the Treasury headed the UJA and was running the meeting. In fact, nobody walked out, and the evening dinner raised around $1.5 million in cash. As Meir recognized, "Not all of them were Zionists, but they all realized what was at stake." The single day in Miami netted between $4 and $5 million.[10]

Miami Jews were not alone in the outpouring of money. In 1948 the UJA raised an enormous sum in comparison to previous levels of giving. Although the UJA maintained a high level of contributions throughout 1949, its receipts for the following year declined. Miami Jews continued to give at a rate far above what had been raised prior to 1948, because of the rapid growth of the community. However, the amount of the funds allocated to the UJA failed to increase.[11] In 1949 Miami Jews accepted an ambitious goal of raising a million dollars for the UJA, but the fund drive fell far short of its aim.[12] The following year fund raisers lowered their sights, but they still failed to reach their self-imposed quota. Seeking stabilization, Miami's Federation voted in 1951 on a precampaign allocation formula that gave 58 percent of the first million dollars raised to UJA; the remaining 42 percent went to local and national Jewish agencies. Miami was one of the first cities to make a precampaign commitment to the UJA, a sign of Zionist strength within the Federation.[13]

The decision to inaugurate a campaign for Israel Bonds occurred against this background of stabilizing or declining contributions to the UJA. In the spring of 1951 the Israeli minister of Trade and

10 Golda Meir, Oral History excerpt, *American Jewish Memoirs: Oral Documentation*, ed. Geoffrey Wigoder (Jerusalem: Institute of Contemporary Jewry, Hebrew University, 1980), 85–87.
11 Minutes of the Board of Governors, Greater Miami Jewish Federation, 30 December 1952.
12 Only $1,101,000 was raised, so the UJA contribution was $530,000 or 53 percent of the total for 1949. *Jewish Floridian*, 13 January 1950.
13 The formula was worked out with the aid of UJA "top brass," including Henry Montor. *Jewish Floridian*, 26 January 1951.

Industry visited Miami to initiate planning for the bond campaign.[14] Two members of the local professional fund-raising staff of the Federation left to work for bonds.[15]

The Federation's executive director ruefully recognized the "friendly competition" and Israeli leaders' preference for bonds, despite the comparative superiority of the UJA.[16] Israel's decision to back the bond drive meant not only competition for funds but the development of an unmediated relationship by American Jewish bond purchasers with the State of Israel. Rather than supporting Israel through a contribution to Miami's Central Jewish Appeal, which also provided funds to local and national American Jewish organizations, Miami Jews now possessed a vehicle of direct support of the state.

When Golda Meir returned to Miami in 1951 as Israel's minister of labor, she came to speak at a local "Salute to Israel" bond rally. Two thousand turned out to hear her. Meir's effective oratory produced the "Miracle of Miami": the sale of over $500,000 of bonds in the first ten days of the drive.[17] This sum came close to the total annual Miami contribution to the UJA.[18] Before the year ended — a year that included several bombings of Miami synagogues — Miami Jews had purchased over a million dollars of bonds. They responded warmly to an array of rallies and concerts, and to speeches by such Israelis as Avraham Harman and Abba Eban.[19] In February the State of Israel honored Joseph Cherner for his role in the bond drive. Henry Morgenthau, Jr., now national head of Israel Bonds, came down for the luncheon, featuring Lena Horne, the black entertainer. Yaakov Shimshon Shapiro, Israel's first attorney general, represented the young state at the event. The press billed the affair

---

14 *Jewish Floridian*, 13 April 1951.

15 *Jewish Floridian*, 6 April 1951.

16 *Jewish Floridian*, 14 September 1951.

17 *Jewish Floridian*, 18 May 1951.

18 In 1950 UJA received $583,487 from the CJA fund raising. *Jewish Floridian*, 5 January 1951. The goal had been $810,000. *Jewish Floridian*, 13 January 1950.

19 *Jewish Floridian*, 16 November 1951 (Elban and funds raised), 25 May 1951 (rally), 14 September 1951 (Harman), 30 November 1951 (Damari concert).

as the first time Israel had paid "official tribute" to an American citizen.[20]

In 1952 Miami Jewish leaders sought to replicate the success of the initial year. They repeated the parade of Israeli visitors to Miami on behalf of bonds. In January the chief rabbi of Tel Aviv arrived; Golda Meir returned in March, followed by Gershon Agron, editor of the *Jerusalem Post* in April and, in June, Moshe Sharett, Israel's foreign minister. As 1952 drew to a close, a final "Big Day" for bonds was scheduled. The Florida Power and Light Company dedicated its downtown window on Northeast 2nd Street, off Flagler, to a special display honoring Miami Jews' efforts on behalf of the Jewish democracy. The mural depicted a background montage documenting the progress of industry, agriculture, and port facilities in Israel. In the foreground stood an American Jewish man and woman jointly watering the flower of the newly flourishing land.[21]

The image of nurturing the economy of the new state reflected nicely the sense of partnership bond campaigns inspired in Miami Jews. They saw bonds as a form of patriotic investment in the State of Israel, as the purchase of United States Liberty Bonds had represented an investment in America's future. Coming only a few years after intensive bond drives in the United States during World War II, Israel Bond campaigns evoked similar sentiments. Morgenthau's presence as head of Israel Bonds reinforced a sense of continuity with his years as secretary of the Treasury, when he orchestrated the successful hoopla surrounding U.S. Saving Bonds. The implied similarity between the two investments combined elements of patriotism and faith, fused American and Jewish experience, and suggested a pleasing parallel between the national struggles of the United States and Israel. Yet purchasers also understood that bonds were in fact redeemable, with interest. Unlike contributions to the Central Jewish Appeal, bond purchases could not be written off as charity. Indeed, by the mid-1950s Miami Jews increasingly gave Israel Bonds as payment on their pledges to the Central Jewish

20   *Jewish Floridian*, 1 February 1952.
21   *Jewish Floridian*, 12 December 1952.

Appeal.[22] Israel Bonds also resembled one of the highest forms of *tzedakah*, interest-free loans designed to help individuals achieve self-sufficiency.

Solicitation of bonds often occurred within a festive and heroic milieu, unlike requests for UJA funds, which tended to stress Jewish suffering, misery, and pressing needs of rescue and rehabilitation. Such differing appeals for money amplified the contrast between a bond investment as opposed to a charitable contribution. In 1952, in response to Israel's critical need for cash, the Central Jewish Appeal responded to an emergency request from the UJA by borrowing $200,000 from local banks.[23] Similarly, during the Suez crisis in 1955 and 1956, local Miami leaders raised over $500,000 in emergency funds through borrowing.[24] In contrast, after the Sinai campaign Israel Bonds sent over a number of Israeli military heroes, including Ezer Weizman, then the fighter wing commander of the Israeli Air Force, and Mordecai Gur, at that time a battalion commander of Nahal paratroopers.

Miami Jews saw Weizman as the personification of the "indomitable spirit of the Jewish State and its people."[25] He had already appeared briefly on television, interviewed by Edward R. Murrow in a "See It Now" program on Israel and Egypt. Standing beside an old plane, Murrow asked Weizman how he managed with such obsolete aircraft. Weizman admitted he would like to have high-speed aircraft, and that it was difficult to shoot down the new Egyptian planes. The discussion then turned to how few minutes and seconds it took to fly over Israel.[26] For American Jews watching the program, Weizman broadcast a clear message of heroism, danger, and need — a message reiterated when he appeared before Miami Jews in person. Weizman represented the living reality of the new

22 Minutes of the Executive Committee, Greater Miami Jewish Federation, 23 April 1956.

23 Minutes of Executive Committee, Greater Miami Jewish Federation, 26 February 1952.

24 Minutes of Executive Committee, Greater Miami Jewish Federation, 22 March 1955; *Jewish Floridian*, 22 June 1956.

25 *Jewish Floridian*, 15 June 1956.

26 "See It Now," 13 March 1956, at Jewish Museum's Broadcast Archives.

Jew who had risen from the ashes of the destruction of European Jewry.

In fact, bond drives generated mutual interaction. A native-born sabra, Gur recalled that "it was the first time I saw Jews living outside Israel. It was the first time I saw American Jews and understood what it meant to be one." American Jews generally impressed Gur.

> I thought at the time that they didn't really know exactly what had happened in Israel and what being an Israeli and what life in Israel really meant. For them, the period between the War of Independence and the Sinai Campiagn was something quite obscure.

He concluded that "the Sinai Campaign brought Israel and the Israel Defense Forces onto the world map as a military power, as a partner to the British and French forces; that created a certain pride and a sudden feeling of belonging." Gur's visits up and down the East Coast, from Miami to Montreal, affected him. "For the first time I felt a part of the Jewish world, which was a new phenomenon for me." Even when he returned to Israel, "I felt for the first time that I was as much a Jew as an Israeli." Bonds engendered a mutual sense of belonging shared by American Jews and Israelis, albeit one unconnected to Zionism. Gur "didn't feel there was any difference between those who considered themselves Zionists and those who did not." He thought that involvement in Jewish and pro-Israel activity was crucial, not membership in a Zionist organization.[27]

By 1958, competition of bond campaigns with local fund raising had eased in Miami. Bond leaders accorded recognition to important figures in the Federation as co-workers on behalf of Israel by including them on the dais at public events.[28] Indeed, by 1958 Miami's bond campaign had achieved such prominence that it could afford a generous gesture. Bond drives even entered Miami synagogues, with great success. The appeals for the purchase of bonds made from pulpits during the High Holy Days signified Israel's centrality for Miami Jews. Synagogues normally reserved the High Holy Day

27   Mordecai Gur, Oral History Interview, 24 June 1979, 1–7, Oral History of the United Jewish Appeal (OH–ICJ).

28   "Editorial," *Jewish Floridian*, 9 May 1958.

appeal for funds to help cover congregational expenses, and many counted on the extra money raised at this time. By urging the purchase of bonds instead, congregations implicitly gave Israel's needs priority over their own. "The sale of bonds is the closest tie between Israel and Judaism during the High Holy Days," affirmed Miami's rabbis.[29] Not all rabbis accepted the consensus, of course. Joseph Narot rejected the plea that he urge the purchase of bonds from the pulpit of Temple Israel, and the Reform congregation's lay leaders agreed. By 1958 Temple Israel stood alone among Miami synagogues in its refusal to support bonds from the pulpit.[30]

Israel became the spiritual home of Miami Jews. They raised record amounts during the High Holy Days. Sales of over $700,000 in 1958 placed Miami among the top three cities in the United States.[31] In January 1959 and again in 1960, Miami received recognition as the leading American city for its increased rate of bond purchases.[32] That year the head of the UJA attacked Miami Jews for their "negligence" and long record of "sluggish giving" to the city's "major philanthropy." Miami failed to support adequately its Central Jewish Appeal. The city ranked the lowest of the largest Jewish cities in funds raised annually for the UJA and the Federation.[33] The contrast between Miami's standing in the UJA with its prominence in selling bonds underscored Israel's significance for uprooted Miami Jews.

Unlike the Central Jewish Appeal, Israel Bonds gave Miami Jews a direct, continuous, and powerful tie with the Jewish state and a concrete means of building the Jewish homeland. Increasingly Miami Jews responded to the message of the constant campaigns. Israel became their homeland, too, through their wholehearted investment in its economic future. Lacking strong ties to their new homes,

29 *Jewish Floridian*, 1 June 1956.
30 Minutes of the Executive Committee of the Board of Trustees of Temple Israel, 1 July 1958.
31 *Jewish Floridian*, 31 October 1958.
32 *Jewish Floridian*, 22 January 1960.
33 *Jewish Floridian*, 19 February 1960. This represented a significant decline for Miami's CJA fund-raising. In 1956 a survey of eighteen large cities in the United States and Canada indicated that only Miami and Cleveland exceeded the total funds raised in 1948, the peak year for contributions. Ibid., 10 August 1956.

Miami Jews preferred to purchase bonds that gave them a stake in a surrogate home. Although government speakers often presented Israel as besieged, an island of democracy in a hostile sea, this imagery always accompanied an emphasis on defense, on action, on an aggressive preparedness. Jews in Miami could appreciate this stance in other Jews, especially when those others were ready to face the dangers. Israel provided an arena to implement frontier visions they could not imagine pursuing in Miami. Israel offered them a future, a chance to help create a new Jewish society, and the power and glamor of statehood. Since they could not seize these perquisites in Miami or even in Miami Beach, they encountered little resistance to adopting Israel as the source of their redemption. Israel guaranteed the Jewish future, and bonds guaranteed Israel. The link was simple, the identification was direct. Bonds were a powerful vehicle to implement dreams.

The imagined Israel of Miami Jews displaced New York City as the source of authentic Jewish culture. Israel offered itself as an attractive new love. Distant and exotic, a young country of pioneers and soldiers, Israel was utterly unlike the New York that Jews knew so well. American Jews projected on Israelis an image of a new Jew nurtured in the soil of the recently recovered homeland, a Jew who bore an uncanny resemblance to the heroic American pioneer farmer. This new Israeli Jew, paraded on the podium of countless bond rallies — unafraid, outspoken, and rooted — possessed vision and purpose, the drive and dimensions of heroism.

As a new society, Israel beckoned to them; Israel suggested the possibility of rebirth. Having recently uprooted themselves and turned their backs on the homes of their youth, Jewish newcomers in Miami proved particularly receptive to the drama of Israel's pioneering statehood because it let them come to terms with their Jewishness. Distance placed few restraints on their imagination. Through Israel they seized the opportunity of fashioning anew the substance of an American Jewish identity.

Israel also allowed Miami Jews to reimagine home and to project roots in an alternative homeland. Israel even became their insurance policy, despite the state's precarious political and economic situation. Frontier visions of pioneering, striking roots, building a new democratic society, and defending it against enemies, spoke to Miami

Jews' specific situation as newcomers as well as to their need to define themselves as American Jews in a post-Holocaust age.[34] Israel entered their consciousness first through its commitment to rescue survivors. But Jews in Miami secured Israel's place by transforming rescue into a promise of redemption.

34 Urofsky, *We Are One!*, 240–241.

Part IV

The Cultural Connection

Homelands of the Heart:
Israel and Jewish Identity in American Jewish Fiction

Sylvia Barack-Fishman

This article examines depictions of Israel in current American Jewish fiction, using as a case study Philip Roth's two powerful recent works about Jews and Jewishness, a 1986 novel, *The Counterlife*, and a 1993 book, billed as "a confession," *Operation Shylock*. Roth's books are fertile examples of the interaction between works of fiction and the social, religious, and cultural trends that surround the writer of fiction. This essay places *The Counterlife* and *Operation Shylock* into the context of the current American Jewish environment and illuminates their exploration of the conflicting impact of the State of Israel, Eastern European origin, and America's open economic and social opportunities as factors defining the identity of Jews in the United States today.

In exploring Roth's depiction of Israel and Israelis, I focus primarily on the position of Israel in the American Jewish obsession with Jewish identity. A search for the essence of Jewish identity has become a focal point of contemporary American Jewish literary and intellectual exploration, spanning all brow levels, in works from the most complex fiction to the soap-operatic life-cycle angst of popular films and television programs. Jewish self-definition is salient in different ways to Diaspora writers and readers than it is to their Israeli counterparts. Unlike Israeli fiction, in which a character can be assumed to be Jewish unless he is identified as belonging to some other group, characters in fiction written outside Israel are not assumed to be Jewish without some indication of their Jewish identity. Sometimes only a distinctive Jewish name identifies literary characters as Jewish in American fiction. Other characters are equipped with some constellation of distinctive Jewish characteristics; for example, a Jewish character is recognized as such because he/she is a Holocaust survivor or a Mosad agent or a *hasid* or a talkative Jewish intellectual.

Among the characteristics that lead people to define themselves and others as Jews, are residual European attitudes, tastes, and habits to which some American Jews of Eastern European origin ascribe centrality. One of the most talented chroniclers of the American Jewish experience, Alfred Kazin, at mid-century embodied Jewish identity in the Eastern European intellectual and emotional Jewish characteristics of his unmarried cousin and her friends. For Kazin, the epitome of Jewishness was found in such characteristics as political attitudes (socialist), physical attributes (dark complexion and hair), cultural mores (ceremonial eating, intense verbal interaction), and not least, vibrant intellectualism and idealism.[1] In contrast to this focus on the Eastern European wellsprings of American Jewish identity, some analysts have suggested that American Jewish identity is increasingly defined by identification with Israel, citing as evidence the ubiquitousness of references to Israel in nonfiction books and essays, in the Jewish and general press, and in recent popular and serious American Jewish fiction. Diverging from emphasis on ethnic or nationalistic factors, some insist that adherence to religious observances defines and links Jews around the world, serving as a passport

---

1   They were all dressmakers, like my mother; had worked with my mother in the same East Side sweatshops; were all passionately loyal members of the International Ladies Garment Workers Union; and all were unmarried...there they were in our own dining room, our cousin and her two friends...arguing my father down on small points of Socialist doctrine. As they sat around the cut-glass bowl on the table — cracking walnuts, expertly peeling the skin off an apple in long even strips, cozily sipping at a glass of tea — they crossed their legs in comfort and gave off a deliciously musky fragrance of face powder that instantly framed them for me in all their dark coloring, brilliantly white teeth, and the rosy Russian blouses that swelled and rippled in terraces of embroidery over their opulent breasts.... I was suddenly glad to be a Jew, as these women were Jews — simply and naturally glad of those Jewish dressmakers who spoke with enthusiastic familiarity of Sholem Aleichem and Peretz, Gorky and Tolstoy, who glowed at every reminiscence of Nijinsky, of Nazimova in *The Cherry Orchard*, of Pavlova in "The Swan." Alfred Kazin, *A Walker in the City* (1951), quoted in *Writing Our Lives: Autobiographies of American Jews, 1890-1990*, ed. Steven J. Rubin (Philadelphia and New York: Jewish Publication Society, 1991), 134–137.

into Jewish peoplehood. Still others have asserted that Jews in the United States are a unique hybrid group who are fundamentally different from their coreligionists living in other countries now and in the past.

Particularly salient to this dichotomy between Israeli and Diaspora Jewish identity is a primary principle of literary deconstructionism; that whenever people perceive and articulate a given reality in terms of a binary opposition, they are also, consciously or unconsiously, ranking the two halves of that opposition.[2] When analysts contrast Israeli Jewry with Diaspora Jewry, a hierarchy is implicit or explicit in their comparison. Either Israeli Jewry or Diaspora Jewry is seen as occupying a superior, nationalistic, political, religious, cultural, or moral position, depending on the observer. This type of hierarchical perception of ranking of world-wide Jewry has important ramifications for the relationship between Jews in Israel and in the Diaspora, of course; and it also has particular ramifications for Diaspora Jews who struggle with the issue of which factors define Jewish identity today.

Defining an Identity for America's Jews

Defining Jewish identity attained urgency in the 1980s, when the government of Israel considered narrowing the Law of Return — which grants automatic citizenship in the Jewish state to all persons claiming to be Jewish. In the face of escalating rates of mixed marriage, large portions of the American Jewish community exploded in anger and outrage, articulated by national Jewish organizations, at the idea that they or their descendants might be deprived of the privileges of the Law of Return. Although attempts to change the Law of Return were tabled, partially in response to pressure from the American Jewish community, the controversy left unhealed wounds in the United States.

2   Jacques Derrida, *Margins*, 329, cited in Deborah Eskin, "Deconstruction," in
    Redrawing the Boundaries, ed. Stephen J. Greenblatt and Giles Gunn (New
    York: Modern Language Association of America, 1992), 376.

Just as unrest over the Israeli episode was subsiding, some results of the 1990 National Jewish Population Study conducted by the Council of Jewish Federations increased levels of American Jewish anxiety.[3] The study showed that secular Jewish activism had declined among younger American Jews. It suggested that the American Jewish community is polarized between Jews who define themselves as "Jewish by religion," and tend to be identified with the Jewish community, people, and/or religious customs, and those who say they do not think of themselves as Jewish by religion, who tend to have few if any ties with Jewish life. Strikingly high levels of overlap between Israel-centeredness and social, sacred, and communal Jewish behaviors and attitudes were seen among younger American Jews.[4] Young American adults who volunteer time for Jewish organizations, work for and give money to philanthropies that distribute funds to Jews in Israel and world-wide, and have many Jewish friends, for example, also tend to belong to synagogues. This religiously and institutionally active group is far more likely to express a deep attachment to Israel. In contrast, another large group of young American Jews have few Jewish friends, do not belong to synagogues, do not volunteer time for Jewish organizations, have never visited Israel, and do not give money to agencies working for world-wide Jewry.

The results of the 1990 NJPS were deeply disturbing to many American Jews, especially to older American Jewish liberals. American Jews had long cherished the concept of "the Jewish heart." For

---

3   The first national study of American Jews undertaken since 1970, the 1990 NJPS, conducted by the Council of Jewish Federations, studied over 5,000 Jewish households, which were found after extensive screening through random digit dialing techniques. These households represent Jews across the country living in communities of diverse size and composition. A summary of the findings is provided by Barry A. Kosmin, Sidney Goldstein, Joseph Waksberg, Nava Lerer, Ariella Keysar, and Jeffrey Scheckner: *Highlights of the CJF Jewish Population Survey* (New York: Council of Jewish Federations, 1991). More detailed examinations of the 1990 NJPS data are being published in the form of a series of monographs.

4   In the context of the demographic analysis, "younger" is defined as ages 18 to 44. For an interesting analysis of these patterns, see Steven M. Cohen, *Content or Continuity? Alternative Bases for Commitment* (New York: American Jewish Committee, 1991).

twentieth-century American Jews who had chosen the middle road of acculturation rather than either a total rejection of American mores or total assimilation, a spectrum of communal and religious options had provided both focus and support for Jewish identification. A network of local and national Jewish communal organizations provided secular outlets for Jewish identity and concern. Persons who described themselves as "not religious" could still express their commitment to Jewish destiny and Jewish peoplehood by working for Jewish federations, the American Jewish Committee, the American Jewish Congress, the Anti-Defamation League, and scores of other organizations.[5] In combination with either communal or religious expressions of Jewish identification — or both — the Jewish commitment of American Jews often coalesced around personal and communal support for the Jewish state.

One of the primary articles of faith supporting the concept of civic Judaism was that Jews could retain their passion for the Jewish people and Jewish ideals without any of the overt trappings of the Jewish religion or culture. Thus persons with a "Jewish heart" might work hard for civil rights in the United States and Israel, reflecting their commitment to Jewish prophetic ideals of justice, and contribute large amounts of money to rescuing Jews in countries where Jews are persecuted, without participating in other forms of Jewish religious or communal life. In contrast to these widespread beliefs, data from the 1990 NJPS indicated that while persons with such secular "Jewish hearts" were fairly common among American Jews over age forty-five, the faith of the Jewish heart unsupported by more Jewishly particularistic forms of identification did not seem to be effectively transferred to younger generations of American Jews.[6]

Many concerns loomed large: Until modern times, it was seldom necessary to separate out the ethnic, religious, and social strands

5   Jonathan Woocher, *Sacred Survival: The Civic Religion of American Jews* (Bloomington: Indiana University Press, 1986).

6   See, for example, Sidney Goldstein, *Profile of American Jewry: Insights from the 1990 National Jewish Population Survey*, North American Jewish Data Bank Occasional Papers No. 6 (New York: Mandell L. Berman Institute North American Jewish Data Bank, Graduate School and University Center, City University of New York, May 1993).

that made Jews distinctive. For most of Jewish history, a variety
of Judaisms incorporated the attributes of peoplehood, civilization,
and religion, and a Jew was an individual who followed a life style
shaped by Jewish laws, cultures, and societies. Although Jews were
often Jewish because they had no choice but to be Jewish, the
complex fabric of Jewish culture did much to define each Jew as
an individual. America's egalitarian and open society, the evidence
suggested, might have irrevocably weakened Jewish commitment.
"Who is a Jew?" and "Who is an American Jew?" suddenly seemed
very urgent questions indeed.

Socioreligious changes in American Jewish life were paralleled by
changes in American Jewish literature and film. Despite expressions
of Jewish identification, by the middle of the twentieth century the
personal assimilation of American Jews was proceeding briskly and
had become the subject of lively exploration by American Jewish
authors. Artists such as Philip Roth, Bernard Malamud, Saul Bellow,
and Woody Allen established Jewish fiction and film as a species
of regional American expression — like fiction and films about
life in the South — in which the Jewish characters were particularly
interesting and appealing because they stood both inside and outside
mainstream American culture. Jewish male protagonists became the
new American antihero. For decades the angst-ridden assimilation
of American Jewish men was depicted as being the interesting part
about being a Jew in America. Brilliant, neurotic, sensitive, funny
— and articulate — Jewish men loved and hated American culture,
and provided Americans with an irresistible commentary on and
illumination of the world they inhabited.[7]

7   The protagonists of such fiction as Philip Roth's *Portnoy's Complaint* and
such films as Woody Allen's *Annie Hall* voiced emotions that resonated for
American Jews. In the words of Roth's Alexander Portnoy: "How do they
get so gorgeous, so healthy, so *blond?* My contempt for what they believe
in is more than neutralized by my adoration of the way they look, the way
they move and laugh and speak — the lives they must lead behind those
goyische curtains! Maybe a pride of *shikses* is more like it — or is it a pride
of *shkotzim?* For these are the girls whose older brothers are the engaging
goodnatured, confident, clean, swift, and powerful halfbacks for the college
football teams.... Their fathers are men with white hair and deep voices who
never use double negatives, and their mothers the ladies with the kindly smiles
and the wonderful manners...these blond-haired Christians are the legitimate

However, in the late 1970s and 1980s, the assimilatory struggle was beginning to lose its bite, as new generations of American Jews matured who had no memories of — and no rebellion against — more intensely Jewish communities. Both established and emerging American Jewish authors began struggling with the transformation of Jewish identity and found compelling new elements to weave into their work, especially explorations of the impact of the Holocaust and the State of Israel.[8] Few events changed the self-image of American Jews as comprehensively as the existence and physical triumphs of Israel. A people derided for centuries as being weak and cowardly and unable to relate to pride of land was now briefly extolled and then often criticized as being aggressive, expansionist, and overly concerned with nationalistic considerations. Some Jews were proud of Israel, some embarrassed by it — but few now thought, like Philip Roth's early heroes, that only gentile boys knew how to fix cars and fight.

Israel became a wellspring for a variety of enriching experiences and myths — paradoxically, making American Jews feel both more Jewish and more like physically empowered citizens of the Western world. Because of Israel, as well as because of rapidly expanding

---

owners of this place.... O America! America! it may have been gold in the streets to my grandparents, it may have been a chicken in every pot to my father and mother, but to me... America is a *shikse* nestling under your arm whispering love love love love love!" Philip Roth, *Portnoy's Complaint* (New York: Fawcett Crest, 1969), 163–165.

8   Rather than the largest output of expression about the Holocaust coming in the decades immediately after World War II, it came much later, at a point when the generation of survivors was beginning to die. The American Jewish reading and viewing public seemed more willing to confront the horrors of the Nazi years and to think about what they might mean to them on a personal and communal level. This preoccupation with the Holocaust helped to fuel vocal American Jewish activism on behalf of Jewish as well as American civil rights causes: Israel and world-wide Jewry. For a time, the definition of Jewishness seemed to be someone who had internalized the motto "Never again." Among the many fine books dealing with the Holocaust, see Hugh Nissenson, *In the Reign of Peace* (New York, 1968); Cynthia Ozick, *The Messiah of Stockholm* (New York: Knopf, 1987), and *The Shawl* (New York: Knopf, 1989); and Saul Bellow, *Mr. Sammler's Planet* (New York: Viking Press, 1970), and *The Bellarosa Connection* (New York: Penguin Books, 1989).

American social and occupational opportunities, Jews had a new vision of themselves. At the same time, however, older visions of the Jewish character persisted. The image of the valorous, forthright, aggressive Israeli Jew existed simultaneously with the image of the sly, overly intellectual, adaptable Europeanized Jew.[9] The quintessential Jewish character might be a product of centuries of Diaspora life or a citizen of the Jewish state. Could a nation — or individuals in that nation — live two lives at once?

Israel as an Existential Setting in American Jewish Fiction

Philip Roth's dazzling ventriloquism, which we will explore shortly, articulating a multiplicity of voices in the complex political and philosphical twistings and turnings of contemporary Zionism, does not take place in a vacuum. Indeed, one of the most striking aspects of American Jewish fiction dealing with Israel today is how interested it is in ambiguities and complexities, and how particularistic it is. Israel, both as a separate subject and in combination with other aspects of Jewish history, including the Holocaust, continues to figure prominently in American Jewish fiction, albeit no longer through the romantic glow it enjoyed earlier in Leon Uris's *Exodus* (1958). While Uris himself continues in the "Jews equal good, Arabs equal bad" mode in *The Haj* (1984), a historical novel depicting the Arab–Jewish struggle leading up to and following the establishment of the State of Israel, the works of Israeli novelists and poets in translation have worked to counteract the stereotype of Israel as an idyllic and morally untroubled land.

It is certainly true that translations of classical, poetic, tradition-steeped works by S. Y. Agnon tend to intensify feelings of the mystical connection that Jews around the world may feel toward Jewish tradition and the Jewish homeland. However, each year

---

9   The persistence of the Europeanized Jewish image is hilariously captured in Woody Allen's film *Annie Hall,* when protagonist Alvy Singer sits at his quintessentially gentile girlfriend's quintessentially gentile dinner table in Chippewa Falls, Wisconsin, and imagines that, in the eyes of her anti-Semitic grandmother, he is suddenly transformed from a nervous, neurotic, New York Jewish agnostic into a red-bearded, black-hatted Hasidic Jew with *payot.*

numerous translations of works by such realistic contemporary Israeli artists as Amos Oz, A. B. Yehoshua, Jacob Barzilai, Yehuda Amichai, Yaakov Shabtai, Shulamith Hareven, Amalia Kahana Karmon, Yosef Haim Yerushalmi, Yoram Kaniuk, David Shahar, Yehoshua Kenaz, Sami Michael, David Grossman, Amos Kenan, and others instruct American Jewish readers in the perception that Israeli society is as complex and troubled as that of any other land. Moreover, left-liberal publications influential in intellectual and academic circles, such as the *New York Review of Books*, have repeatedly included many articles that were intensely critical of Israel and focused on the internal and external challenges to Israeli society.

Fictional pictures of Israel are far from limited to translations from Hebrew authors, however. Israel has provided an immensely fertile focus for American Jewish writing. Ted Solotaroff cogently notes that "the survival of Israel has been the paramount concern of organized Jewish life and probably the paramount source of Jewish identity" for many American Jews during the past quarter of a century.[10] This centrality is emphatically reflected in American fiction. American Jewish fiction dealing with Israel, which has increased in recent years, can be divided into three basic types: serious explorations of Israeli life, society, and history; popular fiction, including romances and mysteries, which make use of Israel as an exotic and appealing locale; and works that, rather than portraying Israeli life as an entity unto itself, present the Jewish state in its relationship to American Jewish life, as an alternative or as a source of revitalization. Israel figures prominently in fiction by such authors as Saul Bellow, Chaim Potok, Elie Wiesel, Jay Neugeboren, Hugh Nissenson, E. M. Broner, Tova Reich, Mark Helprin, and many others.

Both authors and readers of American Jewish literature were profoundly affected by news from Israel, especially after the "Six-Day War" in 1967 marked a watershed in American Jewish involvement with Israel. The acquisition of such historically evocative sites as the Old City of Jerusalem and the Etzion Block, the Yom Kippur War in 1973, the ill-fated war in Lebanon, the occupation and settlement of

---

10   Ted Solotaroff, "American-Jewish Writers: On Edge Once More," *New York Times Book Review*, 18 December 1988, pp. 1, 31, 33.

the West Bank, and the Intifada were continuing preoccupations of the American Jewish public. The early wars awakened in American Jewry a terrified recollection of the Holocaust; the reunification of Jerusalem and the apparent strength of the Israeli state created widespread feelings of nationalistic pride and confidence; the growing and much-publicized strength of right-wing religious nationalism among some factions of Israeli society disturbed the placid surface of American Zionism. On a less edifying plane, note must be taken as well of the extraordinary proliferation of thrillers, mysteries, and political fantasies set in Israel. Paul Breines terms this "the Rambowitz syndrome" and comments that he knows of "roughly fifty" novels that "are linked by their idealized representation of Jewish warriors, tough guys, gangsters, Mosad agents, and Jews of all ages and sexes who fight back against their tormentors."[11]

Many American Jewish writers link the events and the lessons of the Holocaust to their depictions of Israel, following the powerful lead of Elie Wiesel. In observing current events, Wiesel is prompt to draw the lessons of his own history and the history of the Jews, and he remains one of the most alert, passionate, and articulate defenders of Jews around the world, confronting world leaders and intellectual faddists alike to speak up for the dead Jews of Auschwitz and the living Jews in the State of Israel. In a condemnation of the United Nations resolution on "Zionism and racism," for example, Wiesel comments bitterly that the resolution is "shocking and revolting," and that it reflects a "process" that "is not new; it has endured for some two thousand years."[12] Wiesel can never forget — and he never lets the reader forget — that the Holocaust has profound spiritual implications for contemporary Jews. Indeed, one recurring motif in Wiesel's work is the agonizing conflict between the prophetic ideals of justice and mercy, on the one hand, and the physical and emotional strength that is necessary if the Jewish people are to survive in a grossly imperfect world, on the other hand. Having witnessed the utter indifference of much of the world to the near destruction of

---

11   Paul Breines, "The Rambowitz Syndrome," *Tikkun* 5 (6) November–December 1990, 17–18.
12   Elie Wiesel, "Zionism and Racism," *A Jew Today* (New York: Random House, 1978), 41–43.

the Jews, Wiesel comes down unflinchingly on the side of Jewish survival. However, he is ever cognizant of the spiritual price that survival exacts. Ultimately, one may say that Wiesel's anguished argument is at least as much with God as with humankind, for having created a world in which even caring and kindly people are forced sometimes to kill innocent creatures.[13]

The moral dilemmas that Wiesel explores have particular resonance for post-Holocaust Jewish communities. For many contemporary Jews, Jewish survival has become the primary moral obligation. Israel occupies a paramount position when Jewish writers contemplate Jewish survival, but Israel's position in the constellation of factors defining contemporary Jewish identity is less clear. Because of perceived divergence between the demands of physical survival and the definition of Jewishness in the modern world, Israel has become a catalyst for spiritual self-examination among American Jewish authors. Even the titles of many American Jewish books about experiences in Israel are evocative. Consider the existential aura of such titles as Vanessa Ochs's *Words on Fire: One Woman's Journey into the Sacred* (1990), Hugh Nissenson's *In the Reign of Peace* (1972), Jay Neugeboren's *The Stolen Jew* (1981), Elie Wiesel's *A Beggar in Jerusalem* (1970), Meyer Levin's *The Harvest* (1978), Alice Bloch's *The Law of Return* (1983), Marcia Freedman's *Exile in the Promised Land* (1990), and Saul Bellow's *To Jerusalem and Back: A Personal Account* (1976).

The State of Israel provides the physical, intellectual, and emotional setting in which many American Jewish writers confront and re-examine the nature of Jewish peoplehood and the role of Jewishness in defining their being. American Jews who have every intention that their journey will be "to Jerusalem — and back" find

---

13 In Elie Wiesel's *Dawn*, the protagonist demands, "Don't judge me, judge God," because God "created a universe and made justice to stem from injustice. He brought it about that a people should attain happiness through tears, that the freedom of a nation, like that of a man, should be built upon a pile, a foundation of dead bodies." Wiesel's protagonist comes to the startling conclusion that Jews must learn "the art of hate" in order to guarantee their physical survival. "Otherwise," he argues, "our future will only be an extension of the past." Elie Wiesel, *Dawn* (New York: Hill and Wang, 1960), 18, 26, 28–30, 40, 67–69, 86.

themselves exploring both sides of that equation: what ties them to Jerusalem — and what ties them to the United States?

Philip Roth on "Who Is a Jew?"

During the past decade, one American Jewish author who has devoted enormous amounts of creative energy to exploring issues of Jewish identity and the role of Israel in the forging of that identity is Philip Roth. For Roth's Jewish characters in *The Counterlife* and *Operation Shylock,* personal identity is intimately tied up with Jewish identity and with Israel. In his books (as in reality) secular and traditionalist Jews in Israel and America each have very different assumptions about what makes a Jew Jewish. For assimilated American Jews such as *The Counterlife's* Henry Zuckerman, a responsible dentist-businessman-family man, the simple bottom line of being a Jew is dichotomous — a Jew is not a Christian; gentiles "observe Christmas and we do not" (41). For irreligious but profoundly Zionistic Israelis such as Shuki Elchanan and his father, a nationalistic Israel is the answer to what is a Jew, because only in Israel is all of existence suffused with Jewish identity: "See that bird? That's a Jewish bird. See, up there? A Jewish cloud. There is no country for a Jew but here.... We are living in a Jewish theater and you [Diaspora Jewry] are living in a Jewish museum."[14]

In the "Judea" segment of *The Counterlife,* for the literally born-again Henry being Jewish means identifying spiritually and ethnically with the most fundamentalist, distinctive, particularistic — and putatively most "authentic" — Jews he can find, the ultra-Orthodox Israeli Jews of Me'ah She'arim and the Israeli *yeshivot.* Pointing out squat, black-garbed, bearded men, sexless women, and pale children with long earlocks, he declares: "I am nothing, I have never been *anything,* the way that I am this Jew.... I am not *just* a Jew, I'm not *also* a Jew — *I'm a Jew as deep as those Jews... that is the root of my life!*" (61). For West Bank militants, such as the fiery Rabbi Lippman, Jewishness must be redefined as a blending of piety with

14   Philip Roth, *The Counterlife* (New York: Penguin Books, 1986), 52.

biblically based ferocity. He warns Jews that they must relinquish the role of victim, that there is no morality without survival (116).

Anti-Semitism is a virulent force that continues to define the Jew no matter where he lives, in both *The Counterlife* and *Operation Shylock.* Israelis feel anti-Semitism keenly, Roth suggests, because on the world stage anti-Semitism has been transformed into anti-Zionism. Worse, in an ironic twist, it is politically correct to lambast Zionism, because Zionism is "racist." In *The Counterlife*, Buki, an Israeli metalworker, tells Nathan:

> I am in Norway on business for my product and written on a wall I read, "Down with Israel." I think, What did Israel ever do to Norway? I know Israel is a terrible country, but after all, there are countries even more terrible...why is this country the most terrible? Why don't you read on Norwegian walls, "Down with Russia," "Down with Chile," "Down with Libya"?.... Sir, why all over the world do they hate Menachem Begin? Because of politics? In Bolivia, in China, in Scandinavia, what do they care about Begin's politics? they hate him because of his nose! (123)

Nathan Zuckerman does not actually share the politics of a West Bank militant, but he learns to share his passionate understanding of the enemy, the infinite permutations of anti-Semitism, as Lippman explains:

> Can a Jew do anything that doesn't stink to high heaven of his Jewishness? There are the goyim to whom we stink because they look down on us, and there are the goyim to whom we stink because they look up to us.... First it was Jewish clannishness that was repellent, then what was preposterous was the ridiculous phenomenon of Jewish assimilation, now it is Jewish independence that is unacceptable and unjustified. First it was Jewish passivity that was disgusting, the meek Jews, the accommodating Jew, the Jew who walked like a sheep to his own slaughter — now what is worse than disgusting, outright wicked, is Jewish strength and militancy. (128–129)

Each of the four segments in *The Counterlife* presents an alternative version of the destiny of the Zuckerman brothers. Roth links the sections with references to a ceremony powerfully symbolic and evocative of the most basic elements of historical Jewish identity, the "biblical injunction" in Genesis 17 that God marks his covenant with the Jewish people through the act of fathers circumcising their male children. The secular Israeli Shuki warns Nathan that if his "English rose," his pregnant gentile mistress, gives birth to a boy, Nathan will find it "difficult" to "have a son who wasn't circumcised." When Nathan is skeptical that circumcision will matter to such a secular, liberal, and liberated Diaspora Jew as himself, Shuki asks: "Why do your pretend to be so detached from your Jewish feelings? In the books all you seem to be worrying about is what on earth a Jew is, while in life you pretend that you're content to be the last link in the Jewish chain of being." (73)

The Israelis in *The Counterlife* turn out to be good prophets of Nathan's ineradicable Jewishness. In an unforgettable moment ("Christendom"), in an elegant, refined, and understated British restaurant, Nathan Zuckerman actually stinks to high heaven of his Jewishness — as Lippman has predicted — when an English matron loudly demands that a waiter open the window because "there's a terrible smell in here.... The stink in here is abominable." (291) Moreover, his wife's mother and sister reveal themselves to be deeply anti-Semitic as well. Later, Roth has Nathan's wife Maria ask him, "Why do Jews make such a bloody fuss about being Jewish?" (300) She decides that since all Jews seem to retain a Jewish consciousness, they are all the same, in an unknowing reformulation of the Jewish religious injunction that every Jew is connected to every other Jew. "You are your brother!" she accuses. "You are Mordecai Lippman!" (304)

In a stunning epiphany, Nathan commits himself to Jewish identity and concludes the novel by declaring that his newborn son must indeed be circumcised, because that covenant in the flesh of the infant makes a Jew of him by linking him irrevocably to Jewish history:

> Circumcision is startling all right...but then maybe that's what the Jews had in mind and what makes the act seem quintessen- tially Jewish and the mark of their reality. Circumcision makes it clear as can be that you are here and not there, that you are

out and not in — also that you are mine and not theirs. There is no way around it: you enter history through my history and me.

By the end of *The Counterlife*, Nathan Zuckerman has determined that he is, in his deepest core of being, more than he is anything else, "a Jew" (323–324). This discovery, however, does not resolve his questions about the nature of Jewish identity. In *Operation Shylock* Roth moves in a new, but related, direction: given the "irreducible" element of Jewishness in the soul, what is more consonant with American Jewish identity, feelings of connectedness to Israel or to the peculiarly creative insider–outsider posture of Diaspora Jewry?

Through a Glass, Darkly

Roth has often been subjected to the claim that, because he usually focuses his comic aim at Jewish characters and societies, he is a primary example of the self-hating Jewish anti-Semite. In *Operation Shylock*, Roth links those readers' frequent literary obtuseness with the distortions of Judaism and Jews propagated for centuries by anti-Semites. For centuries the lives of Jews changed and shifted, but the non-Jews around them persisted in considering every Jew to be Shylock:

> This is Europe's Jew, the Jew expelled in 1290 by the English, the Jew banished in 1492 by the Spanish, the Jew terrorized by Poles, butchered by Russians, incinerated by Germans, spurned by the British and the Americans while the furnaces roared at Treblinka.... [now these Jews live] in the Mediterranean's tiniest country — still considered too large by all the world. (275)

The Jew, putatively personifying every characteristic that Europeans had hoped to expunge from themselves, became the Christian European's *Doppelganger*, his "savage, repellent, and villainous" (274) dark shadow. In this assertion, Roth anticipates current historical and literary analysis of the legacy of the Shylock character, which points out that *The Merchant of Venice* was a favorite play of the Nazis; they seized upon it gleefully. "'There,' they could say, 'is the

286 *SYLVIA BARACK-FISHMAN*

Jew!'"[15] Despite the Jew's victimization by the Nazis and despite his victorious transformation into a member of a sovereign, militarily powerful nation, in the pervasive vision of the anti-Semite the Jew will always be Shylock, Roth asserts.

Roth connects the anti-Semitic need to see the Jew as Shylock with contemporary revisionist historians' attempts to erase the reality of the Holocaust itself. As one of *Operation Shylock's* characters declares: "Did six million really die? Come off it. The Jews pulled a fast one on us again, keeping alive their new religion, Holocaustomania." (253) Sometimes revisionism takes the form of disbelieving that former Nazis ever committed their horrendous acts because they later, like Ivan Demjanjuk, became their own doubles: banally normal, responsible, family-oriented citizens in midwestern American towns. The Jews perpetrating the trials of these seemingly innocent gentiles appear to be Shylocks, bent on collecting their pound of flesh.

If this seems confusing to you, dear reader, suggests Roth, think of how strange it is that multiple realities permeate the very air we breathe. Realities multiply horizontally and vertically. That is, people and societies can experience a variety of different existences sequentially, as did both the perpetrators and the victims of the Holocaust, who moved from a nightmare existence into seemingly ordinary American daylight. In Jerusalem, as Moishe Pipick watches Philip Roth watching Demjanjuk and his accusers, it becomes clear that the realities of Jews are especially strange. The name "Jew" is used for different types of people: American Jews and European Jews and Sephardi Jews and Israeli Jews and the grotesque image of Jews who inspired the character of Shylock are all called by the name "Jew." What is even stranger, Roth insists, the Jewish people include many disparate individuals and disparate societies as well. The Jewish people war amongst themselves as to how Jewishness is defined because each Jew is comprised of numerous Jews:

> Divided is nothing. Even the goyim are divided. But inside every Jew there is a mob of Jews. The good Jew, the bad Jew. The new Jew, the old Jew. The lover of Jews, the hater of Jews. The friend of the goy, the enemy of the goy. The arrogant Jew,

15   Louis Simpson, "There, They Could Say, Is the Jew: *Shylock: A Legend and Its Legacy*, by John Gross," *New York Times Book Review*, 4 April 1993, 7, 9.

the wounded Jew. The pious Jew, the rascal Jew. The coarse Jew, the gentle Jew. The defiant Jew, the appeasing Jew. The Jewish Jew, the de-Jewed Jew.... Is it any wonder that the Jew is always disputing? He is a dispute, incarnate! (334)

Israeli Jews and Diaspora Jews are creatures so different that they are not even recognizable to each other as Jews, several characters in *Operation Shylock* insist. Characters who are anti-Zionist use the differences between European and Israeli Jewish characteristics to deride and delegitimate Israeli Jews, claiming that Israeli Jews are not "really" Jewish. Although the Jews in Eastern Europe were tormented by their enemies, they had Jewish souls, one character asserts, but Jews in Israel "are Jews in a Jewish country without a Jewish soul." (109)

The setting of *Operation Shylock*, even more than *The Counterlife*, is Israel, and the book explores, among other issues, connections between the Holocaust and the establishment and continuing development of the State of Israel. Interwoven with themes of Jewish identity are considerations of historicity, as embodied in the relationship between the narrative, the narrator, and the historical context. All of these themes are tied together with metaphors of multiple identity even more complex than those in *The Counterlife*. *Operation Shylock* prickles with splintered narratives, as characters with widely divergent historical perspectives wrestle with questions about who represents the "real" Jew and which of the very different cultures depicted comprises a genuine Jewish peoplehood and civilization.

Several characters in *Operation Shylock* argue for a Diaspora-centered rather than an Israel-centered foundation of Jewish identity. Moishe Pipick proposes a theory called Diasporism, in opposition to Zionism. Smilesburger, a Mosad executive posing as an addled Holocaust survivor, mockingly claims that Jews of Eastern European Jewish ancestry — even Ashkenazi Israelis — are in fact totally defined by being Jews from Poland or Ukraine:

The roots of American Jewry are not in the Middle East but in Europe — their Jewish style, their Jewish words, their strong nostalgia, their actual, weighable history, all this issues from their European origins Grandpa did not hail from Haifa —

Grandpa came from Minsk. Grandpa wasn't a Jewish nationalist — he was a Jewish humanist, a spiritual, believing Jew,
who complained not in an antique tongue called Hebrew but
in colorful, rich, vernacular Yiddish.[16]

Moishe Pipik notes that although American Jews can see that they
have almost nothing in common with Israeli Jews, they are willing
to do almost anything for Israel. He warns that any American Jew
is in danger of being a Jonathan Pollard, because American Jews
are obsessed with saving Jewish lives, and helping Israel means
saving Jewish lives. Thus Israel, by its very existence, endangers
the lives of contemporary Diaspora Jews. (81) Even worse, the
disguised Mosadnik Smilesburger sardonically claims, the State of
Israel endangers the lives of Israeli Jews as well. Because they are
like the Jews of the Bible — Jews in a Jewish land who are not acting
Jewishly — God will punish them with the sweeping retribution with
which he punished biblical Jews. The Arabs will sweep down upon
modern-day Israel just as their enemies served as God's avenging
hand and swept down upon the sinning Israelites and Judeans of the
past.

To avert this seemingly inevitable catastrophe, Moishe Pipik,
posing as Philip Roth, goes about Israel preaching the gospel of
Diasporism: he urges all Jews of Eastern European origin to return
to the true homelands of their hearts, the Eastern European countries
from which they came. (87) Outright enemies of the State of Israel
praise the Eastern European Jewish character as well. A University of
Chicago-educated Palestinian now living on the West Bank, George
Ziad, rants passionately in *Operation Shylock* about the fraudulence
of Israeli claims for Jewishness and the superiority of the Eastern
European Jews. The true and valuable Jewish character, claims Ziad,
is the Diaspora Jewish character, that of "real Jews...truly superior
people," who displayed "vitality," "irony," "human sympathy,"
"human tolerance," and "goodness of heart." Israel, in contrast, is
the only place Ziad has ever been "where all the Jews are stupid."
Israel is "a country lacking in every quality that gave the Jews their
great distinction":

16   Philip Roth, *Operation Shylock: A Confession* (New York: Simon & Schuster,
      1993), 47.

These victorious Jews are terrible people. I don't just mean the Kahanes and the Sharons. I mean them all, the Yehoshuas and the Ozes included. The good ones who are against the occupation of my father's house, the "beautiful Israelis" who want their Zionist thievery and their clean conscience too.... What do they know about "Jewish".... Jews without tolerance, Jews for whom it is always black and white, who have all these crazy splinter parties, who have a party of one man, they are so intolerant of one another — these are a people who are superior to the Jews in the Diaspora?.... Here they are authentic, here, locked up in their Jewish ghetto, and armed to the teeth? And you there, you are "unauthentic," living freely with all of mankind.... As if speaking Hebrew is the culmination of human achievement!.... Who do they think they are, these provincial nobodies? (124–125)

Ziad, percolating with utter hatred for Israelis and the State of Israel, agrees with Moishe Pipik that Eastern European Jews should all go back to Poland and Austria and Ukraine.

Ziad, *Operation Shylock's* lapsed and then politically reborn Palestinian, insists that the plight of the Palestinians has been immeasurably worsened because of the cynical way in which Israeli politicians have used the Holocaust for propaganda value. After the Israeli victory in 1967, Ziad insists, members of the government, who had previously been embarrassed by their victimized progenitors, found it expedient "to remind the world, minute by minute, hour by hour, day in and day out, that the Jews were victims before they were conquerors and that they are conquerors only because they are victims."[17] The conquest and continued occupation of the West Bank and Gaza, says Ziad, has been facilitated because "There's no business like *Shoah* business." (132–133) As a result of the extended occupation, and its accompanying brutality, the lives of the Palestinians frequently parallel the lives of oppressed European Jews.

Operation Shylock suggests that the Palestinian has become in

---

17 For a nonfiction, Israeli exploration of similar ideas, see Tom Segev, *The Seventh Million: The Israelis and the Holocaust*, trans. Haim Watzman (New York: Hill & Wang, 1993).

290 SYLVIA BARACK-FISHMAN

some ways the double of the Jew. Roth's empathetic skill in rendering these parallels deceives at least one critic, Harold Bloom, into seeing Israel-hater Ziad as the book's most sympathetic character.[18] On the contrary, in the context of the plot as a mystery quest for Jewish identity, protagonist Philip Roth says he listens to anti-Israeli diatribes "with coldhearted fascination," as if he were "a well-placed spy" (129) — which he later becomes. He understands exactly how Ziad and men like him feel, exactly what they are experiencing, but he knows them to be in opposition to Israel's welfare and survival. Despite his sympathy and his awareness of the ways in which their experience mirrors his own, he is a partisan to the Israeli cause. The actual author Roth's own partisanship — unlike that of some other American Jewish intellectuals and writers, who publicly hectored or abandoned Israel when they found its behavior politically incorrect — is cryptically signaled in a conversation on the West Bank, in which the protagonist asserts, "Arafat can differentiate between Woody Allen and Philip Roth." (155)

Roth signals his partisanship to the reader in several ways. Plot developments and the actions of characters provide important clues; but perhaps even more significant are the ways in which he delegitimates certain characters. Ziad, like some of Shakespeare's profoundly appealing villains, often speaks to the reader's heart. Roth has almost certainly devised Ziad's name as an inversion of the name of literary critic Edward Said, who often criticizes Israeli policies. The name Ziad also echoes the sound of Jihad, the holy Islamic war against the State of Israel. Protagonist Roth listens to Ziad and transmits the Palestinian's often valid cultural critique of Israeli politics and society. Ultimately, however, through his words and his actions the protagonist rejects the moral validity of Ziad's claim.

The hyperbolic Diasporism of Moishe Pipick and George Ziad is meant to go to absurd extremes. The fact that Arab enemies of Israel would like to see the Jews return from whence they came is one warning alarm about nostalgia for the Diaspora Jewish personality. Protagonist Philip Roth vigorously opposes this plan, insisting

---

18 Harold Bloom, "Operation Roth, *Operation Shylock: A Confession,* by Philip Roth," *New York Review of Books,* 22 April 1993, 45–48.

that all of Christian Europe would be appalled if the descendants of Europe's slaughtered Jewry were to return to their European homelands. (156) Christian Europeans ranging from uneducated common men to the pope are probably secretly happy about the results of Hitler's "little miracle," he insists. Underlying the clever games with mirrors is Roth's warning that many qualities that Jews and non-Jews alike may prize in the Diaspora Jewish personality are based on vulnerability to the ever-present reality of anti-Semitism. The protagonist explodes in anger when contemporary Israelis are compared to the Nazis, who

> didn't break hands. They engaged in industrial annihilation of human beings. They made a manufacturing process of death. Please, no metaphors where there is recorded history. (142)

Yet the author knows that the reader knows full well that people — including himself — are continuously constructing metaphors in the face of recorded history. While Jews may argue among themselves about "who is a Jew" and endlessly examine their splintered identities, Roth suggests, one of the primary defining factors of Jewishness are the boundaries provided by anti-Semitism, embodied on two historical sides by the European anti-Semites who participated in the Holocaust and by those among the Arab population who would happily do away with the Jewish state. Roth suggests that complicating the enmity of the relationship between Jews and the persons who hate them are the emotional and symbolic elements that connect them. He indicates that European anti-Semites hated the Jews with an implacable hatred partly because they envied them and partly because they projected onto the Jewish personality everything they hated about themselves and wished to eradicate from themselves. *Operation Shylock* indicates that some Palestinians, on the other hand, hate the Jews of the Jewish state because they see the parallels between the now stateless Palestinians and the once stateless Jews, and they believe that Palestinians have been turned into the Jews of the Middle East and made to suffer for the deeds of European Christianity.

The author Philip Roth delegitimates Moishe Pipick, the champion of the Diaspora Jewish identity, through the blackly ribald ending that protagonist Roth writes for his pretender. Moishe Pipick, a shadowy character much like Roth yet very different from him as well, is terminally ill from cancer. His life is inexorably entangled with a once virulent anti-Semite of Polish stock, Wanda Sue Possesski, who goes by the name of "Jinx" (a "possessed woman," a "jinx"?). Moishe Pipick has lost his physical manhood and can only have intercourse with his Polish inamorata with a mechanical penile implant. Even after he dies, Jinx Possesski continues to have intercourse with the corpse of Moishe Pipick and his mechanical penis. Moishe Pipick is not only the mouthpiece for but also the symbol of the diseased incarnation of the diseased imagination of Diaspora Jewry, impressively tumescent only through mechanical means, and through that sterile manhood pleasuring an anti-Semitic non-Jewish world before, during, and after his demise.

The reader of *Operation Shylock* need not, I believe, assume that the author Philip Roth has already packed or is about to pack his bags, move to Israel, and engage in espionage work. Within *Operation Shylock's* elaborately plotted and executed narrative, the reader comes to understand why and how the protagonist finally breaks free of his indecision and puts his future on the line for the country that provides a home for those who, like his friend Aharon Appelfeld, bear witness to the horrors of the Jewish past and the hope of the Jewish future.

For Philip Roth and for many of his colleagues, Israel is both an earthly Jewish state and also a state of mind in which one undertakes an evaluation of one's spiritual life. Indeed, when one looks at recent serious and popular American Jewish literature, it is striking how often these works use Israel as a spiritual site for the exploration of the most basic existential issues. As American Jews journey psychologically and physically to and from Israel, they wrestle with their own personal counterforces. Israel is the place where the American Jewish writers confront the counterlife; it has become the sacral center, if not the geographical center, of the American Jewish psyche.

Israel as Reel:
The Depiction of Israel in
Mainstream American Films*

Stephen J. Whitfield

Riding with the Galician cavalry during the Russian civil war, the narrator of Isaac Babel's "After the Battle" (1920) is not concerned with martyrdom — with the ordeal of facing death honorably. Instead he finds himself "imploring fate to grant me the simplest of proficiencies — the ability to kill my fellow men." Such an aptitude was not sanctioned in the *shtetl* or in the literature it spawned.[1] *"The virtue of powerlessness, the power of helplessness,... the sanctity of the insulted and injured* [italics in original] — these," according to one major interpretation, "are the great themes of Yiddish literature."[2] But such an ethos had to be abandoned if the *yishuv* was to survive and to withstand Arab virulence, as manifested in pogroms against Jewish settlers and religious scholars in Palestine in the 1920s. It was an ethos that, had it not been repudiated, would have doomed the nascent Jewish state in the 1940s. But the resort to force, even out of the imperatives of self-defense rather than for aggressive purposes, has been fraught with moral consequences just as portentous as the earlier unwillingness to cultivate the simplest of proficiencies was.

How to reconcile decent ends with inhumane means, how to realize the ideals of fraternity while shedding blood — these have

---

* For their criticism of an earlier draft of this paper, I am especially grateful to Thomas Doherty and Joel Rosenberg.
1 Isaac Babel, *Collected Stories* (London: Penguin, 1961), 163; Mark Zborowsky and Elizabeth Herzog, *Life Is with People: The Culture of the Shtetl* (New York: Schocken, 1962), 55, 301, 307.
2 Irving Howe and Eliezer Greenberg, "Introduction" in *A Treasury of Yiddish Stories*, ed., idem (New York: Meridian, 1958), 38.

been perennial dilemmas of historical experience from which Zionism could not exempt itself. That problem has been addressed at divergent literary points on the Diaspora compass, from Arthur Koestler's *Thieves in the Night* (1946) to Elie Wiesel's *Dawn* (1961), and was also confronted by one of Israel's most authoritative moral prophets. "We cannot refrain from doing injustice altogether," Martin Buber conceded in 1945. Himself a serious student of utopias, he nevertheless warned others in the *yishuv* against "having to do more injustice than [is] absolutely necessary."[3] Whether that standard has been satisfactorily upheld is posed in two American movies that explore, however maladroitly, the tension between Zionist ends and violent means.

Each was adapted from a novel that had achieved best-seller status. One film is set in Cyprus and Palestine in the short period 1947–1948; the other includes only two brief scenes set in Israel, around 1981. But both reflect the dialectic between the irreparable losses of the Holocaust and the will of the Jewish state not to let powerlessness tempt its enemies with fantasies of destruction. Both *Exodus* (1960) and *The Little Drummer Girl* (1984) address a once-marginal feature of Diaspora life — a willingness to shoot, if only in self-defense — and make it central to the meaning of Jewish sovereignty. The logo of the earlier film shows, in silhouette, an upraised rifle — arms and the arms; and the logo of the latter shows, in silhouette, a rifle held by a full-scale figure — arms and the woman — as though proclaiming not only the theme but the inevitability of violence. In both movies a female American gentile is inducted — or seduced — into the turmoil of Middle Eastern politics and becomes conscripted into the Zionist cause and the acceptance of its methods. Both Kitty and Charlie are surrogates for the mass audience to which these pictures have primarily been pitched. As outsiders to the conflict, these products of Indiana and Iowa, respectively, absorb the shocks that wrench them out of their previous positions of innocence; these "Middle Americans" are led to understand the fundamental justice of Jewish claims for survival. As women, they come to accept the

3   Martin Buber, "Politics and Morality," *Be'ayot* (April 1945), reprinted in *A Land of Two Peoples: Martin Buber on Jews and Arabs*, ed. Paul R. Mendes-Flohr (New York: Oxford University Press, 1983), 170.

masculine validation of the instruments of violence and realize that words need not be the Jews' only weapon in seeking to prevail in the Holy Land.

In their different ways, these two films show Israel not only managing to beat the odds but also defying the laws of history. Zionism was not just the ideology of the Jewish Agency but, more importantly, made *agency* an attribute of the Jewish people, once again activating its own destiny. Thus were punditry and prophecy confounded. For example, the most brilliant American journalist of the century, Walter Lippmann, had dismissed Zionism in 1922 as "a romantic lost cause, a good deal like Jacobinism in England or Orleanism in France."[4] *Exodus* is about national liberation from British rule, and Israel therefore subverts the Christian triumphalism of Western civilization, which designated Jews as victims who would eventually disappear. *The Little Drummer Girl* is about a successful intelligence operation against Palestinian terrorism and therefore counters the presumption of Islamic civilization, which expected Jews to be stateless rather than agents of their own fate as a people. How these films show Israel shattering such expectations, within the boundaries of the most popular American popular arts, merits some attention, especially because Hollywood has so very rarely focused on Israel.

It hardly needs to be acknowledged that movies are open to diverse interpretations. They do not come with instructions: Use as directed. But *Exodus* and *The Little Drummer Girl* are noteworthy for their favorable treatment of the birth of a nation and of its travail.

Though released in 1960, *Exodus* is set a dozen years earlier; and the change that it helped promote in the consciousness of the largest Diaspora community can be measured by noting what typified the Jewish "problem" film and novel from that earlier era. Whether in Arthur Miller's only novel, *Focus* (1945), or in Laura Z. Hobson's best-selling *Gentleman's Agreement* (1947), the problem was the perception of Jews as alien, when all they supposedly wanted was absorption into civil society, undifferentiated except perhaps on

---

4 Walter Lippmann to Lawrence J. Henderson, 27 October 1922, in John Morton Blum, ed., *Public Philosopher: Selected Letters of Walter Lippmann* (New York: Ticknor & Fields, 1985), 150.

account of religion. Lippmann had once asked Felix Frankfurter, "What is a 'Jew' anyway?"; and the scholarly attorney, whom Reinhold Niebuhr considered the most intelligent person he had ever known, could do no better than refer to "a person whom non-Jews regard as a Jew."[5]There was little sense that anyone would have freely chosen to be a Jew, or that a historical dynamic — much less a covenant — was at work. Jean-Paul Sartre's well-meaning and acute *Réflexions sur la question juive* (1946), translated in 1948, detected no cultural tradition to be defended or explored; he managed to analyze the Jewish question without citing a single book on Jewish history.[6] (Lexicographers should have noted this striking illustration of the noun *chutzpah.*) Even in so open a society as the United States, the fears of Jews were as strong as their hopes; their memories were still perhaps stronger than their affirmations. The case for Jewish culture and identity as worthy of cultivation and continuation was being fumbled.

This was the general level of ideological sophistication when the manuscript of a lengthy novel by a Marine veteran named Leon Uris arrived in the office of Ingo Preminger. The literary agent's find enabled his brother Otto to experience what countless readers would repeat — in the United States, in the Soviet Union, and elsewhere. *Exodus* proved to be utterly engrossing. The director-producer recalled having "started reading it after dinner and couldn't put it down. I sat up most of the night and when I finished I knew I wanted to make that film.... I couldn't get the book out of my mind." Ingo insisted that Uris's property was unavailable, since Metro-Goldwyn-Mayer had commissioned it. But Otto Preminger was undeterred. By raising the specter of an international Arab boycott of MGM films and by proclaiming the immunity of an independent producer like himself to such pressure, he got the property from MGM for $75,000, and then persuaded Arthur Krim of United Artists to put up the production money ($3.5 million). Preminger recalled that Krim "was interested in Israel," where

5   Michael E. Parrish, *Felix Frankfurter and His Times: The Reform Years* (New York: Free Press, 1982), 6, 129.
6   Judith Friedlander, *Vilna on the Seine: Jewish Intellectuals in France since 1968* (New Haven, Conn.: Yale University Press, 1990), 143.

his wife, Mathilda Krim, had served as a research scientist at the Weizmann Institute.[7]

Uris was an obvious first choice to adapt his best-selling novel. But Preminger realized that, though "a good story-teller," Uris "cannot write a screeplay." He was furious when the director discharged him; and after *Exodus* opened, Uris "declared publicly that I had ruined his book," according to Preminger. A member of the Hollywood Ten, Albert Maltz, then a blacklisted expatriate in Mexico, had also tried in vain to adapt *Exodus*. But Maltz's confrere, the "fast and facile" Dalton Trumbo, succeeded by compressing a pop Zionist epic into an action-packed melodrama. According to his biographer, Trumbo slashed a novel of over a thousand pages by refusing "to go back to Old Testament times and follow the Jews through the centuries of the Diaspora and the horror of the Holocaust." In fact the novel is 626 pages long and does not begin with the Bible. For Mort Sahl the adaptation was still too long; and at a Hollywood screening, the comedian yelled out after three hours: "Otto, let my people go!" Trumbo's craft was efficient enough, however, for Preminger to give him a credit, thus helping to break the blacklist and adding to popular interest in a manner that Ahad Ha'am had considered very American — "big noise and publicity."[8]

By drastically shortening the novel, Preminger and Trumbo skipped the forging of the *yishuv* and the ingathering of the exiles, especially in the Second Aliyah, and instead highlighted the tension between nationalist ends and violent means. The film presents the conflict as nominally between the Haganah and the Irgun,

---

7   Otto Preminger, *Preminger: An Autobiography* (Garden City, N.Y.: Doubleday, 1977), 165, 166; Melvin I. Urofsky, *We Are One!: American Jewry and Israel* (Garden City, N.Y.: Anchor Press/Doubleday, 1978), 242; Stephen J. Whitfield, "Value Added: Jews in Postwar American Culture," in *Studies in Contemporary Jewry*, vol. 8, ed. Peter Y. Medding (New York: Oxford University Press, 1992), 77, 79, 83–84.

8   Preminger, *Preminger*, 166, 167; Bruce Cook, *Dalton Trumbo* (New York: Charles Scribner's Sons, 1977), 274; Helen Manfull, ed., *Additional Dialogue: Letters of Dalton Trumbo, 1942–1962* (New York: E. Evans, 1970), 525; Ahad Ha'am quoted in Shuly Rubin Schwartz, *The Emergence of Jewish Scholarship in America: The Publication of the Jewish Encyclopedia* (Cincinnati: Hebrew Union College Press, 1991), 86.

298 STEPHEN J. WHITFIELD

personified by two brothers who had trekked from Czarist Russia to Palestine forty-seven years earlier. Barak Ben Canaan (Lee J. Cobb) is on the executive committee of the Jewish Agency, a negotiator with the British, a friend of the former *mukhtar* (headman) of the Arab village of Abu Yesha, next to the *moshav* of Yad El that Barak founded. He is a conciliator who, in announcing the news of the United Nations partition plan, urges the Arabs to remain in the new Jewish state. His son Ari is played by Paul Newman (an actor only fourteen years younger than Cobb).

By having Ari bring the very blond Kitty Fremont (Eva Marie Saint) to his parents' *moshav* and to the Valley of Jezreel in the bright sunlight, the film establishes a sharp cinematographic contrast with the previous scene, a meeting with his uncle Akiva in a dark, secret, guarded apartment in Jerusalem. Barak has not spoken to his brother in a decade, counts him among the dead at Yom Kippur, and prohibits mention of his name at the dinner table. Akiva Ben Canaan (David Opatoshu) is a leader of the Irgun, whose representative has met with Ari earlier in the King David Hotel to arrange a rendezvous between him and his uncle. The Haganah's Ari is dressed in white. He is endowed with sandy hair and (if memory serves) blue eyes. The Irgun man, who trusts Barak Ben Canaan "as we trust the Grand Mufti," has dark eyes and dark hair and wears a black tie. Barak is often shown out of doors in bright light; Akiva hovers in darkness, a creature of the shadows. His brother is surrounded by family — a doting wife and a gorgeous Palmach daughter Jordana (Alexandra Stewart), plus Ari. Akiva is alone, a hunted man living under a death sentence that the Mandatory power will impose. Barak's screen introduction is sunlit, as he welcomes the young *olim* to Kibbutz Gan Dafna. But when Akiva finally emerges into the blaze of day, after the daring prison escape at Acre, the "underground man" cannot survive — and dies of a bullet wound.

Yet *Exodus* softens this contrast by narrative arrangements that undermine faith in a political and diplomatic solution to the Palestine Question. Akiva calls his nephew an Irgunist "at heart" and "in methodology." Since Ari is shown planning the breakout from the Acre jail, *Exodus* makes clear that, whatever their partisan rivalries, the Jews will unite against the Arabs. (In fact Uris was well aware that the Acre exploit was the "greatest action" of "the Jewish extremist underground" — not of the Haganah.)[9] On board the *Olympia* (renamed the *Exodus*), Dov Landau (Sal Mineo) explains his wish to go to Palestine: "There Jews fight instead of talk!" Not even the angelic Karen Hansen (Jill Haworth) objects to the young Auschwitz survivor's opting to fight for freedom. One reference work asserts that in *Exodus* Lee J. Cobb "played a Jewish conservative,"[10] which is an odd description for a *halutz* (pioneer) who fights for national independence against an empire, and whose plea to God not to "let my brother die at the end of a British rope" is shown as signaling the most daring of the acts of resistance to the Mandate, an action designed to strengthen the Zionists in their struggle against Arab marauders.

In his dialogue with Ari in Jerusalem, Akiva asserts that no nation ever achieved independence without violence. The Haganah activist does not challenge or contradict him, or cite instances of the effectiveness of pacifism. Nor does the film permit the audience to evaluate Akiva's justifications for the policies of the Irgun, which are not logically or historically contested — not even the most volatile argument, which is that Arab claims for "justice" are as debatable as the Zionists'. Some of Akiva's propositions are self-contradictory: if "justice itself is an abstraction," then how can he want "the next injustice [to] work against somebody else for a change"? That would mean that "justice" is not an abstraction but is discernible. If "justice and Jews" cannot be mentioned "in the same breath," that again implies that "justice" is definable; nor could he mean that the combination of terms is "a logical absurdity" (though it could well be classified as a historical one). However clumsy his handling of the idea of justice, the Irgun leader is all mild-mannered, tea-drinking thoughtfulness. He exhibits neither sadism nor sociopathology, and is such a Russian intellectual that he even plays chess in prison. Though *Exodus* does not specify the connection between violence and political effort, neither does the movie show how Zionism

9   Leon Uris, with Dimitrios Harissiadis, *Exodus Revisited* (Garden City, N.Y.: Doubleday, 1960), 80–91.
10 Darryl Lyman, *Great Jews on Stage and Screen* (Middle Village, N.Y.: Jonathan David, 1987), 69.

achieved a diplomatic triumph with the United Nations vote for partition.

Preminger claimed that leading figures of the Labor party, such as Prime Minister David Ben-Gurion, Foreign Minister Golda Meir, and General Moshe Dayan, objected to the excessive credit *Exodus* would give to the exploits of the Irgun and the Stern Gang. "I said politely that I didn't think Israel would have emerged as a nation without the terrorists," the producer-director recalled. "I don't like violence but that is unfortunately the truth. The British would never have given in without the high pressure from the radical element" — whose tribune, Menachem Begin, had lunch with him during the filming and complained instead of not *enough* credit bestowed on the Irgun.[11]

Such cacophony may be taken as a clue that Preminger was doing *something* right, or it may also be understood as standard Hollywood practice to blur ideological lines and manhandle ideas for the sake of maximizing the size of the audience. (The way American movies tend to ignore ideology was heightened in Preminger's next film, *Advise and Consent* [1962], which makes it impossible to ascertain what Secretary of State-designate Robert Leffingwell advocates, or what his chief foe, Senator Seab Cooley, opposes, or what the president's own politics are either. But if these politicians believe in nothing concrete — not even their patriotism takes a particular form or is manifested in a specific policy — then no one has any reason to support what they stand for, much less be *against* it.) The aim is consensus — an impulse to let sleeping dogmas lie that the Viennese-born Preminger tapped, the tendency that has been so dominant in the American character and the democratic marketplace, from Jefferson's first inaugural address ("Every difference of opinion is not a difference of principle.... We are all republicans — we are all federalists") down to the biggest "political" protest novel before *Exodus, The Grapes of Wrath* (1939), in which Ma Joad expands the proletariat into "the people that live.... Why, we're the people — we go on."[12]

This yearning for a non-ideological consensus animates *Exodus* as well, as its Jews unite — against the British and then against the

11   Preminger, *Preminger*, 169.
12   Merrill D. Peterson, ed. *The Portable Thomas Jefferson* (New York: Viking,

Arabs — to fulfill the dream of national sovereignty. In both cases, however, the influence of "the radical element" is pronounced, if only because its activities are far easier to depict on the screen than the planting of trees, the draining of swamps, the building of the Histadrut, or the tedious discourse of the conference tables.

In its effort to warrant the force to which the Zionists resort, *Exodus* seeks to invoke two favorable responses. The first is sympathy. Those who have come on the *Star of David* to a detention camp on Cyprus are manifestly the victims of the greatest crime of the twentieth century. When the widow Kitty Fremont accuses Ari Ben Canaan of not caring for the Jews who have gone on a hunger strike on the *Exodus*, he coarsely retorts: "Jewish flesh is cheap, lady, cheaper than beef. It is cheaper even than herring!" The British are extending rather than terminating a history of persecution in the Diaspora, though their policy of harassment and contempt does not compare with what the refugees have already suffered. General Sutherland (Ralph Richardson) is kindly and gallant. But his underling, Major Caldwell (Peter Lawford), is an old-fashioned anti-Semite (like the actor's own father-in-law, Joseph P. Kennedy). Caldwell complains of being "up to our neck in Jews" and sees them as troublesome and repugnant. The Cypriot philo-Semite Mandria (Hugh Griffith) speaks for the Jews when he acknowledges that the British are preferable to other masters — but why submit to a master at all?

The most evil figure that the film depicts is the German Nazi working for the Grand Mufti, who expects every Jew to be annihilated. Sneering at the UN and its partition plan, he predicts that 650,000 Jews will be in Palestine only "temporarily," thanks in part to the eighty Arab "storm troopers" whom he has personally trained. Along with some Good Britons are some Good Arabs, especially Taha (John Derek), who fears that the "defenseless children" of Gan Dafna will be "butchered like sheep." Yet even Taha is compelled to break with the Zionists whom he and his family had welcomed into the valley ("I am a Moslem. I cannot go against my own people.

1975), 291–292; John Steinbeck, *The Grapes of Wrath* (New York: Viking, 1968), 383.

I cannot kill another Arab"). This principle of solidarity does not prevent the Arabs from killing *him* for his humane sentiments. General Sutherland, who wishes to be relieved of his command on Cyprus rather than continue to block the *aliyah*, had been proved right: "The Arabs are fanatics on the subject of Jewish immigration." The moderate British soldiers are ineffectual; the moderate Arabs are murdered for betraying the Grand Mufti's cause.

All the Jews are by contrast the Good Guys — especially Karen Hansen, a deutero-Anne Frank. Karen's family had sent her from Germany to Denmark when she was six, and who goes through life believing that people are basically good at heart. She is a "child of light," according to Dr. Odenheim, the Viennese-trained physician who works himself to death caring for other refugees. He is a *mensch* who observes that Karen wishes to become, in effect, a saint (the surname of the actress who plays her mother-surrogate). Nor does Ari himself reveal any faults, besides an understandable impatience in the battle for statehood. In the agit-prop final scene, the "Irgunist at heart" delivers a eulogy in behalf of brotherhood, standing over the graves of his friend Taha, found hanged with a Star of David carved into his chest, and fifteen-year-old Karen, whose throat has been slit by an Arab invader. *Exodus* thus conveys the message that the Jews will have to defend not only their lives but also their vision of a land for two peoples to share.

The second theme of *Exodus* is empathy. The highly successful weekly magazine *People* annually lavishes one issue on "The 50 Most Beutiful People in the World." In the most recent version, forty of them turned out to be Americans — a stunning over-representation of national pulchritude. Exactly half a century earlier, the predecessor of *People* devoted a special issue to promoting support for a totalitarian ally, the Soviet Union, in the war against another totalitarian state. The readers of *Life* magazine were assured that the Russians were "one hell of a people... [who] to a remarkable degree ... look like Americans, dress like Americans and think like Americans."[13]

---

13   *Life* 14 (29 March 1943), quoted in John Lewis Gaddis, *The United States and the Origins of the Cold War, 1941–1947* (New York: Columbia University Press, 1972), 38.

Could any higher praise be uttered? That is also how *Exodus* depicts Israelis, who are mostly portrayed by Americans: Newman (a half-Jew), Cobb (*né* Jacob), Opatoshu (a baccalaureate of the Yiddish theatre), and Mineo. To be sure another American, the dashing John Derek, plays an Arab. But Taha is so conciliatory that, on the kibbutz, he wishes the new children *"l'chaim."* The most disagreeable major role is Peter Lawford's, a bit of casting that is consistent with critic Dwight Macdonald's observation that, in spear-and-sandal epics like *Ben-Hur* (1960) and *King of Kings* (1962), the ancient Romans tend to be played by Her Majesty's subjects and the Hebrews by Americans. The studios, "in a most tactful gesture, gave the colonial parts to the country that is now acquiring an empire and the imperial parts to the country that recently lost one. Jolly decent, I say."[14]

Trolling primarily for the American box office, *Exodus* shrewdly makes the case for Zionism by discrediting Kitty Fremont's initial admission that Jews make her uncomfortable. "I feel strange among them," she informs Sutherland; and the film presents no rational basis for such uneasiness. Palestinians like David Ben Ami are courteous and engaging, and no disagreeable incidents mar her nursing activities in the detention camp in which she meets the adorable Karen. Neither the Jews of Palestine nor the refugees seeking a haven can be differentiated from Americans, except perhaps for the puzzling preference — when Mrs. Fremont offers Karen a choice — for the Galilee over Indiana. Indeed a counterpart to the *moshav* that Barak founded may well be the Indiana farm on which Kitty Fremont was raised. When she predicts the failure of the Jewish national struggle ("You can't fight the whole British Empire!"), Ari mentions an earlier, David-versus-Goliath victory over the same oppressor: seventy-seven colonials had fought at Concord. Language also gives away the film's partisanship. When Palestinian Jews speak to one another in *Exodus* they use English (which becomes the equivalent of Hebrew). But when Taha briefly converses with another Arab, it is in an unsubtitled and untranslated (hence truly foreign) tongue.

14   Dwight Macdonald, *Dwight Macdonald on Movies* (New York: Berkley Medallion, 1971), 465, 467.

This is a film told from a Jewish perspective; and the Arab — despite Taha's initial generosity of spirit — is the Other.

Released a dozen years after independence, the film fails to illuminate the persistent intensity of the Other's enmity. (Perhaps this lapse should be treated indulgently, for such tenacious hatred *is* difficult to explain.) While listening on the radio to the news of partition, Taha interrupts the singing of *Hatikvah* to tell his boyhood friend Ari: "You have won your freedom, and I have lost mine." Since both of them had grown up under the Mandate, Ari's reply makes historic sense: "You never *had* freedom — you *or* I." But Taha, defining himself as a Muslim, not an Israeli, is unpersuaded and offers no further explanation for his sudden alignment with the rejectionists. Perhaps there *is* no rational answer. Taha now includes himself in "a minority" and asks of Ari, "Where should my people go?" He answers with a question: "Why should they go anywhere?" The film's distance from Arab or Muslim culture, the reluctance to explore the basis of such animosity to Zionism (as though the military repudiation of partition were a continuation of Nazism by other means) heighten the impression of one-sidedness that in art, if not in history or politics, impugns the seriousness of artistic intention and gives the effect of propaganda.

The appropriate standard here should be *The Battle of Algiers* (1966), which makes its partisanship clear. It was shot in Algeria, and was directed and co-written by Gillo Pontecorvo, an Italian–Jewish independent Marxist and ex-communist (whose older brother Bruno, a famous nuclear physicist, had defected in 1950 to the Soviet Union, earning a Lenin Prize). The movie is manifestly anti-French colonialist in its politics.[15] Yet it never stoops to sermonizing or speechifying, and refuses to air-brush from the picture the savagery that a people's revolution unleashes. *The Battle of Algiers* shows the willingness of the National Liberation Front to bomb a milk bar in which young *pieds noirs* will be maimed and killed, to avenge crimes that such teenagers had not committed; and the figure of Colonel Matthieu (Jean Martin) is made into a sophisticated and very competent imperialist, a civilized soldier with "dirty hands" who sees a relationship between ends and means. The ambiguity of

15   Pauline Kael, *Reeling* (Boston: Little, Brown, 1976), 210–212, 214.

that relationship is largely absent from *Exodus*, which does not bend over backward to be fair to the "other side."

But because its perspective is so forthrightly Zionist, *Exodus* spikes the most durable theme in American films (and fiction and plays) about Jews, and that is the attraction of intermarriage. The star of the film was himself the product of such a union; and both he and Cobb married gentiles. During the filming of *Exodus*, Preminger's divorce from yet another gentile, Mary Gardner, became final, freeing him to wed an Episcopalian in a religious ceremony in Haifa, which Meyer Weisgal of the Weizmann Institute arranged by swearing to the rabbinic authorities that the bride, Hope Bryce, was Jewish. (One reward for Weisgal was the fun of taking a brief non-speaking role as Ben-Gurion, to whose charms he was immune.)[16] At the center of *Exodus* is a short-circuited love affair between Ari and Kitty. Intermarriage is not an especially pressing issue among Israelis, but it bedevils the assumption that minority survival is compatible with the ideals of an open society like that of the United States. How *Exodus* resolved this dilemma became a breakthrough.

Overlooking the Jezreel Valley where the bones of so many warriors were buried, Kitty proclaims that "all these differences between people are made up. People are the same, no matter what they're called." But Ari disagrees: "Don't ever believe it. People are different. They have a *right* to be different. They *like* to be different. It's no good pretending differences don't exist. They do. They have to be recognized and respected." Yet she nourishes the hope that if Ari can momentarily forget that he is a Jew, she will no longer feel so much a Presbyterian. "There *are* no differences," she whispers as they kiss. She later realizes, however, that Ari is right and therefore *isn't* Mr. Right: "We *are* different." After meeting his parents at Yad El, she sees something in "the way they looked at me, the way your sister talked to me." Ari meets her halfway: "I'd feel the same way in Indiana."

But what, after all, *is* so different about Ari, especially when the thrust of *Exodus* is to equate Zionism, as did Louis D. Brandeis, with Americanism? The earlier films and novels that had exalted

16 Preminger, *Preminger*, pp. 1272, 187–188; Meyer Weisgal, ...*So Far: An Autobiography* (New York: Random House, 1971), 313–315.

intermarriage had minimized the contrast between Jew and gentile in the United States. Was the *sabra* a novelty item in the range of Jewish characters? Because a new identity was being forged in Israel, sociologist Georges Friedmann wondered if that meant — as his 1965 book was entitled — the *Fin du peuple juif*. This is the sort of question that *Exodus* ducks. Ari can play different roles, disguising himself in a British uniform on Cyprus as a captain in the fake 23rd GT Company, and wandering through Acre dressed as an Arab, replete with *kaffiyeh*. But when he tells Kitty that "I'm a Jew," the meaning of that identity is not elaborated. (Indeed that monosyllable was itself so uncommon that when *Crossfire* was released only thirteen years earlier, critic James Agee worried about "the questionable excitement of hearing actors throw the word 'Jew' around.")[17]

Citing Joshua's conquest of the Canaanites in the Jezreel Valley, the Bible-quoting Ari is not asked by the politically challenged Mrs. Fremont whether he is therefore a believer in the truth of that Book, and whether the accents of Jewish nationalism in which he speaks are grounded in divine sanction. Nothing about him exudes piety, or a yearning to incorporate religious observance within a busy life with the Haganah.[18] (Though Uris himself has never lived as a religious Jew either, a pop song that was extracted from Ernest Gold's film score veers off in a different direction. Pat Boone, who was so fervent a Christian that he refrained from kissing women in his films, croons: "This land is mine/God gave this land to me." This formulation manages to be both theologically presumptuous — and indeed it transcends any justifications for the *yishuv* offered in the film — and historically inaccurate, in that it reduces a national struggle to a land grant to an individual.)[19]

17   James Agee, *Agee on Film: Reviews and Comments* (New York: Grosset & Dunlap Universal Library, 1969), 270.

18   Patricia Erens, *The Jew in American Cinema* (Bloomington: Indiana University Press, 1984), 218–219; Lester D. Friedman, *Hollywood's Image of the Jews* (New York: Frederick Ungar, 1982), 191–192; idem, *The Jewish Image in the American Film* (Secaucus, N.J.: Citadel, 1987), 162–165.

19   Thomas Doherty, *Teenagers and Teenpics: The Juvenilization of American Movies in the 1950s* (Boston: Unwin Hyman, 1988), 189; Jill Uris and Leon Uris, *Jerusalem Song of Songs* (Garden City, N.Y.: Doubleday, 1981), 273.

Even Ari's secularist culture as a Jew seems limited. In perhaps the film's most embarrassing scene, his doting mother worries that Mrs. Fremont is too thin, with "not even a thing in the house to eat." Sarah contradicts herself by making a big deal of the apple strudel that she serves to her guest. Ari's mother tells Kitty: "You could stand a little weight on you." After the meal, Sarah ruefully remarks, "Maybe next time you'll be a little hungrier." The object of so much solicitude would, in so many movies located in America, have become her daughter-in-law. Though Ari has propelled himself away from the warmth of this domestic *Yiddishkeit*, he cannot be placed in any distinctive cultural setting.

Both the film and the novel on which it was based nevertheless helped to legitimate pluralism and to honor diversity. *Exodus* contributed mightily to the visibility of Israel on the American Jewish communal agenda and helped many of Uris's and Preminger's coreligionists to live — vicariously — in Israel, without the inconvenience of actually having to move there and have such heroes as neighbors.[20] (Indeed it might be argued that by strengthening Jewish feelings and enhancing ethnic pride among the inhabitants of the largest Diaspora community, *Exodus* helped to undermine Theodor Herzl's premise that the *Galut* was fated to disappear.) But the film failed to depict the birth of a state that was not only a response to a legacy of hate but the result of a people's emerging sense of its own destiny. Zionism was designed not only to be an antidote to anti-Semitism; it was to fulfill Judaic culture and destiny — and this was an Israel that the movie barely revealed.

The tripartite structure of *Exodus* — the struggle against the British on Cyprus, the struggle against the British in Palestine, and the struggle against the Arabs in Palestine — corresponds with Ari Ben Canaan's conquest of three of the four elements that the ancient Greeks enumerated. He first appears emerging from the water, swimming onto the beach at Cyprus; and before the *Exodus* finally docks in Haifa, he has dived over the side and into the Mediterranean. In the second section of the film, he is virtually autochthonous, grounded in the land, able to move about freely within it. "Where do you come from?" Kitty asks Ari over dinner on the balcony

20   Sol Liptzin, *The Jew in American Literature* (New York: Bloch, 1966), 196, 224.

of the King David Hotel. The answer is expansive: "I don't come from anywhere. I'm a *sabra* — a native-born Palestinian," who can identify with ancestors who arrived over three millennia earlier in the valley where Ari grew up. In the final section of the film, he triumphs over fire, marching past a burning truck as the Haganah repels the Arab invaders, as the flames leap up from the screen in the final shot of *Exodus*. The only element that is not mastered is air — the winds of freedom. This is the unanswered question. Ari has assured his Arab friend that all can live as equal citizens in a "free" Israel — an offer that is rejected, leaving the possibilities of liberty unrealized. At the end of *Exodus* the fires of fanaticism have consumed the two advocates of brotherhood — Karen and Taha — who are buried together on the kibbutz, perhaps along with their dream of mutual understanding and their faith in humanity.

How embattled and threatened Israel would remain is the theme of another American film, released twenty-four years later. Most of it, however, takes place in Germany, where John le Carré had been stationed in the 1950s and where he set a grim tale that enabled the British Foreign Service officer, in *Time* magazine's phrase, to become the spy who came in for the gold. *The Little Drummer Girl* (1983), another best-selling novel, was adapted for the screen — and also much shortened — by Loring Mandel, who focused on plot rather than characterization or politics. By coincidence the director, George Roy Hill, had also directed *Butch Cassidy and the Sundance Kid* (1969) and *The Sting* (1973), which had kept Newman's stardom intact as he edged past the age for conventional romantic leads. Uninvolved in the politics of the Middle East,[21] Hill discharged his assignment on *The Little Drummer Girl* with professional skill.

Neither the Palestine Liberation Organization nor the Mosad is mentioned in the script (nor is the word "Mafia" heard in *The Godfather*); but a Palestinian terrorist group is obviously responsible for the ugly act of violence with which the film opens: an Israeli diplomatic family is killed by a bomb in Bad Godesberg in 1981. In the aftermath of the bombing, a German police official gripes that the Jews have "problems with everyone" and is annoyed because the

21   Andrew Horton, *The Films of George Roy Hill* (New York: Columbia University Press, 1984), 173–174.

Mosad agent Shimon Litvak (Eli Danker) is abrupt with him during their collecting and sifting of evidence. As with Ari on Cyprus, Shimon's tempo is accelerated; the demands of Jewish history are urgent. Then the scene shifts to Dorset, England, where a masked Palestinian known as "Michel" presents to a rapt and sympathetic audience the case against Israeli occupation. His grievances — such as the expulsion of Palestinians from their homes — resemble those that had made Israel a necessary haven for Jewish refugees, with the imbalance reversed. The Jews are alleged to exert the preponderance of power, while the Palestinians inflict terrorist bombings only because they have no army or air force. Theirs are the weapons of the weak and the oppressed.

It is a viewpoint shared by Charlie (Diane Keaton), an American actress residing in England. Because of her emphatically "progressive" politics (akin to Vanessa Redgrave's, though far less visibly), a counterterrorist unit recruits Charlie to play in "the theatre of the real," with the aim of trapping the chief bombing suspect, the Palestinian Khalil (Sami Frey). Marty Kurtz (Klaus Kinski), the head of the Mosad unit, professes to be a producer of television commercials named Leslie Gold and praises her acting on stage as *Saint Joan*. (Preminger himself had made George Bernard Shaw's play, about a political martyr with a flair for cross-dressing, into a 1957 film.) Through duplicity the Israelis lure Charlie, a highly politicized actress with a masculine name, to Mykonos, kidnap her, and then "turn" her into an agent of their own purposes. They succeed in breaking down the version of herself that she has constructed, in ripping away the persona that she has pretended to herself she had formed. Their stripping away of the façade resembles the Irgun interrogation in *Exodus* of Dov Landau and his past in Auschwitz.

This is the least convincing part of the film (and of the novel). It requires a belief that Charlie is so alone, so starved for romance — or at least for warmth and intimacy — that the Israelis can make themselves into a facsimile of "a family she can join," according to Marty. This American woman abroad is as bereft of family ties as the widow Kitty Fremont. The Mosad offers Charlie the solidarity and support that her own difficult childhood did not include and that an itinerant and insecure craft, in which identities are provisional, cannot sustain. She accepts the challenge of working for the Israelis, for whom she "plays the role of — and *for* — her life" (as the movie's ad campaign puts it). She participates in a "legend," pretending to fall in love with "Michel," who is played by a Mosad agent named Joseph, or Jose, her name for Gadi Becker (Yorgo Voyagis), who makes the case for Michel, the name that Salim (Moti Shirin) gives himself.

Gadi Becker articulates the Palestinian claim as though he were Michel, the son of the *mukhtar* growing up in what the Israelis call Hebron, watching their tanks rumble through his village in 1967 and destroy his home. Over dinner in Athens, Becker reveals that he himself had been in one of those tanks; but since he is playing "Michel," his historical picture is buffed up. "Michel" does not bother, for example, to inform Charlie about the riots under the Mandate that had initially driven Jews from Hebron. He tells her about the massacre of 250 Arab civilians, including women and children, at Deir Yassin in 1948, without mentioning that Arabs retaliated with an ambush in which seventy-seven doctors, nurses, professors, and students bound for Hadassah Hospital and the Hebrew University were killed. Having an Israeli operative advocate the Palestinian cause has the effect of putting such grievances at the remove of ventriloquism. Such play-acting is part of the theatricality — the shuffling of the cards of identity — that is the central motif of *The Little Drummer Girl* with its tangle of duplicity and multinymity and its trail of betrayal.[22]

Becker himself is exhausted by his lifelong battle against the Arabs ("I just want peace") and doubts the morality of playing with human lives like Charlie's. He has already assured the presumably pro-Palestinian actress: "You have said you want to stop the killing. Fine. So do we." Acknowledging the presence of "madmen" and "extremists" on both sides, Becker tells Charlie of his own wish for "the Palestinians to have their homeland beside us" — a claim that brings a sidelong glance of skepticism between Marty and Shimon. "I've killed all the Arabs I ever want to kill," Becker insists. To save her life at the end of the film, however, he must kill one more: Khalil.

22   Friedman, *Jewish Image*, 241–242.

Because the "legend" stipulates Charlie's romantic involvement with Michel, whom the Mosad has flawlessly captured, interrogated, tortured, and killed (by faking an accident that also takes the life of the bomber responsible for the Bad Godesberg murders), Kurtz tips off the British police to ransack the actress's apartment. (The police commander in that brief scene is identified in the credits as David Cornwell — the novelist whose *nom de plume* is John le Carré. He is indeed in command of the action.) She is soon contacted by the Palestinian network in England, which flies her to Beirut, where she meets another commander: Tayeh (Michael Cristofer). Maimed and one-eyed, he is contemptuous of the Eurotrash who attach themselves to the PLO, "scum" who "want to blow up the whole world" or, failing that, will settle for murdering Zionists. Tayeh is also capable of ordering the immediate execution of Dimitri (Ben Levine), the genial young Israeli operating in Lebanon, whom the terrorists have captured and beaten. His murder heightens the aura of Palestinian cruelty.

Their headquarters in Beirut are shrouded in darkness, as are a couple of the scenes shot in the PLO's training camp, where Charlie learns how to use guns and make bombs. The later scenes with Khalil in the Black Forest are all filmed at night or right before dawn; and this impression of a shadowy and sinister world is reinforced by the shabbiness of the diggings of Khalil's European coconspirators. The ambience of the Israeli unit is by contrast bright and sunlit; even when "Gold" becomes Kurtz, kidnaps Charlie, and induces her to make her nocturnal confession and then remake herself, the room is aglow with light. The squalid world of the terrorists diverges sharply from the glamorous backdrop of places like the Parthenon, where "Joseph" romances Charlie. As if the cinematographic effects are not enough, Arab hostility is linked to a widely disreputable, if historic, European hatred. When Charlie is asked to identify "Joseph," she dismisses him as a "greasy little Jew who tagged on to watch the girls" on Mykonos. Tayeh corrects the new recruit: "We are *not* anti-Semitic. We *are* anti-Zionists." But he does not bother to dispute her scornful reply: "Tell me another."

Khalil is even plotting to assassinate the peacenik professor from the Hebrew University of Jerusalem, who is scheduled to deliver a lecture at Freiburg. Khalil is exultant because, according to the faked news bulletin on West German television, three persons were killed in the bombing and "many Zionist supporters wounded." No humanist like his putative victim, Professor Minkel (or Becker, for that matter), Khalil proclaims this "a great victory," for "tomorrow the world will know that Palestinians will not wait two thousand years like the Jews." But for all his murderousness, Khalil seems to display one badge of moral superiority over the woman with whom he (and, he thinks, his late brother) has slept, the woman who has betrayed him and has led the Mosad to his hideaway in Baden-Württemberg. "Are you Jewish?" he wonders; and when the answer is negative, he then asks: "What are you?" She replies: "Nothing. I'm nothing." The arch-terrorist remains puzzled and almost pitying: "You believe in nothing." In this puzzle palace of deceit, too many identities have been switched, too many shocks to a system of psychic integrity have been absorbed. Only emptiness remains. In an unfortunate tribute to American Jewish cinematic conventions, *The Little Drummer Girl* ends with Becker renouncing his heroic career in Israel and romantically pursuing the broken Charlie in England ("I'm here because I love you"). The last line is hers, as she rebuffs him — but only momentarily: "I'm dead, Jose. You killed me, remember? I'm dead."

Because Diane Keaton could not handle an acceptable British accent,[23] Charlie was made an American. The change in diction meant further slashing of the fiction, in which Khalil's last words to her in the novel (before Becker bursts in) make an ironic reprise of the theme of *Exodus*: "And you are the same English who gave away my country."[24] Casting the apolitical Keaton as the windup toy of the Christmas song ("The Little Drummer Boy") lacked resonance. But the choice had the inadvertent effect of highlighting the gap between Israeli and American Jewry, since Keaton's career was so closely tied with the Woody Allen films that put such a wry spin on contemporary Jewish life in New York. The urbane wit and the self-conscious neuroses, plus the fascination with the cultural oddities that spice up interreligious romance, that are the *schlemiel* ticket of the Allen persona characterize his films with her, especially

23   Harton, *George Roy Hill*, 172.
24   John le Carré, *The Little Drummer Girl* (New York: Knopf, 1983), 420.

Annie Hall (1977). They are a world away from the life-and-death struggle embodied in *The Little Drummer Girl* (though, had it not already been used, Hill's thriller might aptly have been entitled *Love and Death*). The lethal stakes for which the Israelis play — even as Hill's movie gives them the winning hand — suggest their divergence from the experiences of Jewry in the United States.

The intrigue and double-dealing in which the geopolitics of the Middle East conflict has been enmeshed, even when transferred to Europe and England, require that the casting of everyone else exclude American actors. A German got the chance to portray the top Israeli agent, though nothing whatsoever can be said for the suspicion surfacing in *Commentary* that Warner Brothers must have produced "America's first forthrightly anti-Israel movie" because Kinski "has never played a sympathetic role in his life."[25] Greek actor Yorgo Voyagis, a quite wooden performer, was largely unknown to American audiences, and as Becker could hardly be termed "unsympathetic." It must have been slightly amusing to cast Sami Frey, a French Jew once romantically linked with Brigitte Bardot, as Khalil. Though the Israelis are not played by American actors, as in *Exodus*, it is noteworthy that the film is narrated entirely from the perspective of the hunters rather than the prey, and that the lone American in the plot — and the only real star in the cast — volunteers to work for the Mosad. Theirs is the challenge that must be overcome: to find the maker of lethal bombs with the distinctive signature of a twisted coil. Theirs is the quest with which the audience is expected to identify.

Moreover the politics of *The Little Drummer Girl* can be classified as pro-Zionist, because no rationale is provided for the obduracy of the Palestinians in rejecting compromise, and no motives are adduced for their refusal to share the land with the Zionists or to recognize their national existence. The only voices granted to the Palestinian cause are inflected with the accents of terrorism, which initiates the unwinding of the narrative spool and comes from sources that seem instinctual, irrational, and prepolitical — which is very close to the truth anyway. Here is further refutation of Walter Lippmann's 1948 assertion that, "among the really difficult

25 Richard Grenier, "Treason Chic," *Commentary* 79, January 1985, 64.

problems of the world," the Arab-Israeli conflict was "one of the simplest and most manageable."[26] Not that *The Little Drummer Girl* limns the historical justification for the Zionist ideology either. The lone stab that the script makes at the political and ethical imperatives that fuel Jewish nationalism is to have Kurtz inquire: "Where would you have us go, Charlie? Maybe you would prefer us taking a piece of central Africa? Or Uruguay? Not Egypt, thank you. We tried it once, and that wasn't a success. Or back to the ghettoes?" She has no answer, but his queries imply that the safety of the Jewish people is itself a moral idea. By 1981, when the trap is sprung for the elusive Khalil, Israel was not — or was not merely — an act of faith; it had become a fact. No *raison d'être* for the state is presented, even though, in the vortex of Arab politics, the legitimacy and very existence of the "Zionist entity" could still be questioned.

Both *Exodus* and *The Little Drummer Girl* are designed to suggest, however, that Israel engages in force only to protect its citizens, that the extremism of their enemies sanctions methods undertaken with moral reservations and ambivalence (and with a high level of competence). As Control tells Alec Leamas in le Carré's first novel about the Circus, "We do disagreeable things, but we are *defensive*...so that ordinary people here and elsewhere can sleep safely in their beds at night."[27] The case against Israel is therefore dismissed, since Buber's 1945 standard of justice seems to be intact.

Such a perspective cannot be ascribed simply to the values of the producers, nor accounted for by the vagaries of individual commitment. Though it had taken Barbra Streisand, for instance, fifteen years to adapt a story by Isaac Bashevis Singer into *Yentl* (1983), no such personal dedication energized the making of *Exodus* or *The Little Drummer Girl*. The politics of these films cannot be traced primarily to the obsessions of their makers. Indeed Trumbo complained that Preminger, who had never been associated with Zionism, was easily distracted by other projects and could not concentrate on *Exodus*; and neither Hill nor le Carré is Jewish. The English novelist vehemently condemned the 1982 invasion of Lebanon as

26   Quoted in Peter Grose, *Israel in the Mind of America* (New York: Knopf, 1983), 264.

27   John le Carré, *The Spy Who Came in from the Cold* (New York: Dell, 1965), 19.

"a monstrosity, launched on speciously assembled grounds, against a people who on the Israelis' own admission constitute no serious military threat." He wrote in a London newspaper of "the most savage irony that Begin and his generals cannot see how close they are to inflicting upon another people the disgraceful criteria once inflicted upon themselves." But the tale rather than the teller should be trusted.[28]

No student of Hollywood history deserves any extra credit for underscoring the mercenary motives behind the production of movies. In that sense it would not matter whether the studio heads were second- or third-generation Jews, or were Buddhist bonzes festooned in saffron robes. Hollywood made these films because of its estimate that the potential market for adaptations of these best-selling novels was big enough, and because the cinematic messages did not defy the prejudices, tastes, and moral preferences of the audience. Because of traditional resistance to politically oriented films, Israel has largely been *terra incognita* on the American screen. But in 1960, as in 1984, the jackpot that Uris and le Carré hit in the literary marketplace made United Artists and Warner Brothers less cautious. These films could be budgeted because they satisfied the basic rules of mass entertainment: "Kiss Kiss Bang Bang" — the words scrawled on an Italian movie poster that critic Pauline Kael once noticed, and realized is "the briefest statement imaginable of the basic appeal of movies."[29]

Perhaps it is just as well that Hollywood has usually not tried for greater sophistication and nuance, which would only expose its ineptitude in attempting to clarify, say, the politics of the Middle East. Derived from action formulas, works like *Exodus* and *The Little Drummer Girl* may tell us less about Israel than about the values and visions of a mass audience that is easily diverted and distracted, just as the citizenry is limited in its attention span and in its curiosity. It wants a glimpse not into the reality of Israel but into

28 Dalton Trumbo to Ingo Preminger, 2 January 1960, in Manfull, *Additional Dialogue*, 527; John le Carré, "Memories of a Vanished Land," *The Observer*, 13 June 1982, 10, quoted in Peter Lewis, *John le Carré* (New York: Frederick Ungar, 1985), 186–187; Joel Rosenberg, "Le Carré's Middle East," *Moment* 8, July–August 1983, 58–59.

29 Pauline Kael, *Kiss Kiss Bang Bang* (Boston: Little, Brown, 1968), vii.

another country — one that can fill in the blanks of the imagination. Just as the postwar history of Eastern and Central Europe discloses an anti-Semitism without Jews (just "Jews" will do), so too this brief foray uncovers cinematic evidence of a pro-Zionism without Israel. Ignoring the UJA slogan that "Israel is real," such works instead enlist political sympathies and moral sentiments in behalf of "Israel."

Filmography

Hill, George Roy (director). *The Little Drummer Girl* (1984). Warner Home Video, 130 min. (color).
Preminger, Otto (director). *Exodus* (1960). CBS/Fox Video, 207 min. (color).

Part V

Tangled Relations

Dual Loyalties: Zionism and Liberalism

Naomi W. Cohen

In a discussion of American Jewish visions of Israel it is appropriate to probe the bases for those images. Are images of Israel or assessments of the Jewish state built on Jewish standards or American standards? Jewish standards underlay early criticism of political Zionism and its adherents, criticism that hammered away at the areligious and even antireligious character of the movement. Today there are many, and not only among the Orthodox, who continue to judge the operations and behavioral patterns of the Jewish state according to biblical or rabbinical injunctions. American Christian critics of Israel, too, be they religious or secular, often invoke the same yardsticks when passing negative judgments. For the most part, however, American Jewish responses to Israel's government and society have been grounded and nurtured in an American matrix. Always a very small and accommodationist minority, Jews took their cues on behavior and ideology from American standards. In the matter of Israel their views were shaped specifically by the tenets of American liberalism.

That finding comes as no surprise. The attachment of Western Jews to liberalism, as many have written, is well-nigh exiomatic,[1] and in the United States, ever since the days of the early Republic, liberalism has been a hallmark of American Jewry. For nineteenth-century Jews, classical or "old" liberalism — the creed of individualism that sought to eradicate the restrictions and discrimination of the Old World — was the ideology that legitimated political, economic, and religious rights for the Jew, rights which neither the state nor, for that matter, the Jewish community could violate. As an eminently

---

1   See, for example, the recent analysis in Ruth R. Wisse, *If I Am Not for Myself* (New York, 1992).

respectable American base on which to rest the case for Jewish equality, Jews looked upon liberalism as the passport to full acceptance and integration in American society.[2] Since liberalism was the acknowledged core of the American ethos, Jewish attachment to its teachings served yet another major purpose — it provided a means by which Jews could demonstrate their unalloyed identification with the United States. Jewish loyalty to liberalism became even more pronounced in the twentieth century, when the classical teachings were replaced by the new genre of liberalism espoused by Woodrow Wilson and Franklin Roosevelt, one that enhanced the role of the state in the interest of social justice. Jews gave their political support to liberal candidates and forged alliances with Christian liberals. Unlike other American minorities, most Jews proudly wore the liberal badge even as their rapid socio-economic mobility made liberal causes less relevant to their daily needs. Among some Jews the liberal creed evoked a religious-like loyalty; it became a pseudo-messianic cause that promised an end to exile and alienation.

The canons of liberalism could, and often did, operate in opposition to Jewish nationalism and statehood. Liberals of both the classical and "new" varieties touted universalism over nationalism; they deplored imperialism, militarism, and the subjugation of minorities. For those reasons, Christian as well as some Jewish critics often raised their voices — first against the Zionist movement, then against the *yishuv* under the British mandate, and then against the State of Israel. Such criticisms were particularly blatant in the aftermath of World War I, when disillusioned American liberals, soured by the war and the disappointing peace, saw no need to stoke the fires of nationalist and internationalist rivalries with yet another small state in Palestine. Blaming the Jews for the Arab riots of 1929, the liberal journal the *Nation* charged for example that Zionists wrongly looked to the "Joshua" instead of the "Isaiah" method of progress. That same year Louis Marshall's son James denied that the Jews needed a *"Judenstaat."* The use of that word in

---

2   What Jews, and more specifically American Judaism, paid for that passport is spelled out in Jerold S. Auerbach, *Rabbis and Lawyers* (Bloomington, 1990).

1929, although an allusion to Herzl's treatise, also conjured up the image of the warlike and antidemocratic Wilhelmine Germany.[3]

Zionists and their sympathizers, however, refused to be deterred by logical inconsistencies or by liberal opposition that was openly expressed until the Holocaust. Their affirmations of Jewish nationalism admitted of no contradiction of liberalism. Indeed, since liberalism was so enmeshed with their view of America, they ignored it as a separate issue. If challenged, they retorted that Zionism was eminently compatible with Americanism — and by Americanism they meant loyalty to the country and its liberal teachings — and was no different, they often said, from the Irishman's vision of a free homeland. The Zionist combination of minority nationalism and liberalism was aided significantly by the philosophy of cultural pluralism — itself a liberal product whose protagonist, Horace Kallen, championed democratic rights for the group.[4] From World War II on, when American liberalism in general connoted an acceptance of cultural pluralism, the merger of liberalism with support of Israel was further solidified.

The Zionism fashioned in America never meant *shelilat ha-golah*, or turning one's back on the future of Jews in America. It was a comfortable Zionism, an ideology that called for a Jewish state as a refuge for less fortunate European Jews or, at best, a cultural and religious center that would invigorate Diaspora living. (American Zionists may have preached the laws of Herzl, but in their eyes those laws stopped at the shores of the United States.) Justifying Jewish nationalism to Americans, Zionists projected their American liberal values on to their ideal Jewish state. Early images of *halutzim* as "Pilgrims" or "Founding Fathers," or Louis Brandeis's vision of a Jewish state as a laboratory for social democracy, bespoke an idiom and a commitment to ideals that were rooted in American liberal practices. After 1948 the image of Israel as a microcosm of America or the extension of American liberal values took on a pragmatic dimension. Zionists took pride in portraying the Jewish state as the

3   Naomi W. Cohen, *The Year after the Riots* (Detroit, 1988), 102–106.
4   In 1919 Kallen himself argued the compatibility of Zionism with liberalism in a rejoinder to the antinationalist Morris Raphael Cohen. Horace Kallen, "Zionism and Liberalism," *Brandeis Avukah Annual*, ed. J. S. Shubow (Boston, 1932), 45–53.

bastion of democracy in the Middle East and as the American outpost against totalitarian communism. Indeed, the Cold War reinforced the Zionist assumption that a common set of liberal values linked the American and Israeli communities.

Envisioning Israel as an ideological extension of American liberalism was an obvious reinforcement of both American and American Jewish commitment to the Jewish state. But it had its weakness too. In the first place, were Israel to deviate from the accepted canons of liberalism, it ran the risk of alienating American Jewish support. Second, were liberalism in the United States to modify its course, its new directions might cast Israel in an unfavorable light and thus erode traditional American sympathy; and if American Jews remained firmly within the liberal camp despite those modifications, Jewish as well as American support of the Jewish state could be seriously weakened. At bottom, Jews who justified their Zionism primarily on liberal grounds were embarked on a course of action over whose variables they had no control.

Early anti-Zionists accused Jews of dual loyalties — that is, of watering down their fealty to the United States by their support of a Jewish state; but that charge lacked real substance. There is, however, another and more troublesome threat of dual loyalties: Jewish loyalty to liberalism versus Jewish loyalty to Israel. Historically, the majority of American Jews have been unable to divest themselves of at least some sense of Jewish peoplehood, the teachings of nineteeth-century classical Reform Judaism to the contrary notwithstanding. At the same time, if election statistics are our guide, never since the New Deal has the majority of Jewish voters abandoned a liberal presidential candidate. Therefore the question is plausible: How would Jews line up, at any political juncture, if their political friends and American liberalism in general were arrayed against Israel? Could American Jews continue to honor two essential commitments, one to Israel and the other to liberal causes and liberal allies? The questions became more than academic in the 1970s and 1980s, when three factors converged: the anti-Israel stand of the liberal churches, the flowering of the New Christian Right, and the Jesse Jackson brand of liberalism that sought to capture the Democratic party.

Until the 1960s the combination of liberalism with support of Israel aroused little dissent within the Jewish or Christian communities. Jews, who liked to identify themselves in FDR's terms as "a little left of center," felt comfortable with Israel's Labor government. Viewing Israel as a political and social democracy, they confidently expected the Jewish state to act out the same principles to which they, the Americans, were committed. Christian liberals, whose theological reservations about the legitimacy of a Jewish state had been silenced at least temporarily by the soul-searching and guilt spawned by the Holocaust, and by the romantic image of the Jewish David besieged by the Arab Goliath, were basically in accord. They too supported a democratic state in the Middle East that could act as a counterweight to Soviet ambitions in the region. Since Jewish and Christian liberals fought side by side in the domestic wars for civil rights and against poverty, the Jewish-liberal connection appeared eminently harmonious.

But serious cracks in the liberal coalition soon appeared. In 1966 Lyndon Johnson, for example, did not understand why Jewish liberals who insisted that the United States honor its commitments to Israel opposed his policies in Vietnam. According to the president, those policies represented an analogous situation of America's concern for a tiny ally.[5] The implication was clear: An anti-Vietnam War liberal could not simultaneously expect unqualified support for Israel.

More disconcerting was the "silence" of the liberal churches during the war of 1967. Theologians A. Roy and Alice Eckardt decried that silence as an example of Christian indifference to the threat of Jewish annihilation,[6] but compared with mainstream liberal Christian spokesmen, now more distanced from the Holocaust, they were vastly outnumbered. The executive committee of the National Council of Churches (NCC), the umbrella organization of mainline liberal churches, concentrated on the plight of the Arab refugees and ignored the primary issues. As Franklin H. Littell, a staunch friend of Israel, explained, the NCC neither acknowledged the design

5 *American Jewish Year Book* (1967): 79–80.
6 See, for example, A. Roy and Alice L. Eckardt, "Silence in the Churches," *Midstream*, October 1967, 27–32; Egal Feldman, "American Protestant Theologians on the Fronhtiers of Jewish–Christian Relations, 1922–82," *Anti-Semitism in American History*, ed. David A. Gerber (Urbana, 1986), 373–377.

of the Arab governments, aided by the Soviets, to carry out a second Holocaust, nor did it admit that the Arab refugee problem persisted only because Arab rulers used it for political capital. Protestant churches, whose theology shared responsibility for the Nazi Holocaust, Littell said, preferred the Jew as the "pariah" or "loser" to the Jew "who is a winner, a citizen-soldier of liberty and dignity, who does not have to beg protection of a patron or toleration of a so-called Christian nation."[7]

In the next decade the pro-Israel attitudes of Christian religious liberals cooled perceptibly. The *Christian Century*, a liberal periodical,[8] answered the Eckardts and the Littells. Jesus may have been a Jew, but he was not a militant Israeli. Even if the fate of Israel rested on the Christian conscience, "These claims still provide no warrant for discounting the preciousness of Arab life or for neglecting the kinships at stake in Christian–Moslem dialogue."[9] Concern for the rights of Palestinian Arabs (reinforced by the "liberation theology" of the Third World) and for the stability of their own network of educational and social services in the Middle East mounted appreciably within American churches, both Protestant and Catholic, and was reiterated by group resolutions and individual clerics. The Quakers, adding insult to injury, attacked the Israeli government and the pro-Israel American Jewish establishment while seeking the moral and financial support of "liberal" Jews. In 1972 Jewish representatives at the general assembly of the NCC were scandalized by the anti-Semitic as well as anti-Israel remarks of featured speakers. As one Jewish professional wrote, "the record of the liberal Protestant establishment on Israel reveals at best a lack of sensitivity on Jewish concerns and at worst a latent hostility which is inimical to Jewish continuity and survival."[10]

7   Franklin H. Littell, "Israel and American Protestantism," *Congress Bi-Weekly*, 20 February 1970, 10.
8   This journal had relentlessly blasted Jewish nationalism before World War II. Hertzel Fishman, *American Protestantism and a Jewish State* (Detroit, 1973), chap. 3.
9   "Israeli Munitions and the Jewishness of Jesus," *Christian Century* 11 (February 1970).
10   Judith H. Banki, "Anti-Israel Influence in American Churches," American Jewish Committee (AJC) report, 1979; AJC file: "Israel and the Christian Church"; Marvin Maurer, "Quakers in Politics," *Midstream*, November 1977,

Menachem Begin's assumption of power in 1977 accentuated the tilt against Israel. The Israeli state — aggressive, expansionist, and militaristic — was the oppressor, and the Arabs the innocent victims. Not only were demands for a Palestinian state endorsed by the churches and the needs of Israeli security ignored, but increasingly Israel, and Israel alone, was blamed for the failure to arrive at a lasting peace. In 1980 the NCC summed up those sentiments in a major pro-PLO policy statement. In that statement the 250-man governing board approved the continued existence of the Jewish state, but only by a margin of nine votes.[11]

To be sure, many liberal American Jews, shared the dismay over Begin and his policies, but even the opposition of antiexpansionist organizations like Breira to territorial annexation did not seek to undermine American popular or governmental support of Israel's legitimacy. In the eyes of such critics Israel had veered from an acceptable course and required instruction from its American partners. The Lebanon War of 1982 compounded the strains when, as one reporter wrote, TV images of Israeli bombardments of Beirut "bruised the liberal sensibilities" of American Jews.[12] Disaffection within American Jewish ranks grew in the 1980s. Arthur Hertzberg, a self-proclaimed "dove," who broke with Begin early on and publicly demanded that "Begin Must Go," charged that the prime minister's Arab policies contradicted American moral and democratic ideals. Hertzberg's claim that American Jews by a vast majority backed dovish options did not, however, tell the whole story. According to polls conducted by sociologist Steven Cohen, most American Jews revealed that no matter how embarrassed or outraged they were by Israel's policies, they did not feel any more distant from Israel than they had before.[13] Unlike liberal Christians, their criticisms

44. On Quaker opposition to Israel, see also articles by Maurer and Raul Isaac in *Midstream*, November 1979; Gerald S. Strober, "American Jews and the Protestant Community," *Midstream,* August–September 1974, 47–54.

11   Judith H. Banki and Gary Wolf, "Israel at Risk," AJC report, 1990; AJC files: "National Council of Churches"; *JTA Daily Bulletin*, 10 November 1980; Raul Jean Isaac, "Liberal Protestants versus Israel," *Midstream*, October 1981, 6–7.

12   *American Jewish Year Book* 79 (1979): 139–140; J. J. Goldberg, "Separated by a Common Cause," *Jerusalem Report*, 27 February 1992.

13   Arthur Hertzberg, *jewish Polemics* (New York, 1992), esp. 3–29; Steven M.

constituted more of an in-house affair that posed no threat, at least not yet, to their commitment to the Jewish state. Israel, although it had sinned, was still Israel.

The anti-Israel sentiments of the mainline liberal churches raised other problems. For one thing, the Christian tilt affected the course of Jewish–Christian dialogue, a cause in which the Jewish Establishment had heavily invested.[14] More important, it stirred a round of soul-searching with respect to the very foundations of the Jewish-liberal alliance. How trustworthy were allies who were at best lukewarm about a high if not the highest priority on the American Jewish agenda? Was the warning of the *Christian Century* in 1977 — that Jewish lobbying to force the administration into a rigidly pro-Israel position before the Geneva Conference ill served the interests of American Jews — a threat to American Jewish security?[15] Dependent on allies to further their domestic interests, could Jews afford to abandon their longtime liberal partners for the sake of Israel? Yet, for the sake of Israel, where could they find other allies? One possibility presented itself in 1980 when the New Christian Right, swearing its love of the Jewish state, emerged as a powerful political force in support of Ronald Reagan's bid for the presidency. Small wonder that some concerned Jews began to ponder whether the liberal camp was indeed their proper place.

But for the needs of Israel, most American Jews would have rejected out of hand any dealings with the News Christian Right.[16] The very

---

Cohen, "Amoral Zionists, Moralizing Universalists and Conditional Doves," *Moment*, August 1989; see also Eytan Gilboa, "Attitudes of American Jews toward Israel," *American Jewish Year Book* 86 (1986): 110–125. When the American Jewish Congress openly criticized the Shamir government, the agency came under attack from other American Jewish leaders. *Jewish Week*, 4–10 September 1992.

14 For early warnings on dialogues, see Jacob Agus, "Israel and the Jewish–Christian Dialogue," *Journal of Ecumenical Studies,* Winter 1969, 18–36; Malcolm L. Diamond, "Christian Silence on Israel: An End to Dialogue?" *Judaism*, Fall 1967, 411–422.

15 "Israel and the Evangelicals," *Christian Century*, 23 November 1977.

16 This section draws on material that I have published in *Natural Adversaries or Possible Allies? American Jews and the New Christian Right* (New York, 1993).

words "Christian" and "Right" triggered historical memories of bigotry, persecution, and destruction. Furthermore, the New Christian Right of 1980, an informal coalition of right-wing evangelical groups — of which Jerry Falwell's Moral Majority was but one, albeit the best known — stood squarely opposed to American liberal values and the American Jewish liberal agenda.

Directing their fury at secular humanism, which they saw as the pernicious virus or the Antichrist that bred rampant social ills, the rightists called for the restoration of traditional moral values in government. Specifically, they supported prayer and Bible reading in the schools, a curb on welfare programs, and increased defense spending; they sought government action against pornography and abortion, and they opposed feminist demands and gay rights.[17] Except for some within the Orthodox community, the vast majority of Jews, the most secularized of all religious groups, held antithetical positions on all those issues. Jewish alienation was compounded by the political rhetoric and methods of the Christian Right: talk of the Christianization of society and government, calls for Christian legislators, and the use of "Christian" report cards for grading candidates. Like all good liberals Jews fumed at the moral absolutism of evangelical leaders — both the claim that they knew the proper "godly" response on every issue and their determination to translate fundamentalist piety into political action.[18]

Jews were not a primary target of the New Christian Right; most rightists spoke of "Judeo-Christian" rather than "Christian" moral values, and the Moral Majority even courted Jewish membership.[19] Nevertheless, the evangelical emphasis on missionizing, a cause that

---

17 Robert C. Liebman and Robert Wuthnow, eds., *The New Christian Right* (New York, 1983); Steve Bruce, *The Rise and Fall of the New Christian Right* (Oxford, England, 1988); Richard John Neuhaus and Michael Cromartie, eds., *Pietry and Politics* (Washington, 1987).

18 See, for example, American Jewish Congress position paper, "Where We Stand," October 1981, Congress files. The Jewish response has been culled from numerous articles and editorials in contemporary Anglo-Jewish newspapers and journals.

19 Moral Majority ad in *New York Times*, 23 March 1981. A Jew, Howard Phillips, helped establish the Moral Majority. Seymour Martin Lipset and Earl Raab, "The Election and the Evangelicals," *Commentary*, March 1981, 29.

was aggressively pursued in the 1970s, as well as Bailey Smith's famous remark to the Southern Baptist Convention in 1980, "God Almighty does not hear the prayer of a Jew," were highly offensive. Some evangelical leaders like Falwell publicly disavowed any anti-Semitism, but others (e.g., Tom La Haye, Jimmy Swaggart) were not innocent of Jew-baiting.[20] Thus the image of the Christian Right as the natural adversary of Jews, both as liberals and as Jews, persisted.

Yet just because evangelical leaders loudly supported Israel, defying the popular assumption that anti-Zionist=anti-Semite, many Jews hesitated to denounce the rightists out of hand. Even though evangelical support was grounded in the theology of Christian triumphalism, fundamentalists like Falwell added this-wordly reasons for a strong defense of the contemporary Jewish state. Some Jews, therefore, gladly welcomed those signs of friendship. According to Nathan Perlmutter, director of the ADL, the litmus test for the "real" anti-Semitism was anti-Zionism, and the lineup of the Christian churches dictated a fresh approach on the part of Jews to both the liberals and the evangelicals. Nor were theological concerns of great importance. As spokesman for the neoconservatives, Irving Kristol stated, "It is their theology, but it is our Israel.[21] Israel's government agreed; it welcomed its American Christian allies, and Falwell became a close friend of Menachem Begin.[22]

The more outspoken Jewish liberals ruled at first that evangelical friendship was in fact "trafe." They warned that the rightists would expect Jewish support of their domestic agenda in return, and Jews could not afford to turn their backs on decades of cooperation with the liberal churches on weighty issues like religious pluralism, civil

---

20   Judith H. Banki, "Key 73: An Interim Report," AJC library; A. James and Marcia R. Rudin, "Onward (Hebrew) Christian Soldiers," *Present Tense*, Summer 1977, 17–26; Mark Silk, *Spiritual Politics* (New York, 1988), 159–162; Susan Morse, "The Christianization of America," *Jewish Monthly*, January 1987, 19–28; William Bole et al., "The New Christian Right," *Present Tense*, Winter 1985, 27ff.

21   Merrill Simon, *Jerry Falwell and the Jews* (Middle Village, N.Y. 1984), chap. 2; Nathan Perlmutter and Ruth Perlmutter, *The Real Anti-Semitism in America* (New York, 1982), chap. 7; Noah Pickus, "'Before I Built A Wall' — Jews, Religion and American Public Life," *This World*, no. 15, Fall 1986, 31.

22   David A. Rausch. "The New Fundamentalists," *American Zionist*, December–January 1983): 6; *Washington Post*, 16 September 1981.

rights, and welfare policies. Balfour Brickner, hinting at ongoing Christian conversionist aims, cautioned that if evangelicals had their way "we would be out of business as Jews," and Arthur Hertzberg recalled that some Nazis in the 1930s were willing to solve the German race problem by sending Jews to Palestine. Rabbi Alexander Schindler, president of the powerful Union of American Hebrew Congregations, summed up the liberal opposition when he argued that the very nature of the Christian Right, which aimed at the extinction of Judaism as well as the Christianization of America, made its support of Israel unwelcome and even harmful: "We [Jews] fail to see that one cannot be good for Israel when one is injurious to America and its Jews!... We make a pact with the devil for transient boon, even while we know or ought to know that in the end we serve *his* purposes!" Others agreed; the thought of any dealings with the Christian Right was so distasteful that the American Jewish Congress changed a clause in a position paper from "we acknowledge and welcome" to "we acknowledge" the support for Israel by the Christian Right.[23]

Jews who loudly lectured the community against the pro-Israel blandishments of the Christian Right were those who swam most comfortably with the tide of a changed liberalism — the preachers of egalitarianism, the doves in foreign policy who criticized both American militarism and Israeli hawkishness. Although mute on this point, they doubtless also feared alienating the liberal churches. Indeed, not only did Christian liberals second the arguments against any alliance with the evangelical right, but they candidly reminded their Jewish friends that the mainline Protestants still enjoyed most clout politically, economically, and religiously. Jewish agencies acknowledged the necessity of maintaining good relations with the liberal churches. The National Jewish Community Relations

---

23 Yechiel Eckstein, "Understanding Evangelicals," National Jewish Resource Center, *Perspectives,* May 1984, 24; Brickner in *Reform Judaism* symposium, March 1981, 11; Arthur Hertzberg in debate, "The Moral Majority — Is It Good for the Jews?" *Hadassah Magazine,* April 1981, 20 ff.; *Report of the President of the Union of American Hebrew Congregations,* 21 November 1980, 4–5, 7; American Jewish Congress, "Where We Stand," 4 October 1981, Congress files. See also Herbert L. Solomon, "The New Right and the Jews," *Midstream,* December 1985, 7–10.

Advisory Council (NJCRAC), for instance, which noted "a marked slackening of contact and involvement" since the mid-1970s between those Christians and Jews, urged its affiliates to work for the renewal of ties at local and denominational levels.[24]

Nevertheless, with Israel in mind, the Jewish organizational network adopted a pragmatic line — work with the right-wing groups on issues of mutual concern, part company where you disagree. NJCRAC formally supported efforts for carving out areas in which to make common cause and for a "rounded relationship" that could generate "mutually beneficial" cooperation. Even the organization of Reform rabbis, from whose ranks some of the harshest critics of the Christian Right sprang, joined the search for a "common ground of faith and commitment." For the sake of Israel the agencies could not ignore the political strength of the Christian Right, and they were prepared to put aside differences on domestic issues. The chairman of the Conference of Presidents of Major American Jewish Organizations explained: "They [the fundamentalists] strongly support a lot of things I think are dreadful for the country, but I'm not going to turn away their support of Israel for that." Indeed, with issues that liberals, and Jews too, found troublesome — like Israel's bombing of an Iraqi nuclear reactor or Israel's rule over the territories — the right-wing evangelicals had no problem.[25]

Accordingly, with some mixed feelings, Jewish defense agencies, particularly the ADL and AJC, broadened their outreach to evangelical churches and leaders. The latter responded positively, and all sorts of activities on behalf of Israel — from public relations work to a pro-Israel film to tourism in Israel — abounded.[26] The pragmatic straddle, or the need to shift from fixed to ad hoc alliances

24   Editorial, *Christian Century*, 23 November 1977; NJCRAC, *Joint Program Plan*, 1986–87, 42: P. Culbertson to J. Banki, 1 June 1981, AJC files.
25   NJCRAC, *Joint Program Plan*, 1987–88, 46; Commission on Social Action of Reform Judaism, *The Challenge of the Religious Right* (New York, [1982]), intro. to sec. 6; A. James Reichley, *Religion in American Public Life* (Washington, D.C. 1985), 310; Simon, *Jerry Falwell and the Jews*, 84–85.
26   Eckstein, "Understanding Evangelicals," 14; Marvin R. Wilson, "An Evangelical Christian View of Israel," *A Time to Speak*, ed. A. James Rudin and Marvin R. Wilson (Grand Rapids, 1987), 173; Rausch, "New Fundamentalists," 7–8; files of the Interreligious Affairs Department, AJC.

according to the issue at hand, bred some discomfort. Not only were Jews unaccustomed to dealing with right-wing evangelicals, but they could hardly forget the underlying threat of the Christian Right to American pluralism. Nevertheless, those who chose pragmatic concerns above ideological purity had found the means for balancing their loyalties to both liberalism and Israel.

Hard put to preserve their traditional image as the natural friends of liberals and liberalism, American Jews were dealt an even weightier blow during the campaign of 1984. A few months before the national conventions, a new factor surfaced, this one in the form of Jesse Jackson's bid for the Democratic presidential nomination. Jackson's candidacy proved that while Jewish liberals were rooted in the same spot, American liberalism had moved, significantly distancing itself from Jewish interests.

The charismatic black minister, who arduously canvassed voters for support of his Rainbow Coalition, enraged Jews by a record of anti-Semitic remarks. Jews fumed in particular over Jackson's association with a black Muslim leader, Louis Farrakhan, a man who admired Hitler and had called Judaism a "gutter religion." More worrisome still was Jackson's anti-Israel posture, highlighted by his embrace of Yasir Arafat, his pro-Palestine statements, and his financial support from the Arab League and from Arab Americans. Some private meetings were arranged between Jews and Jackson in the early part of 1984, but they failed to change the minister's point of view. The problem loomed larger than Jackson alone; surveys disclosed that the black community, notably the more affluent, younger, and better educated, rallied overwhelmingly to his defense on the Jewish issue. The possibility of a black-Jewish polarization was, as one analyst said, "almost too scary to contemplate."

Concerned Jews who bitterly noted the reluctance of the Democrats to repudiate Jackson's stand for fear of alienating the black community urged the party to act. Some warned that a continuing alliance with Jackson could lead only to "disaster"; others asked that front runner Walter Mondale, who was trying to balance the Jewish and Jackson pressures, read Jackson out of the party or at least out of its inner councils. Henry Siegman, executive director of the American Jewish Congress, personally told Mondale that if he failed to repudiate Jackson, he, Mondale, did not deserve the presidency. Only if the Democrats openly rejected the "racism of Farrakhan and...Jackson," New York's Ed Koch insisted, could they hope to win in 1984. On the eve of the convention Mondale spoke up publicly and urged Jackson to renounce Farrakhan, and shortly thereafter the platform committee roundly defeated Jackson's proposal for Palestinian statehood. At the convention, however, thanks to Jackson's supporters, a resolution denouncing anti-Semitism failed to pass.[27]

Jackson's power within the party haunted Jewish voters. Should they adhere to their traditional liberal, Democratic loyalties if that party refused to repudiate Jackson? Was Jackson, the symbol of a new Democratic and liberal trend, a greater danger to Jewish interests than the Christianizers in the Republican party who at least defended Israel? Jews were generally unhappy with their options. To be brushed aside within their traditional political home was painful and demeaning. On the other hand, if they deserted the liberals for the unfamiliar conservative camp it was uncertain how comfortable their new hosts would make them feel. As Irving Kristol pointed out: "For the first time in living memory, Jews are finding themselves in the old condition of being politically homeless." The theme of homelessness was picked up by others, testifying to the alienation of Jews from elements in both parties.[28]

During the spring and summer the implications of Jackson's candidacy were carefully scrutinized by Jewish defense agencies. In May, Nathan Perlmutter used the annual meeting of the Conference on Jewish Social Studies, usually an academic forum, to warn of the new anti-Semitism typified by Jackson. The influence of the black leader also supplied grist for the neoconservative mills. In an article printed in *Commentary*, Kristol focused not on Jackson the individual but on Jackson as the symbol of a changed liberalism.

27   *American Jewish Year Book* 86 (1986): 65–68; AJC files: "Jesse Jackson," "Politics/Elections," in DGX; letter from David Gordis to *Commentary*, October 1984, 4–5; letter from Henry Siegman to *Commentary*, May 1985, 6, 8: *Middle East Policy Survey*, no. 108 (13 July 1984).

28   Irving Kristol, "The Political Dilemma of American Jews," *Commentary*, July 1984, 29; Milton Himmelfarb cited in *Los Angeles Times*, 2 October 1984.

Critical of liberal programs in general, he judged them to be particularly inimical to Jewish interests. Claiming that the New Christian Right baffled Jews precisely because it was neither anti-Semitic nor anti-Israel, he advised Jews to free themselves from the "liberal time warp" and to rethink their "habitual reflexes" about church–state separation and their misplaced commitment to secular humanism, and their blanket condemnation of the rightists' social agenda.[29]

While some observers expected a shift by large numbers of Jews to the Republicans, the latter delightedly prepared to capitalize on the Jackson factor. To show their own good faith, they played up to the Jews in the party's platform and convention. When, however, eight national Jewish organizations appealed jointly to the Republican platform committee to reject "the current divisive assault on the First Amendment's separation of church and state," their attempt to distance the party from the Christian Right failed. Republican strategists never considered dumping the rightists in deference to liberal concerns. Gambling on the recognition of Jewish interests by the platform and on Jewish disaffection with Jackson and his supporters, the GOP hoped to increase its share of Jewish voters (from the 40 percent that had supported Reagan in 1980) without alienating the evangelicals.[30]

Confronted by the partnership of the Republicans and the Christianizers on the one hand and the partnership of the Democrats with a temporarily muzzled Jackson on the other, American Jews chose the latter. The Jackson issue receded in importance, and the Christianization of America, highlighted by the influence and strength of the New Christian Right in the Republican campaign, became the primary concern. Whatever momentum had developed to shift Jews in large numbers away from the Democrats petered out after the Republican convention. In the end, Jewish allegiance to the more liberal party remained virtually unchanged, as 35 per cent of Jewish voters, fewer than in 1980, supported Reagan. Perhaps, as one observer remarked, some liberal Jews were inclined "to overlook

29 Perlmutter's remarks were not printed, but I was a participant at the conference. Kristol, "Political Dilemma of American Jews," 23–29, Kristol's article drew numerous and mixed responses, see *Commentary*, October 1984, 2–17.
30 Reports by Hyman Bookbinder and Milton Ellerin in AJC file: "Politics/Elections," DGX.

anti-Semitism on the Left even when it flourishes, and to detect it on the Right even in those cases where it does not exist."[31]

Jewish neoconservatives as well as spokesmen for the Christian Right deplored the inappropriate Jewish response. Liberal stand-patters, however, were delighted. Henry Siegman summed up the results as follows: "Jews understood... that of the two dangers, Falwell represents the greater, for all of his professions of love of Jews and Israel. However gutless the behavior of the Democratic leadership... no one seriously believed that they shared Jackson's anti-Semitism.[32] Had Jackson's position on Israel captured the Democratic party, the story might have ended differently.

Two major conclusions may be drawn from this account. First, events of the 1980s showed that American liberalism had shifted. Now liberals in the mainline churches and among Jackson's supporters, undeterred by a history of alliances with Jews, no longer felt impelled to defend Israel's basic security. The pro-Arab tilt grew stronger, especially with the *Intifada*,[33] proving that the changed liberal position was more than temporary. Second, although the ultimate test of Jewish loyalties — to a changed liberalism or to Israel — did not materialize, the election of 1984 gave credence to the distinct possibility of such an eventuality. How American Jews would then react is, of course, open to debate. Whatever the outcome, the need to choose would doubtless be accompanied by a dramatic and perhaps devastating split within Jewish ranks. Marking the end of the congenial Jewish-liberal nexus, such events would doubtless result in more extreme (both positive and negative) assessments of the Jewish state by American Jews.

31   AJC file: "Politics/Elections," DGX; Sidney Blumenthal, "The Righteous Empire," *New Republic*, 22 October 1984; Werner Dannhauser, "Election '84," *Congress Monthly*, December 1984, 5.
32   Lucy S. Dawidowicz, "Politics, the Jews and the '84 Election," *Commentary*, February 1985, 25-30; Siegman's letter to *Commentary*, May 1985, 9.
33   Michael Lewis, "The American Mainline Churches and Israel," *Midstream*, April 1988, 5-8; *Interreligious Currents*, Winter/Spring 1988, 1-8; See also references to Christian opposition to Israel in the annual *Joint Program Plan* of NJCRAC for the 1980s.

Are We One?
Menachem Begin and the Long Shadow of 1977

Jerold S. Auerbach

American Jews, according to the conventional wisdom, have always been impassioned and faithful in their attachment to Israel. "We are One!" the popular fund-raising slogan, has also served as a description of the historical relationship of American Jews to the Jewish state. Melvin Urofsky's standard history of American Zionism, published in 1978, cited the indissoluble bonds of Jewish unity, growing stronger over time, between the American Diaspora and Israel.[1]

But historical reality is more complicated than the myth of unity suggests. Indeed, by the time Urofsky's volume was published, its account of Jewish unity had already been superseded by the dramatic consequences of Israel's political revolution of 1977. Menachem Begin's election as prime minister shattered the thirty-year-old Labor party monopoly on governance. It simultaneously challenged the unity that Urofsky, like so many others, had assumed to be a permanent attribute of the relationship between Israel and the American Diaspora. For that "unity" rested on unstated assumptions about loyalty and liberalism no less than on Jewish identity. Its limits would be severely tested during the Begin era.

The overriding concern of the American Jewish community always had been to demonstrate its undivided allegiance to the United States. From Isaac Mayer Wise before the Civil War to Stephen S. Wise during World War II, the perennial challenge to Jewish communal leadership was to enunciate acceptable terms of Jewish accommodation to American civic and patriotic norms. Long before

---

1   Melvin I. Urofsky, *We Are One! American Jewry and Israel* (New York, 1978), 443.

1948, the very idea of a Jewish state had activated loyalty anxieties that were deeply embedded in American Jewish life.

The earliest official statement of American Zionist policy, nearly a century ago, carefully noted that Zionism was reserved for Jews in places where it was "impossible for them to live." (The United States, by clear implication, was excluded.) American Zionists also suggested, in an evident display of their American self-interest, that a Jewish refuge in Palestine might insulate American Jews from the deleterious political and social consequences of a continued influx of Russian Jews to New York.[2]

Louis D. Brandeis, the revered American Zionist leader during the World War I era, was no less uneasy about Zionism. Brandeis carefully steered the American Zionist movement toward the junction of Jeffersonian liberalism and Wilsonian Progressivism. Herzl's arguments for a Jewish state had no appeal, for Brandeis wanted no such outcome. "I neither advise nor desire an independent state," he wrote on the very day the Balfour Declaration was issued. Jewish statehood, he warned, was "a most serious menace." Indeed, Lord Balfour's declaration generated intense anxiety within the American Jewish elite. Henry Morgenthau, the American ambassador to Turkey, warned that Zionism "would cost the Jews of America most of what they had gained in liberty, equality, and fraternity."[3] Although Brandeis and his Zionist followers vigorously rejected any incompatibility between Zionism and Americanism, the persistence of their denials suggests the irrepressibility of their loyalty concerns.

Affirmations of the undivided allegiance of American Jews to the United States, endlessly reiterated during the prestate years, revealed a deep uneasiness lest Jews seem insufficiently American. The birth of Israel, to be sure, was a moment that many American Jews joyously celebrated. Yet Israel immediately, and immeasurably, complicated American Jewish life. A Jewish state, posing the implicit alternative between American home and Jewish homeland, could not help but

---

2   Richard Gottheil, "The Aims of Zionism," in *The Zionist Idea*, ed. Arthur Hertzberg (New York, 1975), 499–500.

3   Brandeis to Jacob Schiff, 2 November 1917, quoted in Yonathan Shapiro, *Leadership of the American Zionist Organization, 1897–1930* (Urbana, 1971), 115; Barbara W. Tuchman, "The Assimilationist Dilemma: Ambassador Morgenthau's Story," *Commentary*, May 1977, 61.

activate some of the deepest anxieties of American Jews about national loyalty. They were, after all, the children and grandchildren of immigrants; and the struggle for American acceptance was central to their experience as Jews in the United States.

There have been three pivotal episodes in the unfolding historical relationship between American Jews and Israel: (1) Jewish national independence, when a brief flurry of Zionist enthusiasm was followed by prolonged American Jewish detachment from Israel (1948–1967); (2) the Six-Day War, which elicited an impassioned identification with the Jewish state that lasted for a decade (1976–1977); and (3) Menachem Begin's election as prime minister in 1977, which provoked a rising crescendo of American Jewish criticism of Israel that did not subside until the Labor party returned to power in the summer of 1992. These sharp swings, from avid identification to indifference to sharp criticism and back, suggest that confident assertions of Israel–Diaspora unity may distort a far more complex, and therefore more intriguing, relationship.

Nor is this surprising. The birth of Israel, after all, recast American Jewry as a Diaspora community. Not only did 1948 mark the renewal of Jewish statehood; it simultaneously re-created a symbiotic relationship between homeland and Diaspora that had been absent for nearly two millennia. After 1948, for the first time, American Jews confronted a Jewish state claiming the authority, at least implicitly, to define Jewish authenticity in political and religious terms. Its new definitions might challenge, contradict, or even undermine, American Jewish norms.

American Jews had no recent precedents, or clear guidelines, to follow. Had they been inclined to look to Jewish antiquity, they might have found some instructive admonitions from the prophet Jeremiah regarding the etiquette of Diaspora behavior. After the first Babylonian exile, in 597 B.C.E., Jeremiah sent a letter from Jerusalem to the Babylonian captives. It conveyed the prophet's understanding of God's prescription for life outside the Land of Israel:

> Build houses, and dwell in them; and plant gardens, and eat the fruit of them. Take wives, and beget sons and daughters...that you may be increased there, and not diminished. And seek the

peace of the city into which I have caused you to be carried away captives, and pray to the Lord for it; for in its peace shall you have peace. (Jer. 29:5-7)

Jeremiah's prescription for Jewish life in exile still resonates in the modern Diaspora. By transforming loyal citizenship into a religious duty, Jeremiah deflected the dangerous possibility of divided loyalty. His legacy, according to David Biale, was "the prophetic model of accommodation," ultimately transformed by the rabbis into "a viable political theory" of Jewish survival outside the Land of Israel.[4]

After 1948, the pattern so novel to Jeremiah's time — Diaspora and homeland — once again characterized our own. American Jews internalized his model: they were already accustomed to balancing the tasks of normal life (build, dwell, eat, marry, parent) with their own distinctive mixture of American civic and Jewish religious responsibility. They knew that Jews could live in the American Diaspora and live as Jews.

Within weeks of statehood, however, even the most devoted American Zionists "envisioned" Israel by recasting the new Jewish state in familiar American terms. Israel, predicted the leading American Zionist journal, would promote "the American ideals of freedom, peace, and prosperity" — a curious mission, indeed, for a Jewish state. Zionism, in a reflexive application of the old Brandeis formula, was praised as "good Americanism." It is not surprising that Prime Minister Ben-Gurion would observe, six months later, that American Jews still had not adjusted to "the revolutionary fact" of the existence of a Jewish state.[5]

Ben-Gurion's bold appeal, the following year, for the *aliyah* of American Jewish children confirmed his perception. Some Jewish community leaders were aghast that a Jewish Pied Piper in Tel Aviv

4   David Biale, *Power and Powerlessness in Jewish History* (New York, 1986), 33. See also Ralph W. Klein, *Israel in Exile* (Philadelphia, 1979), 51–52; *Jeremiah*, with commentary by H. Freedman (London, 1977), 189 n. 4. From Israel, however, Jeremiah looks quite different. For a critique of Jeremiah's "prophecy of subjection," see Yehezkel Kauffmann, *The Religion of Israel* (New York, 1972), 410–112, 422.

5   Naomi W. Cohen, *American Jews and the Zionist Idea* (New York, 1975), 115; Ben-Gurion to Abe Feinberg, 30 December 1948; Ben-Gurion to Jacob Blaustein, 14 November 1951, Ben-Gurion MSS, Sede Boqer.

might lure their children away to the siren song of "Hatikvah." Any insinuation that American Jews belonged in Israel was anathema. To American Jews, the prime minister was sharply reminded, "America is home." The controversy simmered until Ben-Gurion finally conceded the right of American Jews to express "their own needs and aspirations," the better to assure their "security and stability" in the United States. These concessions, he was instructed, were necessary to free American Jews "in the minds of other Americans from the serious charge of dual nationality."[6]

During the "golden decade" following the end of World War II, American Jews seemed to have harmoniously reconciled their feelings for Israel with American norms. Preoccupied with economic opportunity and social integration, their fears of divided allegiance receded. American Jews, Arthur Goren has suggested, could meet "their dual responsibilities as Americans and Jews admirably." But this comfortable reconciliation may have been possible only because Israel was so remote from American Jewish concerns. For most American Jews, the new Jewish state flickered only dimly. Nathan Glazer, in his classic survey of American Judaism, observed in 1957: "The two greatest events in modern Jewish history, the murder of six million Jews by Hitler and the creation of the Jewish state in Palestine, have had remarkably slight effects on the inner life of American Jewry."[7]

In the spring of 1967, the comfortable insulation of American Jewry from the Jewish state was abruptly shattered. After weeks of mounting anxiety, the stunning Israeli victory during the Six-Day War was a transforming moment. Anguish gave way to wonder, wrote Rabbi Abraham J. Heschel; "*terror* and *dread*" became "exultation." For a decade after that momentous week in June, American Jews basked in the glow of their new identification. Israel, for so long a source of American Jewish uneasiness or indifference,

6 *American Jewish Year Book*, 53 (1952), 564ff.
7 Arthur A. Goren, "A 'Golden Decade' for American Jews: 1945–1955," in Peter Y. Medding, ed. *A New Jewry?, Studies in Contemporary Jewry*, vol. 8 (New York, 1992), 8, 10; Nathan Glazer, *American Judaism* (Chicago, 1957), 114.

suddenly became a tangible symbol of Jewish pride and power, even the new religion of American Jews.[8]

Yet what is remarkable in retrospect is the brevity of the attachment. For a victorious and powerful Israel was, if anything, likely to intensify the loyalty anxieties of American Jews. Even after the war, Charles S. Liebman could still identify "the ambivalent American Jew," torn between the desire for "acceptance into American society" and "Jewish group survival." American Jews might try to reduce their ambivalence by insisting that American and Israeli values were entirely compatible; but, Liebman suggested presciently, they were likely to be disappointed.[9]

The latent quandary of American Jews was rooted in their resolute identification of Judaism with liberalism. The origins of this attachment, which remains a distinctive attribute of their Jewish identity, can be traced back to the Brandeis era. The accession of a Progressive reformer to Zionist leadership, and then to the Supreme Court, marked an important turning point in American Jewish history. Before Brandeis, American Jews were as likely to be identified with political conservatism as with liberalism, with no sense that their preference represented a betrayal of Judaism. Well into the twentieth century, the pillars of the American Jewish community, both lay and religious, were political conservatives. To lawyer Louis Marshall, rabbi Solomon Schechter, and philanthropist Jacob Schiff — the towering Jewish figures who were Brandeis's contemporaries — Judaism meant respect for the authority of Jewish law and tradition, not an identification with liberal reform.[10]

The American Jewish embrace of liberalism, which began with Brandeis, peaked during the 1930s. Franklin D. Roosevelt's New Deal pulled second-generation Jews into the American political mainstream, forging an attachment to liberalism as the fundamental component of their Americanism -- and their Judaism. Jews repaid their debt to Roosevelt with the unswerving identification with

8   A. J. Heschel, *Israel: An Echo of Eternity* (New York, 1969), 195–199.
9   Charles S. Liebman, *The Ambivalent American Jew* (Philadelphia, 1973), vii, 24–25, 27.
10   Jerold S. Auerbach, *Rabbis and Lawyers: The Journey from Torah to Constitution* (Indianapolis, 1990), 99, 103.

liberalism for which they have been so conspicuous in American politics ever since.

Liberalism enabled American Jews to overcome their minority vulnerability by submerging parochial Jewish interests in the greater American good. As liberals, Jews defended civil rights, social welfare legislation, church–state separation, and the rights of oppressed peoples everywhere. Doing good for others, they also protected themselves. Long after their socioeconomic status dictated otherwise, they remained tenaciously attached to liberal causes, believing that they were fulfilling the mandate of the ancient Hebrew prophets by voting for the Democratic party.

By 1948, for American Jews, liberalism and Judaism were ideologically indistinguishable. That may explain why Israel won more favor from Jews as an embattled democratic nation than as a distinctively Jewish state. Jews might idolize Ben-Gurion as the founding father of Jewish statehood, embrace Golda Meir as their Jewish grandmother, and admire Moshe Dayan as a modern Maccabee. But only as long as Israel remained faithful to liberal norms could American Jews safely identify with it.

All that changed in 1977. For the first time, Israel had a Revisionist prime minister who symbolized nationalism and religious orthodoxy, an ancient Jewish synthesis that contradicted fundamental modern liberal tenets. Even before Begin took office, American media images depicted him as a symbol of reckless terrorism, unyielding fanaticism, and dangerous demagoguery. The *New York Times* described him as "a former guerrilla" with "a fiery past." That august newspaper, whose venerable anti-Zionism had guided editorial policy for decades, drew solace only from the prospect that the new government "may not last long." *Time*, even less restrained, labeled Begin in successive issues as a "terrorist," "superhawk," and "strong-willed little Polish immigrant," whose name, it crassly noted, "rhymes with Fagin."[11]

Although American Jewish leaders quickly pledged their "support and commitment," affirming "the indissoluble ties" that bound American Jews to Israel, their uneasiness with Begin was evident. The

11 *New York Times,* 19 May 1977, 14, 22; *Time,* 23 May 1977, 45; 30 May 1977, 22–23, 27.

most they could bring themselves to say about the Israeli political transformation was that it had occurred "freely and peacefully," demonstrating "the democratic process at work."[12]

Begin, to be sure, sharply contradicted romantic American images of Israel as the land of muscular kibbutzniks, descended from Amos and Isaiah, who wore *kova tembels* by day, danced the Horah all night, and piloted their planes and tanks to astonishing military victories early the next morning. Instead, Begin resembled a missing Old World uncle who had suddenly reemerged from the shadows of Diaspora history. His ill-fitting suits, Yiddish-accented English, and frequent Holocaust analogies touched deep, often discomforting, feelings among American Jews. His lost world of Eastern European Jewry was, after all, the Old Country that American Jewry had abandoned.

As Begin grafted explicitly Jewish symbols onto Israeli public life, the state of the Jews — at least iconographically — actually began to resemble a Jewish state. He was the first prime minister of Israel, one of his biographers observed, to identify himself "as a Jew rather than as an Israeli." His postelection visit to the *Kotel* graphically symbolized his claim to be not only prime minister of Israel but leader of the Jewish people. One of his first acts as prime minister was to visit a new Jewish settlement outside Shechem (Nablus). There he pledged "many Elon Morehs," claiming Judea and Samaria as part of Israel and insisting that the land be known by its biblical names.[13] Like a vision from Ezekiel, Begin pointedly reminded Jews of their historical attachment to their ancient biblical homeland.

In the process, Begin antagonized the president of the United States. Jimmy Carter found statements by the new prime minister "frightening." Even before the Israeli election, Carter's political sympathies were evident. Urging Israeli withdrawal from nearly all the territory acquired in 1967, he had called for a Palestinian homeland and asked for reparations for displaced Arab refugees

---

12   *Jewish Telegraphic Agency (JTA) Daily News Bulletin (DNB)*, 19 May 1977, 3.
13   Eric Silver, *Begin: The Haunted Prophet* (New York, 1984), 164; Ned Temko, *To Win or Die* (New York, 1987), 198. In fact, Ben-Gurion also identified himself as a Jew first and then as an Israeli. Silver's error on this point is revealing of the popular perception of Ben-Gurion as the quintessential Israeli, while Begin was seen as quintessentially Jewish.

— which even Arab leaders had not yet demanded. Begin, aware of the disquiet that his image generated in Washington, publicly discounted the president's hostility. "Carter knows the Bible," the prime minister declared, "and that will make it easier for him to know whose land this is."[14]

As Begin prepared for his first Washington visit, American Jewish leaders were palpably uneasy. Their effectiveness, after all, depended on an absence of friction between Israel and the United States. They were accustomed to Israeli prime ministers who did not make excessive demands on them as Jews; Ben-Gurion, Golda Meir, and Yitzhak Rabin usually permitted American Jews to identify with the Jewish state, or ignore it, without undue discomfort. With Begin, however, that flexibility diminished. He was, wrote an Israeli journalist, "a different kind of Prime Minister": "a more 'Jewish' leader."[15] The more directly that Begin, speaking as a Jew, implicated American Jewry in the Jewish state, the more fragile became those "indissoluble links" between American Jews and Israel.

The first Begin–Carter visit, in the summer of 1977, was not quite the disaster that many had anticipated. Within weeks, however, the surface geniality between the two leaders dissolved. An Israeli announcement that three West Bank military bases would be converted into settlements provoked sharp criticism from the State Department. The Israeli government, in turn, challenged any assertion that Jewish settlement "in the Land of Israel" could be regarded as illegal. Published reports that the Carter administration was "increasingly alarmed" over Begin's "intransigent views" were followed by predictable White House denials that the United States and Israel were following a "collision course."[16] But even the diplomatic success they shared with President Sadat of Egypt, two years later at Camp David, could not ease their mutual suspicion.

American pressure on the Begin government eased during Ronald

---

14 Time, 27 June 1977, 9; Sasson Sofer, *Begin: An Anatomy of Leadership* (Oxford, 1988), 150–151; Temko, *To Win or Die,* 201.

15 *JTA DNB,* 6 June 1977, 2; Uzi Benziman, "Behind the Headlines," 3 June 1977, 4.

16 Temko, *To Win or Die,* 201–202, 208; *JTA DNB,* 26 July 1977, 3, 4; 22 August 1977, 1; Sasson, *Begin,* 152; *Time,* 11 July 1977, 34.

Reagan's first term. Reagan lacked Carter's determination to resolve the Palestinian problem contrary to Israel's interests; and he welcomed Israel's role as a counterweight to Soviet influence in the Middle East. Consequently, Begin enjoyed greater diplomatic freedom to implement his most controversial policy decisions — to expand settlements, bomb the Iraqi nuclear reactor, annex the Golan, and wage war in Lebanon.

Even Reagan's forbearance, however, had its limits. After the nuclear reactor bombing at Osiraq, the American government suspended its delivery of F-16 fighters. Administration criticism of the Golan annexation provoked Begin's most intemperate outburst. He complained indignantly to American ambassador Samuel Lewis: "Are we a vassal state? A banana republic?" Nobody, Begin predicted, "will frighten the great and free [Jewish] community in the United States. They will stand by us, this is the land of their forefathers. They have the right and duty to support [Israel]."[17]

Begin's assertion of transcendent Jewish unity, irrespective of national identity and citizenship, upset the fragile consensus that enabled American Jews to identify with the Jewish state. As long as Israel was a staunch American ally, a democratic obstacle to Soviet influence in the Middle East, American Jews could comfortably assert a mutuality of interest between the two countries. But once Begin invited them to respond to Israel as Jews, not as Americans or liberals, they backed off. "Anxious American Jews," like children whose parents had begun to quarrel incessantly, were stretched between their attachments to liberal universalism and Jewish particularism.[18]

Until Begin's election, criticism of Israel had largely been confined to the political margins, where New Left anti-Zionism intersected with Black Power anti-Semitism. With Begin in power, the liberal Jewish critique sharpened. Journalist I. F. Stone, who had traveled to Palestine in 1946 with illegal Jewish immigrants, complained in 1978 that the "moral gravity" of Zionism had shifted toward Begin's

17   Silver, *Begin*, 245–246.
18   Edward S. Shapiro, A *Time for Healing: American Jewry since World War II* (Baltimore, 1992), 201–202, 218; Ruth R. Wisse, "The Anxious American Jew," *Commentary*, September 1978, 49–50.

"cold-blooded nationalistic calculation." How, Stone asked, "can we talk of human rights and ignore them for the Palestinian Arabs?" To retain both his liberal and Zionist credentials, Stone pledged allegiance to "the other Zionism," a Zionism of "the deepest ethical motives," which he located in "that spirit of fraternity and justice and conciliation that the Prophets preached."[19]

Rabbi Arthur Hertzberg, responding to Begin's tongue-lashing of Ambassador Lewis, wondered how American Jews could support "a different country from the one its founders had intended," one no longer based on "a moral passion for a better Jewish people." Did Begin, Hertzberg wondered, "define the true meaning of Zionism and will American Jews follow him?" The basic commitment of American Jewry, the American rabbi insisted, was to "the liberal dreams" of Israel's founders, to "a benign society that could be 'a light unto the nations'." Israel must remain "a moral cause, consonant with America's highest ideals."[20] Liberalism, for Hertzberg, must remain the true priority of American Jews.

With Yitzhak Shamir's accession to power, the dilemma of Israel intensified for American Jews. Especially after the eruption of the Intifada, when Israel was routinely pilloried in the American media, liberal Jews joined (and often led) the chorus of denunciation. In a remarkable confession in the *New York Times*, Reform spokesman Albert Vorspan offered an explanation. American Jews, he wrote, were "traumatized" by events in Israel. Suffering "shame and stress," they wanted "to crawl into a hole," where they might escape guilt by association with "the political and moral bankruptcy" of Israeli policy. American Jews, Vorspan insisted, were "implicated" by the actions of the Jewish state. "It's about us."[21]

Implicated by Israel, liberal Jews turned bitterly against it to preserve their liberal credentials. A refrain of liberal disaffection, shading into a myth of Israeli betrayal, emerged. On the Op-Ed page of the *New York Times*, Anthony Lewis relentlessly hectored Israel

19   I. F. Stone, "Reflections and Meditations Thirty Years After," in idem, *Underground to Palestine* (New York, 1978), 239–240, 258–260.

20   Arthur Hertzberg, "Begin and the Jews," *New York Review of Books,* 18 February 1982, 11–12.

21   Albert Vorspan, "Soul-Searching," *New York Times Magazine,* 8 May 1988, 40ff.

for its infidelity to the liberal precepts of Brandeis and Isaiah. The magazine *Tikkun* was founded to save the world from neoconservative defenders of Israel like Norman Podhoretz. A stream of books offered variations on the theme of fallen Israel, compromised by its abandonment of liberal values. The moral decline and fall of the Jewish state became the irresistible allegation of disaffected Jewish liberals.

The theme of this moral melodrama was labeled, by one author, "the tragedy of Zionism." In his story of Zionist decline from liberal democratic promise to Revisionist holy land, Bernard Avishai described the ascendance of an "utterly nationalist, self-absorbed" Zionism, menacingly identified with "power, Bible, defiance, [and] settlement."[22] Journalist Milton Viorst recounted how Israel, after 1967, had wandered into "a moral desert." Ruled by a coalition of Sephardi Jews accustomed to "mob politics," and Orthodox Jews who gave theological legitimacy to Begin's "'muscular Zionism',", a once "humane" Israel had descended into the moral abyss of militarism and imperialism.[23]

The popularity of this polemical genre reached its apogee with Thomas Friedman's *From Beirut to Jerusalem*. Friedman recounted his experiences as a *New York Times* reporter in the Middle East during the turbulent era that began with the Lebanese civil war and ended with the Intifada. The subtext, however, was Friedman's personal odyssey. Growing up in a middle-class Minnesota family as a "three-day-a-year Jew," his Jewish identity had been awakened during the Six-Day War. Thereafter, he claimed, he wore Israel as "a badge of pride" — until Sabra and Shatila, when he was overwhelmed by Jewish shame and outrage. "The Israel I met on the outskirts of Beirut," he wrote, "was not the heroic Israel I had been taught to identify with." In his *Times* articles, he confessed, he "buried...every illusion I ever held about the Jewish state."

Propelling his book up the best-seller list, Friedman offered variations on the theme of Israeli betrayal and his own Jewish disillusionment. Friedman described himself as "a Jew who was raised on... all the myths about Israel," only to witness "an Israel

22   Bernard Avishai, *The Tragedy of Zionism* (New York, 1985), 9, 248.
23   Milton Viorst, *Sands of Sorrow* (New York, 1987), 2, 68, 145–146, 152–153.

he had deeply believed in... recede from gilded, heroic mythology to the shadows of bleak reality." Projecting the self-image of a morally anguished innocent, who suffered a "personal crisis" as the once "heroic" Israel stripped his "illusion" away, Friedman could only conclude that "something had gone terribly wrong" in the Jewish state.[24]

What had "gone wrong," of course, was the Begin political revolution. As an unholy alliance of Revisionists and Sephardim, joined by rabbis and settlers, swept into power, Israel as a light unto the nations became a Jewish state shadowed by political darkness and religious fanaticism. One might have thought that the democratization of Israeli politics, to say nothing of Israel's first peace treaty with a neighboring Arab state, would have elicited a measure of liberal approval for the government whose conspicuous achievements these were. But even as the Sephardi underclass finally entered the Israeli political mainstream, gaining a measure of the recognition that successive Labor governments had denied it, and as land was traded for peace with Egypt, liberal criticism intensified. Israel became a conditional Jewish commitment, endlessly castigated for its violations of liberal norms.

Liberalism, for American Jews, had become a double-edged ideology. Before 1977, it had cut the knot of dual loyalty, persuading them that they were better Jews — and better Americans — the more liberal they became. At the time, liberalism had facilitated their identification with Israel. But once the Israeli political balance shifted to the right, American Jews experienced "the pains of dual loyalty — not, as in the classical model, between Israel and America, but between Israel and liberalism."[25] Their commitment to liberalism, for so long a source of identification with Israel, swiftly provoked their sharpened criticism of the Jewish state.

---

24 For a fuller account, from which these quotations are drawn, see Jerold S. Auerbach, "Thomas Friedman's Israel: The Myth of Unrequited Love," in *With Friends Like These,* ed., Edward Alexander (New York, 1993), 60–62, 65. In fact, as early as his undergraduate years, Friedman had identified with pro-Palestinian "peace" groups. For a more recent example of this journalistic genre, see Robert I. Friedman, *Zealots for Zion* (New York, 1992).

25 Norman Podhoretz, "Israel: A Lamentation from the Future," in *With Friends Like These,* ed. Alexander, 210–212, 214.

This is not to dispute compelling survey data that document the sustained attachment of American Jewry, and its organizational leaders, to Israel thoughout the 1980s. Support for Israel, Charles Liebman and Steven Cohen suggested in 1990, still "dominates public life, is part and parcel of the American Jewish consensus on what it means to be a Jew, and is voiced by a large majority of American Jews." (This after more than a decade of Likud rule.) Yet "the pro-Israelism of American Jews," they also noted, "is limited in a number of ways."[26]

The affection of American Jews for Israel was sharply constrained by their liberal attachments. While identification with Israel waxed and waned, the commitment to liberal values as the functional definition of a "good Jew" remained constant. Back in the 1950s, it had meant support for humanitarian causes; thirty years later, "equality" and minority rights still remained the defining attributes of good Judaism. Support for Israel, like religious observance, trailed far behind the commitment of American Jews to liberal ideology as the measure of their Jewish identity.

The affinity of American Jews for liberalism is not merely a political preference. It is the fundamental component of their Jewish self-definition — and, simultaneously, their American acculturation. American Jews may, in significant numbers, feel attached to Israel. But their commitment to liberalism, which defines them as Americans no less than as Jews, is even more powerful. It is considerably less responsive to the pressure of current events than their more conditional attachment to the Jewish state.[27]

Throughout the Begin-Shamir era, Israeli politics consistently contradicted the tenets of American liberalism. The Israeli fusion of religion and nationality, American Jews complained, violated the separation of religion and state (a liberal, not a Jewish, principle).

---

26   Charles S. Liebman and Steven M. Cohen, *Two Worlds of Judaism* (New Haven, 1990), 84–85; Chaim I. Waxman, "All in the Family: American Jewish Attachments to Israel," in *A New Jewry?* ed. P. Medding, 135–137. S. Cohen's article in this volume, "Did American Jews Really Grow More Distant from Israel, 1983–1993 — A Reconsideration," suggests that they did not. He relies, however, on polling data for American Jews "in the aggregate." I am concerned with public voices, not private opinions.

27   Liebman and Cohen, *Two Worlds of Judaism*, 96–97, 99.

Orthodox efforts to define "Who is a Jew?" — an insulting rebuke to an American Jewish community increasingly plagued by rampant intermarriage — were infuriating. American Jews who remained steadfast in their support for Israel even had their patriotic loyalty challenged, during the loan-guarantee embroglio of 1991, by President Bush.

Harmony between liberalism and Judaism, and between American Jews and Israel, was not restored until the Israeli election of 1992. The Rabin victory resolved the nagging dilemma of American Jewish liberals. Once again they could support Israel as good Jews, committed liberals, and loyal Americans. Allegations of disloyalty subsided. No longer were there complaints about Israel's "Amen" corner in Congress. Instead, there were audible sighs of relief from American Jewish liberals. "Now we can be friends of the government," declared Peter Edelman of Americans for Peace Now. He meant the Israeli government. But his eagerness to suppress the dual-loyalty nightmare, a conflict between American Jews and their own government, was evident.[28]

While liberalism is not nearly as salient in Israeli conceptions of Judaism as it is for American Jews, the identical tension between Judaism and liberalism tormented the Israeli left during the Begin era. That tension, historically rooted in Jewish emancipation and in the process of Western assimilation that it encouraged, erupted after Likud came to power. A decade ago, Amos Oz, with characteristic eloquence, denounced the challenge of "fanatical tribalism" to "the union between Jewish tradition and Western humanism." That rendezvous, he insisted, was "formative" and "irrevocable." Nobody, Oz warned, "will force us to choose...between our Judaism and humanism," for they are "one and the same." More recently, the young writer David Grossman despaired that an "enlightened" Israel had trained itself "to live as a conqueror." He registered a plea for the liberal virtues of "humanity and morality," which encouraged his startling literary transformation of Palestinians into Jews.[29] Oz and

---

28 *Jerusalem Post*, 5 July 1992. See the comments by Henry Siegman, *Jerusalem Post*, July 1992, for additional expressions of relief over issues of patriotism and loyalty in the wake of Rabin's victory.

29 Amos Oz, *In The Land of Israel* (New York, 1983), 138–139; David Grossman, *The Yellow Wind* (New York, 1989), Introduction, 212.

Grossman, needless to say, have reached an appreciative audience of American Jewish liberals.

The Israeli literary critique was accompanied by a New Left historiography of Israel. It narrated how the very founding of the Jewish state was sullied by "original sin": the denial to Palestinian Arabs of their country and national identity. Consistent with this moral homily of Israeli political declension, "the decline of Israeli democracy" during the 1980s has been attributed to the growth of a radical right.[30] From its founding to the present, according to the new Israeli scholarship, Israel has betrayed its democratic promise.

In their chastisement of Israel, Israeli and American writers and scholars spoke the common language of liberalism. American magazines and newspapers opened their pages to criticism of Israel during the Begin years — and in the *New Yorker*, the *New York Review of Books*, and the *New York Times*, Oz, Grossman, Meron Benvenisti, Avishai Margalit, and Amos Elon, among others, were delighted to provide it. So, too, were their American counterparts: liberal rabbis, professors, and journalists, far too numerous to mention, who incessantly wondered whether Israel had lost its soul.[31] With liberalism as their shared ideological heritage, it became all but impossible to distinguish their substantive ideological positions by their national identities.

It is difficult to exaggerate Menachem Begin's role as symbolic catalyst for liberal Jewish disaffection with the Jewish state. He was, after all, a disciple of Jabotinsky with a vision of Israel within the biblical boundaries of Eretz Israel, a Jew who wore a *kipa* and prayed at the *Kotel*. American Jews always preferred Israeli statesmen

---

30 Shabtai Teveth, "Charging Israel with Original Sin," *Commentary*, September 1989, 24–25; Ehud Sprinzak, *The Ascendance of Israel's Radical Right* (New York, 1991), 295. "Radical right," a concept borrowed from American social science literature of thirty years ago, conveniently enabled Sprinzak to link the Likud politics of Begin to Rabbi Meir Kahane's Kach movement.

31 For a critical view, see Ruth R. Wisse, "Israel and the Intellectuals: A Failure of Nerve?" *Commentary*, May 1988, 20–22; and Edward Alexander, "Israel at 40: Wherefore Rejoice?" *Congress Monthly*, March/April 1988, 12–14. There are, of course, conspicuous national differences: American Jews, lacking their own political culture, have not produced a Shulamit Aloni or a Yossi Sarid; Israelis, lacking certain Diaspora neuroses, have been spared a Woody Allen.

who spoke with a British accent, or who capitulated graciously to American definitions of Israel's best interests. Certainly they were uncomfortable when Begin identified himself to President Carter as a proud Jew who would bend his knee only to God. Begin activated some of their deepest concerns about their loyalty as Americans, their identity as Jews, and their credentials as liberals.

Begin era politics, between 1977–1992, offered American Jews disturbing glimpses of an Israeli Judaism that contradicted their own understanding of their Jewish identity. Instead of the Hebrew prophets, whose jeremiads for justice made them the patron saints of Jewish liberals in the modern era, they heard disconcerting calls for the Land of Israel for the people of Israel according to the Torah of Israel. The fundamental premises of Diaspora liberalism were challenged. Liberal ideology, which had once encouraged American Jews to identify with Israel, now undermined their attachment to the Jewish state. Once Israel turned right, Jewish liberals turned away.

For American Jews, the momentous Israeli political transformation of 1977 sharply challenged their conventional understanding of Israel, Zionism, Judaism, and ultimately themselves. Once Orthodox nationalism competed actively with secular liberalism as a legitimate expression of Zionism, the American Diaspora was forced to redefine its relation to the Jewish state. The Begin era remains a prism for viewing the inherently unstable relations between Israel and the Diaspora. It invites us to replace the confident assertion, "We Are One!" with the far more troubling question with which any analysis of Israel–Diaspora relations should begin: "Are We One?"

Did American Jews Really Grow More Distant from Israel, 1983–1993? — A Reconsideration

Steven M. Cohen

Since the early 1980s, the idea has taken hold that American Jews are becoming increasingly remote from Israel. Journalists, social scientists, Jewish communal leaders, and Israeli officials, among others, have surmised that American Jews have grown less enamored of Israelis, less interested in Israel, and less active in supporting Israel by way of travel, study, political activism, and philanthropic contributions.[1]

Admittedly, this proposition — that many elite figures perceive a decline in American Jewish involvement with Israel — rests on only scant and haphazard evidence. It comes mainly in the form of unrecorded informal remarks or occasional articles in a sometimes unfriendly press that, even when taken together, constitute less than convincing proof.

But consider for the moment the counter-proposition. Imagine a public figure claiming that American Jewish involvement with Israel has actually increased and deepened in the last decade. The imagery is ludicrous on its face. The only circumstances under which such a view could be advanced would be those in which both speaker and listeners understood that this claim is not meant to be taken with utter seriousness. An Israel Bonds dinner speaker might tell the

---

1   Steven M. Cohen, "Israel in the Jewish Identity of American Jews: A Study in Dualities and Contrasts," in *Jewish Identity in America*, ed. David M. Gordis and Yoav Ben-Horin (Los Angeles: University of Judaism, 1991); idem, "Are American and Israeli Jews Drifting Apart?" in *Imagining the Jewish Future*, ed. David Teutsch (Albany, N. Y.: State University of New York Press, 1992); and idem, "Are Reform Jews Abandoning Israel?" *Reform Judaism*, Spring 1988, 4–5, 24; For a popular expression of Israeli feelings of distancing, see David Breakstone, "Dear Cousin," *Moment*, February 1992, 46–48.

assembled contributors something to the effect that, "Never before have American Jews so clearly demonstrated their solidarity with Israel." But such statements are meant to be taken as the exercise of poetic license — and everyone knows it. More reflective of the prevailing mood are the familiar articles in news weeklies and other media that ask whether American Jews are abandoning Israel.

These days some pro-Israel activists fear a virtual collapse in widespread American Jewish support for Israel — if not in the short-term, then not too many years down the road. In short, the best evidence for the view that most political and intellectual elite figures perceive declines in American Jewish support for Israel is that none of them, as far as I am aware, makes a serious claim that American Jews in the early 1990s are *more* committed to Israel than they were in the early 1980s.

Given the near-universality of what we may call the "distancing argument," it behooves us to take a close look at the relevant evidence. Have American Jews really been growing more remote from Israel?

The Distancing Argument

What leads many observers to believe that erosion is well under way?

The initial impetus for the distancing argument derived from the mounting criticism of Israeli government policies by American Jewish leaders. The 1970s witnessed only isolated instances of public criticism by what were, in effect, fringe intellectuals in the Jewish community. But by the 1980s, expressions of demurral from Israeli government policies were voiced by increasingly mainstream American Jewish leaders. Four major flash points are particularly noteworthy: the Sabra and Shatilla massacres in September 1982, the arrest of Jonathan Pollard in 1986, the Intifada in late 1987 and early 1988, and the post-election bargaining in the winter of 1988-1989, which raised what became known as the "Who is a Jew?" question.

To many elite figures, American Jews' adverse reactions to these four events signified a growing disenchantment — not just with certain Israeli leaders but with Israel as a state and, even more significantly, with Israel as a Judaic symbol. Many believed that the critical statements of American Jewish leaders could only mean that American Jews as a whole had less regard for Israelis' sagacity, morality, commitment to democracy, and sincerity in the pursuit of peace. Moreover, the argument goes, Israel's unfavorable image among Americans generally could, in time, diminish its standing among American Jews. Eytan Gilboa writes: "Substantial anti-Israel shifts in the attitudes of the general public toward Israel, which so far have not occurred, could cause erosion in the ethnic attitude structure [i.e., attachment to Israel] of American Jews."[2]

The critical reactions of some American Jewish leaders to Sabra and Shatilla, Pollard, the Intifada and the "Who is a Jew" affair — coming so rapidly, one after the other — lent credence to the generalized notion that American Jews were abandoning Israel. Interestingly, this analysis was shared by actors with quite different political agendas. Some journalists — eager for a compelling story — were inclined to attach greater significance to instances of criticism than may have been warranted. Some, who may be unfriendly to Israel, advanced the distancing hypothesis as a way of arguing for a more even-handed American foreign policy in the region. Pro-Israel doves among American Jews also found the evidence of distancing useful for their ends. They could argue (and did) that an Israel that failed to mend its hawkish ways risked alienating its erstwhile supporters among more dovish-minded American Jews.[3] Pro-Israel hawks, for their part, found evidence of American Jewish alienation helpful in their attacks on outspoken doves for helping to delegitimize Israel in the court of public opinion.[4] Despite differences in motivation and inclination among these diverse groups, all

2   Eytan Gilboa, "American Jews and Non-Jews: Comparative Opinions on the Palestinian Uprising," *Jewish Political Studies Review* 2 (1–2) (Spring 5750/1990): 178–179.

3   Leonard Fein, "Days of Awe," *Moment*, September 1982, 13–18; idem, "A New Zionism," *Moment*, April 1989, 48–53; Arthur Hertzberg, *Jewish Polemics* (New York: Columbia University Press, 1992), chap. 5–7.

4   Ruth Wisse, "The Delegitimization of Israel," *Commentary,* July 1982, 29–36; idem, "The Might and the Right," *Commentary*, September 1992, 48–50; and idem, "The Twentieth Century's Most Successful Ideology," *Commentary*, September 1991, 31–35.

could agree that Jewish leaders' criticism of Israeli policies signified increasing detachment from Israel by rank-and-file American Jews.

Jewish leaders' criticism was, of course, not the only reason for the growing popularity of the distancing hypothesis. The sense that American Jews are becoming more remote from Israel is situated within a larger context of pessimism over the future of Jewish life in the United States.[5] The 1980s were marked by rising rates of intermarriage and a foreboding sense as to what they mean for the American Jewish future, to say nothing of what they signify about the quality of American Jewish life today. Most communal leaders and academic observers in the United States and Israel perceive large sections of American Jewry as rapidly losing their Jewish distinctiveness. The image of a growing distance from Israel comports with this larger image of a growing remoteness from Jewish life in all its manifestations.

The declining levels of American Jews' philanthropic contributions provides yet one more argument for the distancing hypothesis. For years the United Jewish Appeal has functioned as a barometer of American Jewish commitment to Israel. Supporting Israel has

---

5   For more on such pessimistic views, see Charles Liebman, "The Quality of American Jewish Life: A Grim Outlook," in *Facing the Future: Essays on Contemporary Jewish Life*, ed. Steven Bayme, (New York: Ktav and the American Jewish Committee, 1989); and Sergio DellaPergola and Uziel O. Schmelz, "Demographic Transformations or American Jewry: Marriage and Mixed-Marriage in the 1980s," in *Studies in Contemporary Jewry*, vol. 5 (New York: Oxford University Press, 1989). For other views, see Steven M. Cohen, *American Assimilation or Jewish Revival?* (Bloomington: Indiana University Press, 1988), chaps. 1 and 8; idem, "The Quality of American Jewish Life: Better or Worse?" in *Facing the Future: Essays on Contemporary Jewish Life*, ed. Steven Bayme (New York: Ktav and American Jewish Committee, 1989); idem, *Content and Continuity: Two Bases for Jewish Commitment* (New York: American Jewish Committee, 1991); idem, "Jewish Content versus Jewish Continuity," in *The Americanization of the Jews*, ed. Robert Seltzer and Norman Cohen (New York: New York University Press, 1994); and Steven M. Cohen and Leonard Fein, "From Integration to Survival: American Jewish Anxieties in Transition," *Annals of the American Academy of Political and Social Science*, July 1985, 75–88.

been understood as the principal single motivation for Jewish philanthropic giving to the local federation campaigns that feed into the national UJA drive. It is for this reason that declines in such giving[6] have been interpreted as additional evidence of erosion in American Jewish commitment to Israel.

The declines have taken place on three levels. First, total giving in real, inflation-adjusted terms has declined fairly steadily since the mid-1970s. Second, the proportion of all funds that are allocated to Israel and other beneficiaries overseas has also declined. In over 200 communities, small groups of highly active lay leaders decide annually (or sometimes less often) on the fraction of dollars raised in the community that will be transferred to the United Jewish Appeal for eventual transmittal to the Jewish Agency for Israel and other major overseas agencies. Over the last two decades, the average fraction for overseas needs has eroded slowly but perceptibly.

Last, philanthropic support for Israel is declining in terms of its meaning for Israel. As a fraction of the budget for the social welfare needs of the Israeli citizenry, or as a fraction of the total economy, the dollars derived from American Jewish donors comprise a far smaller share than in the past. Although this perspective may not constitute a fair and rational way of measuring the American Jewish commitment to Israel, the diminishing importance to Israel of American Jewish philanthropy certainly augments the inchoate sentiment, especially among Israelis, that American Jews mean less to Israel and — as an unstated corollary — Israel must mean less to American Jews.

The fluctuations in American Jewish travel to Israel constitute yet another source of concern over American Jewish support for Israel. Israelis pay close attention to the sharp declines in American Jewish travel to Israel during times of tension. Many interpreted the severe fall-offs in tourism during the first year of the Intifada in 1988 and during the Gulf War in 1991 as signs of the hollowness of American Jewish proclamations of existential solidarity with Israel.

But perhaps more fundamental than all these factors is the implicit comparison of recent times (say, the last decade or so) with

6   Gerald Bubis, "Jewish Dollars Drying Up," *Moment*, December 1992, 28–33.

the unusual period of American Jewish romance with Israel that followed the Six-Day War. The Six-Day War helped produce a profound reorientation in the American Jewish psyche, one that was increasingly political, assertive, and pro-Israel.

In the decade that followed, news reports helpful to Israel's image followed fast upon one another. Jews and other Americans learned of the early acts of urban terrorism in 1968, the War of Attrition in 1969–1971, the Munich Massacre in 1972, the Yom Kippur War in 1973, the proclamation of Arab unity behind the PLO in 1974, the U.N.'s "Zionism is racism" resolution in 1975, and finally, the Entebbe Rescue in 1976. These stories served to reinforce the idealized caricature of Israelis so widespread among American Jews in the late 1960s and early 1970s. The highly critical reactions of American Jewish leaders to the less favorable events of the 1980s took on special meaning precisely because they were in such sharp contrast with the wildly unrealistic images of Israelis commonly held by American Jews (and others) just a decade earlier.

Certainly, far less favorable stories dominated the news in the 1980s: Sabra and Shatilla in 1982, the election to the Knesset of Meir Kahane in 1984, violent clashes between *haredim* and their opponents in the middle 1980s, the Jonathan Pollard affair in 1986, the outbreak of the Intifada in late 1987, the attempt to revise the "Who is a Jew?" law in 1988, and seamy infighting and wrangling over constructing a coalition in 1990. The steady decline in favorable news coming out of Israel comported very neatly with reports (mostly mine) of a significant age-related gap in pro-Israel sentiment. Over several national surveys of the American Jewish population, I found repeated evidence of lower levels of attachment to Israel among younger population groups.

These differences in Israel attachment between old and young, the unprecedented public criticism of Israeli policies, rising rates of intermarriage, erosion in philanthropic support, and fluctuations in Jewish tourism have all helped produce a widely accepted body of expert opinion that American Jews have grown more remote from Israel. According to this view, barring unforeseen reversals in these very deep-seated trends, there is little reason to anticipate a major turnabout in the broad-based, long-term erosion in American Jewish support for Israel.

Orientations to Israel: Three Dimensions

In common parlance, such terms as "attachment to Israel," "involvement with Israel," "support for Israel," "Zionist" and "pro-Israel"
are used almost interchangeably to refer loosely to positive feelings
toward Israel. An analytical approach demands greater precision
than is customary in casual conversation.

Social psychologists readily divide attitudes into three domains:
the affective, the cognitive, and the behavioral. The affective domain
refers to how people feel about a particular object — warm or cool,
close or remote, favorable or unfavorable, attracted or repelled, and
so forth. The cognitive realm refers to beliefs, images, stereotypes —
how the individual conceives of the object, what traits they attribute
to it. Behavioral attitudes refer to the area of action — how the
individual reacts to alternate proposals for actions or policies, either
on his/her part or on the part of the object in question.

This tripartite division readily translates into three Israel-oriented
attitude domains. To wit, with respect to American Jewish attitudes
toward Israel we can distinguish "attachment," "image," and "political orientation." These three domains are sufficiently different from
one another to warrant separate examination; and taken together,
they encompass much of what is important analytically and practically in understanding American Jewish orientations toward Israel.
Beyond the theoretical considerations, these dimensions emerged
from analyses of interitem correlations that testified to the clustering
of Israel-related attitudes under the three broad rubrics.

"Attachment" refers to the salience of Israel in people's consciousness, to emotional ties to Israel and closeness of feelings
toward Israel. Those who are most attached to Israel are those who
talk about, think about, read about, and care about Israel. Given
the centrality of security concerns in American Jews' relationship
with Israel, "attachment" also includes the extent to which the
individual worries about Israel's survival and about the possibility
of its destruction.

It might make sense to suppose that those who are attached to
Israel should also hold positive images of Israelis. In fact, such is not
necessarily the case. Those who are very attached to Israel may easily
hold highly unflattering images of Israelis. Israelis themselves come

to mind as a group who are certainly highly attached to Israel but who may indeed harbor unfavorable portraits of their countrymen. "Image," in fact, constitutes a domain of attitudes quite separate and apart from attachment.

"Political orientation," the third major dimension of Israel-related attitudes, is probably the area that has received the most public attention. It is also one which has been taken (in my view, wrongly) as a proxy for what I have called "attachment to Israel." Empirically, views of Israeli policy directions bear little if any relation to attachment.

The domain of political orientation subsumes such attitudes as readiness to offer compromise to the Arabs; support (or criticism) of tough Israeli responses to Arab threats, violence, and hostility; perception of Arab moderation or extremism; willingness to support negotiations with the PLO and other Arab parties; and impressions of Israeli hawks and doves, of the Labor and Likud parties, and of leading political personalities identified with one or another part of the political spectrum. Responses in one area tend to be strongly correlated with those in other areas, and the same sorts of individuals who are dovish (or hawkish) in one set of issues are the types who hold parallel views elsewhere. (For example, those most supportive of territorial compromise are more likely to perceive Arab moderation and are also more likely to hold favorable views of Israeli doves.)

Consistent with this perspective, the broad hypothesis that American Jews have grown more distant from Israel, then, translates into three subhypotheses: that they have become less attached to Israel; that they have developed less favorable images of Israelis; and that they have grown more critical of Israeli government policies. The available data address all three propositions, albeit with varying degrees of depth and certitude.

The Data Sets — and Their Many Problems

To examine trends in American Jewish attitudes toward Israel, the analysis below utilizes six national public opinion surveys conducted between 1983 and 1993, as well as the 1990 National Jewish Population Survey (NJPS). The five public opinion surveys sponsored by the American Jewish Committee were designed and originally analyzed by me.[7] The most recent one (1993) was conducted by the American Jewish Committee Research Department.

The five AJC surveys just mentioned were distributed and returned through the mails. (For the sake of completeness, it should be noted that AJC-sponsored surveys were also conducted in 1981, 1982 and 1984. Due to the very small number of questions in these studies whose wording was replicated in other surveys, the analysis below does not report results from these three studies.) The 1993 survey was conducted by telephone.

Undoubtedly, all six surveys relied on less than ideal samples. The reason for this circumstance is very straightforward. As the experience with the 1990 National Jewish Population Survey would demonstrate, the effort required to obtain a rigorously representative national sample of American Jews would have cost upward of $400,000; but the budget for data collection for the American Jewish Committee studies never exceeded $15,000. As a result, for the study of American Jewish public opinion we were forced to choose between

---

7   The survey data are interpreted in several publications: Steven M. Cohen, "The
     1981–2 National Survey of American Jews," *American Jewish Year Book* 83,
     (1983): 89–110; idem, "What American Jews Believe," *Moment*, July 1982,
     23–27; idem, *American Modernity and Jewish Identity* (New York: Routledge,
     1983), chap. 8; idem, *Attitudes of American Jews toward Israel and Israelis* (New
     York: American Jewish Committee, 1983); idem, "American Jews and Israel:
     Pragmatic, Critical, but Still in Love," *Jerusalem Letter* of the Jerusalem Center
     for Public Affairs, No. 13 (November 1983); idem, "From Romantic Idealists to
     Loving Realists: The Changing Place of Israel in the Consciousness of American
     Jews," in *Survey of Jewish Affairs 1985*, ed. William Frankel (Rutherford, N.J.:
     Associated University Presses, 1985); idem, *Ties and Tensions: The 1986 Survey
     of American Jewish Attitudes toward Israel and Israelis* (New York: American
     Jewish Committee, 1987); idem, *Ties and Tensions: An Update — The 1989
     Survey of American Jewish Attitudes toward Israel and Israelis* (New York:
     The American Jewish Committee, 1989); Charles Liebman and Steven M.
     Cohen, *Two Worlds of Judaism: The Israeli and American Experiences* (New
     Haven, Conn.: Yale University Press, 1990); Steven M. Cohen, *After the Gulf
     War: American Jews' Attitudes toward Israel — The 1991 National Survey of
     American Jews* (New York: The American Jewish Committee, 1991); and Chaim
     I. Waxman, "All in the Family: American Jewish Attachments to Israel," in *A
     New Jewry? America since the Second World War — Studies in Contemporary
     Jewry*, Vol. 8 (New York: Oxford University Press, 1992).

conducting the research with less than ideal sampling methods, or conducting no studies at all. Obviously, we opted for the former alternative.

Sampling techniques took a decided shift after 1984. Between 1981 and 1984, the surveys relied on distinctive Jewish name (DJN) samples. From 1986 to 1993, the samples were drawn from the Consumer Mail Panel constructed and administered by Market Facts, Inc., a major American marketing research firm.

The 1981–1984 surveys were fielded by A. B. Data of Milwaukee, a firm that specializes in direct-mail fund raising from American Jews. Drawing on the entire nation's telephone directories and, in some states, motor vehicle registrations, and applying a list of roughly 3,100 distinctive Jewish names, A. B. Data drew a geographically comprehensive national sample.

DJN sampling suffers from a bias in the direction of more Jewishly identified respondents. One reason is that the samples overrepresent residentially stable households, the kind who are found in published lists of telephone subscribers or automobile owners. The residentially stable underrepresent younger adults; in addition, the more geographically stable exhibit higher rates of Jewish communal affiliation (such as synagogue membership) than the general Jewish population.

A second problem with DJN sampling is that it underrepresents Jewish women in mixed marriages, who are often listed in public records by their gentile husbands' family names. Last, DJN samples reflect a small influence from the time when less Jewishly identified Jews changed their names from overtly recognizable Jewish names to more Americanized versions (e.g., Cohen became Collins or Cooper). As a group, those who retained their DJNs are probably slightly more Jewishly involved than Jews whose names are less obviously of Jewish origin.

Partially as a consequence of growing concern about the unknown biases associated with DJN sampling of published lists, and partially as an outgrowth of declining rates of response to mail-back surveys during the 1980s, the sampling technique for the surveys conducted between 1986 and 1993 shifted to Market Facts' Consumer Mail Panel.

The Consumer Mail Panel consists of over a quarter of a million

Americans who have agreed to be surveyed from time to time on a variety of concerns, most of which center on purchasing behavior and decision making. Of these, over 5,000 contain at least one household head who is Jewish by religion. That is, on the initial screening questionnaire they completed when joining the Panel, these Panel members indicated that their religion, or that of their spouses, was Jewish. This definition of who is a Jewish respondent is of some consequence, because roughly a fifth of American Jews, according to the 1990 NJPS[8] identify as Jews but declare their *religion* as "Other" or "None." This segment scores significantly lower than Jews-by-religion on most standard measures of Jewish involvement. Thus in terms of many indicators of Jewish involvement, the Market Facts respondents closely resemble the Jews-by-religion in the NJPS. But we need to bear in mind that NJPS Jews-by-religion are somewhat more Jewishly involved than the total Jewish population, including those whom some researchers have called "secular" Jews.

For their surveys, Market Facts drew demographically balanced national samples of about 100,000 households (comprising both gentiles and Jews), chosen to reflect the national distributions of age, income, education, region, city size, and household size. From the Jewish members of these samples, the company then extracted about 1,200–1,500 prospective respondents. Of these, about 75–80 percent generally responded to the mail-back surveys.

These samples were compared with other data sets representing American Jewry, such as the *Los Angeles Times* survey of Jewish respondents identified over several months of national surveys or, in 1991, the NJPS. The comparisons demonstrated that although the Consumer Mail Panel underrepresents Orthodox Jews, it reasonably resembles the American Jewish population in other significant dimensions (region, income, education, ritual practice, affiliation, and age for those over 25). As a result, the analysis applied sampling weights to increase the Orthodox representation so as to equal that reported in the more authoritative national studies such as the NJPS.

---

8   Barry Kosmin et al., *Highlights of the CJF 1990 National Jewish Population Survey* (New York: Council of Jewish Federations, 1991); and Sidney Goldstein, "Profile of American Jewry," *American Jewish Year Book* 92 (1992).

The Findings — More Stability Than Change

The results clearly point to a moderate impact of sampling technique on the composition of the sample. On most indicators of Jewish involvement, the 1983 DJN sample scores a few percentage points higher than the subsequent samples drawn by Market Facts from its Consumer Mail Panel. For example, 43 percent of the 1983 sample had visited Israel, as compared with 33–37 percent of the other samples (see Table 1). In 1983, as many as 59 percent claimed synagogue membership as opposed to 48–53 percent of respondents in the 1986–1991 surveys. The most striking contrast is found in the proportion who identify as Orthodox or Conservative Jews, designations that carry with them higher probabilities of Jewish involvement in several spheres, including attachment to Israel. In 1983, 59 percent saw themselves as Conservative or Orthodox (even if they were not at the time official synagogue members) as contrasted with just 42–45 percent in the four later studies.

Table 1: Trend Analysis, in American Jewish Attachment to Israel, 1983–1993

	1983	1986	1988	1989	1991	NJPS*	1993
Background Measures							
Visited Israel	43	33	35	35	37	33	34
Orthodox & Conservative	59	43	42	42	45	46	
Synagogue member	59	51	48	48	53	45	
Seder	89	84	78	78		73	
Hanukkah candles	77	82	80	80		72	
Fast Yom Kippur	59	61	58	58		59	
Separate dishes	22	20	20	20		17	
Israel Attachment							
Feel close:							
Very		20	28	21	31		27
Fairly		42	42	48	41		48
Very & Fairly		62	70	69	72		75

	C1	C2	C3	C4	C5	C6	C7
Feel emotionally attached:							
Extremely					16	14	
Very					44	46	
Somewhat					23	25	
Not					15	15	
Not sure					1	2	
Care about Israel	78	63	76	72	68		79
Talk about Israel	75	64	55	59	68		
Greatest tragedy	77	61	64	64	65		68
Zionist	39	27	23	24	26		29
Thought about aliyah	15	14		14	17		

Policy Orientation

	C1	C2	C3	C4	C5	C6	C7
Territorial compromise:							
Agree	40	29	42	38	35		32
Disagree	36	36	33	30	34		35
Don't criticize:							
Agree	31	22	31	22	30		
Disagree	57	63	56	63	55		
Israeli Arabs treated:							
Fairly		42			58	55	
Unfairly		28			58	23	

Images of Israelis

	C1	C2	C3	C4	C5	C6	C7
Industrious	81				70		
Heroic	66				71		
Peace-loving	53				54		

*   The NJPS results reported here are limited to respondents who report their religion as Jewish, consistent with the sampling definition used by the other studies. The NJPS subsample has been weighted by the product of two factors: the number of adult Jews-by-religion in the household and the household weight used to take into account national demographic variations in noncooperating or unreached households. Except for the question on emotional attachment to Israel, the NJPS question wording differs from that used in the other surveys in the table.

Key to 1983–1993 AJC-sponsored surveys
(in some cases questions underwent slight changes in wording over the years):
Visited Israel = Whether respondent has visited Israel.
Orthodox & Conservative = Jewish denomination identification of respondent; includes those who are not synagogue members.
Synagogue member = Whether respondent claims to belong to a synagogue.
Seder = Attended a Passover Seder at home or elsewhere previous year.
Hanukkah candles = Lit previous year.
Fast Yom Kippur = Respondent fasted Yom Kippur previous year.
Separate Dishes = Respondent uses separate dishes for meat and dairy products.
Feel close = "How close do you feel to Israel?"
Feel emotionally attached = "How emotionally attached are you to Israel?"
Care about Israel = "Caring about Israel is a very important part of my being a Jew."
Talk about Israel = "Do you often talk about Israel with friends and relatives?"
Greatest tragedy = "If Israel were destroyed, I would feel as if I had suffered one of the greatest personal tragedies in my life."
Zionist = "Do you consider yourself a Zionist?"
Thought about aliyah = "Have you ever seriously considered living in Israel?"
Territorial compromise = "Israel should offer the Arabs territorial compromise in the West Bank and Gaza in return for credible guarantees of peace."
Don't criticize = "American Jews should not publicly criticize the policies of the government of Israel."
Israeli Arabs treated = "In your view, how fairly is each of the following groups being treated in Israel?"
Industrious, Heroic, Peace-loving = "To what extent do you think each of the following descriptions applies to Israelis?" (To a great extent.)

With these considerations in mind, it should not be surprising to find an apparent drop in pro-Israel attitudes between the 1983 and the 1986–1993 surveys. The reported decline probably derives more from methodology than from a genuine change in orientation among American Jews. From 1986 to 1993, identically worded measures of Israel attachment fluctuated in a narrow range in apparently near-random fashion. To take a key example, the proportion saying they feel "very close" or "fairly close" to Israel stood at 62 percent in 1986, 70 percent in 1988, 69 percent in 1989, 72 percent in 1991 (following the heightened concern occasioned by the Gulf War), and 75 percent in 1993 (following the hugely popular Rabin–Arafat ceremony on the White House lawn). These data, then, indicate no significant change in American Jews' attachment to Israel.

Since some of the most disturbing events took place in the late 1980s, it stands to reason that if such events had damaged Israel's standing among American Jews, then an erosion in Israel attachment should have been evident between 1986 and 1993 as well as between 1983 and 1986. The apparent stability between 1986 and 1993 suggests that at least in the short run, developments such as the Intifada and the "Who is a Jew?" controversy exerted only a negligible impact on the overall levels of attachment to Israel by American Jews.

Further evidence for the contention of no short-term impact of events can be seen when we look for changes in the policy domain. Over the years, the balance between support for and opposition to the proposition that Israel ought to make territorial compromises for real peace has shifted erratically. For reasons that are not at all obvious (at least to me), the 1986 sample was the most "hawkish," with opponents of compromise exceeding supporters by seven percentage points. In 1988, perhaps because the Intifada was in full swing, supporters of compromise exceeded opponents by nine percentage points. The views of samples in the other years lie between these two poles.

Similarly, attitudes toward the acceptability of public criticism of Israeli policies by American Jews fluctuated erratically over the six surveys. (To be sure, although majorities find public criticism acceptable, as the 1991 survey determined, they fail to find it desirable or helpful.)

One component of distancing might be evident in diminished good feelings toward Israel's presumption of fair treatment of its Arabs, especially in light of the outbreak of the Intifada. In three surveys

(1986, 1988, and 1989), pluralities of American Jews expressed their confidence in Israel's fair treatment of its Arab citizens. But, contrary to the expectations of the distancing hypothesis, belief in Israel's fair treatment actually grew in 1988 and 1989, relative to 1986. The balance between those perceiving fair and unfair treatment shifted markedly in the direction of a greater perception of fairness in 1988. Possibly some American Jews reacted defensively during the height of the Palestinian uprising to express support for Israel's approach to its principal minority group. Perhaps the Intifada implanted unfavorable images of Israel that will emerge only in time. All we can tell from these data is that in terms of support for putatively "hard-line" Israeli policies, the American Jewish population continued to express levels of solidarity with the Israeli government to those it had in the past.

Proponents of the distancing hypothesis have spoken about the disenchantment of American Jews with Israelis or, in other terms, their "de-heroicization" and "de-idealization" of Israel and Israelis. Some shreds of evidence from the 1983 and 1991 surveys argue against this formulation of the distancing hypothesis as well. Both surveys asked respondents the extent to which they saw Israelis as "industrious," "heroic," and "peace-loving" (as well as other characteristics that were not replicated on both studies). Recalling that the 1983 sample was biased in the direction of more Israel-involved and Jewishly active respondents, the results here are particularly damaging for the distancing hypothesis.

Between 1983 and 1991, perceptions of Israelis' industriousness fell somewhat, perceptions of their heroism grew a bit, and their image as peace-loving stayed much the same. Certainly, these findings run contrary to what one would expect were American Jews' image of Israelis adversely affected by the unpleasant events of the 1980s.

To be sure, any individual trend line associated with a single attitude item offers less than convincing evidence of the inadequacy of the distancing hypothesis. But taken together, the overall stability of many attitudes toward Israel, Israeli policies, and Israeli people strongly suggest that American Jews, in the aggregate, hardly diminished their professed attachment to Israel during the turbulent period of the 1980s.

Having come to this conclusion, it would be foolhardy to project the stability of American Jewish attitudes toward Israel too far into the future. The major nagging question, of course, concerns the attitudes of younger adult Jews, those inevitably destined to replace their elders in the ranks of American Jewish leaders and public. Here the results do in fact point to an impending decline in American Jewish attachment to Israel at some point in the future.

Analyses of all the surveys produce the same essential results: a weak to moderate direct relationship between age and Israel attachment. Older American Jews are somewhat more attached to Israel than their middle-aged counterparts, who in turn are more attached than younger Jewish adults (see Table 2) The patterns vary somewhat over time and by the particular measure being utilized, but the essential contours of the relationship emerge in all surveys and with almost all measures of Israel attachment.

Table 2: Index of Attachement to Israel, by Age

Age:	18–39	40–59	60	Total*
	39	46	56	46
Visited Israel				
Twice or more	74	75	75	75
Once	57	46	57	53
Never	29	41	47	36
Never visited Israel, controlling for Jewish involvement	31	38	45	36

*   All respondents, irrespective of numbers of age.
Source: 1990 National Jewish Population Survey, weighted by household weights and by number of Jewish adults in the household.

The 1990 National Jewish Population Survey provides an excellent illustration (again, any of AJC-sponsored studies would do as well). The NJPS questionnaire provided three modules of questions designated for randomly selected subsamples. One of the modules contained three items especially pertinent to the study of Israel attachment. One question explicitly asked respondents how closely attached they felt Israel. Two other questions asked whether the respondent spoke about Israel with friends and family members and, if so, how often. By calibrating the answers to the attachment question and to a combination of the two questions on talking about Israel, I devised an index that ranges from 0 to 100, measuring extent of attachment to Israel. High scores represent greater attachment.

Those aged 40–59 scored an average of 46 on this index, as contrasted with a mean of 39 among those under 40, and 56 for those aged 60 and over (see Table 2). Significantly, more detailed analysis of the 10-year age cohorts (not shown) demonstrates that the slide in Israel attachment occurs over the entire age range and is not concentrated in only one or two adjacent age groups. If only the events of the last decade or so had been responsible for the depressed levels of Israel attachment among the young, then we might expect to find a sharp drop in attachment at a certain point in the age spectrum, say those who are now in their 30s or early 40s. That is, we might expect that the older group, those who came of political age earlier, would report high levels of attachment, while those whose memories of Israel were forged primarily in the 1980s would feel more distant from Israel. But instead of a sharp differentiation between older and younger Jews, we find a gradual and nearly uniform slippage in Israel attachment as we descend the age ladder, from older, to middle-aged, to younger Jews. This pattern argues against assigning prime responsibility for the apparent erosion in Israel attachment to the disturbing events of the last decade.

It is especially noteworthy that the age-related decline in Israel attachment is limited to those who have never been to Israel. Among those who have traveled to Israel, be it once or more often, age and attachment are unrelated; younger Jews who have traveled to Israel are as attached as their older counterparts. Only among those who have never been to Israel do we find a clear relationship between (younger) age and (lower) Israel attachment. (Again, these NJPS results replicate and confirm the findings from the earlier, AJC-sponsored studies.)

Apparently, trips to Israel both reflect and provoke increased attachment. Those who visit Israel do so in part because of their prior attachment to Israel; in addition, the Israel experience undoubtedly leaves a pro-Israel imprint on most travelers. To be sure, the direction of the relationship between involvement and travel to Israel is far from clear, but the higher levels of attachment among visitors is indisputable.

The NJPS data can also be used to address the question of the likely endurance of the lower levels of attachment to Israel among younger Jews. Is this feature something they will grow out of as they mature, or is it relatively permanent and enduring? After all, many younger adults have yet to experience Israel firsthand. Many will come to be more involved in Jewish life as they marry, have children, and remain in one location long enough to acquire and thicken formal and informal relationships within the Jewish community. Perhaps as they enter the community in greater numbers with greater commitment, they will come to take on the distinctive attitudes of the active Jewish community, one of which is certainly attachment to Israel.

Contrary to this line of thinking, the analysis clearly lends support to the notion that the age-related differences in Israel attachment are *unlikely* to evaporate once younger Jews come to approximate their elders' levels of Jewish involvement (if, indeed, they ever do). The Multiple Classification Analysis for those who have never been to Israel reports a gap of nearly 18 points in the Israel attachment index between those under 40 and those 60 and over. Once we control for Jewish involvement (a composite index made up diverse items pertaining to ritual practice, holiday celebration, communal involvement, and informal affiliation), the gap in Israel attachment between older and younger respondents remains almost as large as before. In other words, even if we imagine (if only statistically) that younger Jews are as Jewishly involved as their elders, they would still manifest significantly less attachment to Israel. Younger Jews are not less attached to Israel *because* they are less involved in Jewish life at the moment. Rather, these results indicate that younger Jews' lower levels of attachment to Israel are better viewed as an enduring feature, one that may derive from long-term historical processes rather than being a transitory consequence of their youthfulness.

If such is indeed the case, then the apparent stability in aggregate Jewish involvement with Israel through the 1980s may well be followed by a slow and gradual but persistent erosion in Jewish support in the early part of the twenty-first century. Theoretically, the age-related differences in pro-Israel feelings should have exerted some influence even on aggregate levels of attachment during the period under study here. However, it is entirely possible that the measures and sampling techniques employed were simply too crude to detect small changes in support levels over just a few years. Alternatively, the genuine perturbations associated with measurement at discrete moments may also have obscured trends occurring during the limited period of study.

The key point is that evidence of stability in Israel-related attitudes during recent years constitutes no guarantee of continued stability in the near future. The patterns in Israel attachment associated sociated with age certainly point to the possibility of broad-scale erosion among the American Jewish population over the medium term.

Why the Misreading?

The data presented here attest to the stability in American Jewish attitudes toward Israel. At a bare minimum, they contradict the prevailing assumption that American Jews must have grown at least somewhat more distant from Israel during the turbulent 1980s. If such is indeed the case, how is it that so many perceptive observers came to the opposite conclusion, that distancing from Israel in that period characterized significant portions of American Jewry?

The answer may lie in the distinctions between the (publicly expressed) opinions of elites and the opinions of the rank and file. On one level, elites and publics may (and often do) diverge substantively; that is, the two groups simply have quite different views. With respect to American attitudes toward Israel, Eytan Gilboa has concluded that U.S. foreign policy elites did in fact adopt a more critical view of Israel in the 1980s, while the American public demonstrated far more stable attitudes, remaining almost as sympathetic with Israel as it had been in the past.[9]

9   Eytan Gilboa, *American Public Opinion toward Israel and the Arab–Israeli Conflict* (Lexington, Mass.: Lexington Books, 1987).

Insofar as elite figures take their cue from other elite figures, those who are in the business of interpreting the public mood may have been overly influenced by their personal networks of friends and professional associates. Studies of national Jewish lay leaders and professionals that I helped conduct in 1987, 1989, and 1991[10] demonstrated that these groups — with the exception of the Orthodox — are substantially more dovish on Israeli political issues and substantially more critical of then prevailing Israeli policies. If these are the people shaping the impressions of American Jewish public opinion (as they might well be), then they helped generate the widespread impression that American Jews generally (and not just leaders) were more remote from Israel (not just more critical) than they were in reality.

Not only might elites harbor different attitudes than the rank and file; they also tend to construct more stable and more consistent configurations of attitudes.[11] Highly specialized elite figures (such as party officials in Jennings's study of political attitude consistency among the American public and convention delegates) maintain far more consistent, ideologically driven attitudes on a wide range of issues than even the most aware and active members of the rank and file. Accordingly, prominent observers of American Jewish public opinion may have erred in inferring an increasing remoteness from Israel when all they were observing was an increasing (and time-bound) discomfort with Israeli policies. They may have (inaccurately) reasoned that the Jewish public's attitudes are as consistent as are those of elite figures. In fact, the Jewish public's feelings about

10   Steven M. Cohen and Gerald B. Bubis, "The Impact of Denomination: Differences in the Israel-Related Opinions of American Rabbis and Jewish Communal Workers," *Jewish Political Studies Review* 2 (1–2) (Spring 1990); Steven M. Cohen, *Israel-Diaspora Relations: A Survey of American Jewish Leaders* (Tel Aviv: Israel-Diaspora Institute, 1990); and Steven M. Cohen and Seymour Martin Lipset, *Attitudes toward the Arab-Israeli Conflict and the Peace Process among American Jewish Philanthropic Leaders, 1991* (Los Angeles: The Wilstein Institute of Jewish Policy Studies, University of Judaism, November 1991). For a synthetic presentation of leaders' complex reactions to Israeli policies, see Steven M. Cohen, "Amoral Zionists, Moralizing Universalists and Conditional Doves," *Moment*, August 1989, 56–57.

11   M. Kent Jennings, "Ideology among Mass Publics and Political Elites," *Public Opinion Quarterly* 56 (4). (Winter 1992): 419–441.

Israel may remain instinctual (that is, instinctually pro-Israel) and largely divorced from Israel's policy judgments (even if those feelings are critical).

We cannot be sure as to why a misapprehension took hold among certain observers. What we can be sure of is that survey research findings to this point fail to support the contention that American Jews in the aggregate have grown more "distant" from Israel, whatever that might mean.

Weakening Ties:
American Jewish Baby-Boomers and Israel

Chaim I. Waxman

When one examines the official literature of the three major American Jewish denominations, Orthodox, Conservative, and Reform, it is evident that a number of interesting and significant changes have occurred over the years in the way each relates to the State of Israel. Some of these changes will be briefly indicated.

In contrast to Eastern European Orthodoxy, which was characterized in the prestate era by its anti-Zionism, American Orthodoxy was always highly supportive of the establishment of the Jewish state. Mizrachi, the religious Zionist movement, was one of the major forces in American Orthodoxy, more influential by far than the non-Zionist Agudath Israel[1] During the interwar period, Yeshiva Torah Veda'ath, one of the first higher yeshivahs in the United States, was strongly Zionist.[2] And as late as 1949, *Hapardes* (the oldest extant Torah journal in the United States) contained regular reports on religious Zionist developments, both within Mizrachi and beyond it. Among the features in the April 1949 issue, for example, was a detailed report on an address delivered by Rabbi David Lifshitz to the annual convention of the Union of Orthodox Rabbis of the

---

1   Menahem Kaufman, *Lo-ziyonim beamerica bamaavak al hamedinah, 1939–1948* (Non-Zionists in America and the Struggle for Jewish Statehood: 1939–1948) (Jerusalem, 1984), 7; samuel Halperin, *The Political World of American Zionism* (Detroit, 1961), 65–71. For a historical overview, albeit somewhat romanticized, of the Mizrachi in the United States, see Aaron Halevi Pachenik, "Haziyonut hadatit bearzot haberit," (Religious Zionism in the United States) in *Sefer haziyonut hadatit* (The Book of Religious Zionism), ed. Yitzchak Raphael and S. Z. Shragai (Jerusalem, 1977), 2: 226–241.

2   Jenna Weissman Joselit, *New York's Jewish Jews: The Orthodox Community in the Interwar Years* (Bloomington, 1990), 17.

United States and Canada (Agudath Harabbanim), in which strong sentiments of religious Zionism were expressed.[3]

Today, much of that picture has changed dramatically. American Orthodox Judaism is now heavily influenced by Agudath Israel. Religious Zionism, if not loudly condemned, is rarely mentioned in the aforementioned Torah journal; the leadership of Agudath Harabbanim is wholly of the Agudath Israel persuasion; and the *yeshivishe velt*, the "world of the yeshiva," is virtually synonymous with the world of non-Zionism. This is a result, in large measure, of the post World War II immigration to America of the survivors of Eastern European Orthodoxy — including those of the scholarly elite who headed the higher yeshivahs in Russia, Lithuania, and Poland, as well as a number of Hasidic grand rabbis and their followers, most of whom came from Hungary, Czechoslovakia, and Poland.[4] Establishing a network of day schools and yeshivahs in America that socialized a new generation in accordance with their non-Zionist version of Orthodoxy, these new arrivals soon took over the ideological leadership of the Agudath Israel of America and provided it with a following from within the rank and file of yeshiva students and Hasidim. By the 1950s, Agudath Israel had grown to be one of the largest and most influential organizations of American Orthodoxy, whereas Mizrachi's leadership had stagnated and its membership and significance had declined markedly.

Not only within "the world of the yeshiva"[5] but within much of

---

3   *Hapardes* 23(7) (April 1949): 12–15. See also p. 10, which contains a report of the New York visit of Rabbi Yoseph Kahaneman, "one of the great heads of yeshivahs, of Ponivezh, and now of the State of Israel." The last phrase, in Hebrew, is *medinat yisrael*, not *eretz yisrael*.

4   Somewhat surprisingly, there is still no thorough study of American Orthodoxy, especially since World War II. The monograph by Samuel C. Heilman and Steven M. Cohen, *Cosmopolitans and Parochials: Modern Orthodox Jews in America* (Chicago, 1990), contains virtually nothing on the relationship of American Orthodoxy with Israel and Zionism. For suggestions as to what a study of American Orthodox should encompass, see Charles S. Liebman, "Studying Orthodox Judaism in the United States: A Review Essay," *American Jewish History* 80(3) (Spring 1991): 415–424.

5   William B. Helmreich, *The World of the Yeshiva* (New York, 1983). This is the "world" known as *haredi*, "black-hat," "right-wing," or "ultra-Orthodox." Helmreich includes Yeshiva University's Rabbi Isaac Elchanan Theological Seminary (RIETS) in his analysis. However, RIETS is clearly peripheral to the

American Orthodoxy in general, the ideology of religious Zionism is
now much less frequently espoused. Indeed, when ArtScroll Publishers, a highly successful publisher of traditional Judaica that caters
to the Orthodox public, put out a new edition of the traditional
prayer book, it omitted the prayer for the welfare of the State of
Israel. Although the organization of modern Orthodox rabbis, the
Rabbinical Council of America, issued its own special edition of the
ArtScroll *siddur* that included this prayer, it appears that the regular
edition has become the standard one for the Orthodox public in the
United States. Likewise, there seems to have been a decline in the
religious celebration of Israel Independence Day within Orthodox
congregations across the United States.[6]

---

world of the yeshiva and not considered part of it by the overwhelming majority
of that world. As Helmreich suggests, it "is viewed by many in the other major
yeshivahs as not being part of the community because it not only permits secular
education but maintains a college on its campus that is a required part of study
for all undergraduates" (p. 36). Although Helmreich makes no mention of it,
there is every reason to suggest that the religious Zionism espoused in RIETS
only confirms its "deviant" status. On the growing influence of the *haredi*
perspective within Orthodoxy, see Menachem Friedman, "Life Tradition and
Book Tradition in the Development of Ultra-Orthodox Judaism," in *Judaism
Viewed from Within and from Without: Anthropological Perspectives*, ed. Harvey
E. Goldberg (Albany, 1987), 235–255; Chaim I. Waxman, "Toward a Sociology
of Psak," *Tradition* 25(3) (Spring 1990):12-25.

6   It is perhaps even more revealing that ArtScroll Publishers blatantly omitted
a phrase implying religious Zionist sentiments from its translation of Rabbi
S. Y. Zevin's *Hamo'adim behalakhah* (The Festivals in *halachah*). See Reuven
P. Bulka, "Israel and the State of the Religious Mind," *Morasha: A Journal
of Religious Zionism* 2(2) (Spring–Summer 1986): 30–34. For another critique
of the ArtScroll phenomenon, see B. Barry Levy, "Judge Not a Book by Its
Cover," *Tradition* 19(1) (Spring 1981): 89–95, and the response by Emanuel
Feldman, *Tradition* 19(2) (Summer 1981), 192. For a more extensive version of
Levy's critique, see his article, "Our Torah, Your Torah and Their Torah: An
Evaluation of the ArtScroll Phenomenon," in *Truth and Compassion: Essays
on Judaism and Religion in Memory of Rabbi Dr. Solomon Frank*, ed. Howard
Joseph, Jack N. Lightstone, and Michael D. Oppenheim (Waterloo, Ont., 1983),
137–189. For an analysis of the Conservative, Reform, and Reconstructionist
perspectives, see the article in this volume by David Ellenson, "Envisioning
Israel in the Liturgies of North American Liberal Judaism." For a group of
essays which deal with a number of issues flowing from the perspective that Israel
does have religious significance, see Chaim I. Waxman, ed., *Israel as a Religious*

Such developments, however, do not indicate a decline in support for Israel within American Orthodoxy. Rather, there seems to have been a *transformation* in the role of Israel within American Orthodoxy, although its precise nature is not yet quite clear. It may be that there is a decline in the tendency to define the State of Israel within the context of modern (albeit religious) Zionism and an increasing tendency to define Israel traditionally, as Eretz Israel — a trend that has also manifested itself within Israel, especially since the Begin era.[7] Alternatively, the transformation may be characterized as the secularization of Israel. Perhaps because Israel has become

---

Reality (Northvale, N.J., 1994). A recent incident that I personally witnessed reinforced for me the validity of the above assertion. A group of several hundred religiously observant Jews, overwhelmingly modern Orthodox, were gathered together at a hotel for Pesach. When, after several days, the leader of the prayer services was asked why there was no recitation of the prayer for the welfare of the State of Israel (*Tefila lishlom hamedina*), he replied, "We don't have any time for it; we have to be finished at [a specified time]." That individual, and indeed virtually everyone present, was highly supportive of Israel. He simply did not relate to it religiously and thus felt no religious need to include a special prayer for its welfare. One other piece of evidence in support of the argument is from the *Ezras Torah Luach*, the annual Orthodox synagogue ritual calendar published in Hebrew and English by Ezras Torah, a prominent Orthodox relief society established to provide financial assistance to needy individuals who are studying Torah. The calendar has become the closest thing to an "official" calendar of Orthodox synagogues in the United States. Neither its Hebrew nor its English editions contain any reference to either Yom Ha'atzma'ut or Yom Yerushalayim. Lest it be argued that the reason lies solely in Orthodoxy's approach of maintaining the centuries-old synagogue traditions and not incorporating new ones, but has nothing to do with Orthodoxy's perspective on Israel, it should be noted that the *Ezras Torah Luach* does include reference to the *yahrzeit* of both Rabbi Eliyahu Henkin, founder of Ezras Torah, and Rabbi Moshe Feinstein, a former president of the society. Moreover, the calendar states that there is an "old custom" of having an appeal for Ezras Torah on Shabbat Shekalim (the Sabbath six weeks before Passover), and that it is forbidden to infringe on the custom of the society. This prohibition is stated in the same linguistic style as all of the other laws and customs included in that synagogue calendar. Obviously, then, at least when it comes to Ezras Torah itself, incorporating new rituals is not an issue.

7   See Charles. S. Liebman and Eliezer Don-Yehiya, Civil Religion in Israel: Traditional Judaism and Political Culture in the Jewish State (Berkeley, 1983), 123–166.

so modernized, American Orthodox Jews increasingly relate to it as a modern secular society to which, nevertheless, they attach strong allegiance because it is a state in which Jews are sovereign.[8]

In all, religious Zionist ideology that defines Israel in religious terms has lost influence, so much so that today most American Orthodox Jews no longer overtly conceive of Israel in ritualistic-religious terms. They remain strongly attached to Israel as the state of the Jewish people and therefore deserving of high communal priority, but the state per se is not part of the specifically religious realm.[9] In any event, even the traditional Orthodox can now openly express their attachment to Eretz Israel and the people of Israel without fear of being tainted by secular Zionism.

Founded in the nineteenth century by moderate traditionalists, Conservative Judaism appealed to large numbers of young immigrants, and later, children of immigrants, from Eastern Europe who found Orthodoxy too confining and inhibiting and Reform too lacking in tradition.[10] Given their strong ethnic self-definition and

8   Such an approach is somewhat similar to the religious Zionism espoused by Rabbi Jacob Reines, as opposed to the approach of Rabbi Abraham Isaac Kook. See Michael Zvi Nehorai, "Rav Reines and Rav Kook: Two Approaches to Zionism," in *The World of Rav Kook's Thought*, ed. Benjamin Ish-Shalom and Shalom Rosenberg, tr. Shalom Carmy and Bernard Casper (New York, 1991), 255–267.

9   For evidence that there is a correlation between religiosity and national Jewish identity and identification, see Simon N. Herman, *Israelis and Jews: The Continuity of an Identity* (New York, 1970); John E. Hofman, "Hazehut hayehudit shel no'ar yehudi beyisrael" (The Jewish identity of Jewish youth in Israel) *Megamot* 17(1) (January 1970): 5–14; and Rina Shapira and Eva Etzioni-Halevy, *Mi atah hastudent hayisraeli* (Who is the Israeli student?) (Tel Aviv, 1973). See also a series of surveys conducted in Israel in 1974 by Shlomit Levy and Louis E. Guttman, and published (in Hebrew) in Jerusalem during that year in four parts by the Israel Institute of Applied Social Research (part 4, *Values and Attitudes of Israeli High School Youth*, contains an English summary); Eva Etzioni-Halevy and Rina Shapira, "Jewish Identification of Israeli Students: What Lies Ahead," *Jewish Social Studies* 37(3–4) (July–October 1975): 251–266; Simon N. Herman, *Jewish Identity: A Social Psychological Perspective*, 2nd ed. (New Brunswick, N.J., 1989); and Eva Etzioni-Halevy and Rina Shapira, *Political Culture in Israel: Cleavage and Integration among Israeli Jews* (New York, 1977), 157–178.

10   See Marshall Sklare, *Conservative Judaism: An American Religious Movement*, aug. ed. (New York, 1972). For a Conservative ideological perspective, see

the fact that many of them were familiar with Zionist groups in Eastern Europe (even if they themselves had not been members), it was natural for many Conservative Jews to join the American Zionist movement that was beginning to take form. Here, too, they opted for the mainstream. Mizrachi was for the religious Zionists and Poalei Zion was for the socialists, but for the majority of recently arrived immigrants who were ethnic rather than ideological Zionists, the much less ideologically sophisticated General Zionism, embodied first in the Federation of American Zionists and later in the Zionist Organization of America, was the logical choice.

These tendencies were reinforced by the fact that the leaders of Conservative Judaism were virtually all self-proclaimed Zionists who defined Zionism as an integral part of Judaism. As Moshe Davis aptly put it,

> Zionism was an integral part of the program of thought and action which the Historical School developed in the closing decades of the past century and which it transmitted to the Conservative Movement. Conservative Judaism and Zionism developed separately, but their interaction was constant. As a result, both were stimulated conceptually and organization-ally.[11]

Given the deep interconnections between Conservative Judaism and American Zionism and the explicit definition of Zionism as integral to Judaism, it is not surprising that Conservative Judaism came to be seen as the most Zionist branch of American Judaism.[12] The depth of Conservative Jewry's Zionist commitment was apparent in its staunch support of the Zionist movement as well as the State of Israel.

Officially, it would appear that this commitment to Zionism and Israel remains unattenuated. Indeed, in *Emet Ve-Emunah*, its recent *Statement of Principles*, the movement's leadership extensively

---

Mordecai Waxman, ed., *Tradition and Change: The Development of Conservative Judaism* (New York, 1958).

11 Moshe Davis, *The Emergence of Conservative Judaism* (Philadelphia, 1963), 268.

12 Naomi W. Cohen, *American Jews and the Zionist Idea* (Hoboken, N.J., 1975), 10.

reiterates its deep — albeit not unequivocal — commitment to Zionism and Israel:

> This zealous attachment to *Eretz Yisrael* has persisted through-out our long history as a transnational people in which we transcended borders and lived in virtually every land. Wherever we were permitted, we viewed ourselves as natives or citizens of the country of our residence and were loyal to our host nation. Our religion has been land-centered but never land-bound; it has been a portable religion so that despite our long exile (*Galut*) from our spiritual homeland, we have been able to survive creatively and spiritually in the *tefutzot* (Diaspora)... We staunchly support the Zionist ideal... The Conservative movement is a member of the World Zionist Organization. We have undertaken major efforts in Israel... Increasing numbers of Conservative rabbis and laypersons have gone on *aliyah*, and we cherish and encourage *aliyah* to Israel as a value, goal, and *mitzvah*... Both the State of Israel and Diaspora Jewry have roles to fill; each can and must aid and enrich the other in every possible way; each needs the other. It is our fervent hope that Zion will indeed be the center of Torah, and Jerusalem a beacon lighting the way for the Jewish people and humanity.[13]

The fact that the statement does not endorse the classical Zionist notion of the centrality of Israel is neither surprising nor a devi-ation. Neither Conservative Judaism nor American Zionism has ever sincerely supported it.[14] More noteworthy is the fact that the statement goes on both to decry existing conditions in Israel and to distance the Conservative movement from Israeli government policies. For example, it emphasizes that "the Conservative move-ment has not always agreed with Israel's positions on domestic and foreign affairs."[15] If such statements are seen as representative of the movement as a whole, a certain subtle shift has in fact taken place among Conservative Jewry.[16]

---

13 *Emet Ve-Emunah: Statement of Principles of Conservative Judaism* (New York, 1988), 38–40.

14 Chaim I. Waxman, *American Aliya: Portrait of an Innovative Migration Move-ment* (Detroit, 1989), 65–76.

15 *Emet Ve-Emunah*, 38.

16 See Steven M. Cohen, *Ties and Tensions: The 1986 Survey of American Jewish*

Of the three major branches of American Judaism, it is unquestionably Reform Judaism that has made the most radical strides in coming to terms with Zionism and Israel, from the early antipathy of classical Reform to Zionism to the movement's acceptance of Israel's statehood on the eve of its creation.[17] It is true that some outposts of classical Reform opposition remained into the 1950s (as Sklare and Greenblum found in the "David Einhorn Temple" in "Lakeville"), but even there most of the community professed a sense of attachment and concern for the Jewish state.[18]

By the end of the 1960s, it was already hard to imagine that only a relatively short time earlier there had been such strong opposition to Zionism and Israel within the movement. In 1897, the Reform rabbinic body, the Central Conference of American Rabbis (CCAR), had issued a declaration stating: "We totally disapprove of any attempt for the establishment of a Jewish state. Such attempts show a misunderstanding of Israel's mission."[19] In 1917, in response to the Balfour Declaration, the CCAR had demurred:

> We do not subscribe to the phrase in the declaration which says, 'Palestine is to be a national home-land for the Jewish people.'... We are opposed to the idea that Palestine should be considered the home-land of the Jews.[20]

Only fifty years later, in June 1967, the CCAR declared its "solidarity with the State and the people of Israel. Their triumphs are our triumphs. Their ordeal is our ordeal. Their fate is our fate."[21] Some eight years later, in 1975, this new identification with Israel

---

Attitudes toward Israel and Israelis (New York, 1987), 18–21, in which he notes a growing percentage of low levels of attachment to Israel on the part of Conservative Jews.

17 A good analysis can be found in Howard R. Greenstein, *Turning Point: Zionism and Reform Judaism* (Chico, Calif., 1981).

18 Marshall Sklare and Joseph Greenblum, *Jewish Identity on the Suburban Frontier* (New York, 1967), 214–249.

19 W. Gunther Plaut, *The Growth of Reform Judaism: American and European Sources to 1948* (New York, 1965), 153.

20 Ibid., 154.

21 *Central Conference of American Rabbis Yearbook*, vol. 77 (New York, 1967), 109.

manifested itself officially in the inclusion of prayers for Israel's Independence Day, in the new Reform prayer book, *Gates of Prayer*.

By the 1980s, one could find one of the most prominent Reform theologians, in a book published by Reform Jewry's temple and synagogue organization, the Union of American Hebrew Congregations, affirming not only the significance of the State of Israel but also the value of *aliyah*, even if not as an imperative. Thus Eugene Borowitz suggests:

> The Covenant, being a collective endeavor, can best be lived as part of a self-governing Jewish community in the Land of Israel. A good Jew will seriously consider the possibility of *aliyah*, immigration.[22]

Impressive as all of these statements are, anyone familiar with the sociology of religion knows that one cannot draw any conclusions about people's beliefs from the statements of their religious functionaries, just as one cannot draw conclusions about what the citizens of a country believe from official pronouncements of their leaders. At best, the foregoing reflects the beliefs of the elite with respect to Israel. What about the folk — *amkha*, if you will?

At the outset, it may be stated conclusively that America's Jews are strongly pro-Israel. I have culled the empirical evidence for this and analyzed it elsewhere.[23] Indeed, that should come as no surprise given that the American people as a whole are largely pro-Israel.[24] What some may find surprising and others disturbing, however, is the evidence that there have been significant changes in the degree to which America's Jews are attached to Israel.

For the purposes of this paper, I present data on two groups, baby-boomers, that is, those born in the period 1946–1964, and middle-agers, those born in the years 1926–1944. The former group represents those currently ascending to dominance (the election of Bill Clinton as U.S. president was widely seen as symbolic of the

22   Eugene Borowitz, *Liberal Judaism* (New York, 1984), 135.
23   Chaim I. Waxman, "All in the Family: American Jewish Attachments to Israel," in *A New Jewry? American Jewry since World War II*, ed. Peter Y. Medding, *Studies in Contemporary Jewry* 8, (1992), 134–149.
24   See, for example, Peter Grose, *Israel in the Mind of America* (New York, 1984).

ascendancy of the "baby-boom" generation to dominance) while the middle-agers are the generation on its way out of dominance. From the 1990 National Jewish Population Survey (NJPS), I have selected all respondents who identified themselves as Jewish by religion. Those who, in 1990, were aged 26–44 are the baby-boomers, and those who were aged 46–64 are the middle-agers. Both samples were weighted, so they represent almost 1,700,000 Jewish baby-boomers and more than 830,000 Jewish middle-agers. What follows is an analysis of their responses to questions relating to Israel and then of their responses to related matters.

Table 1: Number of Times Been to Israel

	Ages 26–44	Ages 46–64
Once	12.8%	19.8%
Twice	4.8	5.0
Three times	1.9	1.5
4–9 times	3.3	3.2
10+ times	2.0	2.0
Born in Israel	1.4	0.3
Never	75.3	68.3
Total	100.0	100.0
Weighted N	1,692,550	836,080

Respondents were asked how many times they had been to Israel. When the responses of the two groups are compared, we see (Table 1) that a higher percentage of the baby-boomers (75.3%) than middle-agers (68.3%) were never in Israel. By itself, this may not be all that significant, since by the time the baby-boomers reach the middle-ager years they may have traveled to Israel at least as frequently as today's middle-agers. This seems a reasonable assumption because at least toward the end of the 46–64 years age period, children are usually

married and out of the house, allowing their parents greater time
and resources for travel, including travel to Israel.

However, the comparative responses with respect to emotional
attachment to Israel suggest that something more serious is involved.

Table 2: Emotional Attachment to Israel

	Ages 26–44	Ages 46–64
Not attached	24.2%	15.0%
Somewhat attached	47.0	38.0
Very attached	18.2	33.2
Extremely attached	10.6	13.7
Total	100.0	100.0
Weighted N	1,461,080	123,860

Table 2 indicates that American Jewish middle-agers are significantly
more emotionally attached to Israel than are the baby-boomers. A
higher percentage of the baby-boomers feels not attached, and lower
percentages feel either very or extremely attached to Israel.

Moreover, as Table 3 indicates, emotional attachment to Israel
varies considerably with denominational affiliation. Specifically,
Reform and unaffiliated Jews, who are the increasing majority of
America's Jews, have significantly weaker emotional ties to Israel
than do Conservative or Orthodox baby-boomers.

Table 3: Emotional Attachment to Israel of Jewish
Baby-Boomers, by Denomination

	Orth.	Cons.	Reform	Unaffil.
Not attached	8.1%	20.1%	24.2%	48.6%
Somewhat attached	18.5	41.4	58.8	44.2
Very attached	28.6	25.6	13.8	7.2
Extremely attached	44.8	12.9	3.3	—
Total	100.0	100.0	100.0	100.0
Weighted N	79,390	362,100	78,926	68,970

In brief, then, the mainstay of America's contemporary Jewish community has significantly weaker ties with Israel than their predecessors. This may be the reason for the apparent readiness of today's American Jews to consent to public criticism of Israel much more than were their predecessors. The Conservative movement's *Statement of Principles* is one striking example. And on the individual denominational level, Gerald Bubis and Steven Cohen, in a survey of American Jewish leaders, found widespread agreement with the statement, "Jews who are severely critical of Israel should nevertheless be allowed to speak in synagogues and Jewish Community Centers." Among the Orthodox, 42 percent of the rabbis and communal workers agreed; among the Conservative, 62 percent of the rabbis and 63 percent of the communal workers; and among the Reform, 82 percent of the rabbis and 74 percent of the communal workers.[25] Cohen also found widespread criticism of Israel among American Jewish leaders on a number of specific issues, including Israel's stance toward the PLO, the settlements on the West Bank, and the issue of "Who is a Jew?"[26] For example, a clear majority (59%) stated that the Arabs on the West Bank are being treated unfairly, and "As many as 77 percent affirmed that

25 Gerald B. Bubis and Steven M. Cohen, "What Are the Professional Leaders of American Jewry Thinking about Israel?" *Jerusalem Newsletter* 107 (15 March 1989): 6, Table 3.
26 Steven M. Cohen, *Israel-Diaspora Relations: A Survey of American Jewish Leaders* (Ramat-Aviv, 1990): 37, 48–59; Steven M. Cohen, *Ties and Tensions:*

they have privately criticized 'Israel's handling of the Palestinian uprising'."[27]

Of course one might argue that the Bubis and Cohen survey was conducted when Likud was in power, and American Jewish leaders' acceptance of public criticism of Israel was simply a manifestation of the general degree of discomfort that America's Jews had with the Likud. The political liberalism of American Jewry is well documented,[28] and it is thus understandable that the democratic, socialist tradition of the Labor party — even if not its present policies — is much more appealing than the assertive nationalism of Likud.

Be that as it may, comparative responses to other questions in the NJPS suggest that this does not quite explain the growing weakness of American Jewry's emotional attachment to Israel. The NJPS data reveal, for example, that Jewish baby-boomers are somewhat less likely to be active in American Jewish organizational life or even be members of American Jewish organizations. As can be seen in Table 4, slightly fewer baby-boomers volunteered for Jewish organizations during the previous year than did middle-agers.

Table 4: Volunteered for Jewish Organization in Past 12 Months

	Ages 26–44	Ages 46–64
Yes	21.7%	22.9%
No	78.3	77.1
Total	100.0	100.0
Weighted N	1,692,550	836,080

Here, too, there is a strong relationship between volunteering in

An Update — The 1989 Survey of American Jewish Attitudes toward Israel and Israelis (New York, 1989), 19–32, 47–52.

27   Cohen, Israel-Diaspora Relations, 67–70.

28   Chaim I. Waxman, America's Jews in Transition (Philadelphia, 1983), 147–151.

Jewish organizations and denominational affilation, as indicated in Table 5.

Table 5: Baby-Boomers, Who Volunteered for Jewish Organizations in Past 12 Months, by Denomination

	Orth.	Cons.	Reform	Unaffil.
Yes	69.5%	26.1%	16.3%	14.4%
No	30.5	73.9	83.6	85.6
Total	100.0	100.0	100.0	100.0
Weighted N	81,890	1,416,140	1,638,530	99,060

The difference in volunteering between the baby-boomers and the middle-agers might not in itself be thought very significant, given that percentage wise it is very small and that middle-agers usually have more time and resources and are thus better able to afford to be involved in volunteer organizational work.

However, as Table 6 indicates, a significantly higher percentage of baby-boomers belong to no Jewish organizations all. For a community that is known to be joiners to have such a high percentage of nonmembers starkly reinforces the distinction between the American Jewish population and the American Jewish community.[29] Even more, the significant decline in organizational membership appears to fit a pattern, of which the decline in emotional attachment to Israel is another component.

29   Waxman, *America's Jews in Transition*, 139–140.

Table 6: Number of Jewish Organizations Respondent Belongs To

	Ages 26–44	Ages 46–64
0	71.8%	63.5%
1	16.5	19.7
2 or more	11.5	16.8
Total	100.0	100.0
Weighted N	1,692,550	833,550

Since there has, historically, been a correlation between denomination and socioeconomic status among America's Jews, with the Reform being the highest and the Orthodox being the lowest, and since the more religiously traditional Jews pay a higher percentage of their incomes to synagogues and Jewish schools, one might have expected that a larger percentage of traditional Jews would belong to fewer organizations than less traditional Jews, or that there would be no relationship between denomination and number of Jewish organizations to which one belongs. Yet, as Table 7 indicates, the trend seen previously continues here as well.

Table 7: Boomers: Number of Jewish Organizations Respondent Belongs To, by Denomination

	Orth.	Cons.	Reform	Unaffil.
0	53.6%	68.1%	75.0%	83.5%
1	6.2	19.9	14.7	16.5
2 or more	40.3	12.0	10.3	—
Total	100.0	100.0	100.0	100.0
Weighted N	81,890	526,630	824,200	97,580

Lest it be assumed that the decline in affiliation among baby-boomers, as compared to middle-agers, is related only to secular Jewish organizations but not religious ones, Tables 5, 8 and 9 show the comparative rates of synagogue membership.

Table 8: Anyone in Household Currently Synagogue Member

	Ages 26–44	Ages 46–64
Yes	33.7	43.4
No	66.3	56.6
Total	100.0	100.0
Weighted N	917,180	416,710

Predictably, rates of synagogue membership vary denominationally, with Orthodox having the highest rates and unaffiliated having the lowest.

Table 9: Boomers: Anyone in Household Currently Synagogue Member (by Denomination)

	Orth.	Cons.	Reform	Unaffil.
Yes	76.2%	41.6%	28.3%	10.5%
No	23.8	58.4	71.7	89.5
Total	100.0	100.0	100.0	100.0
Weighted N	44,090	296,040	437,420	55,720

The lower rate of synagogue membership among baby-boomers is one more component in the emerging pattern. Similar differences are found when patterns of ritual observance are examined. Nor are those differences limited to the formal organizational sphere. They manifest themselves in friendship patterns. As can be seen in Table 10, a significantly lower percentage of baby boomers state that all or most of their closest friends are Jewish (33.9%) than do middle-agers, among whom more than half (50.9%) do.

Table 10: Closest Friends Who Are Jewish

	Ages 26–44	Ages 46–64
None Jewish	6.3%	5.2%
Few or some Jewish	60.2	43.6
Most Jewish	24.2	35.1
All Jewish	9.0	16.1
Total	100.0	100.0
Weighted N	1,686,000	831,000

Just as the trend of weaker identificational patterns among baby-boomers, as compared to middle-agers, persists, so too does the trend of a denominational relationship (Table 11). The one unusual manifestation in the denominational pattern is that a higher proportion of the Orthodox said that none of their closest friends are Jewish than did even the unaffiliated. The reason for this is puzzling; but in any case this deviant finding is a minor one. The overall trend remains clear.

Table 11: Boomers: Closest Friends Who Are Jewish, by Denomination

	Orth.	Cons.	Reform	Unaffil.
None	8.9%	5.2%	6.4%	7.7%
Few or some	9.7	55.1	70.2	68.2
Most	27.3	30.2	19.7	24.1
All	54.1	9.5	3.7	
Total	100.0	100.0	100.0	100.0
Weighted N	81,890	526,630	824,200	99,060

In sum, then, it appears that the phenomenon we are dealing with is rather pervasive and is indicative of a decline in both Jewish identity and Jewish identification. Despite the optimistic pronouncements of various "transformationist" social scientists during the 1980s, the NJPS data appear to confirm the deepest fears of the "assimilationists."[30] Although American Jewry as a distinctive group will almost unquestionably survive into the distant future, it seems at least as certain that the group that does survive will be a much reduced one. Nor should this be very surprising to anyone familiar with religious and ethnic group patterns in American society. The data presented indicate that although American Jewry is not about to disappear in the foreseeable future, it is undergoing a process similar to that which a number of researchers have found for American Catholics — namely, a significant decline in their attachment to the church and its doctrines; especially among the young, Catholic identity is increasingly a matter of personal choice entailing rather amorphous "feelings."[31]

30 Chaim I. Waxman, "Is the Cup Half-Full or Half-Empty? Perspectives on the Future of the American Jewish Community," in *American Pluralism and the Jewish Community*, ed. Seymour Martin Lipset (New Brunswick, N.J., 1990), 71–85.

31 See William D'Antonio, James Davidson, Dean Hoge, and Ruth Wallace, *American Catholic Laity in a Changing Church* (Kansas City, 1989); and Patrick H. McNamara, *Conscience First, Tradition Second: A Study of Young American Catholics* (Albany, 1992).

In terms of the ethnicity as well, the pattern of America's Jews does not appear to be unique. For example, Richard A. Alba found that Italian and other European-Americans are in "the twilight of ethnicity"; and the social significance of ethnicity is becoming increasingly irrelevant — that is, it has less and less significance in terms of socioeconomics, language and mate selection.[32] Interestingly, this seems to suggest that when the public ideology in America was the melting pot, the reality was cultural pluralism; and now that the ideology is cultural pluralism, the reality is the melting pot. The NJPS data seem to lend further support to Alba's conclusion:

> The general outlines of symbolic ethnicity offer a far better fit to the emerging nature of ethnic identity — essentially in the desire to retain a sense of being ethnic, but without any deep commitment to ethnic social ties or behaviors.[33]

Obviously, the findings presented above have very serious implications for the relationship between Israel and the American Jewish community. They do not mean that America's Jews will not continue to be pro-Israel. On the contrary, the available evidence suggests that they will continue to be generally supportive of Israel.[34] Americans in general are rather pro-Israel, and America's Jews will probably continue to be even more so. What is at issue here is the nature and intensity of that support. While non-Jewish Americans are pro-Israel,[35] Israel is hardly central to their concerns, much less to their identity. They do not, as a rule, lobby on behalf of Israel; nor

---

32   Richard D. Alba, *Ethnic Identity: The Transformation of White America* (New Haven, 1990). For an earlier theoretical statement of essentially the same thesis, see Herbert J. Gans, "Symbolic Ethnicity: The Future of Ethnic Groups and Culture in America," in *On the Making of Americans: Essays in Honor of David Riesman,* ed. Herbert J. Gans, Nathan Glazer, Joseph R. Gusfield, Christopher Jencks (Philadelphia, 1979), 193–220. About a decade ago, I questioned the validity of Gans's thesis: Waxman, *America's Jews in Transition* (Philadelphia, 1983), 228–236. The 1990 NJPS data indicate, however, that his analysis was right on target. See Chaim I. Waxman, *Jewish Baby Boomers* (Albany, forthcoming).

33   Alba, *Ethnic Identity,* 306.

34   See article in this volume by Steven M. Cohen, "Did American Jews Really Grow More Distant From Israel, 1983–1993? — A Reconsideration."

35   Grose, *Israel in the Mind of America.*

do they personally contribute to Israel-oriented causes. As American Jews continue to "melt" even as they espouse the ideology of cultural pluralism,[36] Israel will be an increasingly less significant part of their identity and they will become increasingly less emotionally attached to and involved with Israel.

One of the major consequences of the pattern of American Jewish identity and identification for the relationship with Israel will be a shift in the relative positions of the parties involved. Specifically, despite organizational rhetoric proclaiming the two communites either as one or as brothers with (implicitly) equal standing, America's Jews have traditionally thought of themselves as the dominant partner in the relationship. This assumption was frequently reinforced by propaganda from Israel that sought to enlist the support of America's Jews in a variety of activities in Israel's interests. Some of that changed, especially under Likud leadership; but even the most committed of America's Jews continue to think of themselves as Israel's "big brother." Although this places responsibilities on them to act in behalf of Israel, that activity, in turn, feeds their image of themselves as the dominant partner.

The sociological pattern of America's Jews is likely to bring that sense of dominance to a halt — for at least two interrelated reasons, one demographic and the other socio-psychological. Demographically, the decline of the American Jewish population as a result of identificational assimilation combined with the continued growth of the Israeli Jewish population will mean Israel becoming, in the foreseeable future, the world's largest Jewish population center. Simply in terms of size, it might be difficult for America's Jews to retain their self-image as dominant.[37]

36 Chaim I. Waxman "America's Jews: Ideology of Cultural Pluralism/Reality of Melting Pot." *Shofar: An Interdisciplinary Journal of Jewish Studies* 12(3) (Spring 1994): 66–79.

37 Of course, when I speak of America's Jews, I am speaking about the overwhelming majority. Those who are more religio-culturally traditional and/or have visited Israel, especially those who have visited more than once, are likely to remain strongly attached to Israel, perhaps even increasingly so, as Steven Cohen's paper suggests. It must, however, be remembered that about 75 percent of American Jewish baby-boomers have never been to Israel, and another 13 or so percent have been there only once.

However, as anyone familiar with dominant-minority relations knows, dominance is not dependent on size. There are a number of countries that have dominant minorities. In terms of the relationship between Israel and American Jewry, however, the leadership of the American Jewish community is becoming increasingly aware of its dependence on Israel for continuity. Thus at the 1992 General Assembly of the Council of Jewish Federations, there were loud calls for increased travel to and experiencing of Israel — not for Israel's sake but for the sake of the American Jewish community. When Charles Bronfman declared: "The Israel experience holds great promise for heightening awareness, strengthening identity and making a significant contribution to contemporary Jewish life, education and Jewish continuity,"[38] he was referring to *American* Jewish life and *American* Jewish continuity. Perhaps more than ever before, identified Jews — and they are the ones who are likely to be members of and active in the American Jewish community — realize that they *need* Israel. Whether, in the final analysis, Israel will have the ability to accomplish that which the American Jewish communal leadership hopes for, is another question. Several decades ago, Eugene Borowitz argued that it is preposterous to presume that American Jewry will be able to survive and thrive Jewishly solely by implanting an Israeli-based Jewishness in that community.[39] Whether an "Israel experience" can provide what a transplanted Israel-based Jewishness cannot is highly questionable. The denominational evidence presented suggests that "continuity" will be a reality when there is internalization of the UJA Federation slogan of more than a decade ago, "Survival means Sacrifice." The requisite sacrifice appears actually to be espoused by those with very firm and very self-conscious ideological commitments, rather than mere slogans and symbols. Whether, therefore, after all the rhetoric, there actually will be significant increases in those experiencing Israel is an additional important question. For the present, however, it is to that remedy that growing numbers of American Jewish leaders

38 Larry Yudelson, "CRB Foundation Launches Major Effort to Send Every Jewish Teen to Israel," *JTA Daily News Bulletin*, 17 November 1992.
39 Eugene Borowitz, *The Masks Jews Wear: The Self-Deceptions of American Jewry* (New York, 1973).

are looking. This should strengthen Israel in a number of ways, by making it less dependent on both the emotional and the material 'donations' of American Jewry.

There are, indeed, a number of indications that this is the way an increasing number of Israelis now view the Israel-American Jewry relationship. For example, one of the findings of a major study of Israeli Jews is of a shift, between 1975 and 1991, with a significant increase in the percentage who believe that Jews in the Diaspora need Israel for their survival, and a corresponding decrease in those who believe that Israel is dependent on the Jewish people world-wide for its survival.[40]

Another example is the assertion by Yossi Beilin, in his capacity as deputy foreign minister, to American Jewish leaders that Israel is a modern, growing society and no longer needs American Jewish charity.[41] Much as he might have been misunderstood, his statement was an expression of Israel's growing independence and assertion of its position as a full partner in its relationship with the Diaspora, even the American Jewish community.

One final factor that is likely to lead to an increased divide between Israel and American Jewry is the growing secularism and estrangement from tradition of the Israeli government. To the extent that the ideological secularism of many activists in Meretz, such as Shulamit Aloni and Yossi Sarid, comes to reflect the government and its policies, it is likely that the core of the American Jewish community will become increasingly alienated from Israel. As indicated above, it is the more religio-ethnically traditional who have the strongest ties to Israel; and, by definition, it is precisely that segment which is the most estranged from ideological secularism. Nor is there any evidence that such a shift will be successful in winning the

40 Shlomit Levy, Hanna Levinsohn, and Elihu Katz, *Beliefs, Observances and Social Interaction among Israeli Jews* (Jerusalem, 1993). Although this is clearly not the place for an elaborate discussion of this work, it should be noted that there are reasons to suspect that the general picture it conveys — namely, of a basic and deep-rooted amity and unity between the religious and secular segments of the Israeli population — is highly questionable, despite the empirical data presented by its authors.

41 *Long Island Jewish World*, 11–17 February 1994, 2.

CHAIM I. WAXMAN

deep emotional and material support of those who are now weakly
affiliated with Judaism, the Jewish community, and Israel.

Of course, it might be argued that such a development would be
a very positive one for Israel as it seeks its own national cultural
identity and destiny. Similar views were maintained by such thinkers
as Yehezkel Kaufman and Yaacov Klatzkin, among others. But those
are not the dominant views either in Israel or in the Diaspora today,
and they are certainly not the views of those who are concerned
about the future of the relationship between Israel and American
Jewry. For them, developments both within American Jewry and in
Israel should be cause for concern.

Finally, it should be noted that the relationship with Israel is
likely to be affected by shifts and patterns that now appear to
be occurring within American Orthodoxy. Specifically, American
Orthodoxy, and its religious Zionist sector in particular, appears to
have become much more reactionary-nationalist, especially vis-à-vis
the Territories (Judea, Samaria, and Gaza Strip/Gush Katif) and
the Palestinians. The developing trend, at least as evidenced by
statements published in the Orthodox weekly *Jewish Press*, raises the
specter of a major rift between that segment of American Orthodoxy
which has been the most actively pro-Israel and the government of
Israel. Should that rift grow, it will have a major impact both on
American Jewish-Israel relations and on the position of the Orthodox within the organized American Jewish community. Although
the Orthodox will continue to have the most extensive and intensive
ties with Israel, their break with the government and, much more
seriously, the encouragement of antigovernment activity, will serve
to isolate Orthodoxy from the rest of American Jewry. That, in turn,
may also have consequences for the Orthodox in Israel, especially,
for secular-Orthodox relations there. At the present juncture, one
can but speculate how all of this will eventually unfold.

Breaking the Taboo:
Critics of Israel and the American
Jewish Establishment

Jack Wertheimer

> What does the wicked child ask? "What does this ritual
> mean to you?" To "you" and not to "him." Since he takes
> himself out of the community and denies God's essential
> role in the Exodus, shock him by replying, "This is done
> because God did for *me* when I went out of mitzrayim."
> For *me* and not for *him*. Had he been there he would not
> have been redeemed.
>
> — Passover Haggadah

The vituperative struggle that surrounded the eventually successful
bid by Americans for Peace Now to join the Conference of Presidents
of Major American Jewish Organizations in late March of 1993,
brought to public attention once again a bitter, often vicious, battle
that had raged in the organized Jewish community of the United
States for two decades. Since the founding of Breira in 1973 and
continuing with the establishment of such groups as the New Jewish
Agenda and the New Israel Fund, as well as Americans for Peace
Now, the American Jewish community has been challenged to define
the limits of diversity and pluralism, by groups that have publicly
dissented from the official policy of the State of Israel and the
consensus of American Jewry's established leadership. Perhaps no
other set of issues has provoked such intemperate denunciations
and mudslinging in the American Jewish press and organizational
world; even the highly charged religious confrontations of recent
decades have paled by comparison. Opponents of these dissenting
groups have publicly cast them as traitors to the Jewish people,
collaborators with the enemies of Israel (constituting a branch of

"Jews for al-Fatah"), and a fifth column within the American Jewish community. Their defenders, in turn, have vilified the critics as "witch-hunters," "McCarthyists," and slanderers.

Decades from now, historians will assess the charges and counter-charges; perhaps with some historical perspective it will be possible to sort out the motives of the antagonists and evaluate their contentions. But even in the absence of such judgments, students of contemporary Jewry, and particularly those interested in the "tangled relations" between American and Israeli Jews, need to examine this conflict from a different perspective — namely, how has the organized American Jewish community responded to dissenters, and what do such responses tell us about the community and its relationship with the State of Israel? Which types of dissent are judged acceptable and which types place a group outside the tent![1] What sanctions does the contemporary Jewish community exercise to delegitimize a group? And what is the relationship between American Jewish and Israeli elites in this process of delegitimation?

The formation of Breira in 1973 raised a new set of issues for the organized American Jewish community, even though criticism of Zionism and Israel were not new to the American Jewish scene. In the past, anti-Zionist organizations such as the American Council for Judaism and the friends of Neturei Karta, rejected any identification with the State of Israel and at times vehemently criticized the policies of the Jewish state. Breira, however, represented a new phenomenon, one that resulted from the far-reaching Israeli conquests of 1967. According to its in-house, official history:

> The creation of Breira was an indication that its founders and members honestly believe that there can be an alternative to

---

1　In a different context, I plan to analyze the responses of American Jewish leaders to different types of dissenting groups. These groups include those on the right of the political spectrum, such as the Jewish Defense League, as well as groups that were highly critical of the Israeli government and the American Jewish leadership for their lack of militancy in rescuing beleaguered Jews — groups such as the American Association for Ethiopian Jews and the Union of Councils for Soviet Jews. Each of these groups collided with both Israeli and American Jewish leaders — and the dissent of each group was treated with considerable brutality.

the endless cycle of war and violence between Israel and the Arabs, and that American Jews committed to a strong Jewish state could actually encourage Israel to do more than it was doing to initiate peace talks. This meant in practice that Breira would break the "taboo" on public criticism of Israel within the American Jewish community. In particular, Breira gave American Jewry its first serious introduction to the "dovish" perspective on Israeli affairs...by hosting...prestigious Israeli advocates of mutual recognition of Israeli and Palestinian rights as the basis for Middle East peace negotiations.[2]

Indeed, in Breira's self-understanding, it differed from all other groups because it posed an internal challenge to the Jewish community. Precisely because it represented a movement of concerned Jews, including Zionists, it was "a child of the establishment, and [therefore],...caused a serious reevaluation of the future of Diaspora-Israel relations."[3]

Breira also raised the hackles of the organized Jewish community because it directly challenged the legitimacy of established organizations and leaders within the American Jewish community. Breira's commission on Jewish life, chaired by Arthur Waskow, defined the organization's goals within American Jewry as follows:

[To find a] means of freeing debate, especially through a newly independent Jewish press; new forms for doing tzedakah (fund-raising and allocation) that are both democratic and which serve the needs of those now ignored; ...the creation of a grass-roots based democratic structure for American Jewry[4]

By repeatedly charging the organized community with muzzling honest debate and by portraying itself as the true spokesman for grass-roots sentiment, Breira sought to delegitimize the official organizations and leaders of the organized community. Breira promised to democratize Jewish life by providing a forum for "those Jews who

2   *Proceedings of Breira's First Annual Membership Conference* (New York: Breira, 1977), 3.
3   "Factual and Other Errors in 'Why Breira?' by Joseph Shattan, *Commentary*, April 1977." Issued by Breira, unpaged, 1977.
4   *Breira Report*, June 1977, unpaged.

have not found a voice or place in existing structures (particularly youth, women, and the poor)."[5] To express further their displeasure with the established leadership, some Breira leaders urged that Jews withhold financial support from the official community to signal their protest. Arthur Waskow asked rhetorically: "Do we have a responsibility to oppose the giving of money or support through conventional channels, if that means adding to the political power of those presently in power who we feel are blindly marching toward the destruction of Israel?"[6]

The critique of Israeli policies, then, was intertwined with a rebellion against the leadership of American Jewry. Both Israeli and American Jewish leaders were misguided in their policies; the only recourse for concerned Jews was to alter the entire system of American Jewish support for Israel and the undemocratic system that produced such an inadequate American Jewish leadership. Breira's public pronouncements explicitly noted the entanglement of Israeli and American Jewish public life:

> This attitude of "my country right or wrong" was reflected in all areas of American Jewish life because Israel is the "glue" that holds the disparate elements of the community together, as well as the "cause" which unites separate and faltering fundraising efforts into an effective campaign. The lack of news and analysis in Jewish journalism, the one-dimensional level of Jewish education, the growth of the checkbook "mentality" as the basis of communal life, and the hierarchical and exclusive nature of Jewish organizational structures all mirrored an increasingly intolerable rigidity in Jewish affairs. Believing that

5 "An Open letter from Breira's Executive Board." undated (c. May 1976). From a historical perspective, we can gauge the shifts in the organized American Jewish community by noting that in the decades prior to the Holocaust it was the Zionist organizations that intertwined their ideology with a call for democratization; Zionism, they claimed, would revitalize the American Jewish community by bringing genuine democratic representation. By the last quarter of the century, it was the Zionist left and their non-Zionist allies that promoted democratization. By contrast, support for Israeli policies was now viewed as an expression of non-democratic process.

6 Quoted by Rael Isaac and Erich Isaac, "The Rabbis of Breira," *Midstream*, April 1977, 15.

Diaspora Jewry has more than a charitable stake in the future of the Jewish state, and more than an impersonal interest in the quality of Jewish life everywhere, this situation could not be ignored.[7]

Breira broadcast its dual critique of Israeli and American Jewish leaders through advertisements in the *New York Times* and the *New York Review of Books*, mailings to concerned Jews, public testimony to congressional committees, and press releases.[8]

In the winter and spring of 1977, a strong counterattack was launched against Breira's provocative challenge. The precipitating factor was a shift in outlook that took place at Breira's first national conference in Washington in February of that year. In the words of one activist, Breira "ceased to be merely a 'position pamphlet' organization and publicly defended its right to act on its principles by meeting with modedrate Palestinians."[9] At a time when the Israeli government rejected contacts with the PLO and insisted that the U.S. government keep the PLO at arm's length, it was a particularly brazen provocation for an American Jewish group to participate in such talks.[10]

The first — and most public — phase of the confrontation was waged on the printed page, in pamphlet and periodical literature. Spearheaded by writers associated with Americans for a Safe Israel, a group founded in 1971 to persuade American Jews to reject a "peace for territory" solution and only accept "peace for peace," the critics of Breira focused exclusively on the dangers the group posed to Israeli interests. Americans for a Safe Israel published a

7   *Proceedings of Breira's First Annual Membership Conference*, 4–5.
8   Elenore Lester, letter to the editor of the *Jewish Week* (New York), 1 May 1977, 1–2, in the files of the American Jewish Committee's Blaustein Library.
9   Carolyn Toll, "American Jews and the Middle East Dilemma," *Progressive*, August 1979, 33.
10   The entire matter came to public attention through a frontpage article by Bernard Gwertzman entitled "American Jewish Leaders Are Split over Issue of Meeting with the PLO," *New York Times*, 30 December 1976. Gwertzman reported on meetings in-Washington and New York between PLO representatives and ten American Jewish individuals. When the Conference of Presidents denounced such meetings, Breira defended contacts with the PLO and particularly the role of two of its prominent members in those meetings.

detailed pamphlet by Rael Jean Isaac entitled *Breira — Counsel for Judaism*, which linked some Breira members to pro-PLO groups and castigated Breira as more dangerous than the anti-Zionist American Council for Judaism, because even as they claim "to save Israel... they in fact facilitate her destruction."[11] Rael Isaac and her husband, Erich Isaac, continued the assault with a hard-hitting critique of "the rabbis of Breira" in *Midstream*, followed a month later by Joseph Shattan's "Why Breira?" in *Commentary*.[12] Around the same time, two former sympathizers published accounts of their growing disenchantment with Breira, particularly stressing the absence of genuine commitment to and empathy for Israel among Breira members.[13] When the *Village Voice* published an article on "the angry debate among American Jews," news of the Breira controversy reached an even broader audience.[14]

The public airing of this debate forced groups within the organized Jewish community to define a policy regarding the rights of its own members to dissent, thus opening a second level of controversy. As the employer of the largest contingent of rabbis associated with Breira, the B'nai B'rith Hillel Foundation was especially pressed to act. Rabbi Joseph Sternstein, president of the Zionist Organization of America, questioned the president of B'nai B'rith as to why "the most articulate spokesmen for the 'Palestinian' position were the Hillel rabbis"; and though he denied any intention to meddle in the internal affairs of B'nai B'rith, Sternstein justified his concern by noting that "many of these rabbis are in contact with the pliable minds of campus Jews."[15] Within the B'nai B'rith, as well, voices were raised urging the organization to discipline its employees. Benjamin Epstein, national director of the Anti-Defamation League, (ADL), called on the

11 Rael Jean Isaac, *Breira — Counsel for Judaism* (New York: Americans for a Safe Israel, 1977), 28.
12 *Midstream*, April 1977, 3–17; *Commentary*, April 1977, 60–66.
13 Lester, letter to *Jewish Week;* Alan Mintz, "The People's Choice — A Demurral on Breira," *Response*, Winter 1976–1977, 5–10.
14 Alexander Cockburn and James Ridgeway, "Doves, the Diaspora, and the Future of Israel: The Angry Debate among American Jews," *Village Voice*, 7 March 1977, 26.
15 Quoted by Cockburn and Ridgeway, "Doves," 26.

B'nai B'rith International [to] take such steps as are necessary to ensure that in matters of fundamental principle and policy of B'nai B'rith, members of the professional staff shall, in their pronouncements and activities refrain from promoting views contrary to those of B'nai B'rith.[16]

The president of the B'nai B'rith, David Blumberg, publicly rejected these demands; he cast aside the ADL recommendation as unnecessary and determined that "participation in Breira in no way violated B'nai B'rith policy." But these assurances failed to still the criticism emanating from local lodges within the organization and from outside groups such as the Zionist Organization of America, the Jewish Defense League, and even Hadassah.[17] Some of the critics demanded that the B'nai B'rith fire Hillel directors associated with Breira. Blumberg finally convened a "blue ribbon panel" to offer recommendations on the internal policy of B'nai B'rith regarding Breira. The panel upheld the rights of free expression of employees but recommended that they not hold office in Breira or use their identification with Hillel to endorse Breira policies or any other group's policies that were contrary to B'nai B'rith's position. Staff members were also warned that they were "expected to take into account the effects of conduct, including the expression of opinions that conflict with the objectives of B'nai B'rith and its maintenance and growth...and also weigh the effects of actions and speech...upon the fulfillment of the responsibilities of [a]...staff position.[18] It is unlikely that Hillel rabbis associated with Breira could have taken much comfort from such a broadly construed code of obligations.

Other Jewish organizations debated yet a third issue: How should they relate institutionally to Breira? Some organizations refused to send speakers to programs that also included Breira representatives.[19] Some agonized over whether they would be granting

16   Quoted in William Novak, "The Campaign against Breira," Part II, *Baltimore Jewish Times*, 1 April 1977, 24.
17   Novak, "The Campaign against Breira," 24–25.
18   Bernard Postal, "B'nai B'rith Rules on Breira: Right to Dissent Is Upheld, but Not to exploit Its Name," *Jewish American–American Examiner,* 11 September 1977.
19   This seems to have been the intention of the National Jewish Community Relations Advisory Council (NJCRAC), which urged all Jewish organizations

legitimacy to Breira if they elected individuals associated with the dissenting group to positions of influence within their own organizations.[20] And still others debated the wisdom of bringing Breira into the communal tent, a step that might provide some leverage to temper the group's provocative policies, or whether to treat Breira as an outcast and thereby make it serve as an object lesson to other dissident groups. Staff members at the American Jewish Committee issued an internal memorandum for the organization's Foreign Affairs Steering Committee that urged the former approach; it suggested the need to "be critical of some of Breira's positions and tactics" but also to recognize its effectiveness in bringing back into the community disaffected academics, intellectuals, and Jewish youth. The memo suggested that

> the best way to test whether or not Breira is prepared to become a truly responsible element within the diverse and multi-faceted Jewish community is to co-opt them into the community structure... One of the groundrules for such co-option might well be...that member agencies direct the exposition of their different views on sensitive Israel-Diaspora issues to the Jewish community itself and refrain from appealing to the general public.[21]

Here at last the fundamental question of communal legitimation and integration was posed explicitly: Should the umbrella organizations of American Jewry treat Breira and other dissenting groups as

---

to avoid participation in meetings with the PLO. Cockburn and Ridgeway, "Doves," 26. According to one report, Rabbi Arthur Hertzberg, then president of the American Jewish Congress, also eschewed participation in a program when he learned that two Breira representatives had been invited without his prior permission. Novak, "The Campaign against Breira," 25.

20   A slate of Breira sympathizers was defeated in elections held by the Conservative movement's Rabbinical Assembly. The RA also debated but ultimately tabled a resolution calling for American Jews — and their rabbis — "to exercise self-restraint in the criticism of Israel's policies on security, defense, borders and the ultimate components of peace." *JTA Daily News Bulletin*, 6 May 1977, 2.

21   George E. Gruen and Marc Brandriss, "Breira: A Background Memorandum," 13 April 1977, 20–21. In the American Jewish Committee's Blaustein Library.

pariahs or as potential constituents? According to the AJ Committee memo, the Jewish community council of New Haven had adopted the latter approach: it admitted the local Breira chapter on condition that Breira keep its criticism within the community. Other Jewish community councils took a more aggressive position and explicitly stigmatized Breira as beyond the pale. The council in Washington, D.C., for example deplored "the activities and policies of organizations which seek to divide and politicize American Jewish support for Israel" and urged its constituents to "advise and caution their members about Breira's activities which are injurious to Israel."[22] It appears that few Jewish umbrella organizations on either the local or national level were prepared to offer Breira their ultimate form of legitimation — admission as a constituent member.[23]

Within a year after the explosion of this controversy, Breira folded its operations.[24] Interestingly, Breira's most avid opponents and defenders agreed that Breira had fallen victim to a campaign aimed at its elimination. The Americans for a Safe Israel proudly claimed that its exposés had destroyed Breira.[25] For their part, Breira activists consistently interpreted the public controversy as an orchestrated smear campaign.

Defenders of Breira have accused Israeli consular officials of actively coordinating a campaign to discredit Breira. It is known that in several cities — notably, New York, Boston, and Philadelphia — Israeli consular officials called in Breira leaders and community officials to warn that Breira was "giving aid and comfort to the enemy."[26] Israel's prime minister, Yitzhak Rabin, pointedly observed to Jewish organizational leaders during a trip to the United

---

22   *JTA Daily News Bulletin*, 2 February 1977, 3.
23   The exceptions were the Jewish community councils of New Haven and San Francisco. Breira did not have enough chapters or members or a broad enough agenda to qualify for the larger umbrella organizations such as the Presidents' Conference or NJCRAC.
24   Paul M. Foer, "The War against Breira," *Jewish Spectator*, Summer 1983, 23. Foer claimed that the Washington chapter held on longest.
25   Joseph Prouder, *The New Israel Fund: A Fund for Israel's Enemies* (New York: Americans for a Safe Israel, 1990), 3.
26   William Novak, "The Breira Story," *Genesis 2* (March–April 1977): 10.

States that "there is no Breira."[27] But there is as yet no public evidence to substantiate the claims of Paul M. Foer that "there were high level meetings between Jewish leaders, and in some instances, the Israeli Ambassador, for planning anti-Breira strategy and to compare notes and dossiers."[28] As with so much else relating to the Breira affair, only the passage of time will provide us with the documentation and perspective to assess whether there was a coordinated campaign against Breira, as opposed to a more limited offensive by sympathizers with the Israeli right, and what role, if any, Israeli visitors in the United States might have played in such a campaign.

It is noteworthy that throughout the public controversy so little attention was paid to Breira's program to undermine the established Jewish community of the United States. Breira was cast as a group subversive to Israel. Its harsh critique of the organized American Jewish community, its program to democratize and rechannel Jewish life in the United States, its denigration of established leaders, were barely noted. The simplest explanation of course is that a group that never numbered more than 1,500 members posed no real threat to the large membership organizations, which counted their followers in the thousands and even hundreds of thousands. Indeed, had opponents of Breira highlighted its subversive intention within the American Jewish community, they would have found it far more difficult to drum up support against so puny an enemy.

An additional reason for this silence may stem from the generational dimension of the conflict. Breira was an outgrowth of the Jewish counterculture, an expression of "the sixties generation" — a generation that had been nurtured in Conservative and Reform summer camps, had found Jewish expression in the Havurah movement, and had been politicized in the struggle against the Vietnam War. Breira drew its rank and file from this rebellious generation, and its mentors from older rabbis and ideologues who sympathized

27 Quoted in Rael Isaac, "An Open Letter to William Novak," *Outpost*, no. 15 (April 1977): 7.
28 Foer, "The War against Breira," 22. Foer claimed to "have in my possession confidential documents from various Jewish organizations" to support his allegations. Until they are released and authenticated, such documents have no more validity than those purported by the late Senator Joseph McCarthy.

with the left. We may speculate that the emphasis placed by Breira's opponents on its subversion of a vulnerable Israel may have served as a convenient means to deflect attention from Breira's announced goal of toppling the established elders of American Jewry.

Be that as it may, it is clear that the leadership of American Jewry did not know how to react to their rebellious youth. Steven Shaw, then a professional with the Metrowest Federation, captured this generational component well in an anguished private appeal to Jewish leaders for understanding of the Breira phenomenon:

> Through its totally inappropriate response to the challenge posed by Breira, our national organizations (with one notable exception — the American Jewish Committee) ...have again proven that many of our constituent bodies have little understanding of a whole generation of young Jews and even less relevance to their concerns and life styles.... Rather than condemnation and hysteria and threats of job loss (presently directed at some of the best Hillel staff), I would expect that a more mature and healthy Jewish community would welcome the intellectual stimulation and youthfully refreshing energy that such individuals could provide for the wider Jewish polity. That this has not exactly been the case bears sad witness to the state of Jewish organizational life in the diaspora and to the potential for misunderstandings that exist between Israel and America through inadequate Israeli organizational structures which seem incapable of dealing creatively or intelligently with such forces.[29]

Shaw's analysis points to an important consequence of the tangled relations between Israeli and American Jewish leaders — an intensification of generational conflict in the organized American Jewish community because of the disparate experiences of younger Israeli and American Jews during the sixties and seventies. Israeli officials may have responded so harshly because they had little experience with, let alone empathy for, "the sixties generation."

29   Memo by Steven Shaw to Albert Chernin, executive vice chairman of NJCRAC, 2 March 1977, 3–4. In the American Jewish Committee's Blaustein Library.

The Breira controversy represented the most heated confrontation in a series of debates within the organized Jewish community over the proper handling of dissenting groups. Three other organizations situated on the left of the political spectrum, which share much of Breira's criticism of Israeli policies and the Jewish establishment, have sparked more recent debates within the Jewish community. The New Jewish Agenda, the New Israel Fund, and Americans for Peace Now have each in turn forced the organized Jewish community to define the parameters of dissent. But each was treated differently within the institutional structure of American Jewry.[30]

The New Jewish Agenda was founded in May 1979, approximately one year after the demise of Breira, by "disaffected members of Jewish organizations, refugees from the non-Jewish left, and former members of Breira."[31] From it inception, the New Jewish Agenda incorporated the vocabulary and rituals of Judaism, as well as those of the political left. Thus at its founding national conference, time was set aside for Jewish study, worship, and cultural expression. The Sabbath was particularly moving to many participants because of "the potential breakthrough in the combination of intense emotional ties to the various Jewish traditions, with no compromising of political and moral ideals."[32] Agenda (as it was called by insiders) explicitly endorsed a program to draw on Jewish traditions in the formulation of its programs.[33]

Agenda's statement of purpose outlined an ambitious and far-reaching program:

> We are Jews concerned with the retreat from social action

---

30 By combining the discussion of these three organizations, this essay does not intend to suggest that they are interchangeable. On the contrary, it will be seen that each group has fared differently precisely because its unique program and behavior raised a different set of issues. They are discussed in tandem because they all framed a critique, from the left of the political spectrum, of Israel's policies regarding peace with its neighbors.

31 On the founding of the New Jewish Agenda and its first national conference, see Ellen Willis, "Radical Jews Caught in the Middle," *Village Voice*, 4–10 February 1981, 1ff.

32 Gerry Serotta, "What's New about the New Jewish Agenda," *New Outlook*, June 1981, 41.

33 Ibid., 42.

concerns and openness to discussion within the organized Jewish community. As Jews who believe strongly that authentic Jewish life must involve serious and consistent attention to the just ordering of human society and the natural resources of our world (*tikun olam*), we seek to apply Jewish values to such questions as economic justice, ecological concerns, energy policy, world hunger, intergroup relations and affirmative action, women's rights, peace in the Middle East, and Jewish education.[34]

In promoting this program, Agenda activists harked back to "the old agenda of American Jews: Jews used to be concerned with social issues and justice. In the last 20 years, the Jewish community has become extremely self-oriented. The more self-oriented it has become, the more self-defeating it has become."[35] The goal was to reorient the Jewish community and set it back on its former course.

In November 1982, Agenda issued a detailed platform outlining the specific ways in which this would be accomplished. Interestingly, the platform first discussed "Jewish communal life in the United States" before turning to foreign affairs. Agenda criticized "the existing network of Jewish communal institutions" for succeeding only partially. It called for "the transformation of Jewish institutions and the creation of new ones to represent the whole spectrum of views of U.S. Jewry." Highest on its list of demands was

the full empowerment of all Jews. Our communal institutions must involve those whose needs have been consistently disregarded: our elders, Jews with disabilities, the poor, Lesbians and Gay Men, Jews not living in nuclear families, Jews of color, Jews by choice, those of mixed marriages, and recent immigrants.[36]

According to Agenda's most visible leader, Rabbi Gerold Serotta,

34 Quoted in Hillel Schenker, "The New Jewish Agenda," *New Outlook*, November — December 1980, 49.
35 Arthur J. Magida, "Radical Gadflies," *Baltimore Jewish Times*, 3 August 1984, 34.
36 "New Jewish Agenda National Platform," 1–2. In the American Jewish Committee's Blaustein Library.

the organization's goal was to serve as "a loyal opposition in the Jewish community."[37]

Arguing that all Jews are responsible for one another, Agenda also offered specific "principles of peace" in the Middle East. It called for mutual recognition by Israel, the Arab states, and the PLO. It urged a cessation of Jewish settlement activities in the West Bank and Gaza. And it called for Israeli recognition of "the right of Palestinians to national self-determination, including the right to the establishment, if they so choose, of an independent and viable Palestinian state in the West Bank and Gaza, existing in peace with Israel."[38] These views, of course, were far removed from the existing policies of Israel's Likud government. Particularly provocative was the repeated assertion by Agenda that meetings must be held with the PLO — this in the era immediately after the U.S. ambassador to the United Nations was forced to resign because of his secret contacts with the PLO.

Agenda evoked much the same response from more conservative Jews as did Breira. Rael Jean Isaac weighed in once again with a scathing pamphlet entitled, "The New/Anti Jewish Agenda"; and once again she traced the pedigree and dangerous fellow travelers of a left-wing Jewish group. Isaac counseled the organized community to shun Agenda: "The Jewish community," she argued,

> cannot prevent the development of groups like the New Jewish Agenda. Agenda itself is an outgrowth of the very similar Breira, which rose to brief prominence in the 1970s.... The reappearance of Breira in the shape of the New Jewish Agenda suggests that a group of this sort, under whatever name, is likely to persist. What the Jewish community can do is to isolate a group that is outside the consensus.... It isolated Breira, which died as a result of the internal dissension that isolation precipitated.[39]

But despite the attacks in the Jewish press, Agenda did not suffer

---

37   Rael Jean Isaac, "New Jewish Agenda — Outside the Consensus," *Midstream*, December 1990, 19.

38   *New Jewish Agenda National Platform* (adopted 28 November 1982), 6.

39   Isaac, "Outside the Consensus," 19.

the fate of Breira. Members were not as besieged as their Breira predecessors; their jobs apparently were not on the line. And they were not roundly attacked or ostracized, as Breira activists had been. In fact, Agenda scored some impressive victories in gaining an entrée into local umbrella agencies. Agenda chapters in Kansas City, New Haven, Ann Arbor, and Santa Fe won admission into local Jewish councils or Jewish federations. In July 1984, the Los Angeles chapter of Agenda was voted into the Jewish Federation Council of Greater Los Angeles, thereby scoring a coup in Agenda's struggle for communal legitimation.[40]

In contrast, the most bitter defeat came when the local Jewish council in Washington, D.C., overturned the recommendation of its own executive board and denied Agenda a place. The chairman of the ZOA's local chapter led the opposition, declaring: "We feel a group like this is not within the mainstream of thinking of the Jewish community.... They don't fall within the kind of thinking that is current in the Jewish community." He charged the New Jewish Agenda with being "pro-Arab rather than pro-Israel" and therefore "so far out we feel they really don't deserve [membership]." Moe Rodenstein expressed his chapter's disappointment, contending:

> We'd like to be part of the debate...to say we are Jews; we're proud of what we're doing.... It's also important for us to work with a wide variety of issues...to try to push the Jewish community to concern with other issues than Israel and anti-Semitism."[41]

The New Jewish Agenda worked to carve out a place for itself in the organized Jewish community by cooperating in larger ventures. It formed a task force to involve itself in the Soviet Jewry movement.[42] At the request of the Reform movement, Agenda activists worked behind the scenes to keep the issue of the Middle East off the agenda of a major civil rights march on Washington in 1983.[43]

40   *JTA Daily News Bulletin*, 24 July 1984, p. 2.
41   "Jewish Council Excludes New Group over Views on Rights of Palestinians," *Washington Post*, 4 June 1983, B4.
42   J. J. Goldberg, "The Graying of New Jewish Agenda," *Jewish Week*, 21 August 1987, 25.
43   Ibid.

And it participated in elections for U.S. delegates to the World Zionist Congress by joining forces with Americans for a Progressive Israel and Israel's Citizens Rights party.[44] The latter effort further enhanced Agenda's stature as a Zionist group.

When it folded its operations in 1992, the New Jewish Agenda could point to a record of legitimation by the umbrella organizations of local communities far beyond anything achieved by Breira. Undoubtedly, it won such legitimation in part because of the greater receptivity of American Jewry to Agenda's message regarding a solution in the Middle East. But it also showed a far greater willingness than Breira to participate in the life of the Jewish community. From its inception, Agenda employed a Jewish vocabulary. Its leaders determined early on that their message would receive a far wider hearing if Agenda joined the Jewish community. Hence, it sought to balance its self-declared role as the "alternative" to the "established" Jewish community with a deliberate program of seeking inclusion within the structure of that establishment.[45]

The New Israel Fund founded in 1979 has provided still another outlet for Jews on the left who are critical of Israeli policies. Unlike Breira and Agenda, which served as critics of Israel and the American Jewish establishment, the New Israel Fund has devoted its energies to disbursing funds in Israel to groups that embody its vision of what is needed in Israeli society. By serving as a conduit of funds, the New Israel Fund enables American Jews to strengthen those sectors of Israeli society that foster the civil rights of Israeli Jews and Arabs, ameliorate the suffering of abused women and children and victims of discrimination, and work toward Arab-Jewish reconciliation. The goal, according to David Arnow, the Fund's American chairman, is to reshape Israeli society: "Our concept of philanthropy for Israel must be broadened to include not only *tzedakah*, providing concrete needs and services, but also *tikun*, the healing, mending and transformation of a suffering society."[46] Here, then, is another

---

44   Isaac, "Outside the Consensus," 18.
45   Kevin Freeman, "New Jewish Agenda to Seek Communal Status," *JTA Daily News Bulletin*, 29 June 1983, 2.
46   Marvin Schick, "New Israel Fund Pours Leftist Salt on Jewish Wound," *Long Island Jewish World*, 19–25 December 1986, 6.

aspect of the tangled relationship — an American Jewish group that takes it upon itself to reshape Israel by supporting groups that conform to its own image.

In virtually all of its public pronouncements, the New Israel Fund justifies its work on the basis of Israel's Declaration of Independence. Israel, it proclaims, must be true to its founders' original dream: "To be a state based on freedom, justice, and peace envisaged by the prophets of Israel"; to be a state that will "ensure complete equality of social and political rights to all its inhabitants irrespective of religion, race, or sex."[47] Thus the Fund legitimizes itself on the basis of Israel's self-declared ideals. American Jews need to serve as guardians of the true Israel: "The fight to preserve the founding vision of Israel has been raging and has finally shaken the American Jewish community," claims Arnow. "Today we stand at the head of a movement to build the kind of Israel we too long took for granted."[48]

The Fund also invokes Jewish tradition and American democratic values to justify its programs. Its publications hark back to the prophets of Israel and then intertwine Jewish traditions with American values:

> In our view, the values of democracy are not merely consonant with Jewish values; they are inseparable from them. In our view, they are not merely afterthoughts to the basic question of Israel's safety; they are part and parcel of that question.[49]

The Fund's president, Mary Ann Stein, conflates three sets of ideals in her description of her group: "We seek what we view as traditional Jewish values; the values of pluralism, tolerance, and equality for all citizens, adopted in Israel's Declaration of Independence, remain promises — just as in the United States they are promises."[50] This approach is then touted as the best means to protect Israel and

---

47   Letter to the editor defending the New Israel Fund against attack by Americans for a Safe Israel, *Jewish Week*, 21 September 1990, 28, 46.

48   *JTA Daily News Bulletin*, 3 July 1992, 4.

49   From the New Israel Fund's *Guide to the Issues, Grantees, and Programs*, 1991, ii.

50   "The New Israel Fund at Ten: An Interview with NIF President Mary Ann Stein," *New Outlook*, March 1990, 42.

strengthen its ties with America. Karen Friedman, media director for the New Israel Fund, contends that with the end of the Cold War, America no longer needs Israel as it once did. "The only thing that the two countries have in common are shared values."[51] Therefore, by supporting organizations that foster democracy, tolerance, and pluralism, the Fund is promoting the best in Jewish and American traditions and binding Israel and America more closely.

The Fund's religious and democratic rhetoric has not spared it the kinds of attack leveled by the right against left-wing critics of Israel. Americans for a Safe Israel once again issued a pamphlet denouncing its left-wing opponents. The author approvingly quoted Ze'ev Chafets's quip that the NIF people wish to transform Israel into a state that will "meet the approval of the ACLU, *The Nation* magazine, and the Sierra Club."[52] More ominously, the pamphlet charges that the NIF "serves to provide the financial muscle to a handful of Israel extremists who, lacking the electoral mandate to radically transform the Jewish State, seek a constituency in New York and Berkeley that they cannot muster in Tel Aviv and Jerusalem."[53] According to this reading, the Fund subverts rather than encourages Israel's democratic process, because it favors extremist groups that have no support in Israel. Another critic of the Fund has charged that the group is "a virtual Who's Who of Israel's American Jewish critics."[54] The Fund is even more dangerous than earlier left-wing groups because it

> actively sponsors those forces that seek to do to Israel from within what Breira and the Americans for Peace Now have sought to do from without. Whereas the political efforts of Jewish doves in the Diaspora have generally had little impact beyond occasional public-relations splashes, the New Israel

51   Alexandra Wall, "The New Israel Fund Comes of Age," *JTA Daily News Bulletin*, 3 July 1992, 4.
52   Joseph Puder, *The New Israel Fund: A New Fund for Israel's Enemies* (New York: Americans for a Safe Israel, 1990), 30.
53   Ibid.
54   Rafael Medoff "The New Israel Fund — For Whom?" *Midstream*, May 1986, 15.

Fund applies a form of subtle financial pressure within Israel that is far more likely to have longlasting effects.[55]

Despite these attacks, the New Israel Fund has flourished; its allocations have steadily increased, from $80,000 in 1980 to over $8 million in 1992.[56] Moreover, it has been publicly defended by leading members of the American Jewish establishment. In response to attacks by Americans for a Safe Israel, a public letter of support was issued in 1990 defending the legitimacy and Zionist credentials of the New Israel Fund. It was signed by past chairs of the Council of Jewish Federations, the National Jewish Community Relations Advisory Council, the United Jewish Appeal, and the heads of all the non-Orthodox rabbinical seminaries.[57]

The New Israel Fund won such legitimation by virtue of its close ties with Israeli institutions and the strong credentials of it supporters as Zionists and workers within the established American Jewish community. When Jerusalem's mayor, Teddy Kollek, publicly endorsed the work of the New Israel Fund and its contribution to Israeli society,[58] it became far harder to delegitimize the Fund. Moreover, defenders of the Fund could claim that "among the people explicitly smeared [by opponents of the Fund] are many who hold positions of enormous responsibility in the most important (and, for that matter, the most mainstream) organizations in American Jewish life."[59] Even the incoming executive of the national United Jewish Appeal viewed the Fund as a constructive force.[60] By working directly with Israeli clients and reaching out to established Jewish communal officials, the Fund has been remarkably successful in blunting its critics' efforts to delegitimize its work.

Indeed, for the first time, right-wing critics were thrown on the defensive by communal officials who pointed out to the Americans

---

55 Ibid.
56 Alexandra Wall, *JTA Daily News Bulletin*, 3 July 1992, 4.
57 *Jewish Week*, 21 September 1990, 28, 46. Although the president of Yeshiva University did not sign the letter, two other leaders of modern Orthodoxy — Emanuel Rackman and Irving Greenberg — did lend their names.
58 Letter to the *Jewish Week*, 21 September 1990, 32.
59 *Jewish Week*, 21 September 1990, 28, 46.
60 Robert Greenberger, "Growing Pains: The New Israel Fund," *Baltimore Jewish Times*, 27 December 1991, 54ff.

for a Safe Israel that it had no right "to call into question the devotion to Israel of those with whom it disagrees."[61] Defenders of the Fund impugned such critics as the Americans for a Safe Israel, asking: "Is it not curious that while Israelis...welcome the Fund and choose to participate in its work, a fringe American organization seeks to damage it?" Thus by working with Israelis, the Fund legitimated itself in the eyes of American Jewish leaders, and right-wing critics were relegated to the periphery by virtue of *their* overstepping the bounds, by their disrespect for pluralism.[62] As we shall see, the organized Jewish community was gradually crystallizing a set of guidelines for dissent that took into account the values of pluralism and democracy.

It is within this context that the admission of Americans for Peace Now (APN) into the Conference of Presidents of Major American Jewish Organizations must be placed. Opponents argued against admission on the grounds that it supported the PLO and tilted too far to the pro-Arab position. In addition, questions were raised about the wisdom of including a group that might paralyze deliberations within the umbrella organization by failing to submerge its organizational views so as to permit the conference to speak out on behalf of the community. (According to Presidents' Conference rules, a dissenting member may prevent the conference from taking public stands with which it disagrees.)[63] But ultimately these concerns were overridden by the compelling case put forward by those favoring admission, which were twofold: (1) How could the American Jewish community refuse to grant legitimacy to a group that had members serving in the cabinet of Yitzhak Rabin? (2) How could the Presidents' Conference work with the new Clinton administration, which had

---

61   *Jewish Week,* 21 September 1990, 28, 46.

62   Andrew S. Carroll, "A Call for Civility," *Washington Jewish Week,* 9 August 1990, 15ff.

63   Seymour Reich, quoted in *Forward,* 26 March 1993, 16. In this newspaper report the claim is made that Americans for Peace Now had pledged to Lester Pollack, chairman of the Conference, its intention to work within the consensus spirit of the Presidents' Conference. Henry Siegman of the American Jewish Congress rejected the need for the APN or any other new member to accept and abide by the consensus position in advance: "It is the Presidents' *Conference* that must uphold its consensus, not the individual constituent members."

placed several prominent supporters of Americans for Peace Now in high government positions, if it refused to work with APN?[64]

There is no single reason for the metamorphosis in the policies of the national umbrella agencies of American Jewry. But clearly, the tent has been expanded in the two decades since the founding of Breira, and the organized community has refined its views of pluralism and dissent. Among the major umbrella agencies, it appears that only the National Jewish Community Relations Advisory Council grappled openly with the issue of dissent. Already in the early 1970s, NJCRAC had to decide whether the Jewish Defense League should come under the communal umbrella of local Jewish councils. (It formally rejected the JDL in 1975.) As we have seen, the New Jewish Agenda formally applied for membership in local councils in the early 1980s. It was in this context that the chairman of NJCRAC, Bennet Yanowitz, devoted his keynote address to "Democracy and Discipline in the American Jewish Community — The Utility and Morality of Unity." Yanowitz strove to balance the conflicting needs for "unity, discipline, honesty, freedom and purposefulness." He defended the rights of dissenters — as long as they kept their dissent "within the tent or within the family." He objected strenuously to dissenters who insist not only on a hearing but also that their views become policy. He berated Israeli leaders for not always listening and for impugning the motives of critics. And he simultaneously called for "maintaining and strengthening those channels of free debate and free expression within the family...[to] reaffirm the concept of *kelal Yisrael.*"[65]

In the years that followed, NJCRAC struggled to define operationally what all this meant, and in October 1989 its executive board adopted "Guidelines for Participating in Jewish Community Events and Decision-Making."[66] The guidelines pose the critical questions:

---

64 David Twersky, "Welcome to Washington: Now, Peace Now," *Forward*, 19 February 1993, 6; Leonard Fein, "American Zealots," *Forward*, 5 March 1993, 7.

65 Chairman's Address, Plenary Session, NJCRAC, Cleveland, Ohio, 15 February 1983, 20–24.

66 I am grateful to Jerome Chanes of NJCRAC for bringing these guidelines to my attention.

Are Jewish communal instrumentalities that undertake community-wide groups events obliged to provide an opportunity for participation to any Jewish group that so wishes?... Are the central bodies of the Jewish community, national and local, which are representative in nature, obliged to permit any organization to participate in their decision-making process?

The paper sets forth four central commitments of the Jewish community that must be considered when answering these questions:

1. To a free, open, and pluralistic society
2. To the survival and security of the State of Israel
3. To *kelal Yisrael*, the integrity of Jewish peoplehood and the interlocking relationships of the community of Israel.
4. To the creative survival and continuity of Jewish life in America.

It then goes on to suggest that groups seeking to participate in community-wide events, seeking public platforms, or seeking participation in decision making should be included provided they are not "fundamentally anti-Semitic, anti-Israel, anti-Zionist, or anti-democratic." In short, NJCRAC, as one of the major umbrella agencies of American Jewry, has in principle come some distance in its willingness to bring Jewish groups under its tent.

The heated, often rancorous, debates precipitated by the appearance of groups critical of Israeli policies thus forced the organized Jewish community to take stock and rethink questions of pluralism. Contrary to the protestations of these groups that they could not receive a fair hearing, it was precisely their far-reaching criticisms of the American Jewish establishment, as well as their challenges to Israeli policies, that drew widespread attention in the American Jewish community. Indeed, they were accorded far more attention than their minuscule membership figures warranted.

Gradually, the consensus of the Jewish community regarding such groups has changed. In part, this is the case because American Jewish leaders have become less monolithic in their approach to the Israeli-Arab conflict.[67] But the dynamic of the American Jewish

---

67   See, for example, Steven M. Cohen, *Israel-Diaspora Relations: A Survey of American Jewish Leaders*, Report No. 8. (Tel Aviv: Israel Diaspora Institute, 1990).

community has also worked to encourage the expression of dissent: a voluntaristic community must find ways to accommodate diversity of viewpoints, lest *it* be marginalized. As Leonard Fein wrote during the debate over the admission of Americans for Peace Now, "The Conference of Presidents has one resource, and one only: It claims to speak on behalf of organized American Jewry."[68] The legitimacy of the umbrella organization is on the line if it cannot formulate a coherent position on dissent.

As for the particular organizations examined here, it is hardly coincidental that their treatment by the organized community was linked to their behavior. The more these groups allied themselves with Israeli groups, the stronger was their claim to legitimacy. Certainly, we see dramatic evidence of the "tangled relations" when legitimacy within the organized Jewish community is earned by a dissenting group when it links up with Israeli counterparts. These same groups have also moved from a confrontational stance vis à vis the organized American Jewish community to one in which they have allowed themselves to be coopted for some tasks. They included themselves in the collective of *kelal Yisrael* and thereby won legitimacy.

68   Leonard Fein, "American Zealots," *Forward*, 5 March 1993, 7.

List of Contributors

Walter Ackerman — Shane Family Professor of Education, Emeritus, Department of Education, Ben-Gurion University of the Negev

Jerold S. Auerbach — Professor of History, Wellesley College

Michael Brown — Director, Centre for Jewish Studies, York University

Naomi W. Cohen — Professor of History, Emeritus, Hunter College, CUNY, and The Jewish Theological Seminary of America

Steven M. Cohen — Associate Professor, Melton Centre for Jewish Education in the Diaspora, The Hebrew University of Jerusalem

David Ellenson — I. H. and Anna Grancell Professor of Jewish Religious Thought, Hebrew Union College — Jewish Institute of Religion, Los Angeles

Sylvia Barack-Fishman — Assistant Professor of Contemporary Jewish Life/ Sociology of American Jews, Near Eastern and Judaic Studies Department, Brandeis University

Allon Gal — Professor, Ben-Gurion Research Center and the Department of History; Director, The Center for the Study of North

American Jewry, Ben-Gurion University of the Negev

Arthur Aryeh Goren — Russell Knapp Professor of American Jewish History, Columbia University

Menahem Kaufman — Ph.D., Senior Scholar of America-Holy Land Studies, ICJ, The Hebrew University of Jerusalem

Deborah Dash Moore — Professor of Religion, Department of Religion, Vassar College

Jonathan D. Sarna — Braun Professor of American Jewish History, Brandeis University

Stephen Sharot — Professor, Department of Behavioral Sciences, Ben-Gurion University of the Negev

S. Ilan Troen — Sam and Anna Lopin Professor of Modern History, Ben-Gurion University of the Negev

Chaim I. Waxman — Professor, Department of Sociology, Rutgers University.

Jack Wertheimer — Professor of American Jewish History, The Jewish Theological Seminary of America

Stephen J. Whitfield — Professor of American Studies, Brandeis University

Nurit Zaidman — Post-doctorate, Department of Behavioral Sciences, Ben-Gurion University of the Negev

Glossary

Agudat Israel (Association of Israel), Orthodox religious party, founded in 1912, which opposed Zionism as the solution to the Jewish problem.

aliyah, Jewish immigration to Eretz Israel; one of the waves of Jewish immigration to Eretz Israel from the early 1880s.

Amidah (standing), the core of each of the prescribed Jewish daily services.

amkha, Heb. and Yid., the common folk.

Aron ha-Kodesh, the Holy Ark.

Ashkenazi, pl. Ashkenazim, West-, Central, or East-European Jew(s), as contrasted with Sephardi(m).

Bet din, rabbinic court of law.

Bet ha-Mikdash, the Temple, in ancient times, the central building for the worship of God in Israel.

DPs, "Displaced Persons", people driven from home as a result of Nazism and World War II; the Jewish DPs universally presented the problem of Jewish statelessness.

dunam, a unit of land measurement, equivalent to 1,000 square meters, c. 1/4 acre.

The Emek (The Valley), the Valley of Jezreel.

Eretz Israel (*Eretz Yisrael*), Land of Israel, Palestine.

fellah, Arab., peasant.

galut (exile), the condition of the Jewish people in dispersion, cf. *tefutzah*

Gedud ha-Avodah (Labor Battalion), pioneering group active in Palestine during the 1920s whose long-range aim was to transform the workers of Palestine into one great commune open to all.

hachsharah (preparation), organized training in the Diaspora of pioneers for cooperative agricultural settlement in Eretz Israel.

Haganah (Defense), the underground military organization of the *yishuv* in Eretz Israel under the British Mandate, which eventually became the basis for the Israel Defense Forces.

Haham, title of rabbi of Sephardi congregation.

halutz, pl. *halutzim*, pioneer(s), especially in agriculture, in the Land of Israel.

halutziut, pioneering.

haredi, of the ultra-Orthodox community.

Ha-Shomer (The Watchman), self-defense organization of Jewish pioneers of the Second Aliyah, established in 1909.

Hasid, an adherent of Hasidism, a religious movement founded in Eastern Europe in the 18th century.

hatimah, end, epilogue, conclusion, signature.

He-Halutz (The Pioneer), world organization of Jewish youth, which trained its members for pioneering work and self-defense in Palestine.

Horah, a very popular folk dance of pioneer Eretz Israel.

huppah, canopy, wedding.

Intifada (Arab. "shaking off"), uprising of Arab Palestinians, began in 1987, in the territories occupied by Israel since the 1967 Six-Day War.

Irgun, an often used abbrev. in the United States for Irgun Zeva'i Le'umi.

kadosh, holy.

Kelal Israel (the Jewish community as a whole), term implies the common responsibility, destiny, and kinship of all components of the Jewish people.

Keren ha-Yesod (Palestine Foundation Fund), a major fund-raising arm of the Jewish Agency and the World Zionist Organization.

kevutzah, small commune of pioneers constituting an agricultural settlement in the Land of Israel (generally evolved later into kibbutz).

khafiyah, Arab., Arab headdress.

kippah, skullcap.

The *Kotel* (The Wall), the Wailing or Western Wall.

kova tembel, a popular hat in pioneering Eretz Israel.

le-hayyim! (to life!), To your health!

Maccabiah, Worldwide Jewish Olympics in Eretz Israel, since 1932.

Mahzor (cycle), prayer book for holy days.

mamlakhtiut, statehood.

matmid, diligent student of religious studies.

Me'ah She'arim, a quarter in Jerusalem, stronghold of extreme Jewish Orthodoxy.

mensch, Yid., a person of ingrained humanistic qualities.

Minhah, the afternoon prayer service, one of the three daily services of the Jewish liturgy.

mitzvah, pl. *mitzvot* (commandment), precept of Jewish law or, generally, any meritorious deed.

Mizrachi, religious Zionist party, founded in 1902.

Mosad (abbrev., Ha-Mosad Le-Modi'in), Israel's Intelligence Service.

moshav, pl. *moshavim*, cooperative settlement(s), based on individual plots of land and individual households.

moshavah, pl. *moshavot*, Jewish village(s) in Eretz Israel.

Mufti, Grand, a supreme Muslim position in Palestine, held for decades by Hajj Amin Al-Husseini, an Arab nationalist leader who collaborated with the Nazis.

mukhtar, Arab., the head or official representative of the village.

Musaf, the additional prayer instituted on the Sabbath and the festivals.

Neturei Karta, ultra-religious group that does not recognize the State of Israel.

Pesak (in Jewish law), judgment, verdict.

Revisionist party, founded in 1925 by Ze'ev Jabotinsky, it demanded a revision of Zionist policy, greater activity, and nationalistic right-wing policies.

sabra, native Israeli Jew.

Sephardi, pl. Sephardim, Jews of Spain and Portugal and their descendants, wherever resident, as contrasted with Ashkenazi(m).

shali'ah, pl. *shelihim*, emissary(ries) from Eretz Israel to Jewish communities or organizations abroad.

shelilat ha-galut (negation of the *galut*), ideology maintaining that the Jewish people cannot have a valid or meaningful existence in exile.

Shomer, pl. Shomrim, abbrev., member(s) of ha-Shomer ha-Tza'ir movement.

Ha-Shomer ha-Tza'ir (The Young Watchman), Zionist youth movement established in Central and Eastern Europe towards the end of World War I. Its members set up in Eretz Israel a kibbutz movement of left leanings.

shtetel, pl. *shtetlach*, Yid., Jewish small-town community(ties) in Eastern Europe.

Siddur, among Ashkenazim, the volume containing the daily prayers, cf. Mahzor.

Talmud Torah (Torah Study), a direction in American Jewish education — it synthesized religion, modern Hebraism, and Zionism — that came to prevail in the afternoon Hebrew schools after about 1905.

tefutza, tefutzot (Diaspora), voluntary dispersion of the Jewish people (as distinct from *galut* — a forced dispersion).

tikkun, mending of a suffering society and restoring it to the right order.

tzedakah, charity.

Urim and Thummim (in the breastplate of the High Priest), oracle.

yeshiva, academy for study of Talmudic subjects.

Yidishkeyt (Yiddishkeit), Yid., Judaism, with an emphasis on the folk elements of the faith.

yishuv (settlement), the Jewish community in the Land of Israel in the pre-State period.

Yom ha-Atzma'ut, The Independence Day of the State of Israel.

yored, pl. *yordim*, Jewish emigrant(s) from Eretz Israel.

Index

Cons.=Conservative; jour.=journal; newsp.=newspaper;
period.=periodical; Ref.=Reform; Recon.=Recostructionist